MELANIE WARD

DREAMS TO COME

A JOVE/HBJ BOOK

First Jove/HBJ edition published July 1978

Library of Congress Catalog Card Number: 77-91253

Printed in the United States of America

Jove/HBJ books are published by Jove Publications, Inc. (Harcourt Brace Jovanovich) 757 Third Avenue, New York, N.Y. 10017

TUNE IN TOMORROW . . . AND TOMORROW . . . AND TOMORROW . . .

Lauren. Paula. Sally. Anne. For them, DREAMS TO COME was more than a network bonanza—it was a story pulsing with a life of its own—inseparable from the exciting women who wrote and played and lived it . . .

Its star-crossed lovers, resident "bitches," villains and heart-throb heroes—all were characters they knew far better than themselves. And its sweet, erotic, dangerous dreams of love, broadcast every day, were the dreams that tormented them too—night after hungry, restless night . . .

DREAMS TO COME

The searing new novel of four talented women adrift in the star-struck, hard-driving world of the television soaps.

FOR THOSE WHO HAVE CARED
AND WHO GAVE ME DREAMS:
   MY MOTHER, ETHEL WARD
   MY OTHER MOTHER, VERA HOLDING
   AND
   MY TEACHER, WILLIAM FOSTER-HARRIS

Chapter One

Lauren Parrow hesitated on the sidewalk in front of a three-story office building on Sunset Boulevard. A narrow structure jammed in between a sleazy disco and the elegant Habitat, a hangout for the upper echelon of current Hollywood stars.

A yawning dishwasher from the Habitat stepped outside with a broom. He paused long enough to give Lauren an appreciative once over, scratched an armpit and halfheartedly began to push the broom over the sidewalk, stirring up little swirls of dust.

Lauren, at twenty-five, was unaware of her own changing beauty. The scrubbed-young-girl look was fading and in its place was the well-formed bone structure of a woman blessed with high cheekbones, wide-set eyes of clear green and a mouth sensuous in its maturity.

The struggle of the last weeks had melted her body down, giving her a streamlined look that was effectively displayed by a bias-cut print skirt over dark boots. She pulled her sweater together over the soft mounds of her breasts and climbed up the narrow stairway.

Lauren was not comfortable about seeing Joe Seals, who acted as her literary agent. Admissions of failure weren't easy, especially in her vulnerable state of mind.

She found the reception room of the small second-floor office empty, the secretary evidently out to lunch. Lauren paused at Joe Seals's door, where she could see him bent over his desk, lips moving in a mutter of words she could not hear.

Joe was fiftyish, with a high, wise forehead emphasized by the loss of much of his medium-brown hair. A man who tended to buy only brown suits, he was never seen without a bow tie tucked under his chin. Lauren liked him.

She took a deep breath, inhaling the musty smell of the old building, and rapped on his open door. "Joe."

He looked up and a pleased smile touched the round face, deepening the lines running from the corners of his nostrils to his mouth. "Lauren! Come in." He came around the desk and ushered her to a chair with the old-style grace that always made Lauren feel she'd stepped back into a nineteen-forties movie. He wasn't a particularly tall man, perhaps five foot nine, with a good twenty pounds more than his frame should carry. Lauren thought the extra weight fit him and his age.

"Well now." Still smiling, Joe seated himself across from her at his cluttered desk. "You aren't carrying a manuscript under your arm."

"No." She looked down at her hands, where slim, tapered fingers laced together displayed her anxiety. "That's why I'm here. The book won't be completed."

"Honey." Joe shook his head. "Lauren, it's good."

"Maybe it is and maybe it isn't." The book had little meaning for her now; it was too soft, too sweet and romantic, a naive story with a happy ending, a thing she had used to escape from the reality of her own life.

"I believe in you, Lauren, in your talent. You can make it, honey."

"Not as a novelist. I can't afford the time, Joe. My husband, Benji, and I have split." She made a weak gesture of helplessness with her left hand. "I'm sorry. I have to earn a living." She hated having to apologize, to explain. It was bad enough that Joe believed in her and had yet to be rewarded financially for that belief. She'd had one sale to *Redbook* of a short story, another to *Good Housekeeping* and one tiny book of poetry printed that had paid $35.29 in royalties.

"So, a divorce?"

"Yes," she answered without further explanations, the wounds still too raw and hurting for casual discussion.

"Tough. Divorce has a way of knocking the props out from under you," he said, as though he knew. Joe nudged a single sheet of paper into a manila file. "So, what are you going to do?"

"Look for a job. I'm leaving here for an appointment with an employment agency."

"Your book will make money."

"Maybe—if it were completed. It isn't." Lauren lifted her chin, displaying the taut muscles in her neck. "The words won't come. I've tried, Joe." She beseeched him with her eyes green and hurting, asking for understanding. "I'm just about broke now. I have to go to work."

"At what?"

She shrugged one graceful shoulder. "At anything I can find. I'll take the first job offered to me."

"I see." He toyed with the manila envelope again, thinking, then glanced up. "Do you do secretarial stuff?"

"Sure. I said I would take on anything." She needed not only the money, but involvement in the world, a place to go, a function, before she drove herself crazy living alone with the stalled book.

"There's a job I know about." His eyes flicked over her face and she thought he seemed hesitant. "A writing job—or at least, it would be eventually."

"What sort of writing job?"

"TV, daytime drama."

"TV." Lauren drew back, somehow frightened of the opportunity. TV and movies were big time, high pres-

9

sure, glamorous; she wouldn't fit in. "I don't know anything about TV."

"Well, honey." Joe grinned. "Maybe you know more than you think. And you're bright and you'll learn fast. Have you ever heard of *Dreams to Come*?"

"Sure, it's a soap opera. My mother watches it."

"My wife is the head writer."

"Your wife?" Lauren echoed hollowly, surprised, for Joe had never spoken of a wife, though she supposed there had been no reason to before now.

"Yes, Paula Cavanaugh."

"I'm sorry. I've never heard of her."

"Nobody ever recognizes the writers." Joe leaned forward, his face and tone serious. "Look, Paula is a real bitch as an employer. But if you're loyal to her and work hard, she'll be fair. The job pays two hundred a week to start. She wants someone with some talent and brains who can act as her assistant, and you'd be in training as a writer. If you can cut it, you'll go on the writing staff. If you can't—" Joe shrugged.

"Two hundred," Lauren repeated, barely hearing the rest. It was more than she had hoped for, starting back to work after five years. She'd never been anything but a receptionist before she married Benji.

"Let me give my wife a call," Joe said, standing up.

"I'll wait outside," Lauren murmured and excused herself.

Lauren closed the door behind her and moved to a grime-laden window that overlooked Sunset Boulevard. At midday, the street was conventional looking, filled with casually dressed business people out for lunch and shopping. It would be dusk before the night people came to take over. "The fucking hippies," Benji had called them collectively, the hookers and pimps, the runaways and dopers, the little boy prostitutes.

Lauren always found them sad and depressing, these people who populated Sunset and Hollywood boulevards, who hung out around the porno shops on Western and ate in the grimy hamburger joints and ignored

10

the Rollses and Bentleys and Mercedes Benzes that crossed through their territory with locked doors.

She wondered if she was any less a failure than they. Or perhaps they didn't consider themselves failures; maybe they measured success on a scale foreign to her.

Stop thinking, she cried in her mind. Stop thinking so much, quit the analyzing. Benji said she analyzed every emotion, every action, until there was nothing left of them. "Can't you just react?" he had yelled more than once, his face contorted with disgust. "Just one time in your life react, just enjoy the moment. You squeeze the life out of everything."

Remembering made her cringe because there was something in her that denied spontaneous reaction, as if something had been left out when she was formed in her mother's womb. No one else in the family she had left in northern California was as introspective. They'd always found her a little odd because she didn't want to settle down and marry a farmer or store owner. Why anyone would give up the fertile valleys and green mountains of northern California for decadent Los Angeles with its smog and traffic and seven million people was beyond them.

Sometimes she wondered, too. But she refused to flee back home to hide away in the safety of the collective family skirt. It was an admission of failure that even she could not make.

They'd ask questions, Mama and her sister, Lila. She could never tell them that the nice young man from Reseda had found her too quiet and too reserved, then had taunted her with his "women who aren't afraid to live."

Benji Parrow liked his women to have flash. He was not impressed with her housekeeping and cooking skills, he made fun of her writing. "How can you be a writer when you've never even lived?" was another of his favored accusations.

Well, maybe she would live now. She could no longer afford to stay home and putter with her plants and writing. Now all she had was the apartment she'd rented in

11

the Valley. She would work, she would be forced to live. Maybe she would have an affair, she thought, with heavy grimness.

It was what Benji wanted of her. He had had his affairs, had asked for an open marriage, had admitted to going to group-sex clubs in the hills.

A delicate shudder slid over her body and for a moment black anguish threatened.

"Lauren?"

Joe's voice startled her. She had not heard him open the door. "Yes." She turned, forcing full lips into a smile.

"Paula can see you this afternoon. Why don't you get yourself some lunch and drive on over. Here's the address." He handed her a slip of paper. "Use my parking place under the building. It'll have my name on it."

"Thank you, Joe." Unexpected tears misted her vision, reminding her of her vulnerability, of the shaky hold she had on life.

"Good luck with Paula." He adjusted his bow tie and dropped a kiss on her cheek. She wanted to hug him in return and could not. "And when you feel up to getting back to work on the book, let me know. We'll have lunch together soon."

She nodded and moved away from him. Joe's kiss meant nothing, but it still bothered her, even though she liked him, had liked him from the beginning, when she'd chosen his name out of an article about agents in the Los Angeles *Times* "Calendar" section. His was a small agency, handling a couple of well-known writers and lots of unknowns, as well as a few actors.

When he agreed to handle her, she was ecstatic. Now she was sorry she had given him so little to handle.

Lauren walked two blocks down to where she'd parked her battered old Chevy. She took Fairfax south. Nearing Wilshire, she pulled into Farmer's Market for lunch.

The clock on the churchlike steeple said it was after one. She ducked under a green awning and walked

12

down a short lane lined with shops into the main building.

Once an area for farmers in roadside stands and trucks, the place had become a proper market years back. The long wooden building housed open-air vegetable bins with the lushest of products, huge, shiny green avocados, bright red tomatoes, oversized heads of lettuce, alongside such exotics as mangoes and papayas from Hawaii.

Sparkling clean glass protected vast arrays of cheeses, thick cuts of prime beef and plump chicken in numerous butcher shops. Throughout the building was a scattering of ethnic restaurants offering everything from pizza to cheeze blintzes. Tourists and locals alike milled through the building, waiting in lines for food and scrambling for tables.

In the east end of the building Lauren ordered a plate of Japanese food from a booth, carried it to a table next to a vegetable stand and checked the address Joe had given her. It was on Wilshire, only a few blocks down, an office building, she assumed.

She nibbled on a won ton and abruptly laid it back on the plate as her stomach convulsed. An interview. She was going for an interview. The enormity of it was mind boggling. Frightened, she put her elbows on the table and pressed her fingers against her temples, then back into the soft brown hair that framed her face.

I can do it, she told herself. I know I can do the job. I am capable. I am not stupid.

The fear came, not because she doubted her abilities, but because they might not be recognized because of her lack of confidence. She knew she could learn to do any job, but only if she first got it. What if Joe's wife dismissed her as too inexperienced? She would have to fill out application papers and there would be so little to put on them.

Behind closed eyelids she could see Benji sneering at her. "You won't last out there alone, Lauren. You'll come back. You'll see."

13

"Never! Never!" she whispered. She tossed her hair back, stood up and plowed through the crowds of people to the nearest exit. She would not go crawling back to Benji.

Lauren was surprised to find the address wasn't an office building at all, but one of the plush condominums that had sprouted up in Los Angeles. An aging attendant in a faded blue uniform like those of security guards took her car after she explained that Joe Seals had said she could use his parking slot.

In the elevator she realized the suite number Joe had given her was for the penthouse. Intimidated, she smoothed the print skirt and wished she'd worn something dressier. She glanced uneasily at the security camera that stared down at her with one unblinking eye.

In a carpeted hallway that looked like the entryway of a home with its fake potted palm next to a table and gold-leafed mirror, she found two unmarked doors. Apprehension tugged at her insides. Either Paula Cavanaugh made a fortune or Joe Seals was even more unassuming than he appeared. Wondering how she could fit into a place like this, she hesitated between the two doors and finally pressed the bell on the first one. Soft chimes sounded and in moments a harried-looking, overweight woman opened the door. "Mrs.—uh—Miss Cavanaugh?" The plump face was overpowered by a mass of brown curly hair in messy disarray.

"Nah, I'm Jenny, Paula's secretary. You gotta be Lauren Parrow. Joe called about you. Come on in."

"Thank you." Lauren found herself ushered into a posh living room that opened onto a terrace.

"This way," Jenny said before Lauren had a chance to take in any thing about the room. "Paula owns the entire top floor. She and Joe live here. She had the second apartment converted into an office and guest rooms. Not that we ever have time for guests. Here we go."

They turned into a reception room decorated with

14

black-and-silver wallpaper and populated with chrome and glass and stark white leather chairs. Black file cabinets and an oversized desk topped with an IBM Selectric filled half the room.

"This is my office," Jenny explained and plopped her chubby body onto a chair in back of the desk. "Sit down. Paula's on the phone. Still."

Lauren began to relax with Jenny. She liked the friendly, open-faced woman of thirty or so. "You aren't leaving, are you?" she asked.

"Me? Goodness no. I've been with Paula for two years. I hold the record."

"The record for what?"

"For the longest employment under Paula Cavanaugh."

"Oh." Lauren's smile faded and a yawning pit opened up in the bottom of her stomach.

"Don't let me scare you," Jenny said. "If you can cope with Paula and stand the pace, it's a terrific job."

"How—how long do most employees last?" Lauren dared ask.

Jenny shrugged a broad shoulder. "Six months or so."

"Oh, God." Lauren's heart compressed and her face reflected her dismay. "This may not be for me."

"It's the pace that drives them away. It's panicsville every day three times a day."

"You're scaring me," Lauren choked.

"I'd just rather shatter your illusions before I train you."

"Oh, God." Lauren closed her eyes in a prayerful attitude.

"God never helps around here."

again, Lauren. Tell me every ... Paula said aloud me"

Chapter Two

Paula Cavanaugh stood behind a mahogany desk, a white telephone receiver gripped in her right hand. She brushed through dyed black hair cut in a sharp Sassoon bob as she listened impatiently. Straight-cut bangs sliced across her forehead and tapered down at the sides to just below the ears and her hair was blunt-cut into a thick swinging mass in back.

Her face was sharp, cut into plateaus and flats, and lightly etched for her fifty-six years. "Ed, would you shut up and listen to me now," Paula cut in, her tone demanding and unpleasant, her attitude one of long-suffering.

"Paula, Paula, baby," the deep voice of her business manager, Ed Epstein, answered. "It's you who must listen. When you negotiate a contract, it is just that, negotiations. You give a little here, you take a little there."

Porcelain nails applied at a boutique on Rodeo Drive impatiently tapped the glossy desk top. "I'm not giving up on a damn thing. They meet my demands or else."

"Paula." Epstein's voice dropped. "The 'or else' means you are out of work."

Paula's dark, almost black eyes, narrowed and the knuckles of the hand gripping the receiver turned white. How dare he threaten her. "I am *Dreams*. *Dreams* can't

17

survive without me. And they know it. Every damn one of them knows it—from the president of the network right down to the grips."

Paula yanked the phone up and, pulling the cord behind her, began to pace. The full skirt of the black dress emphasized a hard, brittle body that could have belonged to a one-time marathon walker.

"What's the matter?" Paula demanded. "You aren't answering me."

"Paula, you don't want to blow this."

"Then you get in there and fight like the crooked scoundrel you are!"

"This show is your life. Without it—"

She cut him off with a flurry of words. "You think I couldn't make it without *Dreams*. You think I couldn't put my own soap together. You think the other networks wouldn't leap for me."

"Don't be stupid, Paula, I never said that. I'm saying we shouldn't blow this."

Paula returned to the desk. She put the phone down and picked up a yellow sheet from a legal pad. "Okay, let's go over this one more time. Just so everything is clear. Are you ready?" She questioned in sarcastic tones.

"Yes, baby," Epstein replied with a long sigh.

"I want seven hundred and fifty a week for new ideas. I'll give them four series ideas a year. They must go to pilot with one."

"That's the easy part, Paula."

"I want a six-hundred-thousand-a-year writing budget for *Dreams*."

"Maybe. Maybe."

"I want it, damn it. And I want complete story control."

Epstein sighed, sounding like a wounded buffalo, Paula thought. "That's the hard part, baby."

"It's the part that matters." He voice was cold, and rigid. "I want Caleb Shepard off the show. He's a pain

18

in the ass. He hasn't contributed a new idea in ten years."

"Paula, Shepard was your mentor. He got you started."

"You mean he used me," Paula countered. She did the work and Shepard took the credit.

"It's his show. He created *Dreams*." Epstein reminded her. "The network and the production people believe in him. He's got a long string of successes behind him."

"Not in the last ten years he hasn't."

"Paula, three of his soaps are still on the air."

"I don't care what's still on the air. I'm *Dreams*. Did you see that last trash he sent, the proposed story line for the next year? We've done it all before. We can't do it again." Paula's voice dropped and she sat down. "He's old. He's through. Make them realize it. I'm *Dreams*, Epstein."

"I'll try."

She hung up without saying good-bye. Her hand lay flat on the desk supporting her weight. You paid people and you paid them and you still had to do the work yourself. There were ways of getting things done. She knew she would come up with the right one. She snapped her body upright. She was *Dreams*. It was her show. She deserved proper recognition and to get it she had to step out and ask. In this business no one handed you anything on a golden platter.

She poured Bristol Cream sherry from a crystal decanter into a stemmed wineglass and lit a cigarette. She puffed rapidly, eyes narrowed, until the anger began to fade.

Bob Silverstein was the key. As head of Silver Productions, Silverstein had the control. He could pay off Caleb Shepard, ease out the old man and get him off everyone's back. Shepard was a drag on the show. He had to go. He'd overshadowed her long enough.

Paula pushed aside a clutter of typed scripts as her buzzer sounded. "Lauren Parrow is here to see you."

19

"Who?" Paula had to pull herself out of her thoughts. "Oh, the person Joe told me about. Okay, send her in. I hope to hell this one has some sense." Good help was impossible to find.

"Looks good," Jenny replied.

Jenny opened the door and Lauren stepped in ahead of her. She suppressed her shock as Jenny introduced them. She had not known what to expect, but certainly not this aged crow, all in black with red claws. She supposed she'd expected some nice middle-aged woman, someone a little old-fashioned like Joe Seals.

"Sit down," Paula said, vaguely indicating a seating arrangement against one wall. "Just dump something," Paula said, removing a stack of blue mimeographed scripts from a chair for herself.

Lauren squeezed into a small space on the cream velvet love seat and tried to smile. "See, we do need an assistant," Paula said, her voice soft and rather sweet sounding. "Jenny doesn't have time to do the filing. We're both so overworked."

"May I ask what you are looking for in an assistant?" Lauren asked, trying to be as professional as possible. "Joe, Mr. Seals, wasn't clear."

Paula leaned back and clasped her hands at her narrow waist. "Everything. If I name it, you have to be able to do it. I'd throw you at Jenny first. She'll teach you the basics."

"I'm sorry," Lauren said and hated herself for saying the words; she was always apologizing for herself. "But I still don't understand what my duties would be."

"I would consider it a rare opportunity, my dear Miss Parrow." The voice took on a sharp edge matching the severe lines of her mouth. "I need another writer for the show. Joe says you have talent. Naturally you couldn't start writing any time soon. It would take six months to a year for you to familiarize yourself with the show, the characters and the past story line. And to learn my style of writing."

"I see." Lauren drew back, cowed.

"I doubt that you do. Daytime drama is a complex writing assignment. We have the man who created it who does the projected story line each year. Not that we ever use what he sends us," Paula said, dismissing him. "Then we have me. I'm the head writer. I write three scripts a week and two outlines for scripts that I farm out to my other writers. I'd prefer to do only two scripts a week."

"I—I never considered writing for TV before," Lauren stammered, wanting to be honest. "Or even for movies. I'm not sure I can do it."

"That's what we would find out, eventually. Meanwhile, you'd be acting as my assistant. You do whatever I say. I have a full-time housekeeper but sometimes I may ask you to go out and buy toilet paper. Primarily you'll be editing scripts and dealing with the studio, once Jenny thinks you can handle it." Paula emphasized this last point.

Lauren nodded. It didn't sound like so much. She eyed the cluttered room and looked back to Paula. Or maybe it would be too much.

"Do you watch soaps?" Paula asked.

"No, I'm sorry." She wanted to bite her tongue. "But *Dreams to Come* is my mother's favorite show," she offered hopefully.

"You'd have to get rid of any prejudice you have against them. As well as any preconceived ideas. Soaps are real life. Nothing ends happily ever after. We involve the viewers in life, and life is an unknown quantity. Bad people become good, good people can have bad problems. People get married, give birth, die, get divorces. What is your marital status, by the way?"

The question came out of context, startling Lauren. She felt her cheeks growing warm. "Divorced."

"Finalized?"

"No, not yet. I've moved out and I'm seeing a lawyer. The marriage is finished." Lauren fought to keep her voice firm.

"You wouldn't bring your personal life into the office, would you?"

"Never," Lauren breathed.

"Good. I don't have the time or the energy to play earth mother."

Nor the inclination, Lauren thought, not liking Paula particularly, but reserving judgment.

"Soaps are the big money-makers for TV. Night shows lose money. We make money, big money. We are important. We are also the forerunners. We handled rape in a realistic manner before nighttime ever considered touching it. We handled VD and Vietnam and drug addiction first."

Paula got up, went to the desk, refilled her own glass and poured another and returned. "One of your prime responsibilities is to keep sherry in the decanter at all times. Don't ever let it run out."

"Yes." Lauren nodded, uncertain if the woman meant the job was already hers. She took the offered sherry.

"Jenny works from nine to five and goes home to the hubby and kids. So will you, most of the time. But if there is a crisis, I'll expect you to stay and see it through. You can take off another time to make up the hours."

"That's fair enough," Lauren agreed. After all, she had no social commitments to worry about; only bleak aloneness waited in her apartment. A demanding job would be therapeutic.

"I take it you have no children."

"No." On top of being a less than adequate lover, she had never been able to conceive, either, which had bothered her more than Benji, though he was not above using her barrenness as a weapon.

"Good." Paula stood up. Lauren found herself being ushered out the door, the sherry glass still in her hand. "Can you start tomorrow?" Paula asked. "Better yet, how about today? You can watch Jenny."

Lauren nodded, unable to say anything. She was

overwhelmed, dazed by the abruptness of Paula's decision. No one got hired this quickly.

The door closed again, then opened. "You do type, don't you?" Paula asked quickly, black eyes boring into Lauren.

"Yes."

The door closed. Lauren stood there, bemused and somewhat terrified as Jenny grinned up at her. "Does she always hire people this quickly?" Lauren asked.

"Every time," Jenny said with a sigh. "I think that's why there's such a high turnover. She believes totally in her own judgment of people. She never asks for a reference or gives one."

"She didn't even ask for a résumé," Lauren said.

"Joe recommended you. That was enough background. Hey, kid, don't you know that's how it works out here? It's who you know that counts. It's the only way anyone ever gets a job."

"I think I need this," Lauren said and finished the sherry in one gulp. The system did not seem fair, but it had gotten her a job.

"Toss your purse here," Jenny said opening a file drawer. "Take off your shoes and pull up a chair. That's my kiddies." She pointed to a silver-framed photograph. "The fat one is my husband. He worships me." Jenny giggled and Lauren laughed out loud in giddy release. It wasn't going to be dull.

Chapter Three

Lauren returned for her first full day at work lugging a stack of mimeographed scripts she had spent half the night reading.

"How did it go?" Jenny asked from behind her desk.

"I'm confused." Lauren admitted with frankness. "I don't know who these people are or what's going on."

"Of course not. If there's time today, you can start watching some of the old shows. We tape all of them. I'll have to teach you how to run the machine, too."

"Should I go in there?" Lauren asked, nodding toward Paula's closed door. She was more than a little apprehensive about approaching her new boss.

"Paula's still in bed. She was up most of the night doing a script. I'm editing it. Not that Paula requires much editing."

"So where do I start?"

"Fix her coffee. I've got a pot made in the TV room across the hall. You'll find a thermal container that goes on her desk. And fill the sherry decanter. You'll find the sherry across the hall, too, in the cupboard."

The small chore took only a few moments and Lauren was back standing at Jenny's desk. "You can go to the bank as soon as it opens. That's a weekly chore and will generally be your job. We have to deposit it immediately, because we always need it."

Jenny handed Lauren the check. "My God," Lauren gasped. "She makes over nine thousand dollars a week?"

"Fifty-two weeks a year, and it will be more. Her business manager is negotiating a new contract now."

"It—it's a fortune."

"You'll find out it isn't. There's a stiff mortgage on this place. Paula paid a quarter of a million, plus the remodeling. There's monthly maintenance fees. Paula pays the two other writers out of this. One gets seven hundred and fifty a script, the other a thousand. Every week. By the way, if you ever make the writing staff, the starting pay is five hundred a script with a guarantee of one a week."

"Lauren swallowed. "It—it's more money than I can comprehend," she whispered, overwhelmed anew.

"Some day it won't be enough," Jenny said with the sound of having seen it all in her voice. "If you make the staff."

Lauren didn't hear her. Yesterday she'd been thrilled at the idea of eight hundred a month. Now she could think in terms of two thousand a month and more, *if* she made the staff.

That kind of money, that kind of life, that was success. If she could make it, no one, not even Benji, could ever look down on her again. No one could call her a failure. A new resolve began to build in Lauren and with it a sense of strength and hope she had not experienced before.

The phone rang and Jenny answered. "Just a moment. It's for Joe," she told Lauren as she pressed the hold button. "His bedroom is the fifth button here. I have them coded." She turned back to the phone. "Joe, line one is for you."

Jenny hung up and turned to Lauren. "This is the deposit slip. And we enter it here." Jenny pulled a journal out. "Paula has an accountant, but we have to give him something to account."

The phone buzzed and Jenny stopped to pick it up. She listened and hung up. "Joe wants us. Something is up. Come on."

Lauren trotted after Jenny down the hall, past the sunken living room and along another hall where they found Joe in trousers and robe standing outside a bedroom door. "How bad will it be if the press finds out she's in jail?" Joe asked loudly into the door.

"Bad enough." Paula's voice called back.

"Who?" Jenny asked.

"Sally Rook."

Jenny shook her head.

"Who is she?" Lauren whispered to Jenny.

"Sally Rook is fairly new to *Dreams*. She's the young love interest. Looks very sweet and innocent on the show. She was just voted teen-age actress of the year by *Daytime TV* magazine."

"Get her out of jail," Paula yelled from behind the still closed door. "Hide her!"

"Okay. On my way, honey," Joe called back. He looked from Jenny to Lauren. "Lauren, you're coming with me."

"Me?" Lauren gulped. "I—"

"Just get your purse, honey." Joe urged her to hurry. "I'll get dressed."

Jenny propelled Lauren back to the office.

"Why is Joe involved with Sally Rook?" Lauren asked, totally confused now.

"She's one of his clients. He got her onto *Dreams*. Through an audition. Paula didn't even know she was Joe's client when she was chosen."

Lauren got her purse and sweater, and in moments Joe was yelling for her. She ran down the hall. She didn't know why she had to go along, but for whatever reason, it was exciting.

She found Joe at the door, still buttoning a plain tan shirt underneath a brown jacket. In his car he popped a dark green bow tie underneath his collar and backed out of his slot, almost hitting the car behind him.

Lauren clutched the seat as Joe threw the car into gear and screeched out into the Wilshire traffic. "Where are we going?"

"Sybil Brand. Where else?" Joe glanced over at her just before he shot out into the Wilshire traffic.

Lauren shrugged. "Sybil Brand?"

"That's the women's jail. Damn traffic," he muttered as he dodged around a slow-moving delivery truck. "I've got to get off this boulevard. Too crowded."

Joe didn't offer conversation, so Lauren fell silent and eased back into the leather-upholstered seats of the Mercedes. At the jail, Joe ordered Lauren to stand outside the building. "You watch for reporters."

Lauren protested, but Joe was gone, disappearing through the doors. Feeling conspicuous, but determined to do her job, Lauren eyed all who came and went. There wasn't a camera or a notepad among them.

Joe appeared. "Give me your sweater."

"Huh?"

"Give me your sweater," he repeated and she obeyed, awkwardly skinning out of it. "Seen any reporters?"

"No, but I wouldn't recognize a reporter—"

Joe didn't hear her. He was gone again.

Lauren moved out into the January sun. The day was warming and the sky was a clear blue thanks to a recent rain that had washed away the smog.

A lanky man approached and eyed Lauren casually. His eyes met hers and she looked away. "Nice," he said as he passed by. Embarrassed, Lauren pretended not to hear him, not knowing how to handle that kind of casual compliment.

Joe finally reappeared, his arm around the shoulders of a slender girl. Head down, her face was hidden by a mat of long, tangled, sunstreaked hair. She wore rumpled jeans and it was obvious that there was nothing under Lauren's loosely woven sweater.

Lauren started toward them as the girl raised her

28

hand. She mumbled something, pulled away from Joe and shot a finger toward the building. "Lousy cops."

"Hush. Or they'll take you back." Joe took hold of Sally's arm. "Sally, this is Lauren."

"Hi," Lauren offered tentatively, unsure of how she was expected to act.

Sullen eyes flicked over Lauren, their color startling, brown, but not dark, almost cinnamon or a tawny tiger color. Sally did not offer a friendly hello back. Lauren did not know if she should feel intimidated or annoyed by this little creature.

"I brought Lauren with me to help figure out what in the hell to do about you. Hustle yourself to the car, love," Joe ordered and Lauren tried another smile. Now she knew why she was here, for all the good it did her.

The sullen mouth trembled and Lauren caught a glimpse of tears threatening just before Sally ducked her head. Sally shook off Joe's hand and walked ahead of them, stalking over the sidewalk on bare feet, reminding Lauren of a child being sent to her room.

Why, she's frightened, Lauren thought. Something stirred in her chest, a vague feeling of kinship. She's just a kid and she had spent the night in jail.

In the car, with Sally in the back seat, Joe started the motor. "You still living in the same place, honey?"

"No," came the muffled one-word reply.

"Move in with your boyfriend?" Joe asked.

"Yeah," Sally muttered and Lauren glanced over her shoulder at Sally. The matted hair again obscured the downcast face.

"Where?" Joe asked, his face and tone patient, his eyes showing concern now.

"I—I can't go back there, Joe. I walked out last night. That was after he knocked me around and burned my clothes in the bathtub."

Lauren supressed a gasp. Her eyes flickered to Joe and back to Sally who was rubbing a bruise on her forearm.

"What did you do to him?" Joe asked.

"Nothing," was the sullen reply.

Joe snorted, his face hardened. Lauren drew back as he rolled around, came up over the seat and grabbed Sally's arm in a painful-looking hold.

Lauren shrunk back as far as she could in her corner, waiting for the girl to explode. "I didn't do nothing to him. Much." The voice was subdued.

"I'll bet. Are you on the show today?" Sally shook her head. "Okay." Joe dropped her arm. "Where to then?"

"I—I don't know," Sally whispered. The lips began to tremble again. Tears gathered in her eyes and seemed to hover on the lashes, then slipped slowly down dirty cheeks.

"A girlfriend?" Joe asked, ignoring the tears.

Sally kept her quivering chin high. "I don't have any girlfriends." She wiped at the tears with the back of her hand. "Women don't like me much."

Aching for her, Lauren reached back. "I like you," she offered.

"You do?" The tears stopped and Sally sneered. "Where'd you get the weirdo, Joe?"

"She's a writer. One of my clients. Also one of the nice people in the world. She works for Paula.

"The Witch?" Sally asked with disdain.

"The Witch," Joe acknowledged.

"That's what we call her," Sally said, turning to Lauren, friendly now. "She looks like a witch, all the time wearing black."

Embarrassed, Lauren glanced over at Joe, who showed no reaction to his wife's being called names. "Come on, kid," he growled. "Where to?"

"I—I don't know," Sally whispered. She changed again, back into the scared little girl. "I lost my purse last night, not that it had much money in it anyway."

"Tough. I put up your bail. You aren't getting any more money out of me."

"My clothes are at Jake's," Sally muttered.

"I thought you said Jake burned them."

30

"Well, he did. Part of them. Most of them, I guess." The words trailed off in a sniffle.

"You know you can't go back there," Joe told her. "The guy is no good."

"She—she can stay at my place," Lauren blurted out without thinking. "At least for today and tonight, until she can get things straightened out."

Sally raised a skeptical eyebrow. "Why would you do that for me?"

"I—I really don't know," Lauren admitted and shrugged, already wishing she could take the words back.

"You're an ever-loving doll, Lauren Parrow," Joe said, and the smile he flashed went deep into her eyes. His glance moved down to where her skirt was hiked up above her knees. Lauren tucked the skirt back down. Joe cleared his throat and turned back to Sally. "Look, brat, this gal is your savior today. But remember, you keep getting into trouble and one day there won't be a savior."

"I'll be good." Sally sat forward, eager to please now. "Honest, Joe, I'll try real hard. It was Jake that set me off."

"Then stay away from Jake. I swear, I'll drop you if I find out you're seeing him."

"Can—can I get my clothes?"

"Buy new clothes," Joe ordered.

"I like my old ones," Sally wailed.

"Maybe he's burned the rest of them by now," Joe suggested.

"Maybe." Sally slumped down in the back seat. She wiggled dirty toes. The bottoms of her feet were black. "I bet he didn't burn my shoes."

"Just don't go alone," Joe told her. "And if Jake is there, don't even go in. Understand?"

Sally looked to Lauren. Lauren made a helpless gesture, wondering what she had let herself in for. She did not know how to handle girls like Sally—and certainly not men like the high-tempered Jake.

couple against him. His face was always scratchy with whiskers, even if he had shaved that day. He wore

Chapter Four

"You'll have to share my bedroom," Lauren told Sally. "I've got two, but I haven't set the bed up in the other one yet." She had been half planning on selling the second bed and turning the room into an office in hopes of one day starting a new book.

"I don't have to have anything fancy," Sally said and walked into the smaller bedroom where a mattress and box spring leaned up against the wall. "Here, Joe," Sally said. "Give me a hand." The two of them put the spring and mattress on the floor. "There. I've got a bed. Just give me a blanket and I'll be fine."

Instead, Lauren found clean sheets, a blanket and a robe and gown for the girl. "Use whatever you need in the bathroom," she told her. "I'll be home by six. There's food in the refrigerator."

Lauren turned to leave. "Hey," Sally called. "Hey, thanks."

Lauren nodded, struck again by the little-girl quality of her. The belligerent hippie was gone and a child was left. A lost lonely child, one like those she saw drifting along on Hollywood Boulevard, the unwanted runaways.

Back in the car again, Joe headed for the San Diego Freeway. "Thanks," Lauren," he said. "Sally's basically

33

a good kid. And she needs a friend. I appreciate this."

"I owe you one," Lauren reminded him. "You got me a job."

"You'd have gotten it anyway. Like I told Sally, you're one of the nice people in the world." He reached across and patted her knee. "Stay that way."

Lauren moved instinctively toward the door, away from Joe's easy familiarity.

"I wasn't making a pass," Joe said gently.

"I didn't think you were," she replied, knowing it was a lie. Any sexual action threw her off guard.

"You withdrew just now. And when I kiss you, just give you a miserable little peck on the cheek, you freeze up."

Lauren did not answer and Joe went on. "Hell, I meant I know I don't have a chance with you. An old guy like me and a beautiful woman like you? But I can look, can't I? I can admire you, I can dream."

"Joe, please," she whispered. There was so much pain in his words, so much confusion in her mind.

"I mean it as a compliment, not an insult. Did you see *Harry and Tonto*? Harry makes it with a hooker in her car. Harry was an old guy. He hadn't had it up in years. But he still had dreams. He made it with the young chick, because he had dreams. I identified with that."

"You aren't old, Joe," she said, feeling the sadness of him.

"I'm fifty-five to your twenty-five. I'm looking toward seventy. And you're beautiful, Lauren. And I like you."

"I like you, too," she replied softly, feeling oddly tearful.

"Ah, but as a friend," Joe said.

"Joe, please. I—" She stopped. Anything she'd say would only make it worse.

"It's a compliment."

"I—I'm trying to take it that way. I'm not good with men, Joe. I mean, I don't know how to flirt casually."

"You don't take any part of life casually, do you?"

"No, I guess not." Lauren admitted with some pain. "Benji hated that in me."

"He must have been out of his mind. You're lucky to be rid of him. There's better guys around. Men who will appreciate you."

"I don't know if there are or not." Maybe all men were like Benji inside, maybe they all wanted some flash in their women in bed, wanted a sex kitten willing to try anything.

"Believe me, I'm right."

Silent tears glistened in Lauren's green eyes. "You're one of the nice people in the world, too, Joe."

"Yeah, a regular Sir Galahad." He grinned and Lauren let out a deeply held sigh. She felt warmed and strengthened by his friendship.

Joe dropped her at the Wilshire condo and she took the elevator up alone. With a sense of wonder she realized no man had called her beautiful before. Under the unwavering eye of the security camera Lauren took out a compact and studied herself.

She'd never considered herself anything more than wholesome looking. She had a farm girl's complexion, wide-set green eyes and blonde hair that had darkened to light brown. She tanned easily. She liked the thin feel of her body now. Her breasts generally overflowed in a C cup, but weren't quite large enough for a D. With the weight loss they were a nice C. Sometimes she had thought her breasts were the only thing Benji had found right about her.

She snapped the compact shut as the elevator stopped. She was feeling good about herself. She was not going to start thinking about Benji again.

Jenny looked up as Lauren stepped into the office. "Paula wants to see you immediately."

Lauren braced herself, tapped on the door, then opened it. Paula was seated at the smaller of the two desks in the oversized office. The draperies were open to the sun and the view of Wilshire Boulevard running

35

cast. Paula switched off her typewriter in front of her and turned around, black hair swinging. "Why was she arrested?" Paula demanded in a hard voice.

"I—I don't know." Lauren replied with dismay. She had not thought to ask.

Lips that were a red slash across Paula's face formed a sneer. "Stupid little bitch."

Jolted at being called such a name, Lauren took a step backward. "I'm sorry."

"Not you. Sally Rook!" The heavily made-up eyes narrowed as Paula tapped nails on the desk top. "But you should have gotten some facts for me. I'll have to call Joe now."

"I'm sorry," Lauren repeated, still shaken by Paula's harshness.

"You'll learn my way," Paula said with a confidence that said people molded themselves to her. "Damn it, I can't stand seeing anyone waste themselves like Sally Rook does. That kid has more talent than even she realizes. In five years she could be a star. She could have this town at her feet in ten. The waste—"

"Maybe she'll straighten herself out," Lauren offered carefully.

"I hope so. But she has an attraction for the worst sort of men. Bums. Freaks. She's been knocked around too much. Thinks she knows it all. Always playing the wise-ass. Inside she's just a little kid looking for a mama to love her. Or a daddy," Paula added cynically.

Lauren was surprised at Paula's insight and what compassion there had been in her voice. The old gal sounded like she might care a little.

"I've got to get this outline done. Then I want you to run it over to Mel Lorenzen. Jenny will give you directions. Meanwhile, call in these changes to the studio." She handed Lauren several typed pages.

"Yes, Miss Cavanaugh."

"Call me Paula, please."

"Okay." Lauren tentatively smiled, still confused by Paula's abrupt change in mood.

36

As Lauren left, Paula was dialing a number. Jenny explained to Lauren how to call in the changes, gave her the studio number and the name of the secretary to the producer.

"Her name is Sue Bergman. And don't ever tell her anything. She's a terrible gossip," Jenny warned.

Jenny put Lauren in the small office that would be hers, next to the TV room. Lauren was reading over the changes when Paula appeared in the doorway. "I just talked to Joe. Damn it, you didn't even tell me you'd taken Sally to your place."

"I'm sorry. I—I didn't get a chance."

"Are you saying I didn't give you a chance?"

"Well—" Lauren gestured helplessly. That was how it was.

"Are you saying I didn't let you tell me? Did I hold your tongue?" Paula's voice rose shrilly.

"No." Shaken, Lauren tried to make amends. "Was—was I wrong? She didn't seem to have any place to go."

"Just get her cleaned up and make sure she's on the set in the morning."

"Yes, Paula," Lauren said carefully, not wanting any more trouble.

Paula stalked off. Lauren reached for the phone and realized her hands were shaking.

She clasped her hands together and sat very still, willing herself back to calmness, fighting against the overwhelming urge to cry. She'd been yelled at twice this morning. It wasn't a very good start, and it wasn't as though she had done anything on purpose.

Jenny appeared in the doorway. "I heard Paula."

"Yeah." Lauren grimaced. "I can't seem to do anything right."

Jenny's plump face was soft with concern. "Don't take it to heart. Paula yells. It's a fact of life. And let me give you some advice. Don't ever argue with her. When she blames you for something, you should just accept it. Don't make excuses. That only enrages her.

37

You make mistakes, I make mistakes. Actors make mistakes, the studio makes mistakes. Paula does not make mistakes. Understand?"

"I guess I'd better," Lauren said faintly. It was understand or get out, a depressing choice.

"Right." Jenny winked. "Hang in."

Lauren brushed her hair back from her face, took a deep breath, dialed the studio and asked for the producer's extension. I've got to write my mother tonight, she thought. She'll be so excited to know her daughter is talking to the studio, to know her daughter is working for *Dreams*. She even has a real-life actress in her apartment. Lauren stifled a tension-relieving giggle. She couldn't tell her mother about Sally Rook being in jail.

"Silver Production. Sue Bergman."

"Hello. My name is Lauren Parrow. I work for Paula Cavanaugh and she asked me to call in some changes."

"I heard she'd hired a new girl. Welcome aboard." The voice was warm and Lauren responded with a thank you. "Let me get some paper in my typewriter. What's the episode number?"

"Ah. Five thousand, two hundred eighty. Page three. Ah, halfway down the pages where it says—"

"Give me the speech number. Like fourth speech, sixth speech."

"Oh, I'm sorry." She counted down through the dialogue of two actors. "Speech six. I'll catch on," Lauren promised.

"It's okay, honey," Sue answered. "I'm used to breaking in girls for Paula." Lauren ignored the remark and read the speech. She had the feeling she would have to thicken her skin and learn to ignore a lot of things.

During lunch, Lauren took Paula's completed outline to an address in Westwood that belonged to the dialogue writer, Mel Lorenzen. "Just put the outline in his mailbox and ring the doorbell," Jenny told her. "Then leave. Mel's sort of a hermit."

She drove to Westwood, the small village section of

Los Angeles clustered near UCLA with its quaint homes and shops and numerous movie theaters.

Lauren did as she was told and at Lorenzen's town house she placed the outline in the mailbox. She looked back once and a curtain in the front window moved. Very mysterious. She wondered if the other dialogue writer, Germain Gips, was equally eccentric and if she was supposed to establish any sort of relationship with them. How you would establish a relationship with a Westwood hermit?

Taking out time for a sandwich, Lauren returned to the penthouse, where everything came to a stop at two-thirty when the show aired.

Jenny took her in early and showed her how to oper-ate the Sony recorder, and as the opening music began, Paula walked into the room and took the one over-stuffed chair, a big orange monster. Jenny motioned Lauren to the sofa behind and to one side of the chair.

The room fell in silence as a male voice announced over the music, "And now, *Dreams to Come.*"

Lauren leaned over to Jenny. "You'll have to explain some things to me."

Jenny frowned underneath frizzy bangs and put a warning finger to her lips. "Later," she mouthed.

Lauren found the silence awkward and the story line confusing. When the phone rang, it went unanswered. Neither Paula nor Jenny acted as if she had heard it. Paula made an occasional note on a pad and once dur-ing a commercial she turned to Lauren.

"I play off the actors. Sometimes their interpretation is different from what I had in mind. Sometimes better, sometimes worse. I can only build a new character after the role has been cast. If they're good, they give the role a certain feel and direction."

The room remained in silence until the show ended and the last credit rolled over the show's logo. Paula stood up and stretched. "Not bad today. Stu's getting better. Stu's a new director to the show," she explained for Lauren's benefit. "They can make or break you. We use five directors. Did you understand any of what was happening?"

"A little, I think. It's good to have some faces to match the names now."

"They'll all become very familiar to you. Like family. I even dream about them. Jenny, get Germain on the phone for me. Her script played well."

Jenny turned off the recorder and followed Paula out of the room. Lauren trailed behind them, uncertain of her duties for the afternoon. She hoped Sally Rook was sleeping and not getting into more trouble. She hadn't yet found out where the girl had been yesterday or how she'd ended up topless.

Chapter Five

Lauren arrived home a few minutes after six, drove slowly down a driveway that seemed too narrow for any car and maneuvered her way into her designated parking slot.

The building was old, dating back to the early fifties, a dismal green thing of stucco with cracks left over from the seventy-one quake at Sylmar. She walked back up the drive and entered the complex through a wrought iron gate opening near the pool.

A mist wafted over the heated and lighted pool, giving an ethereal quality to the immediate surroundings. The night chill crept through Lauren's clothes and she shivered in the darkening evening that gave a sense that time and the world were out of sync.

Lugging a second stack of scripts, Lauren entered the first-floor apartment. The smell of burnt food filled her nostrils. "Sally?" she called anxiously.

Sally appeared in the kitchen door, a sheepish look on her face. She was wearing Lauren's old cotton robe that was faded and much too large for Sally's tiny frame. Her face was shiny clean and the long sun-streaked hair hung like silk down her back. "I wanted to do something nice for you," Sally said as Lauren laid

41

the scripts down. "I found this recipe in your cookbook and—well, it didn't work."

Lauren was touched and was reminded of her little sister and the first batch of cookies the child had attempted. Lila had sobbed over the blackened mess. Sally looked like she was ready to do the same. "Let's have a look," Lauren said cheerfully, and in the kitchen Sally pointed to a congealed mess of macaroni and cheese in a casserole. Lauren poked the crusted and burnt food. She wrinkled her nose. "It is hopeless."

"We'll never get the bowl clean," Sally said. "I'll buy you a new one, I promise."

Lauren grinned at a sudden thought. "Let's dump the bowl."

"What?" Sally was incredulous.

"In the garbage. Benji's mother gave me this. One of her discards. She was always giving me some pieces of junk that no one else wanted."

"Your ex?"

"Yes."

"He did you bad?" Sally asked.

"He didn't see it that way." Lauren let the bowl fall into the trash sack. It hit with a satisfying bang and cracked into four pieces. Lauren laughed and dusted her hands together. "God, that's a nice feeling. Let's celebrate. We'll have some wine and I'll make grilled cheese sandwiches."

"We—we can't," Sally whispered.

"Why? You drink all the wine?" Lauren teased.

"No. I used all the cheese."

"So? We'll have tuna fish. Who cares?" Lauren felt slightly giddy. "And it wasn't your fault that the casserole burned. It's the oven. It overheats."

"I should have checked it. Or something. Every time I try to cook, this kind of thing happens. You'd think any person who could read could cook."

"You can learn. There's a lot of little tricks to the trade."

"Secrets?" Sally asked, her eyes mischievous.

"Sort of." Lauren smiled at the girl and turned to pour them each a glass of wine from a Gallo bottle with a screw-on top.

They curled up on opposite ends of the sofa. Sally offered Lauren a cigarette. Lauren shook her head. "I bummed them off the guy who lives next door." Sally told her.

"How did you meet him?"

"I was outside. You know, looking the place over. I met him. And a sweet little old lady who lives in front. Did you know the guy in the other front apartment is crippled? He's got an electric wheelchair and his wife sits on his lap and they fly down the driveway."

Lauren laughed. "Sally, you are something else. I've never more than nodded hello to anyone here. How did you meet so many people?"

"I don't know. I guess I talk a lot and I'm nosy," she said matter-of-factly. "Do you like working for the Witch?" Sally asked.

Lauren shrugged, not ready to confide in Sally. "I don't know yet. It's different. This was only my second day."

"And you got me. Some initiation, huh?"

Lauren grinned at her. She was like a stray pup, all friendly wiggles, with eyes full of hope and apprehension. The original pity she had felt was replaced by a genuine affection for the girl.

"Did you sleep?" Lauren asked.

"Like a zombie. That's a terrific bed." Sally folded the old robe tighter around her small body.

"I doubt that. Benji and I bought it secondhand."

"Better than a sleeping bag on the floor at Jake's."

Lauren studied Sally, curious and fascinated. "Who is Jake, anyway?"

Sally looked down at her fingers that began to pleat the hem of the robe. "Oh, he's a crumb I connected up with. I met him at a party. He brought the grass. He's not a bad guy, Lauren. He's a performer. He sings and plays a mean guitar. But he's never had any breaks."

"How does he make a living?"

"He deals some."

"Deals?" Lauren shook her head, not understanding.

"You know, he pushes some."

Her meaning began to sink in. "You mean, he sells drugs?" Lauren was shocked.

"What else would you deal?" Sally asked, puzzled.

There was a dip in the pit of Lauren's stomach. "Oh, Sally."

"I guess you don't smoke, huh?"

"Not even cigarettes, much less grass."

"You mean you've never had a joint?" The sense of shock was in Sally's voice now.

"I've never *seen* a joint."

"Well, I can fix that." Sally announced.

"That's all right." Lauren held up her hands, half expecting Sally to produce one from her pocket.

"Okay." Sally shrugged good-naturedly. "Do you think you could go with me to get my clothes? Joe said I shouldn't go alone. I can't even go if you don't drive me. Unless I hitch. I don't like to hitch at night. They think you're a hooker."

"I can drive you, if you think it's safe to go there." Lauren hesitated, not sure if she wanted to do this. "Sally, what did Jake do to you?"

"Knocked me around. Hit me a couple of times."

"Aren't you angry?"

"I was last night. I hit him back." Sally leaned toward Lauren. "See, there was a big delivery of bad stuff coming down. Coke, mostly. Jake wanted me to make the pickup and I wouldn't. A little grass, maybe even a lot of grass. I'd do that. But not the hard stuff. I didn't want Jake to touch it either. We got into it and he hit me and I hit him back and he hit me again and I started screaming and I said I was leaving. That's when he started burning my clothes in the bathtub. He thought I couldn't leave if I didn't have any clothes. Hell, I'd have walked out of there naked."

Lauren tried not to let her dismay show. She felt like

44

she was hearing something out of a tabloid. "How did you get out?"

"I grabbed a T-shirt and jeans and cut out while he was muttering in the bathroom over his fire. It wasn't hard to get away. He was stoned."

"I see," Lauren said softly, unable to imagine herself getting into such a position.

"I guess I was stoned, too. Cause I went down to this bar that was having a wet T-shirt contest."

"A wet T-shirt?"

"You know, you get up on stage and they pour water over your T-shirt and the guys vote on you. It just happened. I went in the joint cause it was warm and sounded lively. This jock stud started buying me drinks and I was already stoned. The next thing I knew I was up on stage and they watered me down and everyone laughed. See." Sally opened up the front of the robe. "No boobs," she said sadly and touched one of the knobs on her bony chest.

"Oh, Sally," Lauren whispered, aching for Sally's humiliation.

"I started crying and my jock friend got mad and he tore into a guy who was laughing and I jumped in to help him. Then the cops showed up and they found out I was only nineteen. The bar owner was screaming and crying then. He tried to strangle me. My jock guy hit him and the cops arrested the three of us. That's how I ended up at Sybil Brand."

"And you called Joe this morning?"

"Yeah." Sally shrugged. "I didn't want to wake him up last night."

"Wasn't there any family you could call?"

"Nah." Sally's fingers began a new row of pleats.

"Where is your family?" Lauren asked, unable to contain her curiosity.

"I don't know." She glanced up and down again.

"Really?" Lauren pressed for more information.

"Well, my old man, he took off before I was born.

45

My sister's a hooker. She was in Chicago last I heard. My mother is probably still in Kansas."

"You aren't sure?"

"No."

Lauren was feeling confused. "But—but you're only nineteen."

"That's me."

"Then you couldn't have been on your own very long."

"I took off the first time when I was fourteen. I made it to Texas before they caught me and sent me back. The second time, when I was fifteen, I was smarter. The only reason they caught me the first time was because I kept to myself. You've got to be part of a group to survive. If you've got a place to crash and you don't panhandle or hook, the cops don't notice you."

Lauren felt Sally's cinnamon eyes studying her. "You're shocked, aren't you?" Sally asked.

"I guess I am," Lauren answered slowly. Yet it was a common enough story. There had always been runaways pouring into Hollywood, there always would be. But Sally Rook was different. She possessed a very special quality, a kind of charisma Lauren couldn't name.

The girls made what was to Lauren a scary trip to North Hollywood. Sally directed her to a crumbling collection of apartment units that were known as courts when they were built in the thirties.

They walked down a narrow dark pathway that was a crumbling sidewalk bordered by dirt and rocks that must have once been flowerbeds. After Sally made sure Jake wasn't home, they entered a small room, lit by a dim overhanging bulb. The combined odors of dirt and age and grass made Lauren's stomach turn.

The only furniture was a pillowlike sofa covered in some dark material from India and a couple of shabby sleeping bags.

In the bathroom, Sally rooted through a pile of half-burned clothes. "Nothing worth saving here." She rum-

46

maged through the kitchen cupboards and came out with shoes, a purse and a small tin box. She checked the contents, closed it gently and handed it to Lauren. "Take care of this. It's my—you'll think I'm silly—but it's my treasure box. That's what I used to call it when I was a kid. Sometimes I just had a shoe box under my bed. But I always had a few things that were mine and no one else's."

From the single closet in the living room Sally extracted a pair of jeans from a pile of clothes on the floor. "Too bad Jake's jeans don't fit me. But I think I'll take a couple of shirts."

She wrapped the jeans and T-shirts around the shoes. "I'm ready."

It was pitiful. Lauren thought she was going to cry. She couldn't believe they'd driven over here and taken a chance on running into Jake to rescue these meager belongings.

In the car, Sally rode with the tin box held protectively on her lap. Lauren was awash again with pity. She wanted to help Sally.

"You have to be on the set in the morning, don't you?" Lauren asked.

"At eight, for the first dry run."

"Maybe we could take up one of my dresses for you to wear."

"Nah, that's okay. They're used to me showing up in jeans and bare feet." The tone of her voice made Lauren glance over.

"Are you okay?" she asked.

"Yes. No. Damn it, I don't know." Sally burst into tears. "I don't want to ever live like that again. You must think I'm a pig. Your place is so clean and neat. You live nice, Lauren."

"Nice," Lauren echoed helplessly. She had a cheap apartment and some furniture that had for the most part come from secondhand stores.

"I want to change. I want to be a lady like you. I

47

mean it, Lauren. I want you to teach me. Please help me."

Lauren pulled the car to the side of the street. Sally came into her arms. Lauren held her as great wrenching sobs tore out of the frail body.

"I'll help you. It'll be okay," Lauren murmured over and over, though she felt helpless against the onslaught of tears.

The torrent ended and Sally pulled away. Lauren handed her a tissue from her purse. Sally blew her nose loudly. Lauren's blouse was wet from Sally's tears.

"I can be good, can't I?" Sally asked, her eyes pleading liquid pools.

"You can be anything you want to be," Lauren assured her gently, and fervently hoped she was right.

"How?"

"Well, you're an actress. You have steady work. Paula says you're good. She said you have a lot of talent. A lot. She said you can make it big."

"Paula said that? Wow!" Sally sat up straight, her eyes shining. "You're putting me on. The Witch wouldn't say anything nice like that about anybody."

"She said it about you. She said that in five years you can be a big star."

"Unreal!" Tawny eyes stared at Lauren in disbelief. "I just can't believe the Witch would say that."

"She said it."

Sally sank back against the seat. "It's all I've ever wanted to be. I used to do all those corny things, like cut out pictures of actresses and actors and pin them on my walls. I used to daydream about how it would be for me. I decided when I was six years old that I'd be a movie star. I wanted all the things I knew I'd never have if I stayed around Mama and Patty." Sally paused for a moment, catching her breath. "I want clothes and jewelry and neat cars and a beautiful home. But not in Beverly Hills. Up in the canyon someplace, where I can have animals around me. I want horses and dogs and cats."

It is all a fantasy with Sally acting out the part of the central character, Lauren thought. But she'd made it this far against tremendous odds. Maybe she could go all the way.

As Lauren guided the car back into the street, Sally sighed and leaned her head against the seat. "Tell me again, Lauren. Tell me every word Paula said about me."

Chapter Six

Back in the apartment, the girls settled on the sofa with glasses of milk and tuna fish sandwiches. "I want to know how you got your first break." Lauren told her. "Hitting this town at fifteen—how did you survive?"

"I don't know. I just came here. I knew if I could get to Hollywood, I'd find a way into films. Things always work out. You look for ways and you find them."

"I suppose," Lauren said, but she was skeptical. She'd looked for ways to solve her problems with Benji. She'd only found one answer—divorce. The cop-out solution. No, she had to quit thinking like that. Divorce was the only solution.

"I lucked out and connected up with a guy who's an extra," Sally went on. He taught me a lot. He helped me get my first part. I got into the Extras Guild that way. Getting into the unions is the hard part. You can't get a part unless you're a member of the Guild. But you can't join the Guild until you have a part. Anyway, Tony got me the part. I was just a person walking down the street. In an old-fashioned dress with lace and tiny flowers. I loved that dress. I wanted to keep it, but they wouldn't let me. It wãs a western with Paul Newman. Nothing will ever be that exciting again." A shiver ran over Sally's body and she hugged herself. "He spoke to me. Paul Newman spoke to me. He said good morning."

Lauren smiled affectionately at Sally. "I probably would have fainted."

"It was super. Tony paid my initial ducs for me. He was so good to me. I loved him."

"What happened to him?"

"He went back to his lover. See, they'd had a fight and Pete took off with some swish and—"

"Tony was gay?" Lauren injected, shocked again.

"Tony was bi. The sweetest guy in the world," Sally said and went back to her story. "So I lied about my age and used some phony ID Tony had gotten for me. When I got a real role, I joined SAG, the Screen Actors Guild then. Meeting Joe Seals was the best thing to happen to me. He made me take acting classes. Joe even paid for some of them."

Lauren wondered how Sally felt about Joe, how she coped with his friendliness. "Did—did Joe ever make a pass at you?"

"A pass?" Sally frowned. "I've slept with Joe, if that's what you mean." Lauren's consternation showed on her face and Sally leaned over and touched her arm. "Hey, it's not like you're thinking. Joe didn't take me on cause I'd sleep with him. And I've paid him back every cent I've ever borrowed, except the bail money. I've got to pay him that now. I don't barter my body," she ended, sounding half-angry.

"I didn't mean to imply that," Lauren said, a little taken aback by Sally's strong words.

"I sleep with most of my friends. And Joe and I are friends. You're shocked again. I guess you think I'm bad. I'm not. I'm not a hooker like my sister. Sex, it— it's a friendly thing to do. It's for mutual enjoyment. It's nice. I like it." Her tone was half-defensive, half-sincere.

"A friendly thing." Lauren mouthed the words, testing them in her mind.

"You don't understand, do you?"

"No." Lauren looked away. "I take sex very seriously."

Sally's eyes darkened. "I bet—I bet you've never slept with anyone but your ex."

Lauren blushed for reasons she couldn't understand. "That's true."

"Heavy!" It was Sally's turn to be astonished.

She felt as though Sally was looking at her as if she were something foreign, like a bug from outer space. And Sally was almost too bizarre for Lauren to comprehend. The subject was making Lauren tense and anxious, so she changed it. "So, you got on *Dreams* through an audition Joe set up?"

"Yeah. It's good steady money and hard work. Nothing like films."

Lauren touched the stack of scripts on the coffee table. "I'm supposed to be reading those. I'm awfully confused. Reading straight dialogue doesn't tell me much, and there seem to be a lot of undercurrents going on that I don't know about."

"I'm barely getting it straight myself. Hey!" Sally jumped up and got her tin box. "They gave me a thing when I joined the cast."

Sally opened the box and took out some folded Xeroxed sheets. "This is a recap of the last twenty years. This sheet is a sort of family tree. Now, see, Maurice Moran and Rose Jardine are the tent-pole characters. Life kind of revolves around them. They've been married like forty years. They have these three sons, played by Cobb Strong, Lee Trent and Kerry Scott. Everyone is a doctor but Kerry. He's the youngest and doesn't know what he wants to be yet. I'm his current love interest. I'm new to the show. I've been there six months."

"Okay. I've got that." Lauren took the sheets.

"Now, Cobb Strong is the oldest son. His wife is in a mental hospital. And he thinks he's young Timmy's father. Timmy is like six. Only Lee Trent is really the child's father. Cobb Strong is having an affair with a gal named Irene. Irene is the current bitch. Every show has to have a resident bitch."

"I see," Lauren said, though she didn't.

"And every show also has a set of star-crossed lovers. That's Lee Trent and Anne Voll. They have always loved each other, will always love each other, but they are never allowed to marry. Misunderstandings and obligations get in their way."

"Then that's where Belle comes from. She didn't make much sense to me."

"Belle was married to Lee Trent years ago. She's a trampy sort. I guess they brought her back to town because they'd run out of reasons to keep Lee Trent and Anne Voll apart. The viewers want them married. The mail gets very heavy on that point."

"Then why don't they let them get married?"

"I don't know. I mostly know about me. I'm the new girl in town, falling in love with Kerry Scott. Our parts aren't too big right now. I think I'll turn out to be his half sister. From an affair his father had about six years back."

"Six years and you're now supposed to be eighteen?" Lauren gasped.

"Yeah, well, time is strange on soaps. Sometimes we have fourteen-month pregnancies. But kids have to grow up fast. Otherwise they're just clutter. So when they're about eight, you send them off to military school one year and they come back in the next and they are eighteen to twenty-five. All the shows do that."

"How are you paid?" Lauren asked.

"By the day. The regulars all have guarantees, mostly for one or two or even three days a week. They get paid those guarantees whether they're on the show or not, but mostly they work more than the guarantees. Except Kerry Scott."

"He's the young, good-looking brother?" Lauren asked. He was a dark and sexy-looking guy who had caught Lauren's attention on the first show she watched.

"Yeah. He's only guaranteed one day a week. He needs more to live on."

"He's awfully attractive," Lauren said.

"You want to meet him?" Sally jumped to her feet. "I'll set it up. It's easy." She snapped her fingers.

Lauren recoiled. "No. No. I'm not ready for that. And I wouldn't want to come across like a . . ."

"A groupie?"

"Yes."

"You'll meet him sometime. The other girl who worked for Paula was always on the set for one thing or another. You'll meet everybody."

Lauren settled back, feeling good about Sally and her work.

"I think I'm going to like this job."

Sally yawned and stretched. "I gotta go to bed. I'm beat."

"Go ahead. I'm going to read for a while."

But Lauren found it difficult to keep her mind on the endless pages of dialogue. Her thoughts kept flipping to Benji and contrasting him and herself with Sally. Benji and Sally would not like each other if they met. And Lauren did not think Benji would ever take the view that sex was a friendly thing to do. With Benji, it was some kind of obsession, as though he had to keep on proving himself over and over, proving that he was a man who could get it up and make full use of it.

But it was obvious that of the three of them, Lauren was the odd one, the different one. She let the script rest in her lap and wrapped her arms around her body, wondering again if there was something missing in her.

Compared with what she knew now, sex had been based on a simple enough premise back home. You either did or did not save yourself for your wedding night, and if you did not, you tried to be reasonably discreet about it. She'd been brought up by her mother and society to believe sex was something special and sacred between man and woman. The act itself was suppose to be gentle and pleasing, with only the emotions soaring wildly.

With Benji, it had been neither. He was not gentle and there was wildness in the act. She had called him perverted and sick. Was he only honest? Like Sally?

Were people like her mother and her sister one thing on the surface and another in the bedroom? She shook her head. She couldn't believe Lila had a secret cache of sexy clothes like the ones Benji had bought her at Frederick's of Hollywood.

She had been thrilled, truly deeply touched, when Benji told her he was taking her shopping for her birthday last year. Their life had been going badly and they'd had a terrible fight the night before.

Since Benji never liked holidays and never remembered a birthday, she had felt he was trying to make up with her, using the shopping as a peace offering.

Benji, darkly handsome in a new leisure suit, took her to a mall. Her hands went cold in his when they stopped in front of Frederick's. "In here," Benji directed.

"I can't go in there."

"Why not?"

"Benji, you know what kind of stuff they sell. I can't."

Benji's full, boyish face took on a contrite look. "Hey, now, all I want to do is buy you a sexy nightie. Maybe a new bra." His hands on hers urged her forward.

Inside, she fingered a rack of blouses while Benji conferred with a sales clerk. She was aware of the clerk flirting with Benji as the two of them ruffled through a rack of nightgowns. Lauren did not protest when the clerk with her high-piled hair and false eyelashes took her back to a dressing booth.

She silently stripped and pulled a black gown over her head. It wasn't so bad. Incredibly sheer, of course, but it was soft and sexy. Her nipples, hard from the cold, showed through the fabric. Benji would like it, and if it pleased him, if it meant he would be happy, why not?

"Try these now, honey," the sales clerk said and thrust a handful of bras inside.

Lauren was surprised at how well the bras fit. They looked like puffs of nothing, but the straps were sturdy and the underwiring held her up. Of course, they also thrust her up high and formed a cleavage she had never had before. She guessed she could take one to wear at home, but not the one with the cutouts exposing her nipples. That one repulsed her. She carefully put it aside.

"Here we go." The blonde poked her head inside the booth. "He likes these," she said with a suggestive wink. A lacy garter belt dangled from her fingers.

"I—I wear pantyhose."

"Honey, if I had a hunk like him willing to spend money on me, I'd buy these."

Looking away from the woman's gaze, Lauren examined the garter belt. It was actually a type of panty, cut bikini high with the crotch missing. "I—I can't wear this."

"Try it on."

Taking a deep breath, Lauren stepped into the garter belt, pulling it on over her own waist-high plain white panties. The garter belt made her feel dirty. "The garters are too short," Lauren said in relief. "A pair of hose would never reach that high."

"Ours would, and besides, they're only for fun."

"No." Lauren shook her head firmly. "No."

"Have it your way, but I think you're crazy. That is some hunk." She rolled her eyes and disappeared. Lauren heard her say to Benji, "Well, I tried." Lauren hurriedly dressed before the clerk could return with more clothes.

Clutching the black gown and the one acceptable bra, Lauren stepped out of the booth in time to see Benji handing the clerk his card. Her stomach knotted as

Benji touched the woman's chin in a familiar gesture she had once thought was reserved for her alone.

Lauren knew that in that moment, she gave up. It was then she knew she alone would never be enough to satisfy Benji. But she had hung in, hoping, refusing to admit failure, unable to leave until the group-sex thing came up. Only then did she see a lawyer and start divorce proceedings.

The last time she saw Benji was in the lawyer's office. It was to be a simple, uncontested divorce. She did not ask for alimony and he did not want any of the furniture, so dividing the property was an easy enough affair. They would each get half of the small savings account.

They were already in separate housing, she in her apartment in the Valley and he in a furnished place on the edge of Marina del Rey where people were more liberal and swinging than in the Valley.

All very simple and uncomplicated except for the torrent of emotions raging inside her body and mind. It was hard to look at Benji. She was so aware of his nearness, of the familiarity of him, of his maleness, of the faint odor of Brut aftershave, of the way he had of tilting his head and gazing at her.

Don't stare at me, she had wanted to yell. You can't figure me out, and I darn sure don't understand you.

She tried to hang back when they were finished, but Benji took her arm and led her out of the office. In the long, silent hallway he stopped. "Lauren."

"Yes?" She moved away from him.

He came toward her, dark eyes seeming to pin her to the wall. "I'll always miss you."

She had expected anything but that. Jolted, she leaned against the wall for support, unable to stop the hot tears flooding her eyes. "Benji, don't."

"I'm really sorry it had to come to this, Lauren." He took her hand. It was cold and trembling against his warm flesh. He pressed her fingers to his lips. "If you could just give a little—"

"Benji." She snatched her hand back, conscious of the warmth spreading over her body, of her face flaming red. "I gave all I could. I went as far as my nature would allow me."

He shook his head slowly. "Lauren. Level with me."

"About what?" She clutched the handle of her purse with both hands.

"Haven't you ever had a yen for another guy? Hasn't there been one time in your life when you wanted to cut loose?"

"No," she whispered, as though admitting to a sin. Dear God, he made her feel so ashamed of herself.

"Don't any of the things I want excite you?"

"No." It was getting harder and harder to breathe. Her back pressed against the cold wall. She wanted to run, but she was frozen to the spot.

Suddenly he stepped back, breaking the spell. "So be it. If you ever get rid of your hang-ups, call me."

She turned her face to the wall to hide her tears as Benji walked away.

Chapter Seven

Sally Rook lay curled in a tight ball, her face pressed against the softness of the pillow, more frightened than she wanted to admit. Tonight she had a bed, she was safe in Lauren's apartment. But tomorrow she would have to find a place for herself, one without Jake. She knew she was going to miss him, for she missed him already. But she wasn't going back to him. Jake was a dead end.

She closed her eyes against the image of the bearded, long-haired man whose lanky body had possessed hers again and again. She tried to drift off to sleep, but it refused to come. Restless, she twisted over on her right side. The sheets smelled faintly of roses and Sally wondered if Lauren kept those sachet things in her drawers and shelves.

She closed her eyes again, searching for sleep, but the smell of roses always reminded her of home and Kansas City. There had been a tangle mass of wild roses behind their old house, nothing like the oversized California roses. These were wild ones, very tiny with only a few flat and frail petals of the palest pink.

Her mother, who insisted on being called Bunny instead of Mama, used to cut the roses and bring them into the house and stuff them into fruit jars. The flowers never lasted for more than a day.

When Sally was twelve and tiny, she used to hide in the rosebush when Mac, her mother's boyfriend, was around. There was a small space in the back of the rosebush and Sally could just slide into it. She didn't mind the occasional scratches from the bush because the important thing was to remain unseen.

Sally hated Mac, whom she privately referred to as Hairy Belly. Mac worked in the auto plant and was greasy looking with a huge white hairy belly that stuck out between pants and shirt.

At twelve years old, Sally had managed to keep her virginity intact, but no thanks to Bunny or her sister, Patty. Neither of them made much of an effort to protect the child from the various men who came around.

Sally was a small, agile and fast little girl who could pass for a boy. Her lack of development worried Bunny. After all, Patty was hooking by the time she was fifteen.

Sally couldn't remember when she was not aware of sex and the physical act involved. It was an ordinary occurrence at their house. She was both fascinated and repelled, especially as she grew aware of her own sexuality.

She waited for her breasts to develop, but she never got more than small knobs. In a way, it was a form of protection. Most men did not pay any attention to her, except for Hairy Belly, whose comings and goings she avoided as much as possible.

Harry Belly reminded Sally of Raymond Burr in a part he had played in an old movie she had seen on television. In it the young Raymond Burr was a child molester. Hairy Belly had that look about him, only he was worse. He always smelled of stale beer and moldy sweat. His lower lip was fat and tended to flap when he talked; his hands were rough and huge.

Everyone reminded Sally of an actor or actress. The movie world was sometimes more real to her than Kansas City. Bunny was Shelley Winters, overweight and loudmouthed with bleached hair and big boobs spilling over the front of her dress.

Patty was Jane Fonda in *Klute*. She was heavier and bustier than Fonda, but there was something similar about them, perhaps the same attitude toward men as the movie prostitute had had.

A loner, Sally slipped in and out of the house like a shadow, keeping out of the way of Mac and Bunny and Patty and whatever men they had in the house. She lived mostly on peanut butter sandwiches, occasionally bologna and cheese. When she had money she spent it first on movies, then movie magazines, then on hamburgers and French fries at a run-down stand near the railroad tracks.

Her only friend was Donny Stillman. She and Donny were a lot of different people. Sometimes she was Elizabeth Taylor in *National Velvet,* her favorite old movie that was generally shown on Sunday afternoon TV. Sometimes they were the kids in the bikini movies, and sometimes they were Lauren Bacall and Humphrey Bogart.

Donny was the same age as Sally. He lived across the alley from her with his father in a rancid-smelling boarding house. Mr. Stillman was crippled, a disabled veteran who drank each night in order to sleep. Mr. Stillman was the only person she knew whom she could not typecast as an actor.

He was a tall man with broad shoulders pulled into a permanent stoop. He moved about on two metal walking sticks, his gait a lunge from one spot to the next.

At thirty-eight, Mr. Stillman was prematurely gray with a wild thatch of silver-white hair. Once in a while Sally and Donny would lean a chair back against the kitchen sink and maneuver Mr. Stillman into it. The two kids would shampoo his hair and rinse it. Afterward Mr. Stillman would allow Sally to comb it until it was dry. Those were her happiest moments, Stillman's words of praise her only glories.

She loved him as she would have loved her father if she had known him. He was the only grown-up who talked to kids as if they were people. who listened to their problems and accepted their arguments without putting them down.

She liked it when he would sit on the sofa and let her cuddle against him. His face was always scratchy with whiskers, even if he had shaved that day. He wore rough-feeling wools from the local Salvation Army thrift shop and always smelled faintly of whiskey.

No matter how hard she tried, she could not pin him down. Sometimes she would see him as Clint Eastwood, a silent, hard-fighting man before he was crippled in the Korean War. But the hair made him more like Peter Graves from *Mission Impossible*.

In the most secret part of her heart she carried another kind of fantasy. In it Bunny and Mr. Stillman fell in love. Her mother changed into one of the women who picked up their daughters after school in station wagons.

In Sally's daydreams Bunny devoted herself to Mr. Stillman, adoring him. With the help of a famous doctor, Mr. Stillman was restored to his robust self. Of course, she and Donny would be brother and sister. Daddy would go off to work every morning in a gray suit wearing a tie Sally had picked out for him. And of course, she was the only one who could comb his hair. She would get up extra early every morning so she could comb Daddy's hair for him. Daddy would hug her, and before he walked out the door to his shiny car, he would whisper in her ear, "You're the best daughter in the whole world. No one else is as good as you."

She would slip from his arms and he would kiss Bunny good-bye, then Donny. And the three of them would wave him off to work from the front steps of their beautiful brick home.

It was a childish fantasy; even at thirteen she knew that. But she loved it and played it over and over in her head, adding little bits and pieces from time to time.

Sometimes she was the heroine who found the doctor for her daddy, begging for his help with tears sliding silently down her cheeks.

It helped her cope with the reality of Mr. Stillman's being a crippled alcoholic, and of Bunny who worked in various cafes and bars. Donny and Sally walked to school and back together, shared small secrets and hopes and found ways to survive. The summer they were thirteen they exchanged their first fluttery kisses and by winter were tentatively exploring each other's bodies.

It was a bitterly cold winter with the winds sweeping off the plains and into the very bones of her body. Sometimes the snow blew in between the cracks in the windows of the Stillman apartment.

The cold made Mr. Stillman's pain almost unbearable. The pill he got from the VA hospital helped very little and even the whiskey could not stop the pain when it was cold.

The only relief was to get him warm, a nearly impossible task. Watching him suffer tore Sally apart. One night she got an idea. "Why don't we get in bed with him?" Sally asked Donny.

"What?" Donny shook his head. He was a skinny kid and short for his age. His hair was a tangle of dirty blonde and he wore a tattered sweater that was too small for him.

"Sure. I saw it in a movie one time. These people were going to freeze to death. They were lost in a blizzard. But they didn't because they got into bed together. I think they took off their clothes and wrapped themselves together in animal skins. Bear skins or something."

"That's dumb," Donny said.

"No it's not," Sally insisted. "We don't have to get undressed. But we'll get on each side of your father and we'll make him warm."

She brought Donny around in a few minutes, and it worked. Mr. Stillman grew warm and drowsy, then drifted off to sleep. It became a ritual with them. Nearly every night Sally would slip into their apartment and the two kids would get into bed with Mr. Stillman.

"Make me warm," he would say. "Then I can sleep."

"Daddy, are you getting warm?" Donny would ask every few minutes.

"It's better," he would answer. "I'm better. You're good kids, helping me like this."

Sally would press her face against his scratchy cheek and hug him tighter and tighter. "Sleep, Daddy. Sleep," she whispered. "Sleep and tomorrow it will be better."

Her voice and body were full of soft yearnings and desires and funny little prickly sensations she didn't totally understand. He would drift off to sleep and in time become restless. Then Donny and Sally would get up and cover him with the extra blanket kept on the foot of the bed.

"Can't anyone help him?" Sally asked as she watched the man. Even in sleep the pain was etched on his face.

"I guess not, or they would at the VA hospital. It's all that shrapnel, you know. It caught him in the back. He's got scars, really ugly scars. Some of the shrapnel is still in there," Donny said.

Hot tears flooded Sally's eyes. "Oh, Donny. If only we could help him."

"But how?" he asked, his young, unflawed face taking on a bewildered look.

"I don't know," Sally answered in exasperation. "I don't know."

The next winter Mr. Stillman began failing. The night finally came when Donny couldn't get him up from his chair and into bed, and the ambulance came to take him to the hospital. Two days later Donny was in a foster home out in the suburbs.

Sally was wild with grief she kept hidden inside herself. She took the bus to the VA hospital once, but they wouldn't let her in because she was too young. At first she talked to Donny every day on the phone at the hamburger stand. Gradually the conversations dwindled off and she carried her desolation alone.

Hairy Belly, who hadn't been around much, suddenly returned. He was more persistent than ever and without Donny and Mr. Stillman, Sally had no place to hide.

By spring Mac's advances became unbearable. Every time she turned around he was there, trying to press his smelly mouth against hers, grabbing her behind in his huge hands and squeezing her until it made tears come to her eyes.

She begged Bunny to call him off, but Bunny only laughed, her huge breasts jiggling. She thought it was funny, especially when she had been drinking.

In May Sally came home from school and stopped on the back stoop when she heard Bunny and Mac talking. "You got to let me break her in," Mac was saying. "I mean, she's probably already started and if she's got a man she won't be wasting herself on them runny-nosed kids."

"I don't know, Mac," Bunny slurred.

"Hey, I'm all right. I'm clean," he insisted. "I'll be good to her. No telling what she might pick up by herself. She's not like Patty. Patty can take care of herself."

Sally ran away that night. She made it to Texas, where a man in a plain white Chevrolet picked her up on the highway. He was wearing worn jeans and a soiled Stetson and had an easy way of talking.

"Where do you live, kid?" he asked her.

"New Mexico." It was becoming her standard story. She used the next state as her destination. "I've been visiting my grandmother in Oklahoma. She's been awful sick."

"Yup," he drawled, reminding Sally of Gary Cooper. "How old are you?"

"Eighteen," she answered without hesitation.

"Yeah, you are." The skepticism was plain. He reached into his shirt pocket and pulled out a badge. "I'm undersheriff of this county. What say we just stop in and make a few phone calls?"

Sally closed her mouth and did not open it again. They kept her at the county jail for a week, then took her to court and finally to a foster home where she stayed until a missing persons report on her turned up.

Bunny got drunk her first night home. "Mac left me," she whined to Sally. "He left me because you wouldn't stay."

Fat tears streaked down Bunny's heavily roughed cheeks. "I hate you!" Sally choked. Bunny's broad hand lashed out and struck Sally full across the face.

"I ain't supporting you no longer!" Bunny said vehemently. "You get out on the street. Patty will help you."

She went to Donny the next day. It was hot in Kansas, dry and burning. She had to change buses three times and then walk almost two miles out into the new suburb where he now lived with his foster family.

She wiped the sweat off her face with the tail of her shirt before she rang the bell of the two-story house. A woman in an apron answered. Sally asked for Donny, feeling dizzy at the thought of his not being there.

The woman invited her in. Sally was tempted. She could feel the coolness of the air conditioning coming through the door. She shook her head. "I just want to talk to Donny," she told the woman.

A few moments later he was standing on the wide porch with her. He stood back, hands behind him. He looked different. His hair had been cut off and seemed to be a lighter color.

"You're taller," she whispered, feeling far, far away from him.

"I guess I am."

They faced each other, both awkward. "How's your daddy?" she asked.

"He just had surgery. There was still some pieces of shrapnel in his spine."

"Can he walk?" she asked.

"Not yet. Maybe some day. He has therapy every day."

Sally's small heart twisted, her body filling with

68

yearnings for what might have been, for the fantasies she had dreamed so many times. "Oh, Donny!" she choked, grabbed him by the arm and pulled him down onto the steps. "I've got to talk to you. I want you to run away with me. I did it once. I ran away, but they caught me and sent me back."

He did not look at her. He watched a dirty sheet of newspaper the wind was skittering down the street. On the opposite side of the street raw housing frames stood on dry, heard earth, waiting for the next wave of workmen. Beyond those were wheat fields where heavy heads hung on golden stalks in silent preparation for the combine crews.

Sally waited, her head down now, too. "Donny." She tugged at the sleeve of his shirt that was new and freshly ironed. She felt like a rag picker compared to him.

"What?" he asked, his eyes darting to her then away again.

"Go with me," she pleaded.

His hands hung limply over his knees. His head dropped down. "I can't, Sally. I can't leave Daddy. He needs me, needs me now worse than any time. If I went off, what would he do? Who would he have to visit him?"

I need you, too, she thought through the haze of loneliness enveloping her. But she did not say it. "Sure, Donny," she said instead. "I guess I knew that all along. I just wasn't thinking."

"Where are you going?" Donny asked, glancing back over his shoulder at the house. She could feel him pulling away from her.

"Hollywood," she answered.

"You gonna be in the movies?"

"Sure I am!" She flung her hair back, making it float up and around her face in a silken curtain. The wind caught it; she grabbed her hair and pushed it all to the back of her neck.

"Will I ever see you again?" he asked.

"I don't know, Donny. Maybe if you come to California. I'm not ever coming back here. Never!"

She left Donny and never returned. She did not know if his father ever walked again or not. She lasted another two months at home. She spent the summer days working in the hamburger stand, coming home at night with her hair and skin smelling of fried grease. She saved her money, forgoing movies and movie magazines and eating mostly at the stand.

She left in August, taking a bus into Oklahoma City and hitchhiking from there. There were a lot of kids on the road in the summer. She did not stand out now, and she did not travel alone.

She bought a backpack, putting in the clothes that she had brought with her in a cardboard box. There was also her treasure box, a little tin box she had found on the street one day. All it contained was the old high school picture of her real father and a necklace Donny and Mr. Stillman had given her the previous Christmas.

She met two college boys from New York. She slept with both of them, and though the sex was not particularly exciting to her then, she did find it a warm and satisfying experience. She liked the closeness of the bodies. Her only regret was that she had never done it with Donny. It would have been something special to remember.

She parted with the boys in Las Vegas. They were going north and invited her along, but she held her eyes on only one place—Hollywood. She managed to hitch a ride with an older man straight into Los Angeles. He dropped her in North Hollywood and she headed for an address the boys had given her, a place where she could crash.

She wondered if Bunny had put out another missing persons report on her. Probably not. They were probably glad to be rid of her. She wondered if Bunny and Patty ever saw her now on TV or in a movie. She hoped they did. She hoped they knew she was somebody.

Chapter Eight

In a bedroom in the Encino hills, *Dream*'s star-crossed lovers sprawled naked on a king-size bed. Violent red and green flowers danced in mayhem over the sheets. A gold velvet spread had been kicked to the floor of a room done in spindly legged French Provincial. A bath, dressing room and walk-in closet took up as much floor space as the bedroom.

The occupants of the bed were both in their mid-thirties and blessed with a certain youthful appearance. Through rigid dieting, Anne Voll managed to maintain a size seven figure. Her small breasts were firm, her black hair curly, and tumbled from their lovemaking.

She cuddled against Lee Trent, her head on his stomach that had a tendency to protrude if he didn't stand up straight. His carefully styled sandy-colored hair was only slightly mussed.

Lee yawned and touched Anne's bare shoulder. "I should go home," he said.

"Don't go. Spend the night." Her voice was low and husky, a trademark her fans adored.

Lee felt vaguely annoyed. He wanted to go home, where he could sleep alone. "We have to be discreet," he reminded her. "You know that. If one of the fan magazines got hold of this, we'd be splattered across every cover."

"Oh, who cares?" she pouted prettily.

"Silverstein cares. The network cares. The viewers care. You know the kind of audience we have. We're an old-fashioned show."

She flipped over and bumped her forehead against his tummy. "I don't care what they think. I want you here," she insisted.

"Anne!"

"Well, I don't care."

"Anne. Anne," he muttered. He removed her head from his stomach and sat up. He gazed down into her dark violet eyes. God, she was beautiful. "What am I going to do with you?" Lee asked softly.

"Just go on doing what you've been doing all evening," she purred.

"You're a crazy little wench."

"Crazy in love with you."

A knot formed in Lee's stomach. "Maybe we're both crazy."

"Just crazy in love," she teased and made kissy sounds with her lips.

He began to trace a flower on the sheet with a fingertip. "We aren't just hung up on our scripts, are we?" he asked thoughtfully.

Her violet eyes darkened. She scrambled up, knelt in front of him and took his face between her palms. "No. No, Lee. I love you!" The perfume she wore was made of plumeria blossoms, shipped in at her order from Hawaii. "Lee." The violet eyes sought his. "You aren't having second thoughts about us, are you?"

"I don't know," he said and rolled away from her. It had been nagging at him for weeks now, but he had not worked up enough nerve to talk to her about it. He sat on the edge of the bed, toes rubbing the pale shag carpeting. "It happens, you know," he said without looking at her. "We play *them* more than we play ourselves. Since you joined the show three years ago, it's been—

well—our relationship has moved along the same lines.

"Lee," she pleaded, "don't talk like this." There was a tiny catch in the husky voice. "You're scaring me."

"Remember, we hated each other on the show and off. You were blackmailing Kerry Scott, my little brother. And honest to God, Anne, I was so protective of him. On and off the show. I found myself looking after him."

"Protective of Kerry Scott!" Anne laughed out loud. "He needs about as much protection as a—a barracuda or a lion. Kerry Scott was born knowing how to look after Number One."

"That's not the point, Anne." He swung around to face her. "The point is that I felt protective of him. And I didn't like you until you started seducing me and we had all those kissing scenes."

"And then we started kissing on our own time," Anne whispered and rubbed up against him like a kitten.

Lee pressed back against her. Anne was a sexy, loving woman. Her voice and eyes could melt him, but he was not sure he loved her. The idea of being married to her did not sit well. The truth was, Anne was not a bright woman. She chatted too much about nothing. She never read anything beyond the next day's script. She didn't play chess or backgammon or even bridge. Lee knew two people had to have more in common than sex to make a marriage work.

"It's like I said, Anne," he said, "we keep following that miserable script."

"You're scaring me now, Lee." Anne drew back slightly. "I love you. I love you, Lee. You're everything to me."

He swallowed. "Everything? What about Reenie?"

"That's another kind of relationship." She put her arms around him and he went rigid. "A mother and a child relationship. Reenie is fourteen. She won't need me forever."

"Don't—don't cling so, honey."

73

The violet eyes widened. "That's it. That's why you're upset. I'm smothering you. I'm sorry, Lee. I don't mean to cling. I have been pressing you too much to move in, haven't I?"

Lee sighed. He was not sure where they were going or why. "We've been over that. We're together too much to live together. Four and five days a week, we put in eight hours on the show."

Anne's lips began to tremble. The eyes, those vivid, stricken eyes that seemed to have a life of their own, pooled with tears. He softened and pulled her into his arms. "I'll be okay," he whispered. "I'm just in a bad place tonight. We'll work it out."

A timid knock on the closed door startled Lee. Anne patted his chest. "It's only Reenie."

"Mommy?"

"Just a minute, honey." Anne rolled off the bed, snatched matching robes out of an oversized mirrored closet and tossed one to Lee.

He knotted the maroon velour robe around his waist and pulled the covers up over himself. This was the third time Reenie had come knocking at their bedroom door and he didn't like it. It was embarrassing to have a fourteen-year-old girl know you were sleeping with her mother.

Anne shrugged it away when he mentioned it to her. "Kids aren't dumb nowadays. Don't worry about it. Reenie is old enough to know her mother can have a mature relationship with a man."

Lee still didn't like it, mostly because he couldn't figure out what Reenie wanted. She didn't seem to be jealous, but why else would she come knocking at the door?

"What is it, baby?" Anne asked, putting her arm around her daughter and drawing her into the room.

Lee tensed at the sight of Reenie backlighted in the doorway. She was wearing a tiny, sheer nightie that hid nothing. She was taller than her mother and more voluptuous. High, firm breasts showed through the gown;

74

large, hard nipples poked against the fabric. Moisture gathered in Lee's mouth and he had to swallow.

Reenie pressed her face against her mother's cheek. "I—I had a nightmare. After I woke up, I kept hearing sounds and I got scared."

"Ah, poor darling." Anne hugged her.

"Can—can I get in bed with you? Please, Mommy. I'm so scared."

"There's nothing out there," Lee said, his voice too gruff.

"Please, Mommy."

Anne hesitated. "Oh, I guess so. For a little while."

Reenie darted ahead of her mother and slipped under the covers and into the middle. Rigid, Lee moved closer to the edge.

Anne got into bed, plumped up the pillows, and the two women lay down. "Cuddle with us," Anne urged.

"I gotta go home," Lee muttered, horribly uncomfortable.

"I'm cold," Reenie whined. "I'm so cold and scared, Mommy."

"You're safe here. Lee won't let anything or anybody get you."

Lee kept his distance as the two of them settled into just the right spots in the bed. He felt the softness of a hand on his thigh. The robe was nudged apart and the hand firmly clasped him. Reenie smiled up at the ceiling. "I feel safe now, Mommy."

In the Wilshire penthouse, Paula paced restlessly in front of the terrace windows. Joe glanced up from a book in his hand. "Would you sit down? You're making me nervous."

"I can't think when I'm still. Damn it." She paused to light a cigarette with a sculptured lighter from a glass table. "There has to be a way to get rid of Caleb Shepard."

"Why?" Joe asked. "You just ignore him now. You do the show as you please."

"I want the credit, too."

"So make an appointment with Silverstein. He's the producer. He holds the reins."

"Epstein hasn't been able to deal with him," Paula muttered.

"You may have to give some, too, you know. You can't expect every demand to be met."

Ignoring him, she began to pace again. "There must be a way. Some way. Some dirt, maybe."

"He had an affair with you once."

"Go to hell," Paula tossed at him, more annoyed than angry. "I'm serious."

"So am I."

"You aren't. You're being cruel. I can't hold that over Silverstein's head."

Joe feigned mock astonishment. "You mean there's no lingering fondness left in his heart?"

"We never meant anything to each other and you know it. It was only a form of insurance, to make sure I'd become head writer." It was one of the disgusting things women always had to do to get ahead. She did not like it, but she coped with it. The dark eyes probed Joe's. "What's the matter? Are you jealous? Do you think he was able to satisfy me?"

"Did he?"

"None of your business." She arched one dark brow. "Maybe Sue Bergman knows something," she said, deliberately bringing up the name, making it a challenge.

Joe's eyes did not waver. "If she did, it would have been common knowledge by now."

"Not necessarily. Even Sue Bergman has been known to keep a secret."

"Sue?"

Paula's stomach tightened at Joe's feigned innocence. "For God's sake, Joe. Don't play stupid games with me. I know you sleep with Sue Bergman. Every third Friday of the month, the two of you cut out for Palm Springs. You spend three nights at the Fireside Inn."

Color rose high in Joe's usually pale face. "Who told you?"

She shrugged and a catlike smile curved her lips. "Word gets around."

"Who saw us?"

"Everybody sees everybody in Palm Springs. You don't think I bought that trash about your weekend therapy group, did you?" Joe shrugged, not seeming very perturbed at being found out. "It seemed like a good story. And I did go a couple of times."

"I don't care who you sleep with," Paula said pointedly, "as long as it isn't me."

"So I get it elsewhere. What else can I do? You've retreated from sex—and love."

She shrugged. She didn't want to discuss it. "Let's drop it."

"Suits me."

Paula ground out her cigarette and turned her mind back to the immediate problem. "If I can't get something on Silverstein, maybe I can make Shepard walk."

"How?"

"I don't know." She threw up her hands. "Maybe he molests six-year-old midgets. There has to be something he doesn't want known."

Joe stood up abruptly. "I'm going to bed."

"Joe." Paula moved to him and touched his arm. "Keep your ears open, please."

"Sure, honey," he said and walked away without looking at her.

She watched him until he disappeared, not knowing if he would help her or not. Maybe. Thoughtful, she sank down on the sofa and lit another cigarette. She did care for Joe in her own way, the way she might care for a brother who had never quite become successful. Joe could not seem to bring himself to enjoy their life together; he always had to get nasty and remind her of the lack of sex and affection between them. She was willing to be affectionate; she was not a cold woman, but sex with Joe was the one thing she could no longer tolerate in her life. She could not endure it now or ever again. Joe should be grateful; she pulled him out at a point in his life when he was killing himself with alcohol. He should be willing to exist with her in a friendly way, as two friends who happen to live together.

Chapter Nine

Lauren, seated on the floor at the oversized coffee table in Jenny's office, had the week's scripts and outlines spread out in front of her as she worked out the guarantee table for Paula. Small minus and plus signs went before the numbers beside each name, indicating whether the actor was over or under his guarantee. Paula could juggle the actors in and out of the show accordingly.

Jenny was humming a jaunty but unidentifiable tune. "Why so happy?" Lauren asked her.

"It's Friday. George and I are taking the kids up into the snow tomorrow."

"That's nice." Lauren silently counted up another actor's days. She was feeling good about her job and her new friendship with Sally. She had shaken the bleakness of the night before and was proud of herself for coming out of it so quickly. She was beginning to realize that she had been in a depressed state. She had been down so long over Benji that her mind had begun to accept depression as the norm. Acknowledging that was scary and she vowed never to let it happen again.

She had driven Sally in to the studio this morning, leaving an hour early over Sally's protests. "I'll just hitch it. I can get a lift on Ventura Boulevard, then I'll make it through Laurel Canyon."

"A lady doesn't hitch," Lauren said.

"Being good is going to complicate my life." Sally teased.

"You'll make it," Lauren promised her with a quick smile.

The phone rang, breaking into Lauren's thoughts. Jenny answered, then turned to Lauren. "It's for you. Joe Seals."

Lauren took the call in her own small office. "Good morning, Joe."

"How's our jailbird doing?"

"I got her to work on time."

"Can I see you at lunch? I did promise you a lunch, you know."

Lauren hesitated. She alternated between feeling warm toward Joe and being uneasy with him. "I don't know."

"I do need to talk to you about Sally."

"All right." That was fair enough. They were both concerned about Sally and what was going to happen to the odd girl.

"Meet me and we'll save time." He named a small soup-and-sandwich place and Lauren arrived there a few minutes before twelve. She hesitated in the doorway, the sun backlighting her. The three-inch platforms she wore raised her height to five foot ten. She wore a multicolored scarf swept back around her throat, and its colors complemented the simple gray dress of lightweight wool.

A deli counter on her left beckoned to the appetites of all who entered, displaying beautiful sliced meats and huge mounds of salads. The smell of spices mingled with the faint odor of draft beer.

Lauren spotted Joe in the back. She dodged an overweight woman who was stabbing at her selection through the glass of the counter.

"Hi," Joe said. "You're looking beautiful."

"Thank you," she answered with lowered eyes.

Joe reached across and touched her hand. She stilled. "Lauren." She looked up, but not at his eyes; she focused instead on his balding head. It was odd how smooth and wrinkle-free his high forehead was.

"Yes?" She wished he would remove his hands from hers.

"Oh, Lauren. You don't know it, do you? You don't know you're beautiful."

"Joe, please, I'm just an average looking girl."

"Don't you ever believe that, young lady. Ah," he said when he glanced up, "here's our food. I hope you don't mind. I ordered my favorites for both of us."

"It's fine," she said as a bowl of thick split pea soup was placed in front of her. "It looks delicious." She tasted the soup, and before she could put the spoon back into the bowl the waiter dropped an avocado and Jack cheese sandwich in front of her. The wine arrived last.

Joe shrugged good-naturedly. "I never said the service was good. Just the food." He smiled across at her and she smiled back. He had such a pleasant, open face, she knew she should not feel uneasy with him.

Joe seemed to inhale the soup and shoved the bowl aside. "Sally called me from the studio this morning. She has a proposition for you. But she's afraid to broach it herself."

"Sally is afraid?" she asked. "I find that hard to believe, Joe."

"You're a new breed of cat for her. She'd like to stay on with you. Live there, share expenses."

Lauren toyed with her wineglass. "That has occurred to me, too, Joe. It popped into the back of my mind last night. But the things she's into—men and drugs. I couldn't handle that."

Joe's voice dropped low. "She wants to break away from all that, Lauren. With you around she could make it. She'd have a real chance."

Lauren drew her lower lips slightly between her

81

teeth. "It's a scary responsibility, Joe." It was almost like taking on a child to raise.

"She needs you, Lauren. And I think you need her." Joe leaned across the table. "You're so terribly alone. The loneliness is like an aura around you. I can sense it. Almost touch it."

Lauren stared down at the alfalfa sprouts sticking out from between the dark slices of bread. She didn't like it when people saw through her so easily. She thought she presented a good façade; but obviously she didn't.

"It's the truth," Joe said, driving his point home gently. "You are lonely. Tell me, what have you done with yourself since you and Benji split?"

"I cleaned. I sorted. I moved. I saw my lawyer." She felt herself edging toward a breaking point. "And I cried a lot," she admitted at last.

"It's lonely as hell, being divorced. I know. I've been there. Even when you know it was for the best you can't shake that sense of failure. You keep thinking that if you'd just tried harder, if you'd been patient . . ." Joe's words trailed off.

Lauren's eyes caught his. "You're very wise," she said softly. "You see right through me."

"I just see myself," he said, bleakness in his tone. "Well," he smiled crookedly, "you have to change all that. You have to get out. Have you been dating at all?"

"No." She had not met anyone to date, had not considered it yet.

"Have you made an effort to meet anyone?"

"No. It's too soon."

"It's not," he said emphatically. "See, you do need Sally. She'll be good for you. She won't let you live like a hermit. You need her."

It wasn't easy to face, but she knew Joe was right. She had been living totally within herself and it wasn't healthy. "We—we could give it a try," Lauren said.

Joe's face brightened. "Good. Good girl." He patted her hand. "Now, eat!" He glanced at his watch. "I've got another appointment."

A few minutes later on the sidewalk she thanked Joe for the lunch. "My pleasure," he said, leaning over to kiss her cheek. She surprised herself and leaned forward, accepting his kiss.

Joe took her hand, squeezed it and winked. "There, that wasn't so bad, was it?"

"No. It wasn't so bad." Lauren stood on the sidewalk a moment, watching the tidy man walk away in his immaculate brown suit that had no class at all. He would be comical if he was not so endearing.

Hoping she'd done the right thing and remembering to report to Paula this time, she went into the woman's office. Paula was having a small salad at her desk. The sherry bottle was one third down.

"I approve," Paula told her after Lauren had explained. "Keep Sally straight."

"I'm not sure I can do that. I'm not her keeper."

"You can be firm with her. Guide her in the right direction. Gently, of course." Paula emptied her glass of sherry and poured another. "They're all children, you know."

"Who?" Paula had lost her again.

"Actors. Actresses. Most of them are children. They live in pretend land. They don't have a strong sense of self. Their personalities are too fragmented, which is the reason they can act."

Lauren found herself bristling protectively. "Sally is very young," she said.

"They are all very young. You'll find out," Paula assured her with her usual annoying smugness. "How are you coming with the show?"

"I'm getting people and plot sorted out," Lauren answered, feeling as though she was standing at attention making a report to a first sergeant and, like any new army private, had no right to disagree or ask questions.

"Good," Paula said with a nod. "I want you to take this script to the studio for me. Now. Give it to Sue

Bergman and tell her I said to show you around. Be back by show time."

Lauren's heart quickened with pleasure. "Thank you."

Paula frowned, deepening the wrinkles around her eyes. "This is exciting for you, isn't it?"

"Of course. It's new. Different."

"You'll get over that. That's all, dear." She dismissed Lauren with a wave of her hand.

"Yes, Paula." Lauren moved to the door.

"Oh, yes. One more thing," Paula said. "You are to remember to keep track of your mileage. You can file an expense account once a month. You'll get back fourteen cents a mile."

Lauren nodded and slipped from the room. The woman always made her feel off balance. She could never be certain what turn a conversation would take. But who cared? She was going to the studio. Darn it, it was exciting. Why shouldn't it be? She would not let Paula take away the pleasure.

Jenny glanced up at Lauren. "I was eavesdropping. You think Paula's cold and uncaring, don't you?"

"I'm not sure what I think of her yet," Lauren replied, knowing it sounded as though she was hedging. Which she was, a little, but she certainly did not have Paula Cavanaugh figured out.

"She isn't cold. She couldn't write soaps if she didn't have compassion. Compassion and caring about people are what it's all about in soaps. Everyone cares."

"Yes," Lauren said. "I see that in the show. Their involvement with each other is mind-blowing." But not very realistic, Lauren thought.

"But you don't think it exists in her." Jenny's round face reflected her loyalty to Paula.

"I guess not," Lauren admitted reluctantly.

"I won't pass her off as the hooker with a heart of gold, but Paula comes through. Last year when my husband was out of work and my mother died, it was Paula who slapped me out of hysterics. It was Paula who got me through the arrangements and wrote a check for the funeral. She never let me pay her back."

Lauren nodded. I'll bet you were back at this desk the day after the funeral, too, she thought. Lauren couldn't believe Paula ever did anything for anyone unless it benefited her first.

Sue Bergman looked and sounded like a typecast American Jewish Princess from New York. She attempted to conceal overly wide hips with blazers and A-line skirts. Everyone knew she had had her nose done when she was sixteen. It was generally the first thing she confided to a new acquaintance, coming just before the newest gossip she had picked up about one of Hollywood's finest. She never wore a piece of jewelry that was less than eighteen karat gold, most of it purchased at a downtown wholesaler. Thick dark hair swung just above shoulder length, cut in the latest fashion, swept slightly back off her face.

Lauren had been prepared to dislike Sue Bergman. Instead she found herself responding to her endless chatter and quick smile. Sue led her through the oversized cinder-block-and-concrete building to a sound stage.

Lauren had been on a sound stage before, but only as a tourist at Universal and once at CBS game show. "You arrived at a good time," Sue was telling her. "Everyone is drifting back from lunch."

Sue opened a heavy steel door and they went through dressing rooms and onto the set. Lauren stopped. This was different.

"It's a closed set," Sue told her. "No audience, no spectators. We don't have the room. There're too many sets involved and we work on too tight a schedule."

The sound stage was ringed with sets. Cameras were set up in the center, so they could be moved quickly from one set to another. Lauren had to look twice to recognize the rooms that were already becoming famil-

85

iar to her. They were so small and exposed without four walls.

Sally and a man were obviously working together on a scene. Lauren saw him caution Sally and bring her back and show her how to make a turn around a sofa.

Sally glanced up and saw Lauren. Her lips parted in a wide smile. She waved and poked the man with her, whom Lauren recognized as Kerry Scott. He nodded but did not smile. His eyes caught Lauren's and a dart of excitement hit her.

Sally grabbed Kerry's arm and pulled him towards Lauren and Sue. Sue moved away to speak to the person who was evidently the director just as Sally and Kerry came up to her.

"Lauren, Kerry Scott. Lauren Parrow."

"Miss Parrow." He took her hand and Lauren smiled up at him. He was taller and far more striking than she had anticipated. He held her hand longer than necessary and seemed reluctant to drop it. There was speculation and admiration in his eyes.

"Isn't she pretty?" Sally asked.

"A lovely lady," he agreed.

"Sally," Lauren murmured, "please." She felt her face burning.

"Who are you?" Kerry asked.

"She's the Witch's new assistant," Sally answered for her. "She's going to be on the writing staff."

"Congratulations," Kerry said dryly. "I hope you find a way to enjoy the work."

"Well, we'll see," Lauren said, not wanting to gossip about Paula. It would be disloyal.

"Oh, she'll manage," Sally announced confidently. "Lauren is smart. She will last."

Kerry gave her a sidelong look. "How can you be so sure? You know how Paula goes through employees."

"This one is different."

"She is different," Kerry said, his eyes catching Lauren's again. "So you're close to Paula." He had a way of cocking his head slightly to one side that was

86

highly appealing. She had seen him do it on the show. The way he did it put a catch in her throat.

"Sure she is," Sally answered for her again. "Just like this." She held up crossed fingers.

"Sally!" Lauren laughed in embarrassment, but she was enjoying the attention.

Kerry gave her a lazy smile that was reassuring and somehow intimate. Sue swooped down and pulled Lauren away to meet the director, then guided her to the older couple seated on one of the sets. Maurice Moran and Rose Jardine were as gracious off camera as on. Lauren had the sensation she was actually meeting the couple she had seen them playing.

Sue led her back over camera cables to Cobb Strong, who was sitting alone munching a sandwich and studying a script. He was fortyish, with an outdoorsman's rugged features. He could not be called handsome, but there was strength in his face.

His handshake was firm and he did not come on strong like Kerry Scott. Lauren liked him.

"He's nice," she told Sue as they walked away.

Sue shrugged. "He's okay. But he doesn't *do* anything. He's not any fun." She checked her watch. "You'd better get out of here. Paula will have your scalp if you aren't back in time for the show."

"Okay. Thanks for introducing me around."

"You'll be around a lot," Sue said with a smile. "Try to get back sometime so you can watch a taping."

"I will."

They started to leave just as the director called out to Sue. "Just a second," Sue said. "You have to have a guide to get out of this place."

Curious, Lauren decided to peek into some dressing rooms while she waited. She headed toward them. "Wait up," a man called. She turned and saw Kerry Scott trotting up to her. Lauren's pulse rate picked up.

"Hey, you don't have to cut out, do you? Can't you hang around?"

"No, I can't," Lauren said. "Duty calls and all that."

"Paula calls. I understand." He placed one hand on the wall and leaned over her. "Why don't you come back later."

"I will," she smiled. "At five o'clock to pick up Sally. She's staying with me."

"Hey, terrific! I'll buy you both a drink."

His direct gaze was unsettling and all she could do was nod. "See you then," he said and she watched him walk away. She glanced down at her blouse. Her heart was beating so hard it was making her left breast rise and fall.

It was not until she was back in her car that she realized she had not told Sally about her talk with Joe Seals.

Chapter Ten

A few minutes before five, Sally rang Lauren. "Hi, me and Kerry and Cobb are at J. Sloan's Saloon. You meet us here, huh?"

"Where is here?" Lauren asked.

"On Melrose. Hey, somebody, where are we?" There was a flurry of yelling, then Sally came back on the line. "It's not far from Doheny and Santa Monica in West Hollywood. Eighty-six twenty-three. The drinks are cheap and the popcorn is free. Maybe they'll buy us a hot dog, too. Oh, hey, Kerry thinks you have a terrific body."

"Oh, dear," Lauren breathed.

"It's a compliment. Enjoy it," Sally said.

"I am." I think, she added to herself, uncertain how to feel about Kerry and Sally discussing her body and in what terms.

"You meet us, huh?" Sally asked.

"I'll be there," she promised. She felt a little scared, a little excited, and didn't want to make too much of a simple drink with Kerry Scott. Joe was right about one thing, Sally would not let her sit at home and brood.

Lauren found traffic bumper to bumper, but moving. She found the corner bar and drove around the residential area behind it until she found a parking place.

Inside, she paused to let her eyes adjust. It was not what she had expected. Kerry Scott was too sleek for this kind of place. "Funky" was the only name for J. Sloan's Saloon. A clutter of junk and antiques leaped out from every wall and hung from the ceiling. She glanced up, wondering if the ancient wheelchair ever fell from its ceiling perch.

Sally's head poked out of a booth. She saw Lauren and jumped up. "Back here," she called, but came to meet her, her thin body jiggling with energy. She was wearing her jeans and a faded blue T-shirt again. The makeup from the show had been washed from her face, but her hair was softly curled and gave the illusion of floating around her face. It drifted down her back in silken waves.

"Did—did you talk to Joe?" Sally whispered.

Lauren smiled. "Yes, and you're my new roommate."

"Far out!" Sally squealed, making people turn to look. She engulfed Lauren in a giant hug, then grabbed her hand and rushed her to the booth. "Guys, this is a real celebration now. I'm going to live with Lauren. I'm her roomie!"

"Nice," Kerry said to Sally, but his eyes were on Lauren. Just his look sent an immediate rush through her body, and she had to fight for composure. Sally let her slide in first. She grabbed Cobb Strong's hand, then Kerry's. "Isn't it wild? I'm so happy. Come on, Kerry. Dance with me. I have to dance when I'm happy."

"There's no dance floor, honey."

"I don't care. We'll dance in the aisle. That's what you're supposed to do when you're happy, isn't it? Come on, please," she coaxed prettily.

"What's a guy to do?" he asked with a shrug. "If you'll excuse us."

They stood, then Sally leaned back to Lauren and Cobb. "Hey, you two met, didn't you? It's really something for us to get Cobb out like this. He's a real loner."

They smiled at each other. "Would you call her brash?" Lauren asked him.

"Refreshing, I think."

"Lively at the least. My life won't be dull any more."

"Has it been?" he asked.

"Hmmm." She made a noncommittal sound. "Let's just say it's looking up now." Today she wasn't about to explain about her divorce; today was for living.

"Sally's a nice kid," Cobb offered.

"I think so."

"Have you seen her on the air?"

"Yes."

"She's got it," he said. "That undefinable quality that makes an actress something special. She won't stay on the show very long."

"Because she's too good?" Lauren asked. Cobb flinched visibly. Lauren flushed, wishing she could take back the words. "I'm sorry," she said. "That sounded awful. I'm so ashamed. You're all good."

"It's okay. Don't beat at yourself so. Besides, I've learned to live with that attitude. But it's not just that Sally is good, it's that she won't be satisfied. She wants a lot."

Lauren glanced out at Sally and Kerry boogying. Sally looked about fifteen years old. "Are you sure? I don't think Sally even knows what she wants out of life."

"She knows," Cobb assured her. "She wants it all." His hazel-colored eyes darkened. "So did I—once."

"I think you must be a very perceptive person," Lauren said.

"Maybe," he answered, but she could tell he liked the compliment and she was relieved to be back on better footing. "And maybe I've just been there," he said. He looked directly at her. "I'm sorry, I've been neglecting you. What would you like to drink?"

"A Collins, I guess. I'm afraid I'm not much of a drinker."

"One Collins coming up. And some more popcorn." He took the empty bowl from the table and headed for a popcorn machine near the front entrance.

The taped song ended and Sally and Kerry returned to the table. He sat down beside Lauren without making a big deal of it.

Cobb approached, and Lauren thought she caught a look of disappointment in his eyes, but then it was gone and he was smiling and handing her the drink. He had a closed smile which didn't tell her much. It wasn't at all like Kerry's, whose smile was open and admiring as he talked to her.

Sally, still bubbling, tried to coax Cobb out to dance with her. "I can't boogie," he told her.

"I'll teach you."

"No way. That's not my style."

Kerry turned to Lauren. "Let's make an evening out of this. We can have an early dinner, maybe see a movie in Westwood."

The suggestion triggered some warning device in Lauren. She didn't want to go too fast, she had to have time to think. "I really can't," she said, aware she was withdrawing from him.

"Why not?"

"I have to go home."

"Why?" Kerry insisted, making her squirm. Her tongue seemed frozen to the roof of her mouth. She didn't have a good reason for turning him down, not one she could voice.

"Let's go out," Sally interjected. "We could have such fun."

"I can't make it either," Cobb said. "I have to get home."

"Please," Sally pouted prettily again.

"Nope. I have a lot of things to do."

"So do we," Lauren reminded Sally, relieved to find a viable excuse. "You're moving in with me tonight."

"I'm already in," Sally protested. "I've got all there is. Please, let's go out," she coaxed.

"Not tonight," Lauren said. "I'm beat." She had had all the excitement she could handle in one day. And there was something frightening about Kerry Scott.

He moved so fast and was so sure of himself, like some beautiful wild beast who knew he was invincible.

"So be it," Kerry told Sally. "We can't fight both of them."

"Ah, all right," Sally said, giving it up. "But you guys are no fun."

"Nor are we as young and impetuous as you," Cobb said, like a father reminding a child of bedtime.

Sally cupped her hand around one side of her mouth. "We're being watched," she said in a pseudowhisper.

"So what else is new?" Cobb sighed.

"Watch out, here she comes," Kerry said, grinning.

Confused, Lauren looked around to find an overweight girl stuffed sausagelike into tight jeans approaching their table.

"Excuse me," the girl said, flustered but determined. "Aren't you Bill Reese?" she asked Kerry.

"Who?" Kerry gave her a blank look of total innocence.

"Bill Reese?" the girl repeated.

"No. Never heard of him. My name is Scott."

"You're cute and you sure do look like Bill." She pressed her lips together and frowned. She looked to Lauren and dismissed her with the briefest glance. Her eyes flickered from Cobb to Sally and back again. She clapped her hands together and squealed. "Ned! And Bill, and Janie. You are! You are! You're from *Dreams to Come*. Oh, my God!" She pulled out the exclamation in a shriek. "My God, nobody is going to believe me." She turned. "Monica! Monica, come here. It's Bill Reese and Dr. Ned."

Lauren observed a look that passed from Kerry to Sally to Cobb, who barely nodded his head.

The girl named Monica slid up to the table gushing. The girls scrambled and found paper and pens, then the three actors signed their names.

"Who are you?" Monica asked Lauren.

"Nobody," Lauren answered with a mischievous grin.

"Oh. Okay. Gosh, thanks. Could—could we join you? I've just gotta ask some questions."

Kerry was already standing. "We were just on our way out. If you'll excuse us now." He was polite but firm.

The first girl followed them toward the door, tugging at Cobb's shirt. "Listen, when are you going to wise up about Irene? She doesn't love you."

"I guess I'll figure it out one of these days," Cobb answered.

"Say hello to your parents for us. We just love them to death," Monica enthused. "We love all of you."

"You're a doll," Kerry said, his voice deep and liquid-sweet. "It was nice talking to you girls." Lauren saw him wink and she thought Monica was going to swoon on the spot.

They escaped outside, Sally giggling. She hugged herself and jumped straight up in the air. "I love it! I love it! They knew me. Me! I get goose bumps every time it happens."

"You're a nut," Kerry scolded. "Once they find you in a place like that they won't leave you alone."

Sally's smile faded at the chastisement. "I know, but it's still nice."

It was night, and the winter chill had spread over the city. Lauren pulled her sweater tighter around her. Kerry put his hand on her arm. "Where's your car?" he asked.

"That way." She nodded in the direction of where she had parked.

"I'll say good night then," Cobb said. "See you all." His glance lingered wistfully on Lauren for a moment before he strode away.

At her car, Kerry held the door for Lauren while Sally let herself in. Lauren looked up to Kerry to thank him. For just a second, she thought he was going to kiss her. An unexpected longing welled up in her. Instead of kissing her, he touched her lips with his fingertips. "I'll be calling you, lovely lady," he said.

She slid into the car and he closed the door. Lauren watched him walk away into the darkness, disappointed because he hadn't kissed her and at the same time considering the almost frightening prospect of seeing him again.

"Hasn't he got the cutest behind?" Sally asked, snuggling down into the seat. "I'll bet he's great in bed."

"Probably," Lauren whispered, wondering if she would have the opportunity or nerve ever to find out.

Sally sat up. "Hey! Know what?"

"What?" Lauren started the car and turned on the headlights. She was an old Chevy, but by some grace, she kept going.

"I never had a girlfriend before."

"You're kidding?"

"You know, I told you most women don't like me. They either look down on me or they're jealous or something."

"I envy you," Lauren said softly, as she pulled out into the street.

"Me?" Sally's face reflected her disbelief.

"I'm not sure I can explain why. Mostly it's your attitude toward life. You just keep reaching out and pulling it in. And you deal with men and sex on such a different level than I can."

"Sex is out there to be enjoyed," Sally shrugged. "I enjoy. So what's the big deal about that?"

"That's the point. I don't know how to enjoy it. That makes it a big deal."

"Benji must have been a real louse," Sally murmured. "He sure got you messed up, but good. Maybe you should try Kerry. I just know he's good."

"How?"

"From the way he treats women. He genuinely likes women. He comes on all the time. And he's got the equipment to make it good."

"How do you know?" Lauren challenged. "You said you never slept with him."

"Oh, come on." Sally glanced over at her in disbelief.

95

"He wears those tight pants. It's all there to see. He's big."

Lauren laughed, embarrassed. Maybe she had noticed.

Sally went on. "I guess you probably don't know how to crotch-watch either, do you?"

"No," Lauren admitted.

"I'll teach you then. It's easy. My faggot taught me. They're all experts at it." Sally paused and sighed deeply. "Tell me again what Paula said. I'm going to be so good, Lauren. I'm gonna take classes, lots of classes. Voice and dance, like Joe wants me to. I'm gonna audition for every part I hear about. I'll work hard."

"So am I," Lauren said, her determination matching Sally's. "Paula said it would take me a year to make the writing staff. I'm giving myself four months."

"Right on!" Sally applauded. She settled back to enjoy the drive home, more content with her life than she had ever been before. So maybe she had laid it on a little thick about friendly sex. But it was there to be enjoyed and it shouldn't be made into a big deal. Of course, she had had some bad times, guys who made her feel cheap, or some macho stud who cared only about satisfying himself. Sex wasn't perfect every time and a realistic girl had to be prepared for the disappointments. Friendly sex had its advantages, too, especially with men like Joe Seals. Her availability made him care about her more than his other clients. And she needed the attention and release, so it was an even exchange. If Lauren ever loosened up, she would come to understand these things.

Chapter Eleven

Lauren hated to admit to herself how disappointed she was that Kerry Scott had not called her that weekend. She was so mopey at work on Monday, Jenny asked her if she had gotten enough sleep over the weekend.

A few minutes later Sue Bergman called from the studio. They had given Kerry Scott permission Friday night to be out of the show for two weeks. He had gotten a last-minute chance to replace a drunk actor filming a cop show in San Francisco. Lauren's quick relief was tremendous. Her mood perked up immediately.

"Hustle time," Jenny told her. "Check out the dates and get out the scripts for those two weeks. Pull any that Scott is in. They'll have to be rewritten."

Lauren took the news in to Paula, expecting an outburst of anger.

Instead, Paula only shrugged. "They have to make a living, too. Nobody can exist on one day's work a week. I want to start picking up more on Kerry and Sally before we lose both of them to greener pastures."

Lauren nodded, suppressing a rush of excitement at the prospect for Sally's sake. And for Kerry's, she admitted.

Sally squealed and hugged her when Lauren relayed the information. "You're so good to me, Lauren."

"Well, it wasn't me. I didn't have anything to do with it," Lauren insisted.

"Yes. Yes, it is you. Nothing but good things have happened to me since I met you. I'm going to buy you a gift."

"Don't be foolish," Lauren told her. "You can't afford it." Sally had never said she was broke, but Lauren had assumed she was from her attitude. So Lauren was astonished when the girl pulled nearly two thousand dollars out of her tin treasure box. "I forgot about it, till now. I didn't need it. And if Jake had seen it, he would just have spent it."

"That much money should be kept in a bank," Lauren rebuked her. "Don't you have a checking account?"

"No."

Lauren was surprised at the number of simple things the girl did not know. She had never written a check in her life, much less opened an account. She did not even know how to get a telephone installed in her room.

They spent Saturday shopping for clothes for Sally. Lauren did not try to change her style. The girl liked funky clothes and she wore them well, they suited her. But Lauren was able to control her taste when it tended to run to gaudy.

"If I just had some boobs," Sally complained when she tried on a low-cut black dress, "then I could wear things like this."

"There's always falsies," Lauren reminded her.

"No, I want real ones. I'll get some some day. You know, those silicone ones."

"You're crazy," Lauren laughed.

"You'll see," Sally predicted. "You'll see."

Sally was enrolled in her classes and was working hard at home. Lauren taught her to make spaghetti sauce and they both stuffed themselves silly. Except for an occasional complaint about the lack of a "stud" in her life, Sally was glowing and happy.

Paula was hard and demanding, and Lauren was beginning to see the necessity for it. The pace was endless, never letting up, the demand for scripts ceaseless. The show went on five days a week. If Paula wanted a vacation or a day off she had to write ahead for as many days as she would be away.

Lauren had met Germain Gips, the other dialogue writer. In her way she was as eccentric as Mel Lorenzen. Germain was a bubbly woman, as fat as Paula was thin, a soft dumpling, and a few years older. She apparently kept as close to home as possible, just like Lorenzen. Germain could be reached at home any time of the day. She not only wrote for *Dreams* but apparently watched most of the other shows. When Lauren talked to her on the phone, Germain gossiped about soap characters as though they were friends and relatives. Lauren found her delightful.

She had yet to meet Mel Lorenzen. His scripts arrived by messenger and the outlines were still hand delivered to his mailbox.

Sue Bergman called on Friday to report that Kerry Scott would definitely be back in town and no more rewrites would be required. Lauren tried not to think about it so much. He had probably forgotten about her by now. It was foolish to let his name creep into her mind so often.

She had given up hope by the time he called on Saturday afternoon. He said he had just gotten back to town and wanted to take her out to dinner. She gave him a giddy yes and hung up the phone humming.

Cat-nervous, she changed clothes three times, berating herself out loud for not asking where they were going. She discarded a slack suit as being too matronly, definitely what some Valley housewife would wear. She pulled out a beige dress trimmed in suede, discovered a small spot on the skirt and tossed it in a corner for the cleaners.

She finally settled on a periwinkle-blue shirtwaist dress with a dipping V neckline. The fabric was soft and hugged and flowed around her slender body. She stood in front of the mirror and ran her hands down her hips. "I love being skinny," she told Sally. "I feel so—so free, like I'm not carrying any excess around."

"You look terrific. Except . . ." Sally screwed up her face. "Can't you do something about your front?"

"My front?" Lauren looked down at her breasts.

"Yeah, the V just vees. You need to pull yourself together."

"Oh!" Lauren ran her fingers down the neckline. In the bottom of a dresser drawer was the bra Benji had bought for her at Frederick's. She did not like the memories surrounding it, but it would work.

Lauren let the dress fall down around her waist and changed bras quickly, her back to Sally. It was a provincial thing to do, especially considering the fact that Sally was as likely to walk nude through the apartment as she would clothed.

Lauren eased the dress back up over her shoulders and turned around. Sally clapped in approval. "Now! That's the way. Kerry will love it."

"I hope so," Lauren said, pressing her hands together. They were ice cold. "Sally, I'm scared. This—this is my first date in over five years. I won't know how to act, what to say."

Sally pulled her legs up into a lotus position on Lauren's bed. "You're only going out to dinner, for cripes sake! You're not signing a contract with him."

"I know." Lauren ran fingertips over the softness of her breasts. She had cleavage now. Her skin glowed golden in the dim light of the room. Was she pretty enough to go out with Kerry Scott? Was she dressed right?

A thousand doubts darted through her mind. This was important; a first date after a divorce was some kind of a milestone. And she liked Kerry Scott so much it frightened her.

Sally nudged her. "Hey, settle down and quit looking like you're on your way to the electric chair. Kerry is just a guy. So he's better looking and smoother than most. So what?"

"Sure, so what," Lauren muttered wryly.

"Just keep it casual with him," Sally suggested. Then her face changed, becoming solemn. "And take that as a warning, Lauren. Don't get serious about Kerry. He's not the serious kind."

"I won't do anything foolish," Lauren said, but it was more of a hope than a statement.

"Just consider yourself warned."

A tap at the door brought both of them out of the bedroom. Lauren let Kerry in and Sally grabbed him in a hug, coming up on tiptoe to plant a kiss on his cheek. "Hi, kid," he said to Sally. His eyes went to Lauren, moving quickly up and down her body. He grinned and nodded in silent approval. The relief inside made Lauren feel weak.

"Guess what?" Sally asked, drawing Kerry into the small room.

"What?"

"Lauren is going to get us both more work!"

Kerry turned to Lauren. "You mean it?"

"Sally, please," Lauren scolded.

"Well, you are. Paula is going to use us more. And I think Kerry should know about it. Isn't it neat?" she asked.

"It's super, kid." He patted her behind and she squealed good-naturedly.

An hour later, Lauren and Kerry were seated at a table at the Aware Inn on Ventura Boulevard. Lauren was heady from the drinks he had ordered and warmed by the glow from the brick fireplace near them. It was a small restaurant, an intimate, rosy bistro with a menu featuring organically grown fruits, vegetables and poultry and dark, heavy bread made fresh daily from a variety of grains.

After they had ordered dinner and the waiter had whisked away the menus, Kerry reached across the red-and-white checked table cloth and laid his hand across hers. "I would have called you sooner, but when a chance for a part came up, I jumped at it."

She was conscious of the heat of his hand and her own erratic pulse. "Did you like San Francisco?"

"It was cold. I'm glad to be back, but I have to take out-of-town stuff like this. I can't make it on one day's work a week. That's all I'm guaranteed. But you know that," he said with a shrug. His hand tightened on hers. "I hope Sally was serious about you working on the Witch."

"Well, I don't have a lot of influence with Paula," Lauren said. "But we have discussed it. She wouldn't want to lose either of you."

Uneasy, she tried to draw her hand away. She was not lying, but she knew she was letting him believe she did have some influence. She knew she should tell him she was just a flunky, but she could not do it. She wanted Kerry to think well of her.

He tightened his grip on her hand. "You know, you have a way of popping in and out of my mind at the oddest moments."

Lauren did not know how to respond to that. She stared at his hand on hers, studying the dark hairs on the broad fingers.

"Lovely lady," he said. "You've thought of me, too. Haven't you?"

She raised her head. "Yes," she admitted and he smiled, pleased. The wine steward appeared, then the salad and a basket of dark bread and a saucer of butter was placed before them.

After the meal of curried shrimp and brown rice they held hands over cups of Capuccino in the quiet and dimly lit room. Kerry had moved his chair closer to hers and the silence was companionable.

She studied him as he watched a flaming dessert being prepared at the next table. Kerry was dark, but not swarthy; his complexion was more golden. Incredibly thick eyelashes added to his appeal. For the briefest moment, he reminded her of someone else, but the image came and went so fast she could not identify it.

"You want one of those?" he asked.

"Dessert? No, I couldn't."

He moved closer and put his lips next to her ear. "You know what I want, don't you?" he asked, his voice low and husky.

A jolt darted through her. She remained very still as his breath on her neck made her vibrate. "No," she lied.

"I want to take you to my place," he said, brushing her hair with his cheek. I want to undress you. Very, very slowly, so I can savor it. I want to kiss you, to make love to you all night long."

She breathed out and swallowed, but the sense of panic was overwhelming. "Please." She pulled away from him.

"That's what I want, lovely lady." His brown eyes caught hers, but she looked away.

"I—I'm not like Sally," she said, so quietly she could barely hear herself. "I don't get in and out of beds casually. Sometimes . . ." She had to clear her throat. "Sometimes I wish I could, but it isn't in me."

"I didn't say it would be casual. You're the kind of woman I'd want around for a long time."

"Kerry." She whimpered in protest at being fed a line she wanted to believe. The rich male smell of him seemed to envelope her, becoming stronger and stronger until she had to fight for breath.

Abruptly, he drew back. "Come on." He stood and came behind her chair, then leaned over and kissed her cheek while she remained rigid. "Let's get out of here."

She thought she had herself under control, but the minute they were in his Fiat her head began to pound madly. Dark memories cascaded into her mind. Benji jeering, taunting, telling her she was less than a woman. Benji naked, standing over her as she huddled on the bed. "Baby, if I can't satisfy you, no man can. No other woman has ever complained."

The thought of having Kerry look at her with the

same kind of disgust in his eyes was unbearable. "I can't!" she choked and began to cry.

"All right," he said quietly, not touching her. "It's all right."

"I want to be with you," she whispered, her voice ragged with anguish. "But I'm afraid."

"It's okay. I wouldn't pressure you, wouldn't hurt you. There's no reason to be afraid of me."

"It's not you. It's me! Please take me home, Kerry." It would be best for both of them. There would be no real disappointments on either side.

"No," he said. "I won't do that. Not like this. I'm taking you to my place and I'm going to make us another Capuccino while you fix your face. And no pressure, no coaxing. Not even a kiss, unless you want it. We'll listen to some music and we'll talk."

"I—I don't know," she said weakly, but hope was pressing around her heart.

"I'm not taking no for a answer," he said firmly. "We're going."

Lauren sank back in the seat, letting him take over. It was a nice feeling, letting someone else make the decision.

Kerry's apartment was in West Hollywood on the fringe of Beverly Hills in a beautiful old Spanish-style building. They walked up one flight and into rooms that surprised Lauren. The ceiling reached to twelve feet, area rugs were scattered over polished wood floors and a huge fireplace dominated one end of the living room.

Modernistic paintings were hung on every wall. She didn't know if they were good or not, but she walked up to one of the vivid blues. It was something to do, to pass an awkward moment of being in a man's apartment. "It's beautiful," she said.

"Thanks. But I did that a long time ago. I haven't done anything as good in years."

She turned, surprised and interested. "These are yours?" she asked.

"Yeah." He grinned boyishly. "I've tried to quit it, but I can't. So I paint when I can, which isn't often. The hustle to make a buck never stops. The bathroom is back there."

He pointed down a hall, then disappeared into the kitchen. This apartment was another kind of world to Lauren. Not as rich as Paula's, but far different from her own, exotic by comparison.

Lauren splashed her face with cold water, repaired her makeup and felt almost calm when she returned to the living room, where Kerry was placing small logs onto a grate.

"Cold?" he asked.

"A little."

"I'm freezing. I'll have this going in a second."

She was trembling slightly as she eased down onto the rug in front of the fireplace. She leaned her back against the sofa composed of fat cream-colored pillows of artificial suede.

The logs caught and Kerry turned around. He handed her a cup from the heavy coffee table and took the other for himself. He kept his distance, sitting on the hearth. "Tell me about yourself," he said.

"There's not much to tell."

"I don't believe that, a lovely lady like you."

His voice was soft and soothing, coaxing her into a reply. "I'm twenty-five, divorced," she began. "Or almost divorced. It's not final yet. And I'm a writer."

"Published?"

"A little, and I have a novel started."

"I'm impressed."

"Oh, come on." She was embarrassed because she did not believe him.

"No. I am impressed. A published writer, and you're going to be writing for Paula."

"If I can make it," she reminded Kerry with care.

"I suspect you can do anything you set your mind to."

105

"That's not quite true," she said, wishing she could measure up to such a standard.

"Yes, it is," he insisted. "You have that stable look. You might be slow about making a commitment, but once you do, you're right."

"Maybe. It's important to me to succeed," she said, and realized how much she really meant it. I want that more than anything."

"It's important to both of us."

She glanced at him, uncertain. Did he mean her success was important to him, or his own? She did not ask for clarification.

They talked about her writing for several minutes, then about his paintings, and he showed her his studio. They played records and discussed the show.

She was startled when he said it was time for him to take her home. "I have a tennis date at eight in the morning," he explained.

"Oh? Home." She jumped up too quickly, face burning with embarrassment.

Kerry came to her and took her hand. "You don't want to go?"

"Yes, I do. I . . ." The words trailed off in confusion.

"You thought I'd come on again, didn't you? I'm not that kind of guy, Lauren. I said it was up to you tonight, and I meant it."

She felt her face flush and went completely tongue-tied. She let him take her home and cursed herself for having no guts.

Chapter Twelve

Lauren woke up tired. It had been a bad night. She had come home from her date with Kerry to find the apartment empty. There was no note, nothing to indicate where Sally had gone or why. Her concern led to annoyance, then real anger as she lay in bed trying to sleep, yet listening for Sally.

Joe and Paula would hold her responsible if anything happened to Sally. Lauren tossed uneasily, wondering if Sally had connected with Jake again or, worse, if she were back in jail.

Lauren drifted off to sleep about two, only to awake again at six. She lay there, waiting for dawn, thinking about Kerry Scott and herself, and wondered if she would ever come to terms with the confusing concepts of male and female sexuality. She finally drifted into the deepest sleep of the night.

When she woke, she rolled over and frowned at the clock. Noon. She came up out of bed so fast her head spun. "Sally!" she called out. No one answered. She checked the other bedroom. The bed was empty, still unmade from the night before. Clothes were strewn about.

Angry and worried, Lauren let out a deeply held breath. She padded to the kitchen on bare feet. She yanked down the coffee pot instead of making her usual cup of instant. She was plugging in the pot when she heard a key in the door.

Sally, hair shining and swinging, eyes bright, smiled at her. Lauren, weak with relief, clasped the back of a chair. "My God, where have you been?" she demanded, her voice rising. "I was so worried."

Sally's cinnamon eyes darkened, her body went stiff and defensive. "I was out," she answered.

"You didn't leave a note!" Lauren snapped.

"Hey, I'm a big girl. I can take care of myself. I've been at it for a long time, you know. Don't come on to me like a mother."

"A mother!" Lauren paused. "Oh," she said, slightly subdued now, "I guess I did sound like my mother."

"You sounded like somebody's mother," Sally said with a shrug, silently saying "Let's drop it." "What do we have to eat? I'm starved."

"Eggs. And I think there's some bacon."

Lauren laid out strips of bacon in a skillet while Sally took a Coke out of the refrigerator and opened it. "So, you want to hear about my night?"

"If you want me to. I won't pry again," Lauren murmured, somewhat defensively.

"I want to tell you."

"So where did you go?"

"Spark's."

"Isn't that a private club? A disco?"

"Sure, but I crashed. You know how it is. Most of the people who can afford to belong are older guys. The management lets in girls."

"I see," Lauren said, her tone disapproving. The whole conversation was stilted and Lauren did not know how to change it.

"Hey," Sally said. "It's not like that. They don't let in hookers."

"Just a meat market, I suppose," Lauren muttered, aware that she was being cruel and unable to stop herself.

"You're mean, Lauren. How do you think you meet men out here, anyway?"

"I—I don't know," she had to admit.

"Well, that's how! And I decided, why hang around the crummy places when I've got a closet full of new clothes and I can get in a classy joint like Spark's. I'm really changing my ways, Lauren. No more creeps for me."

Mollified, Lauren tried to be nicer. "Did you meet someone?"

"Did I ever! Oh, he's beautiful." Sally swung her arms out, whirled around and landed in the nearest chair. "He's about fifty. He's so pretty, Lauren. He's tall and broad with silver hair. I just know you've heard of him, Alex LaBarre."

Lauren shook her head. "Is he an actor?"

"No, silly. He's a director. A big shot, a top honcho. He took me to his bungalow at the Beverly Hills Hotel. You know, the ugly pink place on Sunset. Only inside, it's real classy. Everybody who is anybody hangs out there."

"Congratulations," Lauren said. "You scored."

"You're being sarcastic."

"I'm not," she protested, but she knew she was. Lauren broke eggs into the skillet and stepped back as they splattered. She hurriedly turned down the heat.

"Well, that's how it sounded. You're mad at me."

"I'm sorry," Lauren apologized. "I didn't get enough sleep. My head is pounding."

"Didn't you get laid last night?" Sally asked, zeroing in with unerring accuracy.

"No!" The answer wrenched out of her.

"No wonder you're in a foul mood. You need to be loved."

Lauren did not answer as she dropped slices of bread into the toaster. She was not sure what she needed, knowing only that she was miserable.

"Anyway," Sally continued. "Alex LaBarre is super.

He's not like any man I've ever known before. He was so good to me, so gentle."

"I'm glad," Lauren said, meaning it this time.

"He was good. I feel good. He isn't a wise-ass like some older men. And he didn't say anything about my not having boobs." She touched her flat chest.

"Are you going to see him again?" Lauren asked, studying the tawny-eyed girl who was at once childishly innocent and worldly wise.

"I don't know. I hope so. I suppose he's married." She twisted a button on the dark blouse. "Most of the good ones are always married."

"I wouldn't know," Lauren replied. The remark came out with fresh disapproval even though she knew she was being unfair to Sally.

"Man, you are in a mood! A real bitch. What happened last night? Did Kerry not ask or did you turn him down?"

Lauren lifted eggs onto a platter alongside the bacon. She did not look at Sally. "He asked. I said no."

"Why?"

"I did't think I could handle it, Sally."

"Scared?"

"Yes," she admitted slowly. She had been scared silly, terrified of failure.

"You're going to have to take the plunge one day. I think Kerry would be good to you. If I got to know Alex better, you could try him. He's warm, gentle, considerate."

"Sally!" Lauren shook her head in exasperation. "I couldn't do anything like that."

"Why not? He's so laid back. Mellowed out. He'd be considerate, and he gives head like you wouldn't believe!"

"Head?" Lauren set the platter on the table too hard.

"Yeah, you know. He went down on me. It's the only way to fly. You know, I don't get off if a guy doesn't do that for me."

Lauren's curiosity overcame her embarrassment. Her back to Sally, she said quietly. "Benji never did that for me." She carefully laid out the toast, positioned it just so on the plate.

"He didn't, huh?"

"No."

"Stupid!"

"Me?" Lauren sat down at the table.

"No, him! My God." Sally looked at her as if she were the dumbest woman she had ever encountered.

Lauren watched as Sally served herself, trying to figure out if the girl was telling her the truth. She swallowed. "Do you mean it? That you can't get off by just having intercourse?"

"It's nice, but I can't get there on that alone."

"And that doesn't make you feel inadequate?" It had made Lauren feel worthless, less than a woman.

Sally swung her hair back from her face. "Why should it? Different strokes for different folks. Besides, lots of women can't come vaginally."

"How do you know?" Lauren couldn't quite believe the girl.

"'Cause I'm that way. 'Cause I've heard it from other men and women. 'Cause I've read it."

"And it doesn't matter to men?" That would be the least believable of all.

"Most of them love it, they like doing it."

"I don't know," Lauren said. "Benji . . ."

"Benji was a rat," Sally said sharply.

Lauren nodded. God knows he'd made her do it to him enough times. But he'd never offered to return the favor. And she had never had the nerve to ask. She could feel the blood leave her face; she went cold and taut with anger. "Damn it!" Lauren slammed her fist on the table.

"Good!" Sally cheered her on. "Get mad!"

"I am mad!" Elbows on the table, she clasped her head with widespread fingers, feeling the pulse beating

111

madly in her temples. "But not at Benji. At myself!" She had been submissive, cowardly. And naive. But after five years of marriage, being naive was no longer a valid excuse. Neither was last night. She had waited for and expected Kerry to take the initiative the second time. He had left it up to her and she had failed herself.

Suddenly Lauren laughed, and the sound was like silver coins tossed in air. She brought down her hands down. Outside of the bedroom and Benji's mouth, she had never heard such words uttered before, certainly not as casually as Sally used them. What a sheltered life she had led. Mama and Lila would be shocked, absolutely horrified. And her friends back on the block where she and Benji had lived—they would be stunned. She had always been secretive about her and Benji's problems because she was ashamed of them. At times she had wondered which of them was the abnormal one. Benji had usually been able to convince her that it was she.

"What's so funny, Lauren?" Sally asked.

"Life," Lauren answered. "Eat it up before it gets cold." She popped a forkful of eggs into her mouth. "Hmm, delicious!"

They cleaned their plates, picked the last crumb of bacon from the platter and topped off the meal with more toast smeared with jelly and peanut butter. Sally picked up the plates.

"I'll clean up," Sally offered. "Then I'm going to take a nap. Don't let me sleep the whole day away, though."

When the apartment was quiet, Lauren settled down on the sofa with a fresh stack of scripts. Outside, someone was splashing in the heated pool. She considered moving out in the warm February sun, then changed her mind.

Notepad in hand, she attacked the scripts. She had stopped her former random reading and was going through the show in sequence, using old synopses to speed up the process. She was beginning to get a grasp on twenty years of background, and the forty-three characters were taking on the reality of relatives.

Head down, frowning slightly, she penciled a notation on her pad. She wondered when, and if, Kerry would call again.

Chapter Thirteen

Tuesday morning, Paula Cavanaugh dressed carefully for her appointment with Silverstein. Like a warrior going into battle, she built her image, choosing a dark gray pants suit, white blouse and black accessories.

The wool pants suit was baby soft, yet held its shape. She snapped on the fifteen-hundred-dollar watch Joe had given her for Christmas and carried a wide-brimmed black hat with her back to the offices.

It was too early to leave for the business meeting that included Ed Epstein. Paula was displeased with herself. Being dressed too early was a sign of anxiety; it made her ill at ease with herself, vulnerable.

The script she had done yesterday also reflected her anxiety. Paula had stayed up half the night writing and re-writing until it was a mass of crossed-out words and cut-and-taped pages. Lauren was having to retype it and Paula did not like that. She prided herself on turning out letter-perfect scripts the first time through.

She paused to discuss some household bills with Jenny, then went into her office and closed the door firmly behind her. At the oversized mahogany desk she poured a glass of sherry and savored the first smooth taste. She drained the glass and poured a second one.

She sat down and tried to make a list of the points

that had to be discussed before she signed the new contract. She scribbled down some figures, then pushed the list aside. This was pointless, because she knew what she wanted, she didn't need a reminder list.

Too nervous to sit, she got up and turned to the floor-to-ceiling windows that overlooked Wilshire. She pressed a button and two layers of sheer fabric slid away.

Her head ached, her stomach was turning queasy. If only Naomi were here. She always knew how to handle this sort of situation. Or any sort of situation.

Paula gazed out the window and up Wilshire Boulevard, a street of banks and churches and more money than any one human being could comprehend. It was a good feeling to be here, to have a Wilshire address and yet to be able to sit above it and look down on it, to know the peacefulness of security and power.

But there was always the haunting knowledge that it could all be snatched away. The show could be canceled. Not likely, but in television it was always a possibility. Destruction almost always came from flagging ratings. It didn't matter if a million fans loved you, a million wasn't enough. In the competitive, profit-based business, the show will be canceled if it drops below the competition, because the sponsors would withdraw their funds. Silverstein would never fire her, but he could die. He could sell out. A new producer might fire her.

And she could lose her touch. It happened to writers sometimes. They dried up, they died; they walked and they moved, but they died inside when they could not write. It was not a business that supplied security. Her stomach turned over and she pressed the edge of her hand against her body, willing away the queasiness.

Fear was not an easy thing to admit, especially for Paula. But today she was scared. Only Naomi could erase that fear. If she were here, they would be laughing and teasing and plotting out how they would take Silverstein.

Paula had loved Naomi for a lot of reasons. The

116

woman was bright, talented, wise. She never made it seem wrong for two women to love each other; she had made it natural and right.

They had met in New York at a cocktail party. Paula was doing radio scripts then and Naomi Weston had just opened a new play off-Broadway. Naomi wrote in the style of Tennessee Williams, dealing in family relationships and fortunes lost. She never attained the status of Williams, but she was well known and respected.

When Naomi accepted an opportunity to turn one of her plays into a movie in the early fifties, Paula moved to Los Angeles with her.

She was proud of Naomi. She liked being seen with her because neither she nor Naomi ever dressed or acted like a butch. Naomi was older by ten years, soft and feminine, with a cloud of smoky-blonde hair. She worshiped Naomi in some ways. She knew she would never be as good a writer as Naomi; she did not possess that special, all-seeing kind of insight.

It was odd how few people guessed at their relationship, because to Paula it was a shining, tangible thing. Two men together that length of time would have caused whispers and snickers, but not two women. For the most part, it stayed their private secret.

Nowadays, they could have been more open about it, but not in the fifties. They were always careful, never indulging in public displays of affection. Naomi dated from time to time, as did Paula, because they needed an escort for some functions. Mostly they stayed home in the ancient adobe house Naomi had ferreted out in the Hollywood Hills. Together they stuffed it full of antiques and Persian rugs.

It was so good, so right. Until Naomi became ill. The cancer destroyed her quickly, eating her flesh down to the bone, turning her skin yellow and bringing the sick room smell of death into the house.

The doctors could have kept her alive in a hospital, but Naomi refused to leave their bedroom. It was December when it ended. Outside their house, Christmas

117

lights flickered on a neighbor's lawn, a dog barked at imagined intruders. Inside it was quiet. In the bedroom fireplace logs burned, snapping now and then as sap was eaten up by the flames.

"I want my pills now," Naomi said.

Paula's body went cold as ice. "Pills?"

"All of them."

"Naomi, not yet," Paula protested, not wanting to look into the skeletal pain-ravaged face of the woman who gave her strength.

"We've discussed it. It's time, Paula."

In Paula's last act of love, with Naomi's strength supporting her one final time, she laid out the pills and held the water glass for Naomi, whose fingers were no longer strong enough to hold it for herself.

When the last pill was down, Naomi leaned back into Paula's arms. "My love, my beautiful girl. Thank you."

"Naomi." Paula choked and buried her face in the gray-streaked hair, letting silent tears slip down her face.

She held Naomi with no concept of how much time passed, until the breathing ceased. When she became aware of the new silence she carefully tucked the frail body down under the old-fashioned quilts in the center of the brass bed and went to call the doctor.

In her grief, Paula sold the house and everything in it. She never looked for another woman to love. Another woman could never measure up. There had been a couple of men, but never anything lasting.

Marrying Joe had been a mistake. But at the time it had seemed like an answer. There was a need for someone in both of them. Joe was on his way down when she met him nearly four years ago. She supposed it was some dormant mother instinct that drew her to him. That and perhaps a fear of growing old and having nobody, knowing there was nothing out there for her besides becoming a pathetic old butch, constantly cruising.

She endured sex with Joe for the first year, then put an abrupt halt to it when it could be tolerated no longer.

He had been an inept lover at best. At worst, he was a wham-bam-thank-you-ma'am male.

There was a young man once, ever so long ago it seemed now. A beautiful young man of twenty with slicked down hair who owned only two suits, both of them too small.

She was eighteen when she fell in love with Henry Day. He was twenty, the year 1939. The Depression was over, but the aftereffects still rippled over the country like aftershocks from an earthquake.

They were both working, she in a millinery shop and Henry as a garage mechanic. He always had dirt under his nails and grease embedded in his hands that never came out, no matter how hard he scrubbed. He was always self-conscious about his hands. They were both attending college, cramming as many hours as they could into studying, and still supporting themselves.

They both wanted to be writers. They were both naive and young and groping in all directions. Nice girls didn't sleep with boys, but Paula slept with Henry, sneaking into the little room that was more of a lean-to tacked onto the back of a boarding house.

War was in the wind even then, and Henry heard its call. She watched him, mesmerized, as he slipped farther and farther away from her. She tempted him to stay, with her body and her mind and the writing and the adventures yet to come. But the faraway look in his eyes was there more and more often.

She could feel his excitement and knew the eagerness of his body when he talked of the war. In the end she let him go, off by ship to be an ambulance driver in Italy. He was dead in less than a year.

A piece of Paula died with him. She took the rest of herself to New York, over the loud protests of her parents. There were other men, men whom she found crude or overly demanding or just plain selfish and inconsiderate.

There was her first startling discovery of women who loved women. And when she thought about it, it did not

119

seem so bad. She had experienced a terrific crush on a woman teacher once in high school. She had had an inkling then of woman-to-woman love.

As her talents grew, she mingled more and more with the theatrical people who did not condemn any type of love. Naomi found her when Paula was bleeding from a disastrous affair with a married man, at a time when she was in need of the kind of tenderness and compassion only another woman could give. It was the most beautiful and precious experience in her life.

She turned away from the window and the view of Wilshire Boulevard. Her eyes were dry, but inside was the ache that never subsided completely. She straightened her shoulders. Naomi wasn't here to help her or encourage her, she had to depend on herself.

Joe, damn him, hadn't come up with anything from Sue Bergman to use against Silverstein or Caleb Shepard. So it was all up to Paula. Epstein was being a shlepper, giving in too easily to Silverstein.

She finished her sherry. They were all bastards. Epstein, Silverstein, Joe, Shepard. But what the hell did they know about women? Nothing really, they were men.

The buzzer sounded and Paula leaned over the intercom. "Yes, Jenny."

"It's time to leave for your appointment."

"Thank you."

She drove herself to Silverstein's office in a Mercedes matching the one she had given Joe. At the studio the guard waved her through and she pulled into the first parking slot she found open.

Inside she found Epstein waiting in the outer office. Sue Bergman was all over Ed, a slender fellow with thick, well-styled hair and a manner that made him seem younger than his thirty-five years. She was serving coffee and chattering like a mindless bird to Ed.

Sue turned to Paula immediately. "It's so good to see you. I was just telling Mr. Epstein that you never come down yourself."

120

"Darling, I hardly have the time." She glanced purposely at her watch. "I'm not early," she said pointedly.

"Oh, you are to be ushered straight in," Sue said, rushing ahead to announce her. Paula nodded to Ed and ran a hand down over her slim hips, pleased to see Sue's were wider than ever. She mentally shook her head, wondering how Joe put up with Sue. Didn't they bore each other in bed and out?

Ed followed Paula into the inner office. He was barely as tall as she and much too polite. She decided that her next business manager was going to be built like a bouncer.

Silverstein, a big, rotund bear of a man, came around his desk and embraced Paula and dropped a kiss on her cheek. "Darling, you're beautiful," he gushed.

"Thank you. You're looking very prosperous yourself."

"Ah, this old shmatte? It's nothing," he said and flicked away an invisible piece of lint from the vest that encased his large belly.

"Shmatte, like hell. Quit trying to sound like some old yenta, Bob. It doesn't become you."

"What can I say?" Silverstein asked, spreading his hands. "It's an old suit. At the prices they charge today, who can afford new?"

Paula sighed. He was so obvious, trying to set her up to take less than what she wanted, while his hands were weighted down with a gold and diamond ring and a watch that cost more than hers and his feet were clad in soft Gucci shoes.

The smile on Bob's face did not shift, but the look in his eyes became more appraising as Paula took a chair across from him. Ed took the matching chair.

Paula drew out a cigarette and both men leaped to light it. Ed diplomatically withdrew and Paula accepted the light from the heavy gold lighter in Silverstein's hand.

She slowly exhaled and sat back in the chair. "I think

Ed has conveyed to you exactly where I stand," she said.

"He has, darling. And I have the contract here." He pushed a many-sheeted packet of legal papers toward her.

"So I see." She nodded to Ed. He picked the pages up and began to read.

Silverstein leaned forward, serious now. "We've gone as far as we can, Paula. You know, things are tight in the industry now."

"You tell me the same thing on every contract."

"This year it's true. Inflation is eating us alive." He gestured to Epstein. "Ed and I have hassled this back and forth. I've talked to my accountants, my lawyers, to the network. The seven hundred and fifty a week for new ideas is in solid. You give us four treatments a year and we'll go to pilot with one of them. Guaranteed!"

Paula nodded, suppressing her pleasure. The "created by" line was essential to a writer's survival. Long-running series, residuals from foreign rights and reruns could support her nicely in her old age.

"That's yours, Paula. But the six hundred thousand a year, I can't do it. You're five hundred thou now. The new contract"—he nodded toward Epstein—"adds another fifty thousand a year. It's the best we can do for you." He paused and smiled for effect.

Impassive, she watched him, the fifty thousand came as no real surprise to her; it was about what she had expected, though she would not admit it to the man. "And what else?" Paula asked, impatient to get on to the most critical point.

"And what?" His feigned innocence annoyed her.

"You know what I want," Paula's voice was cold and hard, even to her own ears. She wished it was not this way, wished for a way to be feminine and soft spoken, but the business would not allow it. Women had to fight constantly to get what any man would be handed as his natural due.

"Paula, baby. Darling. I can't give you story control.

Caleb Shepard created *Dreams*. He has contracts, too."

"He doesn't contribute."

"That's not true, Paula."

"He doesn't. His stuff is old hat. You read the story projections. They're worthless. He wants Cobb Strong to fall in love with a nun. My God, it's been done."

"*Everything* has been done, Paula," Silverstein reminded her.

"It's been done too much. It's old. Old! If we don't stay current, we'll die."

"But Shepard wants to revive the competition between Cobb and Lee. That's good," he argued. "Two brothers at odds and they both love Katherine."

Paula shrugged. "Maybe." It needed to be done and she was annoyed Shepard had thought of it before she could.

"No," Silverstein said. "Not maybe. Yes. We'll go with it."

"We can't!" Paula insisted. She would use it only in her own time and in her own way. "Damn it, Lee and Anne are our major love interest now."

"And something has to prevent them from getting married. The viewers are starting to press for a wedding. In fact, some of them are getting downright vicious. They've been through a lot of hell and anguish with Lee and Anne. They want the reward now."

"But they can't get married," Paula cried. "That's why we brought Belle back into the story. Ex-wife on the scene."

"I think we should go with Shepard's thoughts," Silverstein said, still calm and sure of himself while she remained rigid and as suspicious as a wild animal. "The character of Katherine will be revived. We'll bring her back out of the mental institution. Then she can tear up Cobb's involvement with Irene and shake Lee and Anne apart."

Paula eyes glittered. Silverstein had her cornered and he knew it. "You'll have to find a new actress to play Katherine," she said.

123

"I know. It's been two years since we used the character."

Katherine was a popular character. The viewers had loved her and forgiven her all sins. When the actress who played Katherine wanted out of the show, they wrote in a mental breakdown and shuffled her off to an institution for the incurable because they were afraid the loyal viewers would not accept a substitute Katherine.

"It'll work," Silverstein insisted. "Katherine will renew the old rivalry between the brothers. She'll create some new suspense over Timmy, too. Only Katherine knows Lee is the real father."

Paula's mind leaped ahead, racing to one story complication after another. Of course, it would work. As long as she did it. She'd bring it to life, make it all logical. Then Shepard and Silverstein would pat each other on the back and take all the credit. It had happened before with them. For a moment, wild, unreasonable anger threatened, distorting her features, sending blood racing through her veins.

Paula pulled herself together. "We aren't here to discuss projections. We're here to discuss my control. And the money. It's not enough. Germain and Mel deserve a raise, too. And I'm going to put on a new writer as soon as I have her trained."

"What you pay them is up to you, not me," Silverstein said with a shrug.

The hassling, bargaining, points and counter points went on for two hours. In the end, Silverstein, sweating heavily, pushed the contract at Paula. Angry and exhausted, she signed it. But for one year only. It was her only triumph. Maybe next year she would get rid of Shepard.

Bob Silverstein leaned back in his chair and beamed. "Now, let me take you to lunch, Paula," he said. "We must celebrate."

"You celebrate," Paula said shortly. "I have work to do. Ed?" He stood with her.

Silverstein came around her desk. "Paula, baby." He clasped her face between his hands and kissed her. "I love you."

"Sure you do." It was all she could do to keep from wiping the back of her hand across her mouth to keep from telling him how disgusting she had found his body and bad manners. She felt sick to her stomach again. It would serve him right if she threw up on his plush carpet, then walked out to leave Sue to clean it up.

Ed trotted after her, out of the offices and down a long corridor. "It's not a bad contract, Paula. It's a good one. You're going to make a lot of money, especially with these new tax shelters I've come up with."

"Buzz off," Paula muttered.

"Paula." Ed stopped. "Listen, I work damn hard for you. But if it's not enough, just say so. I'll get out here and now."

Paula's eyes flicked over him. Sure he would, after he sued her for breaking a contract. "I need a drink, Ed," she offered. "How about you?"

"Me, too."

Paula took his arm. "Come on, then." They would have a drink, but it would not be a celebration. She had lost, and deep inside the fear still gnawed her, like a mouse slowly but surely consuming a hard crust of bread.

Chapter Fourteen

Joe Seals met Sally at the door of his inner office. "Hi, honey girl," he said. "You're looking mighty pretty today."

Sally executed a small curtsy. "Why, thank you, Joe."

He stepped back as she entered the office. "Hold any calls that come through while Sally is here," he told Maggie, his secretary, a pimply-faced girl with dirty-blonde hair.

Joe closed the door and turned to Sally. "Got a kiss for your old agent today?"

"Hmmm, every day," she answered, coming up on tiptoe and offering her lips to him. He encircled her and kissed her hard. She kissed back, cuddling against Joe. He was the sweetest and dearest man in the whole world, but he sure didn't know how to kiss. Sally wondered how any man could get to be over fifty without learning how to really kiss.

Joe let his hand slide down over her backside. "Nice." He rubbed her jeaned behind. "I love that rump of yours."

"It's bony," Sally complained, sliding away from him, hoping he would not want to make love today. "I'm bony."

"I think you're delicious. Don't ever change, Sally."

"Well . . ." She wanted to change, she wanted to be rich and famous. She moved across the room.

Joe was always immaculately dressed, always incredibly scrubbed looking, yet his office was a mess. The carpeting was an old floral print that looked as if it had been pulled out of someone's bedroom. The windows were never washed. There was always a thick layer of dust on every surface.

"Joe," she said slowly, leaning against his desk. "I want to look like a woman."

He studied her curiously. "What do you think you look like now?" he asked.

"Like a skinny boy. I want . . ." She held her hands out in front of her chest. "I want breasts, Joe."

"Oh, come on, Sally. You're terrific like you are. You're different, special."

"How much would new boobs cost, Joe?" she went on.

"Oh, a couple of thou, I suppose. Maybe a little less or a little more."

"Ouch!" Sally made her lips pout. "Guess what? I can't afford them. I'm broke again, Joe."

"Not for long, baby," he said, moving closer to her. "You got the part in *Slocum*."

"Oh, Joe!" Sally squealed and leaped on him, almost knocking him down. She locked her legs around his body. "I love you, Joe! You're so good!"

"You nut!" He bounced her to the floor. "You can't go around attacking old men like this. You'll give me a heart attack."

"But I'm so excited." She clasped her hands together. She was bubbling inside, ecstatic with joy.

"It's only a TV movie."

"But it's such a good part. Not just a bit or a walk-on. It's a real supporting role."

"Is it?" he asked.

"Oh, Joe. I wouldn't lie to you. I was good in that

128

audition, Joe. I had a feeling it would come through. They liked me."

"Are you sure it's a good part?" he teased, with a mock scowl.

"Oh, Joe," she complained. "You're being mean. You read the script, you know it's good."

"I know it is baby. It's just that you're so easy to put on."

"There is one thing." She looked down. "I wore a set of falsies. Not big ones, because the character is only in high school. But I wore falsies and a sweater."

"And?"

"What if they want to put something low-cut on me, Joe? What am I going to do?" The small deception had nagged at her ever since she had done it. She had done it before, of course, but so far she'd always gotten by with it. One day she was going to get caught.

"Come on, Sally," Joe coaxed. "Wardrobe people have dealt with figures like yours before. They'll find a way to fake it if breasts are important. Don't be such a crazy kid. You put too much emphasis on boobs."

She shook her head, not believing him. He couldn't know how much it hurt to be a woman and go through your whole life like a flat-chested twelve-year-old. "I got nothing up front, Joe. You know that," she whispered, her voice filled with despair. "Nothing!"

"I know." He patted her on the shoulder and ran his hand down her slender body. "But you're little and thin. You don't want a shelf out to here like some porno queen."

"I want something. A B cup, even an A would make me happy." She gazed up at him with sorrowful eyes.

"So, maybe you should talk to a plastic surgeon. You wouldn't be the first actress to go the silicone route."

She let out a deeply held breath. "It's hopeless, right now anyway. I don't have that kind of money."

"You will some day. And by then you won't care about big breasts."

"Oh, Joe, I care. I'll always care." She rubbed her

face against him, wanting the comfort of his nearness. "I care so much."

"I don't. You're a regular sexpot just like you are."

"I'm not!" she retorted. She put her arms around him. Joe was so sweet and good to her; without him she would be nowhere.

"Yes, you are. Look." He took her hand and placed it over the zipper of his trousers. "Feel how you turn me on. You just walk into a room and I'm turned on."

"You're sweet," she murmured. She rubbed her hand up and down. Poor Joe, she thought. He really was a sexy guy, he needed as much as the next man. It was just too bad he was so small. She slept with him because it made him happy and made him dependent on her; it didn't matter that it did not do much for her.

She let him lift her T-shirt and unbutton her jeans. She wiggled her hips to help the jeans slide down and, leaning against him, she lifted one foot, then the other. Joe cupped her buttocks with a soft groan and pulled her up against his body. She endured his petting until Joe pulled back. "Let me get out of these clothes," he panted.

He took off his jacket but left on his shirt and tie. He hurriedly shed his pants as Sally moved to the vinyl-covered sofa. She sank down and arranged her hair upward out of the way. She spread her legs invitingly and hoped that just this once he would do her first.

He didn't. "God, you're beautiful," he murmured and lifted her legs, then turned her lengthwise on the sofa.

So be it, Sally thought. It was just a friendly lay, anyway. Only why did she feel annoyed, almost angry.

Joe entered her and she wrapped her arms around him and faked a moan. He was a nice guy, but hardly big enough for a girl to know anything was going on.

She held him very close, feeling a certain sense of warmth from the easy engagement of their bodies. She made the proper number of whimpers. Joe was too nice to put down. And he cared about her, like a father, which was all-important to Sally. She liked to give back all she could to people who cared about her. Dear sweet Joe was always there when she needed him.

When Joe was finished, she gave a happy little sigh and nuzzled his neck. "Was it good, baby?" he asked.

"Joe, it's always terrific with you. Always." Poor baby, she thought. He needed some kindness and affection in his life. She was certain he did not get it at home, not from the Witch.

He started to get up when Sally pulled him back and looked into his face. "You're the best friend I have, Joe."

A look came into his eyes, one that shook Sally and she was not certain why. It was a sad look.

"Sure, honey." He jumped off her and ruffled her hair as though she were a little kid. She leaned her cheek against his body, rubbing gently. Silence filled the room and it was Joe who broke away.

He padded across the office in his stockinged feet, hairy legs sticking out beneath his shirttail. Sally had to tighten her lips to keep from grinning.

As he pulled his pants back on, he said, "I have more good news for you. I'm getting my bail money on you back. They're dropping the charges."

"Joe. You are super." She ran across the room and kissed him hard with loud, smacking noises. "How did you do it, Joe?"

"Just by being me, I guess. Naw, you'd never been arrested before. The courts are crowded. They drop a lot of stuff."

"Super. I am so pleased, Joe. It's a good day. I'm happy. The dance teacher says I have real potential, Joe. She said that, honest."

"How about the voice lessons?"

"They're boring, but okay."

"They're important. Very important. I want to try and get you in a stage play. It'll be good training for you."

"Does it pay well?"

"It probably won't pay anything, honey girl. There

are little theaters all over Los Angeles. You'll probably have to pay dues to belong to one of them. But you need that kind of experience."

"Oh, Joe. I don't want to if there's no money in it. It takes all my time scrounging around for parts to make a living."

Joe faked a surprise look. "My God, what's this? My Sally worried about money?"

"Aw, come on, Joe. I know I've been living like a flower child. I guess I'm just a hippie, but I've got responsibilities now. For rent and stuff to Lauren. And I want to dress nice." Those things were becoming important to her. If she was going to be a star, she had to start living and acting like an adult.

"It'll be good for you. Put your jeans on, honey."

"Oh, okay." She became aware of the stickiness between her legs. She snatched a handful of tissues from a box on his desk and cleaned herself up, then crawled back into her jeans and pushed her feet into sandals.

"Hey, I almost forgot. Guess who I was with Friday night?"

"King Kong."

"No, better. Alex LaBarre."

Joe arched one eyebrow and whistled. "Nice! He could do lots of good things for you. He'll be casting *Rainbow* in a few weeks. It's supposed to be the film of the year. The book was on the best-seller list for months. Handle him carefully, Sally. Don't ask for a chance for a part unless he opens it up first. Don't make it sound like blackmail or anything."

"Joe!" She was shocked and hurt. "I wouldn't do anything like that. I like him, Joe. I like him a lot."

There was a warning in Joe Seals's eyes. "Don't get foolish about a man like him, Sally."

"Why?" she asked warily.

"Because you don't move in his circle, and the town is full of young girls willing to slip between the sheets with him."

"Maybe I *will* move in his circles, some day." What was wrong with Joe? Didn't he believe in her?

"Sure, honey girl." Joe flipped through a Rolodex. "I have another audition set up for you. It's for a TV pilot. They need a teen-aged daughter. A skinny type about fourteen."

"I'll look young," she promised. "It's not hard to look fourteen when you don't have breasts," she reminded him with some bitterness. Mostly she'd have to remember to keep her mouth shut and act shy and convey an image.

"And stop worrying about your boobs all the time," he added. "It'll turn into an obsession."

"Okay, okay," she said, but she knew she would continue to worry. There was no way for her to be unaware of her obvious lack.

"You've got it where it counts," he said. "You make it magic for me."

"You're sweet, Joe. I love you." She gave him a wet, mushy kiss, took the card for the audition and left.

She walked slowly down Sunset. There was no comparison between sex with Joe and sex with Alex. Alex had called her his baby girl, and she had liked that. The truth was, she had let him think she was less experienced than she was. She had kept her words clean and let him make all the moves. She had sensed something in him that demanded that, and she had wanted to impress him. Even before she knew who he was, she wanted him to think good things about her. She had been a lady for Alex in her deliberate little-girl way and it had paid off in spades.

On impulse, she darted into a phone booth at a service station. She looked up the Beverly Hills Hotel number and dropped in her dime.

"Beverly Hills Hotel."

"Mr. LaBarre's bungalow, please."

"May I ask who's calling?"

"A friend."

"Mr. LaBarre isn't using his bungalow this week."

"Ah, well." Disappointment washed over her.

"Would you like to leave a message?"

"I guess not. Thank you." She hung up quickly. God, what was she doing? Ladies did not call men, they waited for them to call. But if he did not call, she was going to die.

She shifted her shoulder bag again and moved on. She felt vaguely annoyed with Joe over the stage training he had suggested. Sure, she needed experience, but to pay to act? That didn't make sense.

Paula had said she was good, Paula said she could make it to the top. Annoyed, she wondered why Joe didn't tell her things like that?

Even Alex had been skeptical when she told him she was going to be as big as Barbra Streisand some day. "There's hundreds of girls out there carrying around the same dream, baby girl. To make it, you have to work hard and be hard. You've got to square your shoulders and bull your way through. You can't let anyone get in your way."

"I'm not afraid of work. I thrive on this kind of work."

"Then you may make it," Alex conceded.

"I will make it. I will," she said, silently vowing to stay away from drugs and crumbs like Jake.

"Damn." Sally spoke out loud and stopped in the middle of the street as she realized she had set some kind of record for herself. She had not smoked a single joint or popped a pill since moving in with Lauren. It was a real record.

"Ha!" She squared her shoulders, as Alex had told her she should, and swung along down the street, happy and proud of herself. She glanced up and caught sight of a clock on a building. "Oh, my God! I'm late!" She started running toward the bus stop. Her voice teacher was a sour old broad who would chew her out for sure.

Joe Seals stood at the grimy window. He had watched Sally emerge from the building, his eyes following her until she disappeared from sight. "Damn kid," he muttered against the pain in his chest, against the familiar haunting ache eating at his insides. Sally was a warm, loving little creature, built like a child, but with the sexual attitudes of a woman far beyond her years. He did not kid himself about their relationship: they were using each other. But as long as the using was equal he would take it, it was all he could get.

He did not expect Sally to love him, any more than he thought he could interest Lauren Parrow. He would never mess with Lauren. She was both vulnerable and naive, a woman who took life and love and sex with great seriousness.

Joe sighed. His face relaxed, the muscles sagging and making him look older. His age weighted heavily, a burden all men had to carry and one made especially difficult in a world full of warm, alluring women far too young to consider him as anything more than a friend or a kind uncle. For Sally he wished he could be more. A fierce protectiveness welled up in his chest, surprising him with its intensity. The urge to go after Sally, to pick her up and carry her off to some secret place, welled up in him. He wanted to hide her from the world, take her to a place where she could never be hurt again by men like Jake and those like Alex LaBarre, who could hold her with their position and wealth. He silently damned them and himself for his lack of sensuality, for being forced into the nice-guy role, because he was not one of those men with natural sex appeal.

It was insane for a man his age to be in love with a nineteen-year-old girl, especially one like Sally Rook. He knew she only slept with him because she liked him and perhaps felt a little sorry for him and because he was her agent. He knew she simply tolerated sex with him, without giving of herself.

Joe was certain he could be a good lover if he ever had the chance. It was just that he always felt so uncertain with women in bed. There was an awkwardness in him, even a slight embarrassment. And he could never

135

live up to his fantasies. Brooding, he turned back to his desk and sank down in the chair.

Joe grew up a quiet, studious boy in a religious home where Bible reading was a nightly ritual. He had one dream, to be a writer. As a teen-ager and briefly as a college student, he piled up an impressive collection of rejection slips.

The one professor he trusted to critique his work finally told Joe he had no talent. Sickened and desperate to prove the man wrong, Joe fled to Los Angeles and to Hollywood, where he hoped to become a script writer. With a bit of luck he landed a job at the old RKO studios as a script reader.

World War II rejected Joe as 4-F because of a punctured eardrum. As more and more men disappeared into the military forces, Joe found many jobs available. He considered being a director and worked on various films as an assistant. He wrote nights, alone in a Hollywood apartment, until the end of the war when there was nothing left to do but face up to the truth and give up writing.

He would have left Hollywood then if it had not been for Lorraine. She was a contract actress at MGM, a starlet. Looking back, he could see she was a silly, not very bright girl who giggled too much and never thought beyond her own self. She worried constantly over the hair she kept bleached a white blonde. A pimple could throw her into total despair. But then Joe found her refreshing when compared to the hard, calculating ways of most actresses on their way up.

It took Joe three years of marriage to figure out that Lorraine really did not like men very much. To her sex was a commodity to be bartered. She refused to try anything beyond the standard missionary position.

Still, they stayed together another seven years. Joe went to work for one of the big talent agencies and his connection with the industry held him in good stead. He knew the town and he knew the people. He was a good agent.

Dumb blondes went out of style and Lorraine could not get work. She could not stretch her limited talent in new directions. She turned into a shrew and berated Joe over the slightest infractions. No matter what he said to her, she took it as criticism and began to turn to other men for the reassurance her ego craved.

She divorced Joe and married a director five years younger than herself. She starred in a couple of films, both flops. The last Joe had heard of Lorraine, she and her director had returned to his hometown in Minnesota and his father's bank. Joe assumed she was now the settled housewife of a banker.

He really wished her no ill. They had each married reflected images, not real people. He hoped she was happy, for he was not.

Joe broke off from the big agency and began his own after a salary dispute. He did well for a long time, until one cocktail at lunch turned into three and four cocktails and finally to drinking through the entire afternoon. He began to lose clients and there were serious warnings from friends that he was becoming an alcoholic.

It might have happened. He might have drunk himself into the final oblivion of death if Paula Cavanaugh had not come along.

He woke up in her apartment one Sunday morning four years ago. She was living in Brentwood then, working out of a studio office. Joe came to consciousness slowly and without opening his eyes rolled over and fell off a couch onto the floor. He landed hard and cried out in alarm.

He blinked, then through a red haze saw feet clad in pale yellow mules. He looked up at a sharp-faced, black-haired woman. "Who are you?" he muttered.

"Paula Cavanaugh."

"Oh." He forced himself up. The name was familiar, of course. "Where did we meet?"

"At the party last night. Remember?"

Joe rubbed his hand over his fur-filled mouth. "I

137

only remember arriving. My apologies." He wrinkled his nose. He could smell himself and it was not very pleasant.

"The party broke up early and you didn't look like you could drive, so I brought you home with me," she explained.

"I'm indebted," Joe said as formally as possible under the circumstances.

Cool and composed, she pointed out the bathroom to him, showed him the new toothbrush laid out for him. When he returned she silently handed him a cup of coffee. His hands shook so badly the cup rattled on the saucer. Humiliated, he set it down. "I'm sorry," he said.

"And well you should be, Joe Seals. You used to have a good reputation in this town."

He looked at her, shocked by her honesty. He was more conscious than ever of the stubble on his face and his rumpled clothing. "You've heard of me?"

"Of course. Hollywood is a small town." She sipped her coffee, studying him over the rim.

"And the word on me is bad, right?"

"You're a boozer. A loser."

Joe flinched. "I'll go now. Thanks for rescuing me."

"I'll have to drive you," she reminded him. "Your car is still at the Hillmans'."

"Oh." Joe sank back down.

The pale yellow robe she wore reached to the floor and was knotted around her slim waist. "I'll change," she said. "If you'll excuse me?"

Joe sent flowers the next day, yellow roses. Then he called to apologize and to invite her out to dinner in gratitude.

"Will you be drinking?" Paula asked bluntly. There was no doubt that she would have turned him down if he had answered yes.

"Even a boozer can stay sober for one night," he said.

She accepted the invitation, and it was the beginning of a friendship. Paula's strength, her determination, her belief that a person could accomplish anything nurtured him back into sobriety.

Joe picked himself up and rebuilt his stable of clients, becoming a functioning agent once more. There was not much they did not know about each other by the time they married. His failed marriage, her affair with Naomi. They were the best of friends and they should have stayed friends, Joe thought. Marriage had destroyed that friendship and now they just tolerated each other.

Sex had never been good between them, and now they did not keep up any pretense about it. They had maintained separate bedrooms since moving into the penthouse two years ago.

Joe knew his lack of ambition drove Paula crazy. She wanted to take over and build his agency into one of the biggest and best. She could not understand that Joe was willing to settle for making a living and keeping in close contact with his people, preferring it to being the boss of a large staff.

Last year he had drifted into an affair with Sue Bergman. Joe did not kid himself about Sue any more than he did about Sally. She did not love him. He was simply an escape from the nagging mother she lived with, a Jewish mama who could not adjust to the fact that she had a thirty-year-old unmarried daughter.

Joe gave Sue weekends away she could not afford on her own. He cared about her in his way. She was all he had and she was his escape from Paula and the words and looks that told him he did not measure up to Paula's standards.

Joe had told Lauren he was fifty-five, going on seventy. It was true, frighteningly so. He had yet to rid himself of his fantasy, that one day he would find a woman, the right woman to love. He wished with all his heart that woman could be Sally. Fantasy, pure fantasy, he told himself, and tried to keep her out of his thoughts. It was impossible.

Joe wondered about Paula. He had never asked her

what prompted her to bring home a drunk. Such an un-calculated act was totally out of character. Perhaps in her way she had been as lonely and lost as he. Maybe someday he would ask.

Chapter Fifteen

When Lauren arrived at Silver Productions to deliver scripts, she was told Sue Bergman was in the rehearsal room. She left the scripts with the girl at Sue's desk and followed her directions to the rehearsal rooms in the basement.

She did need to talk to Sue, but it could have been done over the phone. Her real reason for going was a chance to see Kerry again. She was aware of her moist palms and a heart that was racing too fast as she walked down a drab basement corridor.

She stepped quietly into the room where the actors and director were making their dry run of the day's script. There were no props or scenery on hand.

She stepped to one side of the door and stood there, silently watching. Though the actors had studied the script the night before, the words were not committed to memory yet and they stumbled over lines and had to refer to the scripts in their hands from time to time.

The action was awkward as Rose Jardine opened and closed phantom cabinets and poured coffee from an imaginary pot into invisible cups for her husband and youngest son.

The youngest son was Bill. Kerry Scott. Intent on the action and lines, he did not notice Lauren. He looked vaguely rumpled and still bore the appearance of having just awakened. Lauren's heart twisted slightly as a desire to smooth his dark hair hit her.

Rose Jardine's graying hair was hidden under a hastily tied scarf, and Maurice Moran, the family head, was decidedly unpatriarchal looking. He scratched at his belly as he read his lines.

Lauren was struck by a sense of amazement. Taping time was less than five hours away and by then they would have turned this seeming shambles into a smooth-running show, she realized.

Sue Bergman was seated at a table with the director, scribbling notes. She glanced up and Lauren raised her hand. Sue saw her, nodded, smiled and held up a finger, mouthing what looked like "just a minute."

Sally was not in today's show and neither was Cobb Strong. There were some actors who had secondary roles whom Lauren had not personally met, but it was Kerry who held her interest.

He repeated a line twice and laid down his script and turned to the director. "I'm sorry, David," he said, "but I don't think Bill would say something like that to his mother. He's concerned and maybe confused, but he's not going to be cruel to his mother."

"Oh?" The director, a small, balding man Lauren had seen around before, fingered his script. "How would Bill say it?"

Lauren held her breath. The actors did change bits of dialogue from time to time, but if they went too far Paula exploded. How she could remember every word of every script was beyond Lauren's comprehension, but Paula did.

"Softer, I think," Kerry explained. "He'd suggest, rather than order. This is his mother he's talking to. Not a servant."

"Okay," David said, giving Kerry the go-ahead. "Try it your way."

Lauren listened closely as Kerry spoke modified lines, then nodded her silent approval. He was right, his way was better. They went through it twice and the change was noted on the scripts.

"And fade out," David murmured, peering at his script on the table. "Now, next scene. We come in close on Lily. Anne!" His head came up. "You're sad. You're overflowing with unfulfilled yearnings. Let's see it!"

Lauren's pulse rate increased when Kerry's eyes fell on her. She managed a shaky smile. He winked and grinned and whispered something to Rose Jardine, then excused himself as the Lily scene began.

Lauren fought for outward calm as Kerry strode toward her. He stopped in front of her and his broad shoulders blocked her view of the room and locked them into their own private space. "Hey, I'm glad you dropped in," he said with a smile. "I was going to call you tonight."

Were you? she wondered, gazing up at him with questioning green eyes. Or are you only saying it because I'm here? She wanted to believe him.

"Let's step outside. Or we'll get yelled at for talking," he said, leaning close enough for her to inhale his after-shave. He took her hand in his and led her out into the corridor. He left the door open. "I'm having a couple over for dinner tomorrow night. Thursday night. I think you would enjoy them."

"Oh." She felt flustered. She had expected and hoped for another date alone with him. "I'd like to come."

"Great. You want to come early? You can make sure I don't wreck the rice."

Lauren laughed out loud.

"Look," he said, "I've got to get back in there." He dropped an unexpected kiss on her cheek. "I should pick you up, but if I do, dinner will be late."

"It's all right," Lauren whispered, knowing she would do anything he suggested. "I'll drive over. I don't mind."

"You know, you live on the wrong side of the hills," he said.

"Maybe I do," she replied.

"You should move to my side."

"Scott!" the director yelled.

"Bye." He squeezed her shoulder and stepped away. Lauren closed her eyes for a moment and laid her fingers in her cheek where his lips had touched. She exhaled slowly, awed at the wonder of finding herself attracted to him. It was amazing how fast her world had suddenly righted itself.

Lauren stepped back inside and Sue Bergman came over. "He's cute, isn't he?" she said, nodding toward Kerry Scott.

"Yes, he is," Lauren agreed, aware of Sue's curiosity, and not liking the direct invasion of her privacy.

"Not many girls would turn him down," Sue added, frankly eying Lauren.

"Why should they?" Lauren asked, her voice dripping sugar.

"Why indeed?" Sue asked and changed the subject. "What's up with Paula?"

"It's me and the guarantees," Lauren said. "Your figures and mine don't match. I can't find the error."

"Okay." She glanced around. "Uh, want to go up to the studio with me? I've got to check out the sets. We can talk on the way." Their heels clicked on the tile floor as they moved to the concrete stairs. "What's the problem with the guarantees?"

"With Cobb Strong and Rose Jardine. You have them both over guarantee by ten days. I have Cobb over by three days and Rose by six."

"Those damn things are such a hassle, but a necessary evil. Here."

They turned into the huge barnlike studio. Sue's eyes traveled from one set to the next and she excused herself to go speak to one of the workmen.

Lauren watched, still new enough to the business to be enthralled with the commotion taking place. Tables and chairs as well as food for the refrigerator were being carried into Rose Jardine's three-walled kitchen

144

by technicians for the breakfast scene Lauren had watched them rehearse downstairs. Every day these men assembled the home according to the instructions of the director and the scene designer.

The pace was almost hysterically quick as they carted objects, snapped up cables and set up booms. The set had to be completed so the actors could rehearse their lines again on the finished sets and the camera blocking could be done.

Sue darted through the fast-moving technicians, running through a checklist of especially needed props. She was puffing slightly as she returned to Lauren. "You know this isn't my job," she complained. "But David's assistant is down with the flu and I'm filling in. Look, I can't think about guarantees today. Call me, okay? We have a photograph missing. There's supposed to be a framed picture of Lee on Anne's bedside table. We use it for a fade-in. If it doesn't turn up we'll have to use something else. Damn it!"

She took off before the last two words were out of her mouth. Lauren called out a good-bye.

It was a wonderful, pleasant evening. Lauren arrived at Kerry's apartment at seven. He greeted her with a drink and the same sort of casual kiss everyone seemed to indulge in. He put her to work chopping vegetables for a stir-fry. The activity let Lauren feel at ease almost immediately, though nothing could have destroyed the underlying sense of danger and excitement at his nearness.

Kerry showed her how to butterfly shrimp and taught her how to use the wok, a deep, bowl-shaped pot, a cross between a skillet and a saucepan. "I'm amazed," she told him in frank admiration. "Not many men can cook like this."

"Ah, but all the great chefs are men, remember. And I like to eat well. So it's been a matter of survival and of catering to my own good taste," he said, grinning down at her with his head cocked slightly to one side.

Lauren liked the casual way he accepted her into his kitchen, as well as the way he touched her. She liked his friends, too, a couple about their age who were both actors and planning their wedding. Kerry was to be their best man and the dinner was in the way of a small celebration. Lauren was smugly pleased to have been invited to share the intimate function.

Mickey Stevens, built like a football player and with the face of an innocent boy, was instantly recognizable, though she wouldn't have remembered his name. "I saw you on *The Waltons*," Lauren told him. "And you were the killer on *Baretta* last week. You were so good. Vicious and mean, but you don't look mean at all now."

"He's a pussycat," Joyce Mitchell purred and rubbed her face against his shoulder.

"I'm sorry," Lauren said to the petite girl with rather ordinary features and plain brown hair. "You look familiar. But I can't place you exactly."

"Oh," Joyce gestured vaguely. "I'm a forgettable face. But that's all right. Mickey is going to be the star in this family. Aren't you, baby?"

With good humor Mickey conceded that that was undoubtedly true, and they settled down to the beautiful Japanese meal, complete to the chopsticks and rice bowls.

"Did you hear?" Joyce asked. "Chris Betts has been hired as casting director for *Rainbow*."

"Who else?" Kerry asked. "He's the biggest in town and this is supposed to be a big flick."

"I have a friend who knows Alex LaBarre," Lauren offered.

"Alex LaBarre!" Mickey nearly choked on his shrimp. "*Personally* knows Alex LaBarre?"

Lauren glanced over at Kerry. She wished she hadn't brought it up; she had not meant to tell him Sally had slept with LaBarre. "More of an acquaintance, I guess," Lauren hedged.

"I should be so lucky," Joyce said. "Every actor in town will be pounding down Chris Betts's door. It'll take a name reference like LaBarre's to get an audition."

"I don't think so," Kerry said. "Those casting directors are bright people."

"I don't understand about casting directors," Lauren said. "I thought directors and producers chose their actors."

"Well, they do," Kerry explained. "The top stars anyway. Back when we had the old studio contract system of casting, getting unknowns for small parts was easy enough. Every studio had a lot full of them. But that's all gone and now most casting of films is done by a handful of independents."

"And they can make or break people like us," Joyce told Lauren. "The casting director submits a list of candidates for a role to the director and producer."

Mickey poked his chopsticks into his rice. "It gets kind of weird sometimes, too. TV is supposed to be the big training ground for actors. Supposed to get us ready for the real thing, which is films. Yet, if you get too big on TV, many filmmakers and studio executives get the idea that the moviegoers aren't going to pay to see someone they're used to watching for free at home all the time."

"So films is where you all really want to be," Lauren said.

"Or stage," Kerry said. "God, I'd sell my soul for a good stage role on Broadway. That's the only real theater in the world."

"Maybe you'll get it one day," Joyce said. "Your agent has a lot of connections in New York."

"Maybe. Meanwhile, it's hustle to make a living."

"Ain't it though!" Mickey muttered.

Between Kerry and Sally, Lauren was finally gaining a concept of what it meant to try to make a living as an actor. The erratic income and the feast-or-famine aspects were overwhelming.

By the time Mickey and Joyce left, Lauren was tipsy from drinking too much warm *sake*. Kerry moved to pick up a tray from the coffee table to take back to the kitchen. Lauren stood up too quickly to help him and swayed. She reached for the sofa for support.

Kerry caught her arm and steadied her. "You okay?"

"I think I'm drunk," she murmured. "Wow, my head is spinning!"

"I think you're cute," he said. "Here, lie down for a minute." He pushed a cushion to one end of the fat-pillowed sofa.

"This is awful," she mumbled as she lay down. "I never do things like this."

"Maybe it's time you did." He patted her shoulder and left her lying face down.

She closed her eyes and let the soft music move into her head as the world swayed gently. She was drifting and warm and it was all lovely.

She sensed more than felt Kerry kneeling beside her on the floor. She turned her face toward him and opened her eyes. He was smiling gently. "Beautiful lady," he whispered and his lips came down and touched hers tentatively.

"Hmmm." She turned over and put her arms around him. She was surprised at the urgency with which she returned his kiss. Her world spun faster and wilder than before. She wanted the kiss to last forever.

When he pulled away she almost cried out at the pain of his leaving. "Kerry?" she asked.

"I want you," he said, tracing the lines of her cheek bones with a fingertip. "Do you want me?"

Panic knotted the pit of her stomach. She willed it to go away. If she did not do it now, she might never. He might never ask again. "Yes," she said.

"Are you sure?" he asked.

"Yes. I want you," she said, but she was not sure at all.

"You weren't before."

"I know. But I am now." She knew the cocktails and wine helped. She was scared, but the inhibitions had dropped away. "Please, Kerry. I won't fail you."

He frowned. "Fail me? What goes on in that head of yours?"

Her eyes dropped from his face. "Never mind. It doesn't matter." Her fingertips tugged gently at him. "Nothing matters but here and now. Hold me," she choked. "Hold me." And don't ever let me go, she thought. Make it good and right for us, prove Benji was wrong about me.

He looked at her curiously, as if still uncertain. Then the puzzled look disappeared as he flashed her the quick familiar smile she saw so often on *Dreams*. "Come on," he said. "Let's do this right. I have a king-sized waterbed."

She sat up slowly, then Kerry helped her to her feet.

"Are you okay?" he asked.

"I'm floating." She raised her face for another kiss, but the pressure of his hand on her arm urged her back to the bedroom.

The room was masculine but sensuous in rich browns. The waterbed was covered with a thick fur spread. Lauren stroked the fur and the bed moved under her touch. She pressed the bed hard and it sloshed. "I've never slept on a waterbed," she said, her voice still and self-conscious.

"You'll like it," he assured her.

He was pulling his sweater off over his head. Lauren hesitated as doubt pressed around her. What if she froze in his arms? What if she couldn't respond? What if she felt nothing, as she had so often with Benji?

She looked away and heard a rustle of his clothes being removed. She stood very still until she worked up enough nerve to face him. When she did, he stood nude in front of her. She gasped. He was beautiful. She dared to look down at his erection. The air in her lungs refused to move in and out. Her eyes darted away, as though in shame at being excited by the sight of him.

Her fingers fumbled with the buttons on her blouse. Benji used to get mad if she did not get undressed fast enough.

"Let me," Kerry offered and pushed her hands away gently, and he undid her blouse and pushed it back off her shoulders and to the floor. His arms went under hers, then he unfastened her bra and let it slip away.

"Lovely lady," he breathed, his voice a hoarse whisper as he leaned over her. He drew a nipple gently into his mouth.

"My God," she moaned at the exquisiteness of the sensation. "My God." His mouth found the other breast and held there as he unfastened her pants. Then he stepped back and pressed her gently onto the waterbed. He removed her slacks and shoes. She thought she was going to die as a warmth spread into her loins.

"Move up on the bed," Kerry said softly and she obeyed. His weight caused the bed to rock and she tried to turn onto her side to face him. He stopped her, his hands on her hips keeping her firmly on her back. "Be still," he said. "Be very still, Lauren."

He moved up over her, hovering for a moment. She tensed, waiting for him to enter her. He didn't. He let his weight press on her and his mouth found hers again.

Lauren felt herself responding with an ardor she'd never dreamed she possessed. Her hands worked through his hair and down his back. Her mouth demanded more and more. She couldn't get enough of the taste and feel of him.

His hands stroked her gently and his mouth came away from hers. She cried out silently, then let him go. He slid down and cupped a breast in each hand and kissed first one and then the other, turning the warmth of her body into a fire.

"Please!" Her head rolled back and forth. She was begging. For what she didn't know. There were no clear thoughts in her head, only the mindless need and excitement, the incredible joy that was almost painful in its torment.

He moved down again and his mouth sprinkled kisses over the softness of her belly. And down again as she cried out at the shock of his mouth finding the secret, dark place no one had ever kissed before.

"Oh, God, my God," she moaned, then her cry fell into a small whimper. She reached down, her fingers finding his head and spreading through the dark thick hair. She pressed him harder against her.

He made soft, moaning sounds and she raised her buttocks, her legs going out tense and straight under him. The roaring in her head and the movement of the bed turned into a tidal wave. Her back arched, suddenly convulsed and she exploded.

"My God. My God." The words were barely audible, though in her head she was screaming. The sound from her lips turned into a high keening. He stopped all movement and lay very, very still until she moaned and then became as still as he, her mind barely capable of accepting the miracle he had given her.

They lay utterly still for unmeasurable moments. Sally was right, Lauren thought. She was right! It's the only way to fly. It works.

She shifted slightly, wanting to thank him. He moved upward and she welcomed him with her arms upheld. He hovered over her, then eased gently into her, almost teasingly at first. She groaned at the intensity of feeling left in her, at the sensitivity of her body.

"Lauren. Lauren." He stroked her hair and his mouth covered hers in a probing kiss and the mindless rhythm of the ages began. She let herself go, riding with him, wanting to please, clinging and caressing, whispering inaudible words of passion.

The rhythm increased again and again, until abruptly his body stiffened. Then it began again, harder and faster and his mouth moved from hers and their faces were pressed tightly together. Sweat ran from his face and body. His rapid breathing roared in her ear.

His hands became still on her back and suddenly she felt the inner tremors and she knew it was going to happen again. He whimpered as he came and she screamed, nails digging into his back, body arching and arching until she lifted him upward. He collapsed suddenly, breathing hard and fast.

They lay quietly, and gradually the bed also stilled. Kerry rose up on his elbows. "Lovely, lovely lady. I never dreamed." There was an awed look in his dark eyes. "I thought you were shy and inhibited."

"I am," she cried, hugging him tightly in her joy. "I am shy." She laughed aloud and felt the happy tears in her eyes. She gazed up at him through a misty haze. He was incredible, so special there were no words to express it. He had given her heaven, he had made her whole.

"If we could bottle and sell it, we'd be billionaires," Kerry said.

"No," she said. "I don't want to sell it. I'm selfish. I want to keep it."

"So do I. I may lock you up and never let you out again."

She stroked his face, memorizing his handsome features. She was so proud of herself, proud of being a woman, of being female. For the first time in her life she felt strong and powerful, a total woman.

"I love you," she longed to say, but did not dare. Just being here had to be enough for now. She wished for a talisman to ward off any evil that might ever touch and change this.

He moved off her and rested beside her on one elbow. With his fingertips he pushed tendrils of hair back from her moist face. "There's such a quiet, soft beauty about you, Lauren," he said. "You're different from most girls."

"I'm a woman, not a girl. Now." She hoped she was different enough for him to love. She smiled up at him adoringly. "You're pretty unique yourself."

"You're a real tiger," he went on. "I never dreamed such passion was hidden under that cool, composed exterior. You interested me from the beginning. And puzzled me. I guess it was the mystery of you that drew me to you."

She loved him with her eyes. "No one ever called me a tiger before."

"Come on," he said. "You were married."

She hid her face against Kerry's chest. "He was the only man I ever slept with, until you."

"Hey, come on." He poked at her, sounding uneasy.

"It's true. And he was a lousy lover. I . . ." She had to stop and swallow. "I never came before. Tonight was the first time."

"Jesus!" He fell over onto his back, making the bed sway. "Jesus, lady, I don't know how to handle this."

"Don't try." She snuggled against him. "I'm happy."

"I—I don't know what to say. It's like you gave me a gift. It's sort of scary."

"You gave me the gift, Kerry," she said, pressing closer to him, holding her body against him. "I'm so happy. You made me happy."

"I'm happy, too. Me, too." He scooted away from her. "I think this calls for another drink. There's a little *sake* left in the bottle."

"Not for me," she sighed, stretching lazily and watching him stand beside the bed.

"Coffee?" he suggested.

"Yes, I'd like that," she said.

They padded to the kitchen. She felt no embarrassment about being naked with him. They made cups of instant coffee and carried them back to the bed where it was warm.

Kerry pulled back the fur spread and they got in under it, sitting on the heated waterbed with the fur up around their necks. Lauren rejoiced in the quiet contentment of being with him.

"Listen, Lauren," he said, "I came up with something the other day. I can't feed it to Paula myself, but you could present it as your idea. Sally and I are falling in love, right?"

"Right," she replied.

"But she won't go to bed with me and you know

153

there's been a slight flirtation running between me and Irene. Only it hasn't been going anywhere."

Lauren frowned, not understanding where they were headed. "I guess I hadn't really noticed," she admitted.

"Well, Irene is an older woman and she might like to take on a younger man."

"I suppose it's possible," Lauren agreed, catching on to the idea. "Sure, it would be terrific. It's a good complication and it will fit in because Paula told me they are bringing back the character of Belle. She'll mess up the games going on with Cobb—I mean Ned and . . ." Lauren laughed. "How do you guys keep your names straight?"

"We don't. We just all have two names and we answer to either of them. And sometimes I think the characters are more real than we are. At least to each other." Kerry hesitated. He put his arm around Lauren and pulled her close. "You will bring this idea up to Paula, won't you?"

"Well, yes. I will if you want me to."

"But make it your idea," he suggested.

"But that's no good," she protested. "It's your idea. You should get the credit for it."

"No," he insisted. "Paula wouldn't like it. She doesn't give actors credit for having enough ability to do something as complicated as thinking. And I'd be careful about saying much about you and me to her. She might get the wrong idea."

Lauren was puzzled. "About what?" she asked.

"About how you came up with this idea. She'll think you're pushing me, and then she'll balk."

"Well," Lauren said hesitantly. "If that's how you want it."

"It is. Here." He took her empty coffee cup and set it with his on the floor. "I want to kiss that sweet mouth of yours."

They began to make love again, slower this time and with less urgency. And she wanted him. It was incredible that she wanted him again. She was here willingly and she could be pliable in his hands. It was a miracle.

She didn't reach the same highs as before, but it did not matter. She was content, she felt complete.

Later, he held her close. "You've exhausted me, woman. Let's go to sleep."

"I can't," she said.

"Why not?"

"I have to go," she explained.

"Why? Too young to spend the night away from home?" he teased.

"No, I just don't have any clothes or makeup and tomorrow is still a work day, remember? Friday."

"But it's too far for you to drive home."

"I have to, Kerry," she said. "I'm sorry."

"You've got to move to this side of the hills. It would be better for Sally, too. She could ride the buses more easily."

"We can't afford to move now," Lauren said. "Places like this cost twice what we pay. You know that."

"Let old brother Kerry here help you. I'm a genius at finding affordable apartments with good addresses," he said.

"Are you serious?"

"Of course I'm serious," he said. "There's no need for us being so far apart."

"But we can't afford it, Kerry. Sally's income is even more irregular than yours."

He laughed. "No one's could be that bad."

"I have to go now." She leaned over and kissed him, meaning to make it quick, but he drew her down and she lingered a bit longer, savoring the moment. Reluctantly she moved away from him.

She gathered her clothes. "Rock my bed," he said drowsily. She gave it a shove, then carried her clothes into the bathroom to dress. She had to go home. She could not have slept if she had stayed, she was far too excited and needed to be alone to savor the miracle.

She wished Kerry had asked her to move in with him. She had to smile at herself in the mirror. Men, especially men like Kerry, were awfully casual about sex. She would not push him, she would take it easy, do it his way. They would see where this glorious love would take them.

She went back to say good-bye and found him already sound asleep. She stood over him, overflowing with a rush of emotions. He looked like a little boy sleeping. She dropped a single kiss on his cheek. Kerry Scott was indeed a remarkable man, a very remarkable man.

Chapter Sixteen

Lauren was certain she would not be able to sleep at all. Not even the drive back to the Valley tired her. When she stepped into the apartment she was wide-eyed and exhilarated, yet dazed with awe and shock from her encounter with Kerry Scott.

Lauren peeped in on Sally, hoping she would be awake, but the girl was curled up into a ball in the center of the bed. Lauren slipped into her own room and undressed. She paused before putting on a simple nightgown. She examined her own body in the bathroom mirror, turning this way and that. She touched her breasts and ran her hand down to her thighs in a kind of wonderment at herself. She had a woman's body. Now she felt like a woman, too, utterly and completely female.

Proud and pleased, she pulled the nightgown over her head and got into bed to relive the night again and again. Sometime toward dawn she did fall asleep.

The next thing she was aware of was the alarm ringing. She groped for it, her fingertips found it, but abruptly the clock was whisked away. Lauren jerked awake, blinking.

Sally pounced on the bed, her eyes gleaming

wickedly. "Well, tell me! Tell me! When you weren't home by two I was certain it had happened."

Lauren could only smile happily. She stretched out full-length under the covers, still wrapped in the soft cloud of love and sleep.

Sally squealed. "It did happen, didn't it? You've got that fresh-loved glow on your face!"

"I do?" Lauren said, throwing back the covers and sitting up. "I do?" She pressed her palms against her face.

"Yes, you do," Sally said. "A very smug, contented look."

Lauren's arms flew out and she hugged Sally. "It happened."

Laughing, Sally hugged her in return, then sat back on her heels on the bed. "So tell me all the gory details."

Lauren blushed. "Oh, I don't think I can."

"Why not?"

"Well, they—they're private," she said.

"Oh, come on!" Sally cried. "You aren't falling in love with Kerry Scott, are you?"

"Don't look so dismayed," Lauren said. "It's just not something I can discuss freely."

"Are you falling in love with him?" Sally repeated pointedly.

"Yes, I guess I am," Lauren admitted.

"You're crazy!"

"I don't care. I'm too happy to care." Lauren shrugged and pressed her hands together. "It was so wonderful. I don't have the words to tell you."

"I don't suppose I can blame you because it did happen, huh? I mean, it was good for you, too. Not just for him?"

Cheeks burning, Lauren murmured a yes.

Lauren was humming softly as she edited Mel Lorenzen's weekly script. She was seated on the floor of Jenny's office with the scripts spread out on the glass coffee table. There were five copies of each script and they had to be exactly alike. They kept one for their file and Mel and Germain each kept a copy. The other two went to the studio. There they were typed again, mimeoed on heavier paper and bound and handed out to the actors. One mimeo copy was then returned to Paula's office and kept on file.

One of the penthouse rooms was nothing but files. A section for story projections, a file for outlines, another for typed scripts and another for mimeos.

Jenny glanced up from the accounting book she'd been poring over. "You're certainly happy this morning, Lauren," she remarked. "You're glowing, in fact."

Lauren looked up. Jenny's plump face showed her curiosity. "I feel good," Lauren said. "I'm happy."

"Why?" Jenny asked.

Remembering Kerry's warning about letting Paula know about them, Lauren shrugged. "Actually I was thinking about trying a sample script. Paula will do the new outlines for Mel and Germain today. Maybe I'll do one of them over the weekend."

Jenny's face grew somber. "Don't try too soon, Lauren. You'll annoy Paula if you're too eager."

Lauren sighed in exasperation. And Paula annoys me, she thought. Everyone walked barefoot and on tiptoe when it came to upsetting Paula. "I've got a story idea, too," she offered to Jenny.

Jenny brightened. "Now you might try that on Paula. That's a good thing to spring on her first."

"I'll type it up later then." Lauren said. God, she felt good! She began to hum again and turned back to the scripts.

Sally was feeling sexy and it made her edgy. It was all she could do to sit still through a camera blocking. She wished she had some pot to bring her down into a mellow mood. If she had a joint she could sneak off and smoke half of it.

She tapped her foot nervously on the floor. She

159

needed action in her life, she needed a man. She had gone hunting for one last night, but she did not find anything. Or rather, she did not find *him,* the only man she wanted now, Alex LaBarre.

But the night had not been a total loss. She did pick up some other useful information. She had hitched over Laurel Canyon and got the driver to drop her a couple of blocks from Spark's. She had dressed with care in her new boots and the loose-fitting white gauze dress Lauren had helped her pick out. The dress was belted at the waist with a brightly colored scarf. It was cold walking, but her one crummy sweater would have ruined the outfit.

Inside the plush club Sally walked through the disco section, dark except for the flash of colored lights focused on the withering dancers. She left the disco and strolled through the quiet game room which was empty except for two couples playing backgammon.

The bar, done in red velvet and gold gilt in an eighteen-hundreds motif, was crowded. She stood just inside the room, searching for a glimpse of Alex. Craning her neck, she edged around until she saw a man with a leering grin on his face coming toward her. She looked around for a way to escape and spotted a woman sitting alone at one of the tiny tables.

Acting as if she had spotted a friend, Sally headed in the woman's direction. "Can I sit down for a minute?" Sally asked the red-haired woman. "There's a creep closing in on me."

"Sure," the woman said, gesturing to a chair. She was about thirty and wore a bright green dress.

The creep advanced. He was drunk, and rich, judging from the look of his Gucci belt and shoes, but still a creep.

"Wanna go dance?" he asked, weaving over Sally.

"No thanks," Sally replied. "I have to talk to my friend."

"You wanna go dance?" he asked the red-haired woman.

"No, thanks," she said. "I'm waiting for my date."

"Stuck-up dames. I bet you aren't even members. I'm going to tell the manager about you two. Won't even dance with a bona fide member."

"Get lost, turkey," Sally hissed at him. "We aren't B-girls here to please you."

"Why . . . why . . ." he blustered.

The redhead gave him a hard look, daring him to cause trouble. He seemed about to respond when a waiter stepped between them. "Excuse me, sir," the waiter said politely. "May I get you ladies a drink?"

The creep left, muttering. Sally flashed the waiter a relieved smile. "Thanks," she said. "I'll have a glass of chablis." Sally turned to the woman as the waiter left, glad he had not asked for ID. "And thanks to you, too," she said. "I'm Sally."

"Rita." She ran polished nails through thick curly hair, then down to the neckline of her dress. She made an odd little adjustment to her breasts.

Sally stared with frank envy. "That is some set of boobs you have there," she said admiringly.

Rita looked down. "I like them," she replied.

"You should. You can't know what it's like to be built like a stick."

The woman smiled slowly, cat-like. "Can't I?"

"Huh?" Sally was amazed.

Rita leaned closer and kept her voice low. "I know exactly how you feel. I've been there myself."

"You—you mean those are—are—?"

"Yes," Rita said with a smile.

"Far out!" Sally moved her chair closer. "My God, tell me about it! I want to have it done, but it must cost a fortune."

"So get yourself a sugar daddy."

Sally shook her head, knowing she had almost had one in Alex LaBarre. "Naw, come on. What's it cost?"

"Well, that depends on where you go," Rita explained. "Los Angeles doctors with their fancy offices in Beverly Hills charge you a fortune. As much as three

161

thousand dollars. And it's about as bad in Las Vegas. And they run you through like it was a factory of some kind. Zap you in and zap you out while you're still too groggy to walk, much less drive home."

"Is that what happened to you?" Sally asked.

"No, I had good care. The best. Three days of loving care."

Sally could hardly contain her excitement. "Where?" she asked. "Where did you go?"

"Mexico," Rita answered.

"Oh, no!" Dismayed, Sally threw up her hands. "No injections in me. Terrible things happened to Las Vegas girls who had that done."

"No," Rita said. "These are implants. And Dr. Toby is a genius. The man is a renowned plastic surgeon." Rita leaned closer. "He's a good lay, too."

Sally was skeptical. "If he's so great, what's he doing in Mexico? Why isn't he here getting rich like the rest of them?"

"Oh, he's getting rich all right. He makes the same profit. He just doesn't have the same overhead. He doesn't do things the way they do in the States, shoving you in and out in the same day. He keeps you three days at his ranch in the interior. Dr. Toby sleeps right in the same building. There are twenty-four nurses on duty. American nurses. It's like a very exclusive spa. You can swim in the pool, sunbathe, eat, sleep in. It's total luxury."

Sally was interested. But Mexico. "I don't know," she said, beginning to feel wary. "What made him leave the States?"

"He left when the malpractice insurance rates sky-rocketed. Otherwise he would have had to double his fees. He went down to Mexico and lowered them."

"But even there, an operation and three days in a classy joint is still going to cost a lot," Sally said, still skeptical.

Rita smiled. "Eight hundred dollars," she said.

"Eight hundred!" Sally licked her lips. She could

come up with that much. That was nothing like two or three thousand. "How do I get in touch with this turkey?" she asked.

"Let's see." Rita picked up an oversized purse and dug through it. "Here you go." She pulled out a shiny brochure. "Just call this number." She tapped the sheet.

"I just call him up and say I want boobs?" Sally asked.

"That's right."

"How do I get there?"

"You can fly down into Mexico and he'll have his houseboy pick you up at the airport," Rita said. "Or you can take the limousine down."

"How much does that cost?" Sally asked, looking for the catch.

"Nothing. The limo is part of the service."

"God," Sally said, looking at first Rita's breasts, then her own. She clutched the brochure closer. "God."

"You should have it done, honey," Rita said. "It'll change your life."

Sally caught her lower lip between her teeth. "Does it hurt much?"

"No. It doesn't hurt. You'll walk in like you and walk out like me," Rita answered.

"I'm going to do it," Sally said firmly. "If I can find the money, I am, by damn, going to do it!"

"Hang on to that brochure," Rita said. "Don't lose his number."

"I won't," Sally said, putting the brochure into the bottom of her bag.

"And tell them that Rita recommended you. I get a little credit, you know, for sending other women down."

"I'll tell them," Sally promised.

Rita looked up. "Oh, there's my guy," she said. "Excuse me, please."

Sally believed in luck and omens. And here she had been thinking about boobs so much lately and now this had fallen into her lap. It was a sigh, a true sign that she should do it. Life was good when things fell into place.

And not so good when they did not. If Alex LaBarre would just walk through the door, the night would be perfect.

The waiter returned with her glass of wine. "The gentleman at the end of the bar paid for it," he told her.

"Oh." Her interest perked up and she peered around the waiter. It was the creep. He waved baby fingers at her. "No thanks. I don't think I can accept it," Sally said. "Give it back to him. By the way, has Alex LaBarre been in tonight?"

"No, he hasn't," the waiter answered.

"Do you think he will be in?"

"I wouldn't know, miss."

"Okay. Keep the wine. I'm checking out."

Which she did, and now she wished she could check out of the studio as easily. Damn, it was a long day!

Chapter Seventeen

Sunday afternoon Sally lay by the pool with a guy who lived in one of the upstairs apartments. He was a turkey, but a nice turkey, and he did have some grass. Not anything great like Colombian, but it was okay. They shared a couple of joints and lay side by side, not talking very much.

Sally wanted to get lost in the good drowsy feeling that could come with a joint and the sun, but the damned wind wouldn't quit blowing. It made her edgy. Plants popped and snapped in the wind, from somewhere a door clanged back and forth. All the clattering and rustling and whistling sounds kept crowding into Sally's head.

She sat up abruptly and said, "I'm going in." The turkey looked up hopefully. "I'll see you around. Thanks, fella."

"Oh. Okay." Disappointed, he sighed and laid his head back down on his towel. Sally took her first and last dip in the pool to wash away the grime and sweat. She came out and started shivering the instant the wind hit her. She ran for the apartment, the wind licking at her body. Damned Santa Ana winds, Devil's wind was more like it. Full moons and Santa Ana winds always got to Sally.

Her teeth were chattering by the time she got into the apartment. She ran a tub of hot water, wishing she had a guy to share it with, other than the available turkey. Lauren was off with Kerry, in bed, Sally was certain. Lucky girl!

In the tub she examined her nubby little breasts. She began worrying if there was enough skin there to stretch out to hold the implants. My God, what if she called and went down and this doc said he could not help her?

She slid deeper into the hot water to think. She got out, toasty warm, and wrapped herself in one of Lauren's oversized towels. In her bedroom she tossed jeans and T-shirt onto the floor and stretched out with her checkbook. She had four hundred dollars left. She could use it to pay for the doctor and worry about how to pay Lauren her share of the rent later.

Lauren would understand. Sally ran a hand over her breasts. Nobody expected her to seriously go around like this the rest of her life. She had borrowed a hundred dollars from Cobb on Friday for extras. So all she needed was another four hundred. Which meant she would have to con Joe out of it. She would see him tomorrow and it should be easy enough. Joe was a good guy.

She took her calendar out of her treasure box along with the brochure from Rita. The first week in March was free. Almost. She was scheduled to tape *Dreams* on Friday. The dance and voice classes were simple enough to cancel.

She snatched up the phone before she lost the courage. Direct dialing to Mexico, no less. Area code and all. It was far out.

What Sally assumed was either a receptionist or nurse answered the phone. The connection was lousy and they both had to yell. "Who recommended you?" the crackling voice on the other end of the line asked after Sally had identified herself, told her what she wanted and when.

"Rita," Sally yelled. "Rita recommended me."

There was a slight pause. "All right. Come down on Sunday. We'll do it on Monday about nine and you can go home on Tuesday."

God, it sounded so easy! "Can I go to work on Friday?" she asked.

"As long as you don't have to lift your arms."

"I don't."

"You must pay in advance when you arrive." The line crackled with static and Sally lost the next words.

"Can you repeat, please?" Sally yelled.

"Cash or money order. We do not accept personal checks. Will you wish to be picked up by the limousine?"

"Yes."

"Fine. Call this number in Los Angeles that I'll give you."

The arrangements made, Sally hung up and called the limo service. She found out that the women going down to Mexico met in Century City and left their cars in the underground parking lot. She was to be there promptly at nine.

Sally hung up. Limo, plastic surgery. She felt like a real classy lady. She wished Lauren were here to talk about it. Or should she tell Lauren? She had a feeling Lauren was not going to like this at all. Maybe she would just surprise her. Once it was over, Lauren would be pleased for her. Everyone would be. She would have boobs, no behind still, but real breasts.

Her bedside phone rang and Sally snatched it up. "Hello," she sang.

"Hi, baby girl," the smooth voice said.

Her heart almost stopped. "Alex?"

"Who else?"

"Oh, Alex! I didn't think you were going to call."

"I've called several times. No one answered. Don't you know an actress is supposed to have an answering service? You could miss something important." The deep, rich voice delighted her. If she knew how, she would have purred.

167

"Well, everyone goes through my agent," she explained.

"I don't," Alex said. "I always call direct."

"I know that now, Alex. As soon as I can, I'll get a service."

"How would you like to have dinner with me at Chasen's tonight?" he asked.

"Chasen's!" Sally gulped. It had been the *in* restaurant with the movie people for forty years. It was very public, a place to be seen. "Alex, aren't you married?"

"Well, yes. But my wife is out of town."

"But aren't you afraid of being seen with me? Out in public like that. Won't someone tell her?"

"Probably," he laughed. "But I suppose we can call this business. You are an actress."

"Yeah. Funny business. I don't want to get you in trouble, Alex."

"You're sweet, baby girl. But you let Daddy watch out for himself. You're an actress and I'm a director. It must be business. My chauffeur will pick you up at eight."

"Chauffeur?"

"Yes. I have to attend a cocktail party in Bel Air. I'll take a taxi to Chasen's."

"I'll be ready."

"Good girl. Bye-bye."

"What—what should I wear?" she cried, but he had already hung up. Chasen's. Chauffeurs. Arrangements for not one, but two limos to pick her up in the scope of five minutes. It was another omen, a sign of things to come.

Sally plopped backward onto the bed, her body alive with excitement. She popped back up and got out her treasure box. She sat it in front of her crossed legs.

She was extraordinarily possessive of the meager contents she had spent nineteen years accumulating. She had once threatened a guy with a knife when he tried to dig through it. He had backed off quick enough, but she was certain she would have sliced him up if he had not.

There was a small pewter box Tony had given her, a love gift, he had called it. It had not been her birthday or anything when he gave her the delicately engraved box with a pewter butterfly resting on a daisy. There was a pearl-gray feather in the pewter box. She had picked it up during the location shooting of her first film as an extra. She thought it might be a dove feather. She brushed the soft, delicate feather across her face and smiled. The feather, like the pewter box from Tony, was among the beginnings of good things, of her career.

Inside was her most prized possession. When she was younger, she had studied the photograph over and over. It wasn't much of a picture, just the standard high school wallet size taken at graduation.

The guy in the photo wasn't wearing a tux or a graduation gown as they did in most pictures now. He had on a leather jacket and his collar was turned up and his high pompadour was greasy looking. A kid from the fifties, a kid who had gotten Sally's mother pregnant, then taken off.

His name was Rook, too. She had taken the name when she ran away from home the first time. Her mother had named her Sara Hill. Sally hated it. Hill was not anybody, just a name her mother had tacked on.

Sally thought she resembled her father, Barney Rook. Of course, he would not look like that now. He would be old, like Mama, in his late thirties. She had looked for him in every city she had ever been in, but she had never found a Barney Rook in the phone book.

She hoped he was nice like Alex, maybe turning gray now. Or was he too young to be gray? Sally shrugged. It did not matter, she was never going to find him anyway. Except maybe when she was a star. Then she would have enough money to hire a private detective. She bet a good one could find him. She had envisioned him being every kind of person from a hood in prison to a banker.

She closed the lid gently over the photo. There were no pictures of Mama or her sister, Patty.

"I don't want to think about them," Sally said aloud. "So I won't." She was going to Chasen's tonight. She did not have to think about anything else. Oh, my God! She scooted off the bed. What could she wear?

Sally's first glimpse of Chasen's was a disappointment. It was just an ugly white building kind of squatting by a parking lot. Of course, when the limo pulled up, the door was whisked open and a uniformed attendant offered his hand.

She was so nervous, it was all she could do to smile. She pulled the brightly colored shawl closer around her and was ushered inside.

She was led into the large dining room to where Alex was seated. "I just arrived," he said, standing. He was a large, rotund man, but solidly built in the pearl-gray suit with matching vest and a wide tie of muted gray satin. There was a comfortable sense of authority about him, an air of being in constant control.

"Do I look okay?" Sally blurted out.

"You're very pretty, Sally," he said. "And everyone is wondering who you are."

"They're looking at me?" she asked, glancing around quickly.

"Of course they are." His dark gray eyes gleamed in pleased amusement.

"Wow!" She sat up straighter and tried not to play with the long fringe on the shawl. There were drinks, then Alex talked quietly, pointing out celebrities to her, getting up once to speak to a couple at another table.

When the menus were laid in front of them, Sally shook her head. "I'm much too excited to eat," she demurred.

"Order something grand," Alex insisted. "How about lobster?"

"No, I couldn't. I'd make a mess out of it. I just can't eat anyway. I'll get sick."

"No, you won't," Alex said. "And I'm ordering for you. We'll have chili and champagne."

"Together? Really?"

"They go well together."

Sally giggled. "Sure, why not?" Chasen's was famous for their outrageously priced chili.

By midnight they were in Alex's bungalow at the Beverly Hills Hotel. Alex, nude, was stretched out on the bed. He patted the bed beside himself invitingly. "Come on," he coaxed. "Come to Daddy, baby girl. Come to Daddy."

"Alex . . ." she began, stopping when he frowned. "Daddy." It was a hard word to say, foreign on her tongue. He smiled up at her and she went to him, eager to make him happy, to please him. He was so good. He did not come too soon, like some guys, before she could get off. She slid next to him, pressing her thin body against his broader one, going into the security of his arms.

They made love slowly, and it was simple and good, the way Sally liked it. Afterward Alex, wrapped in a floor-length velour robe, studied the nude girl on the love seat across from him.

She was an odd little thing, he thought. Not like the usual young actress on the prowl. She was not sexy. She was all bones and skin, yet she was terribly appealing, this child-woman.

Alex wondered if he was getting kinky in his old age. There were old guys around who would not touch anything over fifteen. Or even fourteen.

Her eyes were the most striking. He had never seen eyes quite that color before, the tawny gold of a tigereye stone or of an old penny. Combined with the hair and skin, she was outstanding. A conversation he remembered from the cocktail party in Bel Air suddenly clicked in his mind. He had paid little attention at the time. The filming of TV commercials did not interest him. All his energy was pouring into *Rainbow*.

He studied Sally, then said, "Sally, I heard of something you might be right for. I was talking to Dick Morris tonight. He's with a big eastern advertising agency. He's out here from New York. They want the California girl look for a new line of cosmetics aimed at the younger market. That's what they're calling the line— California Girl Cosmetics. The model can't be just the average suntanned blonde leggy girl. She had to be that and more. Different."

Sally looked surprised. "Me?" she asked. "You're thinking about me for that?"

"Sure." He reached over and stroked her hair. "You are different, special."

"You're sweet." Sally gave him little kisses. "But you don't have to do things for me. I don't sleep with you because you're Alex LaBarre."

"Well, who said you did?" he asked.

"Nobody," she replied, her small face totally serious. "But I just wanted you to know where I'm coming from. I like you, Alex. I don't want gifts or handouts. I don't want a sugar daddy. So you don't have to take me to places like Chasen's. I'll get there on my own."

Alex studied her intently for a few moments, then said, "You aren't putting me on, are you? You really feel strongly about this, about making it on your own?"

Sally nodded firmly. "Yes, I am." Though it darn sure helped that he was a director and did take her to Chasen's.

"Most girls have their hands out though," he reminded her.

"I don't use sex, Alex." She was becoming aggravated. She stood suddenly, uncertain of her own motivations.

Alex grabbed her hand. "What's with you?"

She sank down on his lap. "I'm sorry," she said. "I'm paranoid, I guess."

He drew her legs up and held her close, making soothing sounds. "I never thought that about you. And I never will. This commercial thing just came about. And I want you to follow up on it. Here, jump down."

Sally hopped to the floor while Alex got his wallet out of his pants and extracted a card. He scribbled on the front and back and handed the card to her.

"You call this number and ask for Dick Morris," he said. "I wrote his name here. You tell him I sent you, and he'll set up an audition for you."

Sally was hesitant, partly for show and also for something more, an odd sort of fear. She did not take the card. "I don't know, Alex," she began.

"Girl, you do as I say," he said with authority. "You want to make it, don't you?"

"Yes," she said weakly, raising the copper eyes to his face.

"Then don't turn away an opportunity. No matter where it comes from. Okay?"

"Okay." She took the card, then put her arms around his neck and nuzzled his face. "I think I love you, Alex. You're about the nicest thing that could happen to a girl."

He patted her bare behind. "And I think you're a nut, but an adorable one," he said lovingly.

"Are you going to take me back to bed now, Daddy?" she asked, because she wanted it and because it was expected.

"If you're a good girl."

"I'll be good, Daddy," she promised. "I'll always be good for you."

He believed her and wondered how he could ever return such devotion. He knew he should send her home and never see her again, because nothing could really come out of this relationship for her. He was very much married and he intended to stay that way, but he was not going to turn her out. He needed her, wanted her, and he would have her for as long as possible.

Chapter Eighteen

The first Sunday in March dawned cool and clear. Sally was both excited and apprehensive as she walked from the bus stop on Santa Monica Boulevard into Century City. The acreage that had once been Tom Mix's ranch, then Twentieth Century Fox's back lot, had been transformed into a modern white city of soaring buildings.

Sally was always struck by the sense of cleanness about Century City. She walked up the Avenue of Stars, carrying a small suitcase she had borrowed from Lauren for her three-day stay in Mexico. She had told Lauren she was going down for a brief vacation.

Across the street was the ABC Entertainment Center, a complex featuring The Shubert Theatre, movie houses, expensive shops, restaurants and a Harry's bar transported from New York. A fountain, shooting spray high into the air, stood between the center and the prestigious Century Plaza Hotel, a soaring skyscraper built for the world of tomorrow. It spread out from a dramatic formal entrance in the shape of a twenty-story-high Japanese fan. Someday Sally intended to stay in that hotel, in one of the suites overlooking the Fox Studios.

Sally kept one arm protectively over her purse. The

eight hundred dollars was inside a folded and sealed envelope deep in her shoulder bag. She sort of wished she had told Lauren the truth and then maybe gotten her to come along. Though she doubted Lauren would leave her job or Kerry. Their relationship had become common knowledge now, and Lauren wasn't a bit of fun. She spent more nights with Kerry than she did at home, while Sally was only seeing Alex twice a week.

Sally cautiously approached a small cluster of women on a corner near the Century Plaza Hotel. "Excuse me." Sally spoke to an elderly woman who was standing slightly away from the others. "Are you going to Mexico?" she asked.

The woman looked at Sally. "Why, yes, dear. I am."

"Good, are you scared?" Sally asked, wanting to share her fears.

The tiny, grandmotherly face wrinkled even deeper as she considered the question. "No, I think not," she replied after a pause. "At my age there's little left in life to frighten me."

Sally persisted. "What are you going down for?"

The woman chuckled. "My face, dear. What else? My whole family is furious with me. My sister thinks I've lost my mind, having a face-lift at my age. I'm seventy, you know. But I don't care what they think. It's my face—and my money."

"Good for you!" Sally cheered the spunky lady. "You hang in there." She tugged at her sweater. "I'm going to get implants," she announced with more bravado than she felt.

A black Cadillac limousine nosed toward the curb. There was a flurry of bag gathering and purses being hiked up on shoulders as it stopped. The driver, an overweight, sandy-haired fellow who introduced himself as George, looked them over. He pushed a scuffy cap back on his head. "Six of you, huh? Luggage back here. How many are staying and how many are going for consultations?"

There were three of each. They arranged themselves

in the limousine and settled back as the car headed up Santa Monica Boulevard to the San Diego Freeway. Names and greetings were exchanged. The two women in the front were both housewives from the Valley. One was going down for a nose job, the other for a consultation about a face-lift.

Sally was seated in the back by the window next to the elderly Mrs. Stokes. The other two women interested Sally. They did not look like housewives.

"What do you do?" Sally asked the flamboyant-looking one who was decked out in French jeans and a tight lacy blouse that showed off huge breasts.

The woman brushed an imaginary piece of lint off her front porch. "I'm going to see if Dr. Toby can make me larger," she answered.

Sally gasped. "Larger?"

"Yes. I'm an exotic dancer. The more the better."

"Oh." Sally eyed her sideways. She was a porno star, Sally guessed. She looked like porn, like she would spread her legs for any guy with a camera and a few bucks.

"And you?" Sally asked the sixth woman, who was the only one in the group dressed in high heels and hose and an expensive wool dress, as though she was going out for a club luncheon.

"Breast implants, too," she said in an unusually husky voice. She was strikingly tall and broad shouldered. She said her name was Tanya.

"Are you a dancer, too?" Sally questioned.

"Me? No, darling. I own a beauty salon."

"I should have guessed," Sally said. "Your hair is just lovely." Actually, Sally thought it looked like something out of a costume movie. It was swept high and done with elaborate lacquered curls.

It was three hours to the carnival-gaudy border town, another six bumpy hours into the interior. It was dark when they arrived and stopped at a locked gate. George got out, inserted a key into a padlock and swung open wide wrought-iron gates.

George drove the black car through, then stopped, got out and relocked the gate.

"Why all the heavy security?" Sally asked him nervously as he got back into the car. "Afraid a patient will escape?"

"No," he answered dourly. "Let's just say we like to keep out uninvited guests."

The tires crunched their way over a graveled drive. In the headlights' path Sally could make out patches of vividly blooming flowers, mostly geraniums in hot pinks and whites.

She leaned forward, eager for the first glimpse of the ranch. It was a low cream-colored adobe with a red tile roof sitting in the midst of a landscaped estate.

George led them through a courtyard and into the villa, where they were welcomed by a round dumpling of a Mexican woman. "This way, ladies," she said with all the authority of a tour guide and only the slightest trace of an accent. "George will take care of your luggage. The bar is in here."

They traipsed after their hostess, following her into the biggest living room Sally had ever seen. Huge windows overlooked a dark terrace that curved around the outer edge of the house.

A black leather and polished wood bar dominated the far end of the room. A young man in a white jacket waited to take their orders. A few other women were already gathered. Two sat quietly and slightly apart in robes and slippers. Both had darkly bruised faces and their mouths were encircled with what looked like a dark stain. "What happened to them?" Sally whispered to Mrs. Stokes.

"Face-lifts and acid peels," the woman answered, touching her own upper lip. "It gets rid of these horrid lines. Don't you hate them? I can't stand it when my lipstick starts edging up into the lines. Nasty!"

"I guess," Sally murmured. She had never thought about it one way or the other. Sally and Mrs. Stokes asked for white wine and sat together at the far end of the bar.

A sudden rising of voices made them turn. A tall broad-shouldered man entered. He greeted every woman by name, touching hands and kissing cheeks and even squeezing breasts here and there.

"Doesn't look sixty-five, does he?" Mrs. Stokes whispered to Sally.

"My God, he doesn't look forty-five!" Sally gasped in surprise. He certainly looked younger than Alex. "How does he do it?"

"He admits to face-lifts, and he also takes cell injections. I don't understand it exactly. Some kind of youth drug."

"He's yummy," Sally said. A good-looking man was always to be admired.

Dr. Toby approached the pair. "Ah, Mrs. Stokes," he breathed. "You're looking awfully bright and chipper. You're going to be a beauty tomorrow." His voice was silky smooth, his eyes intense.

"I'm going to look like hell tomorrow," she reminded him.

"Oh, only for a few days." His eyes moved to Sally. "Now, what do we have here?" He reached out with both hands and clasped her waist. "You're Sally."

"I'm the boobless wonder," she said.

"We're going to take care of that, too." He stepped back and raised his voice. "I'll see each of you separately after dinner, ladies. This way, please."

The group drifted into a formal dining room laid with china and silver. Two black-haired girls with shy eyes stood waiting to serve them.

That Rita was right, Sally thought. This is a real classy joint. She bet it was as nice as the Golden Door, where they starved people to death.

Sally ate until she was stuffed, then waited her turn to see Dr. Toby. She was directed into his office as the well-dressed beauty salon owner came out. Her head was down and she looked like she was crying.

Dr. Toby closed the door hard after he and Sally went in. "Would you believe that was a man?" he asked Sally, his voice dripping with disgust.

"Oh, no," Sally said.

"Oh, yes," Dr. Toby replied. "He wanted me to do implants."

"How sad," Sally offered.

"It's sickening. I wouldn't touch him."

Sally looked at the doctor's face. "Well, I don't blame you," she said hesitantly. "But I still think it's sad."

"He's a freak. But he's not our problem." He turned his silky smile on Sally. "Let's have a look at you, honey. Lift your blouse."

He sat down in a chair in back of a large desk and indicated she should stand beside him. He placed a card with her name on it in front of him. "Let's see," he began. "Did you bring the payment?"

"Oh, yes, sir." She lowered her blouse and scrambled for her purse. She took out the precious eight hundred dollars and handed it to him.

He put it in a drawer, not bothering to count it, and made a notation on her card. "Now, then. Let's have a look at you."

Sally lifted her blouse again. She had not bothered wearing a bra. He squeezed the small nubs with his fingertips, probed her bony rib cage and pulled at the flesh and skin under her arms. Sally's heart was beating so fast there was a pounding in her ears. "Can—can you help me?" she asked timidly.

"Well, I can't make you into a *Playboy* centerfold, but I think I can stuff it enough to make you a B cup."

"Oh, wow!" Her knees went weak with relief. She pulled her blouse down with a small wiggle as he picked up a clear blob from his desk.

"This is a silicone implant," he explained. "A jell. It can't leak, not even if it is broken. And it would take a hell of an accident to break one. It's going to stay all together. I'll make a little incision under your breasts, a

180

half-moon shape, then tuck these up underneath what you have and sew you back up. And that's it."

"That's all?" Sally found it hard to believe.

"Yes, that's all. I see my nurse has you down for nine. I'll be doing Mrs. Stokes first."

"You aren't going to take blood or anything?" Sally asked.

Dr. Toby looked at her curiously. "You are healthy, aren't you?"

"Oh, yes."

"Okay, you'll be fine, honey. Just fine."

"Is it going to hurt?" Sally had to ask the question that had been on her mind from the beginning.

The doctor shrugged. "Oh, maybe a little. But don't worry about it. Now, no breakfast tomorrow morning. Not even water."

With the help of a pill on top of the drinks and wine with dinner, Sally had no trouble sleeping. The instant she awoke another pill was popped into her mouth. It made her feel she was floating in some lovely place.

A sour-faced nurse placed her on the operating table of the attached clinic shortly after nine. A needle was inserted into the blue vein of her arm. The next thing she was aware of was the doctor there, another needle in his hand.

"What's that?" Sally asked, her voice seeming to come from far away.

"Novocain, just like in the dentist's office." She flinched and had to grit her teeth to keep from crying out at each stab of the needle. He massaged her tiny breasts and made soothing sounds until she calmed down.

She was half-awake during surgery, her sense of time distorted. Once she had the sensation of being peeled like a grape and she was aware of the insertion of each silicone bag.

The boy who had served as bartender the day before took her to her room in a wheelchair and tucked her into bed. She lay back, eyes closed, placing one hand over each new breast. Under the tightly wound tape, they seemed awfully small, though larger than before.

She slept, then sometime in the late afternoon awoke in terrible pain. "Oh, please," she begged. "Please, someone!" The room was empty and there was no call button. She hurt, couldn't breath under the bindings. "Please," she cried out louder. "Someone help me!"

Through a haze of pain, she saw Mrs. Stokes leaning over her. The woman's hairline was matted with blood. Her mouth was an ugly brown thing, a grotesque clown's grin.

Mrs. Stokes left and the sour-faced nurse appeared. "What's wrong?" she demanded, her tone hateful.

"I hurt," Sally said emphatically. "Damn it, I hurt! Nobody told me it was going to hurt."

"So it hurts," the nurse shrugged. "Here." She popped a small pink pill into Sally's mouth and held a glass of water for her.

It was a strange evening and night. There were more pills and time was out of warp. There were moments when Sally did not know if she was dreaming or hallucinating. She did not like the pills. She did not want them, but the pain was worse without them. She had to have them.

Tuesday, the tape was ripped from her body by Dr. Toby. Gasping from pain, Sally kept her eyes averted, afraid to look down. "Well?" she asked him feeling the pounding of her heart pulsating through her body in apprehension.

"Lovely, just lovely," he said, his cool fingers probing gently. "I'm very proud of them."

Sally dared to look down. She gasped. Two full round globes were sitting on her chest. Breasts! She had breasts! Gingerly, she cupped each one in her hand. "I actually have boobs!"

Dr. Toby smiled at her. "That you do, Sally. I'm giving you this packet of pain pills to take home with you in case you need them."

182

"You didn't tell me they would hurt," Sally complained in accusing tones.

"Of course it hurts, honey. I cut into your body. There has to be some pain, some bruising." He sat down on the edge of the bed and put his arm around her in a fatherly way. "You seem to have more pain than most."

"But you didn't tell me it would hurt," she repeated. "You lied to me."

"I didn't want to scare you, that's all. You're a sensitive girl. You'll be fine in a few days. Try to limit your arm movement to a minimum for a few days. No lifting, okay?" He tickled her under the chin.

"I'll be good," Sally promised. "I don't want to hurt any more."

A few moments later, the nurse brought in an elastic bra for Sally and charged her an extra fifteen dollars for it. The next morning, Sally was tucked into the limousine by Dr. Toby.

"I still hurt," she whispered to him.

"But you got what you wanted," he reminded her.

"Yes," she reluctantly agreed.

"Look at yourself," he said. "My God, you're terrific!"

"Am I, doctor? Am I?" She wanted to believe him.

"You're beautiful. And don't let those bruises worry you. They'll be gone in a matter of days."

They stopped once in Mexico and again in the States for coffee, and Sally downed pain pills each time. She slept most of the way into Los Angeles. In Century City, she got a taxi to take her home. She was crying when she opened the apartment door with her key. The pain had become all-encompassing, taking over as the center of her being and sending out wave after wave of hot lava.

"Lauren!" she called. "Lauren!" The apartment was empty. Sally took another pain pill and eased her tormented body into bed.

Chapter Nineteen

After leaving Kerry's apartment, Lauren drove through Beverly Hills and took Coldwater Canyon across to Studio City and dropped into the San Fernando Valley. It was after midnight and she was feeling oddly disconcerted. There was no doubt in her mind that she loved Kerry Scott, even stood in awe of him. He had given her a belief in herself as a woman.

He said many nice things to her and also about her, but he never said he loved her. She longed to hear those words, but she had not let it matter. The rapture of each meeting had been enough, more than she had ever expected.

Mama used to tell her to count her blessings when she began to fume over a lack in her life. She had been doing it subconsciously with Kerry. She acknowledged the many blessings to be counted now. She cautioned herself to be satisfied, not to ask for too much too fast, not to want everything.

"Kerry, Kerry." She mouthed his name aloud. You were just in an off mood tonight. That's why you told me to go home.

He had not come right out and told her he had money problems, but she knew something was weighing on his mind and he had not been working as often as he would have liked.

If only Paula would follow through on the idea for *Dreams*. Lauren had typed up the suggestion for an affair between the younger brother and Irene. She had presented it to Paula as her own.

Paula had said it was good, but she had not followed through on it and Kerry was openly disappointed. He felt like he was drifting on *Dreams*. Lauren was afraid to press Paula about it. You simply did not pressure Paula unless you were prepared for a possible explosion of anger. Or of simply being ignored. Paula Cavanaugh was not easy to work for, but Lauren wouldn't quit. The opportunities outweighed the negative aspects.

The car slid through the quiet Valley streets. Here and there, fifty-year-old walnut trees stood gray and leafless, all that remained of what had once been a grove. Sixteen-thousand-dollar houses that now sold for fifty thousand were huddled together on small tract lots. Apartment houses had taken over every available space that was large enough to accommodate one.

At her own faded green complex, Lauren parked the car and walked quickly through the chill of the night. Sally should be home by now. She was anxious to hear about her sudden vacation to Mexico.

Sally had been strangely mysterious about it and Lauren had decided she was going down with Alex La-Barre and he did not want anyone to know because he was famous as well as married.

Lauren opened the door with her key and stepped inside. "Sally," she called. There was no answer, but a pair of platform shoes were in the middle of the living room floor. Lauren set down her purse, picked up the shoes and went back to Sally's bedroom. The door was open and Sally made a curved bump in the bed.

"Sally?" she said softly.

"Oh," came the weak moan.

"Sally?" Concerned and puzzled, she stepped into the room.

"I—I can't turn over. Come around here." Sally's voice was hardly more than a whisper.

Frightened, Lauren circled the bed. "What's wrong? Are you ill?"

"I—no—yes. Oh, God, I hurt so bad, Lauren."

Lauren touched her face. It was warm and damp. She stepped over and turned on the bedside light. "Honey, where do you hurt?" She knelt beside the bed. Sally was hunched up in the fetal position.

"I hurt." The voice was low and husky. "There— there's some pills on my dresser. Get me some water."

"You have to tell me what's wrong," Lauren insisted.

"Please, Lauren!"

Lauren hesitated, then obeyed. She got the bottle from the dresser top. It was filled with pale pink pills. There was no label on the bottle. "What are these?" she asked Sally.

"Pain pills."

"Sally, what's wrong? Please tell me," Lauren begged, confused and more frightened than ever.

"Get me the water, Lauren. Damn it, I hurt!" She was crying now.

Kneeling, Lauren brushed Sally's damp hair back from her face. "Not until you tell me why you need pain pills."

Sally sniffled. "I got breasts, Lauren. I got breasts in Mexico."

Lauren stiffened in disbelief. "You what?"

"Nobody told me it would hurt." The words were a pitiful whimper.

"I—I'll get you the water." Lauren hurried. She returned with the water and helped Sally sit up. It was a slow, painful struggle, with Sally trying to keep her breasts supported with her hands.

Lauren stacked both pillows behind her and Sally eased back onto them. Lauren put the pill in her mouth, then held the water glass.

Sally leaned back. "See, Lauren. I got breasts." She

sounded like a little girl. She unfolded her arms and exposed the surgical bra.

Lauren gazed down at the swollen globes. Her lips formed a hard straight line. "You're bruised," she managed, too shocked by this to say anything else.

"Yeah, I guess I am," Sally admitted. "But they'll heal."

"Oh, Sally." Lauren whispered, appalled. "Why did you do it? Who did this to your body?"

"It was an American doctor. Don't worry, he's okay."

"Are you sure?"

Sally ducked her head and gently touched the tops of her breasts. "The incision is draining a little. I need some new pads. I used the box of gauze you had in the bathroom."

Lauren retrieved the box and took out two square gauze pads. The bra had a front opening and she undid it herself. The breasts poped out, making Sally grimace and moan. "Damn it, they're heavy."

Lauren hesitated, horrified. The flesh was grotesquely swollen and bruised. She controlled her reaction, not wanting Sally to know how dismayed she was. Lauren carefully removed the old pads that were soaked with bloody yellow fluid. She returned to the bathroom for alcohol and cotton, then cleaned the incision that ran underneath each breast, careful not to pull the stitches.

"I think you should see a doctor, Sally," Lauren suggested as gently as possible, not wanting to scare Sally.

"No, I'm okay. I can feel the pill hitting. I just want to sleep now."

Lauren got her back inside the bra and helped her lie down again. She covered the girl, who was asleep before the act was completed.

Sally was warm to touch, but she did not seem feverish. Frustrated and a little frightened, Lauren wanted to call someone. But who? There was no one.

There seemed to be nothing to do but go to bed and

let Sally rest. She slept lightly and woke up twice to check on the girl. In the morning, Sally seemed slightly better. She was stiff, but it did not hurt as much, though she was still draining heavily. Lauren cut up a Kotex pad to use this time. She gave Sally a light sponge bath, got her into a front-opening robe and back into bed before she left for Paula's penthouse. Sally refused food, asking only for the horrible-tasting herb tea she kept on hand.

By Thursday night, Sally insisted that she felt much better. But Lauren did not believe her. Sally did not look good. She was pale and thin. She did get into the bathtub and, with Lauren's help, was soaped and rinsed. The bath exhausted Sally and all she wanted to do was crawl in between the cool, clean sheets Lauren had put on her bed. Lauren noticed the level in the pill bottle was dropping rapidly and it worried her.

Sally was childishly proud of her new breasts and Lauren did not have the heart to say anything negative about them. She could not tell Sally they looked like two bruised oranges screwed into her chest. There was no softness, no flow to the breasts, just two alien protrusions sticking from the thin chest.

She tried to talk Sally into seeing a doctor again, but Sally refused, stubborn in her attitude to tough it out alone. She was equally determined to go to work Friday morning. "I don't want to cause any trouble," she said. "I'll be able to get through the day. I'm only in three scenes. It will be a breeze."

"Sally, I think you should stay home," Lauren insisted, somewhat annoyed.

Sally's upper lip curled. "And have Paula and Silverstein and the director all down on me? No thanks. I don't want any trouble. Besides, I'm ready to go out. I don't like being shut up like this."

"You're pale, Sally. You aren't eating and you've lost weight. You aren't well."

"I've been drinking my tea," Sally said. "It has healing powers, you know?"

"Well, I don't think it's going to heal an infection, which is what I think you have," Lauren retorted stiffly.

"I'm not infected," Sally insisted. "I'm just a slow healer."

"Then let me fix you something to eat, some soup maybe."

"I can't eat. Food just . . ." Sally made a face and shrugged. "I can't eat, that's all."

After three conversations along those same lines, Lauren gave up. Sally went to bed early. Lauren wished Kerry would call, but he did not. She had talked to him briefly at the studio and told him Sally was sick and that she wanted to stay home with her.

Lauren had to assume Kerry was making an effort not to intrude. Maybe he was waiting for her to call him. She had never called him. Which was dumb, she decided. She was not in high school now. She was on more intimate terms with Kerry Scott than she had ever been on with another human being, including Benji Parrow.

Why not? She picked up the phone and dialed Kerry's number. I'm missing you, she would say. I'm lonely.

"Kerry Scott's residence," a female voice said. Lauren was taken aback. She couldn't say anything. "Hello?" the voice said. "Hello? Is someone there?"

Lauren sat very still, her mind reeling. Who was she? What was she doing in Kerry's apartment this late at night? There was only one obvious reason.

"Hello," the voice said again. Lauren replaced the receiver.

Her head began to pound. She crept back into the bed and pulled the blankets tightly around her.

Of course, Kerry knew other women. He was not a monk. He had made her no promises either.

Lauren endured a lousy toss-and-turn night and got up the next morning feeling hung over. Facing Sally didn't help. Lauren's uneasiness grew. Sally was very pale with dark circles under dull eyes. She was also shaky, but she did get down a cup of broth as well as her tea and insisted on going to the studio. "You aren't going to change my mind, Lauren. So just forget it," Sally told her. "Quit nagging me."

Sally's rebuke hurt. "I'm only concerned," Lauren said.

"Let's can it," Sally said sharply.

"All right." Hurt, Lauren withdrew and didn't argue any further.

The drive to the studio was silent. She drove Sally up to the entrance and dropped her off. As she circled the parking lot, Lauren looked for Kerry's car. It was not there. She had hoped they might run into each other this morning.

Depressed, Lauren drove to Wilshire Boulevard and to Paula's place. She was at her desk early and hoped Joe Seals would pop in to say good morning as he did occasionally. She was going to drag him in by the lapels of his brown suit or hang onto his bow tie until he heard her through. Someone had to talk some sense into Sally. She seemed to listen to Joe.

Joe did not appear and Lauren buzzed the kitchen for the housekeeper. "Would you tell Mr. Seals that I must talk to him?" she asked.

"Oh, he left early this morning," Margaret replied in her clipped English accent. "I'm sorry."

"Thank you," Lauren said. She broke the connection and dialed Joe's office number. His yawning secretary told her that Joe was going to be out all day on appointments.

Lauren did not bother leaving a message. She had no choice but to trust Sally to know what she was doing. There was work to be done here. Paula had been up and in her office before Lauren or Jenny arrived. An early rising was ominous on Paula's part. She was on a tear about something and today would be a good time to foul up.

Paula sat in front of the IBM Selectric II, clicking it on and off from time to time with her index finger. She had to get out Germain and Mel's outlines today, but nothing was coming.

She tapped her polished nails on the typewriter. She couldn't afford the luxury of a writer's block. It made her angry when one threatened. The name of the game was daily performance.

She knew the script she had turned out yesterday was lousy. Three a week was simply too much of a drain on her creativity. Both Germain and Mel refused to do more than one a week; it was beyond their capacity.

She had won her right to submit four new story ideas a year to Silverstein and the network. Only, how in the hell was she going to find time to come up with them? New projects were all-important. If she could never get her job down to just doing outlines for *Dreams* . . .

Impulsively, she buzzed for Lauren and asked her to step into the office. Lauren entered a few moments later with pen and pad in hand. "Yes, Paula?"

"I want you to try a sample outline this weekend," Paula announced. "I'll decide which one when I've finished with them."

A look of panic flew into Lauren's eyes, making Paula laugh. "*This* weekend?" Lauren choked.

"Well, I know it's sooner than you expected," Paula said. "But I think you're ready to try it."

"Oh, Paula. I . . ."

Why did she look so distracted, Paula wondered. She ought to be pleased. "Don't pressure yourself," Paula advised. "Just follow my outline. We can find out where your weaknesses and strengths lie. You'll know what to concentrate on then. Aren't you ready?"

Lauren licked her lips. "I'll do it, of course. I'm just a little overwhelmed, Paula."

"Just remember, Lauren. More often it is what you don't say than what you do say. It's the innuendos. It's John being protective of Timmy when he doesn't know he's the boy's father. It's . . ." An idea struck her. "That's all, Lauren."

Paula was not even aware of Lauren leaving the office. Timmy, of course! They had not used the kid lately. It was time they brought him back into the show. Ned was raising the boy alone. He should be having problems. A man alone, his wife in a mental hospital. It was good. It was time to make use of it again.

It was also nearing time to bring the mentally ill wife back, too. A new Katherine would have to be cast. She would have to write an audition scene for that.

Paula ripped out the paper in the typewriter and inserted a fresh sheet. She began to type a scene for Katherine, a woman ready to merge back into sanity. Paula's fingers flew over the keyboard. She was back in control.

Chapter Twenty

Lauren came out of Paula's office. Her first thoughts had been of Sally and Kerry and her need to spend time with both of them this weekend. The reality of what Paula has asked of her began to sink in and she went giddy. Jenny glanced up from her desk and asked, "What's up?"

"I—I get to do a sample script."

"Very good!" Jenny said. "I'm impressed. You've only been here a little over two months."

"Wow, I think I'm impressed, too." Lauren felt as if she had just been injected with a revitalization serum. She glided back to her own office. She wished she could call Kerry, but he was at the studio.

She decided her reaction last night had been crazy. The woman who answered Kerry's telephone was probably a friend. It could have been Joyce Mitchell. Now that she thought about it, the voice did seem familiar. Maybe Joyce Mitchell and Mickey had dropped in and Joyce had happened to answer the phone.

Relieved, Lauren tackled the day's correspondence with exuberance, eager to get it finished so she could edit the script Paula had written yesterday.

Copy streamed out of Paula's office. She skipped lunch and ordered a sandwich from the housekeeper to be served during the daily viewing of *Dreams* on the air.

When the show was over, Paula turned to Lauren. "I hope you paid close attention. That was an outstanding show. I may use it for the Emmy competition."

Lauren followed Paula back to her office while Jenny stayed behind to shut off the recorder and date the cassette.

"Fate is the only real villain in soaps," Paula explained. "Irene is our resident bitch, but she could change and will change in time as we learn more about her background. No one is totally bad or totally good. We—"

The telephone interrupted her. Lauren moved to answer it at Jenny's desk.

"This is Sue Bergman. Lauren?"

Lauren stilled instinctively at the sound of Sue's frantic voice and tone. Something bad was coming down. "Yes?"

"We have a problem. Sally just collapsed on the set. On camera!"

Lauren's knuckles turned white as she grabbed the receiver. "I'll be right there," she said, her only thought to get to her friend.

"No!" Sue ordered. "You stay where you are. We're taking care of Sally. A doctor is on his way."

"But I know what's wrong," Lauren protested.

"Get today's mimeos," Sue snapped. "It's Sally's last scene. Page twenty-three. The scene has to be scrapped. Now, let me explain this to Paula."

Lauren handed the phone to Paula, saying, "Sally has collapsed on the set."

"Damn!" Paula snatched the receiver from Lauren.

Lauren whirled around. Paula had scattered everything as usual. Lauren had fought since she arrived to bring some order to the constant clutter, but it was a hopeless task.

She frantically thumbed through a stack of mimeos on the love seat. The dates were all out of sequence. Today's script was not there. She checked a pile on the floor, then spotted a single mimeo under the coffee table. Success!

Paula took the script after Lauren had opened it to the critical scene. Paula began rewriting the scene over the phone, substituting one of the other actresses for Sally, changing the lines to fit the other character and managing to convey the same information to the viewer.

In fifteen minutes, it was over. Paula hung up the phone. "What's wrong with Sally?" she demanded of Lauren.

"I—I don't know," Lauren stammered.

"Did she have an abortion?"

"No. No, she looked pale this morning and a little feverish. Maybe she's coming down with the flu."

Paula studied her. "Maybe."

Oh, God, Lauren thought. Why was she lying like this to cover for Sally? Why had she let some instinct to protect the girl overpower all else. Paula would be furious if she found out the truth.

"Can I leave now?" Lauren asked. "I want to see Sally."

"I suppose so," Paula said slowly. "Here, take a copy of Germain's outline with you. Do as much as you can over the weekend. I'll have Jenny deliver the outlines to Mel and Germain. Or use a messenger service."

"Thank you," Lauren said.

Traffic seemed to move unusually slowly as she drove from Wilshire to the studio, shredding Lauren's already frayed nerves. Once there, she could not find a parking place and had to circle the lot twice. Anxious and concerned, she ran inside and found Sue.

"Where's Sally?" Lauren asked breathlessly.

"Not in the hospital, which is where she belongs," Sue snapped. "What butcher got hold of her?"

"Let me talk to her," Lauren said, ignoring Sue's question.

"I put her in Bob's office. He's out. He's going to flip when he hears about this."

Lauren stepped ahead, not caring what Bob Silverstein thought. Sue followed her into the office where Sally was lying on her side on the leather sofa. A lean man was standing over her.

"Who are you?" the man demanded of Lauren.

"I'm her friend," Lauren said crisply, kneeling beside Sally. "How are you doing, Sally?" she asked.

"I'm okay," Sally replied.

"She's full of infection," the man said. "But she won't let me check her into a hospital."

"I can't afford it," Sally said.

"We have insurance," Sue reminded her.

"Go to hell, Sue," Sally snapped. "I don't like hospitals." She turned to Lauren. "Take me home," she said.

"I think you should do as the doctor says," Lauren replied.

"No. He gave me a shot. I'll be okay."

"I pumped her full of antibiotics," the doctor interjected, his tone almost hateful. "Here's a prescription. You can have her. She's all yours."

"And you can go screw yourself, too," Sally yelled as he walked away.

He turned around. "Foul-mouthed little creature, aren't you?"

"I give it my best!" Sally shot back at him.

"Shut up!" Lauren ordered. "You make me so mad. I want to shake you." She heard the door close behind Sue and the doctor.

The harshness and anger faded from Sally's face. "I'm sorry, Lauren," she said. "But I just can't take people messing with me and telling me what to do."

"The man was only trying to help you," Lauren said, her tone sharp and full of anger. There was no telling what she had said to the doctor.

"Well, I don't need his help." She tried to sit up. "Oh, goddamn it! I hurt. The bastard wouldn't give me any more pain pills. He told me to try hot packs, the no good s.o.b."

Sally held both her breasts as Lauren helped her to her feet. "Can you walk?" Lauren asked her.

"You're damned right I can," Sally answered.

"Yeah, you can. You're wobbling." Lauren supported her as best she could and got her out into Sue's reception area.

"You know this is costing thousands of dollars," Sue taunted as they left. "Delays like this cost plenty."

"Sue, please. Not now," Lauren begged.

Ignoring Sue's yammering, Lauren guided Sally into the hall. She looked up at the sound of footsteps. "Kerry!" she cried, relieved. Even in the midst of this, her body reacted to his nearness.

"You need some help, girls?" Kerry asked.

"Yes, she can hardly walk," Lauren answered.

"You go get the car and bring it to the entrance, Lauren. I'll handle our girl here."

"Thanks." Lauren took off at a trot and brought the car around as quickly as possible. Kerry had scooped Sally up into his arms and carried her outside. Lauren went around to help him tuck Sally into the front seat. He gave her a kiss on the cheek, told her to mind Lauren and closed the door.

"Thanks, Kerry," Lauren said. "I don't know what I'm going to do with her."

"Certainly no more than she'll let you," Kerry replied.

"I guess not." She looked up into his dark eyes. "Last night she seemed better." Last night another woman answered your phone, she wanted to say.

Kerry touched her arm. "I guess you'll be tied up all weekend, huh?"

"I guess." She nodded in disappointment. "Maybe you could come over and have dinner with us?"

"You give me a call if it's convenient," he said.

She did not want to leave, but she had to. She raised her face for his kiss and let her hand linger on his for a moment.

Sally was crying by the time she was into bed. Lauren stood by helplessly as the tears flowed down the girl's cheeks. "I have one pain pill left," Sally said. "I'm going to have to take it. And don't stand there looking at me like that."

"You should be in a hospital, Sally."

"No! Hot packs and aspirin will help."

Lauren got aspirin and filled a pan with hot water. When she unfastened Sally's bra, she flinched. The drainage was worse. The flesh was red and taut. She looked as if she would explode if poked with something sharp.

Sally winced as Lauren laid a hot wet towel over her breasts. She laid back, clenching her teeth, her eyes closed tightly. Little tears escaped and ran down her temples and into her hair.

Sally downed four aspirin and eventually drifted off into a restless sleep. Lauren stayed with her, stretched out on the floor beside the bed with a book.

The telephone rang shortly after six. Lauren scrambled to her feet and snatched it before it could ring again. "Hello?"

"Sally?" a male voice asked.

"No, this is Lauren, her roommate." She hesitated, then blurted out her question. "Is this Alex LaBarre?"

There was a pause, then a cautious reply. "Yes."

"I need your help," Lauren said. "Sally needs you. She's really sick and I can't do anything with her."

"Sick?" Alex asked. "What's wrong with her?"

"She went to Mexico and had breast implants," Lauren said, deciding it best to level completely with Alex. "She's full of infection and in a lot of pain. She collapsed at the studio this afternoon. She let a doctor treat her there and he gave her some antibiotics, but she's refused to go to a hospital where she should be."

"I'll be right there," Alex said.

"Thank you!" Lauren breathed, relieved. She hung up the phone and looked over at Sally. She was still sleeping; the pillow and sheets were damp from perspiration.

Forty minutes later, Alex LaBarre knocked on

Lauren's door. She opened it and stepped back. "I'm so glad you're here, Mr. LaBarre."

He stepped inside. He dominated the room with his size, his obvious wealth and his authority. The lined face was deeply tanned and rather handsome underneath the silver-white hair.

"Where is she?" he asked, wasting no time.

"Back here." Lauren took him into the bedroom. "She's sleeping now."

He crossed to the bed in three quick strides and touched Sally's shoulder. "Baby girl."

Sally tossed her head. "Hmmm?"

"Sally, it's Alex."

"Alex?" She frowned and opened her eyes. "What—what are you doing here?"

"I heard you were in trouble," he said.

"Lauren." Sally's feverish eyes sought her out. "You had no right to call him."

"She had every right," Alex interjected. "Now stop acting like a stupid little kid and tell me what's going on!"

Lauren watched the normally independent girl take Alex's hand and press it to her face. "I'm scared, Alex," she whispered, her feverish eyes locked on his face.

Lauren stepped out of the room and closed the door behind her. She made herself a cup of instant coffee and waited in the living room until Alex came out.

"I've called a doctor I know," he told her. "He has a small private hospital in Toluca Lake. I'm taking Sally there." He took a card out of his pocket and scribbled down a name on it. "You can inquire about her here. She'll have the best of care."

"Thank God," Lauren breathed. "I'm so grateful to you."

"She's a crazy kid," Alex murmured and looked away, as though embarrassed by his concern for Sally.

"Don't I know it?" Lauren felt ready to collapse out of sheer gratitude. "I'll go see her tomorrow."

Alex returned to the bedroom and came out carrying

Sally wrapped in a blanket. Lauren walked out to Alex's chauffeur-driven car with them. But Alex did not need her assistance, he was in complete control.

She walked slowly back to the apartment, her mind automatically going to *Dreams*. Sally would need at least two weeks off. Paula had to be notified. There were scripts to be rewritten.

Inside, she dialed Paula's home number. Margaret, the housekeeper, answered and told her Paula and Joe were eating dinner.

"This is Lauren, and it's important," she told the housekeeper.

There was a short wait, then Paula answered. "Yes, Lauren?"

"It's about Sally."

"I know about Sally," Paula said, her voice icy cold. "I spoke to Sue. You lied to me earlier, didn't you? You knew what was wrong with Sally all along."

"Yes," Lauren answered with the deep sigh of one reconciled to accepting punishment.

"I thought I could trust you. This is my show, and whatever happens to the crew is important to me."

"That's why I'm calling now," Lauren said. "To explain to you."

"You can't explain away Sally's kind of stupidity."

"I suppose she thought it was the right thing to do. She didn't consult me about it, anyway. I know she felt very inferior because she didn't have breasts."

"She was like a four-year-old wanting chocolate," Paula said. "She reached out and took the first bar that came along."

Lauren couldn't argue with her. It was true. "She'll probably be out of the show for at least two weeks," Lauren said.

"I'm writing her out for a month," Paula replied acidly.

"A month? But surely we could wait and see," Lauren protested.

"One month," Paula repeated firmly.

"I see," Lauren murmured. It was Paula's way of punishing Sally. "May I speak to Joe?" she asked.

"I suppose," Paula relented. The phone went down with a clank that hurt Lauren's ear. She had to wait for Joe.

"Joe," she said when he came on the line. "Sally had some things coming up. I don't know the exact dates. But I'm sure she won't be able to work for a couple of weeks."

"There's no problem on the TV movie," Joe said. "She's not due to film that until April and I hear they're running behind schedule anyway. I think she can scratch the pilot though. She's not going to be able to play a fourteen-year-old with big boobs."

"No, I guess not," Lauren agreed.

"I'll cancel her out on the audition," Joe said.

"I'll tell her when I see her."

"Poor kid," Joe said. "I should have known she was up to something like this when she hit me up for a loan."

"I didn't know what she was up to either."

"She needs a keeper," Joe said.

"I'm not a very good one, I'm afraid," Lauren sighed, wishing Sally had trusted her enough to confide in her. She could have talked her out of going to Mexico.

"Neither am I," Joe replied. "Neither am I."

But maybe she had found one in Alex LaBarre, Lauren thought. "Thanks, Joe," she whispered.

Joe was sweet and she felt better after talking to him. But Paula had left her quivering. The woman could make her feel so stupid.

Lauren toyed with the dial, wanting to call Kerry, needing him. She picked up the receiver and dialed Kerry's number. He had said to call. It was okay this time.

"I'm free tonight," she said when Kerry answered. "Sally is in the hospital."

"That's great," he said. "But how did you ever get her to agree?"

"A guy she knows," Lauren explained. "He wouldn't take no for an answer."

"Good."

"It's where she needs to be, Kerry. Why don't you come over here? The apartment is ours, and I'll fix you something special for dinner. Maybe quiche and salad."

"I've had dinner," he said. "But I can think of other things I'd like to eat."

"Kerry!"

"Don't sound so shocked and prudish," he laughed. "You love it."

"It's you I love," she said quickly, immediately wishing she could take the words back. Her pulse raced as she waited for his delayed reply.

"I'll be over soon," Kerry said, his voice low and controlled and distant. His obvious displeasure over her impulsive statement had a strange effect on her. She felt released, she had said it and it was out in the open. She would take whatever consequences came.

Chapter Twenty-One

Lauren was aggressive in her lovemaking with Kerry, not only responding eagerly but also initiating moves of her own. She had never dreamed she could respond so strongly to a man. She did not just love Kerry, she hungered for him.

The relief of having Sally off her hands, the chance to do a sample script and the fact of having finally blurted out to Kerry that she loved him all gave her a strange kind of confidence. She held nothing back from him. She had said the forbidden words and she did not think she had anything else to lose.

She was thoroughly content and relaxed when Kerry left Saturday morning. Her newly found confidence carried from Kerry over to the script. Following Paula's outline seemed incredibly easy. When once it had taken her hours to get through one page of copy, the white sheets now flowed in and out of her typewriter.

By mid-afternoon she was pleasantly tired. She abandoned the typewriter, made herself a cup of coffee and called the private hospital. The switchboard put her through to a nurse who was polite, but firmly turned down her request to speak to Sally.

"She's resting comfortably and she needs solitude," the nurse said. "I have strict orders not to disturb her."

"Would you please tell her I called then?" Lauren asked. "And could you tell me how long it will be before I can visit her?"

"Perhaps on Monday," the nurse replied. "But that isn't firm."

"Thank you. I'll call back tomorrow," Lauren said.

She considered calling Kerry, just to share her good feeling with him. But last night had gone so well that she did not want to push it. She had agreed to call him when the script was completed, not when it was half done. That would be her reward for working so hard all weekend.

She finished the cup of coffee and stretched out full-length on her stomach on the shag carpeting, a thin, cheap polyester. Happy with herself, she wriggled into a comfortable position. She had told Kerry she loved him and he had not fled or gotten angry with her. And though he had not responded to it, it was now up to him to take the next step. Last night had been beautiful. Surely there was no other couple in the world who satisfied each other any better.

Lauren closed her eyes. Kerry's apartment was big enough for two if they wanted to live together. And maybe one day after her divorce . . . She drifted off into a light sleep.

She came awake suddenly, uncertain of what sound had jarred her back to consciousness. She rolled over on her back and stretched. It was dusk and the apartment was growing chilly. Lauren sat up and yawned. She looked down at her breasts jutting out against the fabric of her T-shirt.

She had always found them so imperfect before. Compared to Sally, she was in terrific shape. And Kerry certainly seemed to like them. Poor Sally. Joe said Sally was a survivor, but Lauren was not so certain that was true. In many ways, she was very vulnerable.

A rap on the door brought Lauren to her feet. "Coming," she yelled.

She ran her hands over the soft brown hair, then

206

opened the door. A tall male figure was silhouetted in the doorway. Coldness sliced through Lauren's body. The pit of her stomach formed a tight ball. "Benji!" she choked, taking a step backward.

"Hi, Lauren." The sensuous lips formed an all too familiar smile.

She gripped the edge of the door. "Why are you here?" she asked.

"Oh, curious, I guess," he said. "I wanted to know how you were getting along. Can't I come in?" he asked, stepping inside as he said the words.

"For a minute," she demurred. Her brain felt numbed by his unannounced arrival.

He looked around the small room. "Not a bad place you've got," he said.

Lauren shrugged, trying to come off as cool and confident. "It will do. I have a roommate."

"Oh, yeah? Where is she?"

"Out," Lauren answered, not wanting Benji to know Sally could not return at any moment.

Benji touched the back of the armchair and leaned against it. Her eyes followed his hand as he reached down to his crotch and made a small adjustment. He was always doing that. It used to drive her crazy. She had wondered if he had to keep checking to make sure it was still there. Did some part of him think it was going to disappear? At night he used to sit and watch television with one hand inside his trousers.

His eyes followed her gaze and he grinned suggestively. "I'm still in good working order, Lauren," he leered.

She flushed and looked away. Damn him! Flustered, she moved away farther from him.

"I miss you, Lauren," he said, his tone going suddenly soft.

"Please," she said, "don't do this to either of us." She didn't want any more pain, she didn't want the memories stirred up.

"Do what?"

"Torment me—us."

"Don't you miss me? Even a little?" He smiled, but it didn't reach his eyes.

She didn't want to play games, so she refused to lie. "Benji, I don't even think about you any more," she sighed.

His eyes widened. "Getting feisty in your old age, aren't you?"

"No, Benji," she said, her tone weary. "I'm only being truthful." She looked up at him. He was good-looking in a slick sort of a way. The eyes were his best feature. Brown and large and expressive, they could be soft and gentle or turn into mean probes.

He toyed with the keys in his pocket. "We had five years together. They must count for something."

"They count as a mistake," Lauren replied, wanting to keep him at a distance. She felt that if he touched her, she would scream.

"So, you never think about me, huh?"

"No."

"I don't believe you."

She swallowed. There were times when he had occupied her mind day and night. Once in love, when they first met, and once in fear, when she wanted the divorce.

"I'm over you, Benji," she said as honestly as she knew how. "I have been for a long time."

"No, it's more than that," he insisted. "You've got yourself another guy, haven't you? You're getting screwed regularly."

She drew herself up straight, hating him for zeroing in on the truth. "Is that the only way you can conceive of a human being functioning?" she asked cynically.

"It's what makes the world go around, babe. And if you think otherwise, you're fooling yourself."

"Would you just please leave?" she asked coldly. She didn't want him around. They had nothing to talk about. What she did and who she slept with was none of his business.

"How about a drink first?" he asked. "For old time's sake?"

"I don't have anything in the house."

"Not even a beer?" he asked, walking into the kitchen.

"Benji," she begged. She wanted him to go away. Talking was pointless. He'd find a way to hurt her again.

He ignored her and opened the refrigerator. "You have wine," he said, taking out the capped bottle.

"Benji, please." She began to feel panicky.

He turned around. "I only want to talk, Lauren. That's all. Can't we be friends?"

"I didn't think you believed in such." He had threatened to hit her the first time she had mentioned a divorce. He called her a spayed bitch when she saw a lawyer. He told her she would come crawling back and finally said he did not want her around because she cramped his style.

Now he said he was lonely. "It's pretty rough coming home to an empty apartment every night. It's cold there and there's none of your good cooking. Lauren, it wasn't all bad between us."

She weakened slightly. "I—I know what you mean," she conceded. "I've had my bad days." There were times she had felt like having anyone who was human around would be better than being alone.

He took water glasses out of the dish drainer and filled them each half full. He handed one to Lauren and she took it. "Toast?" he asked.

"To what?"

"You name it, babe," he grinned.

"To success, then," she said.

"Good enough. To success." He clinked his glass against hers. She watched him sip his wine. He was wearing a new leisure suit, this one with a western cut. He wore it well. Benji was a handsome, sexy man, there was no denying that.

"How's your job going?" she asked for lack of anything else to say, not comfortable with him. Benji worked for a Chevrolet dealer in the west end of the Valley. He was very good at it. He made a great deal of money, but he spent it as fast as he earned it, sometimes faster. They had never been out of debt their entire married life.

"I sold twenty cars this month," he announced.

"I'm impressed," acknowledging his hard work.

"How about you, Lauren. You're working? Let's go sit down?"

She was quick to take the one armchair, so he could not sit next to her on the sofa. She filled him in briefly about her job and began to relax slightly as the warmth of the wine spread through her body.

"So you're still going to be a writer?" he asked.

"Yes, I am, Benji." She tossed her hair back from her face defiantly.

"You're different, Lauren," he remarked. His eyes were studying her again.

"I hope I'm growing," she replied stiffly, not liking the turn the conversation was taking.

"You look good. But then you always had a fine body. You just didn't know how to use it."

Her edginess turned to anger and her temper flared. "Maybe you were the one who didn't know how to use my body," she threw out and immediately wished the words back, because Benji's eyes snapped at the challenge of her remark.

He leaned forward, his bulk menacing. "What gave you that kind of idea?" he asked roughly.

"Nothing," Lauren said quickly, backing off. "Nothing. I'm sorry, Benji. I shouldn't have said that."

He stood. "I don't like this, Lauren."

"Neither do I, Benji," she said. "So why don't you leave?"

"Not yet." He set his glass down on the scarred oak table and walked over to her. "You've got a boyfriend, haven't you?"

She pulled her feet up into the chair. "I'm dating," she said, forcing a casual tone.

Benji's eyes narrowed. "Is he better than I am?"

"Benji." She jumped up and moved around him, hardly daring to breathe. He didn't reach for her. "Benji, let's drop it," she begged.

"I asked you a question."

"Benji, please." She took a step backward and his hand lashed out and grabbed her left arm. The glass in her hand trembled and wine spilled out. His grip hardened and she whimpered in pain.

The glass fell from her numbed hand. He didn't even look down as the glass hit the floor with a soft thud. The wine splattered on his pants leg. "Maybe you need a comparison. We could run a little test. Then you can tell me who is better."

"Benji, you're hurting me," she choked, and from some depths mustered her courage. "I'm going to scream if you don't let me go."

"Are you?" he taunted. "What are you going to scream? Rape?"

"Yes! Yes, damn it!" She screamed and tried to yank away.

He twisted her arm to one side and she fought against him, shoving at him with her free arm. He grabbed it, then with one hard jerk threw her to her knees.

"A husband can't rape his wife. Everyone knows that." He yanked her arms upward and she scrambled to her feet.

"You aren't going to touch me, Benji," she warned. She'd fight, she'd yell and claw.

"I am touching you."

"Damn you!" She kicked out and he jumped back, one foot hit the glass and threw him off balance. His grip loosened and she yanked free and scrambled away, getting the coffee table between them.

She stood, panting, steeling herself for his next move.

"I can take you, you know," he jeered. "If I wanted to."

She tensed, but did not answer. Could she make it to the door? Probably not, she decided.

"Hell," Benji muttered suddenly, giving up. "You were never any fun anyhow. You lay under me like a goddamn dead fish. I wouldn't waste my time on you."

As abruptly as he had arrived, he left, slamming the door behind him. Lauren dashed for the door and double-locked it. Chest heaving, gulping in deep breaths of air, she went down to the floor on her knees.

She had once measured her every action, every response by Benji. He had beat her down with words and disdain so often, she had almost believed him when he said she was the sick one.

"I know better now, Benji!" she said to the empty room. Damn it, I know better! You can't ever hurt me again. I have Kerry now."

She began to cry, then sob. I am a normal human being, a woman, she thought. I am. I am! The sounds of her crying echoed softly through the underfurnished room. Her shoulders shook with the racking sobs.

Chapter Twenty-Two

The second half of the sample script did not go well for Lauren. She berated herself for letting Benji turn her into a weeping shambles. She should have been stronger. She had thought she was stronger than that, but his appearance and attitude and words had brought the past tumbling down on top of her lovely new world.

All the old feelings of inadequacy hung on through the night, haunting her sleep. She dreamed of Benji and Kerry, the two men standing over her with looks of contempt and disgust on their faces. "See," Benji told Kerry in the dark dream. "I told you she wasn't much of a woman."

"I should have listened to you," Kerry answered. "You tried to warn me. She calls herself a woman, but she's a fake."

"No, no," she begged, trying to reach out for Kerry, but he was too far away to touch. She woke up crying and it seemed to take hours to fall asleep again.

She came awake slowly the next morning. She lay still, holding the warmth of the bedclothes. The light outside her window was gray. She rolled over to check the clock, thinking it was predawn, but the clock said it was after nine. She threw back the covers and hurried to turn up the thermostat.

She was exhausted, her body ached as though she had run miles and miles. The depression left her feeling hung over, both queasy and headachy.

In an attempt to revive her body, she took a hot shower. Still feeling dull and achy, she made a pot of coffee and rejected the idea of eating breakfast.

Lauren slipped into jeans and a T-shirt and approached the typewriter. Clearing her head of Benji was difficult. She wanted reassurance from Kerry, but she did not dare call him. She would end up telling him about Benji and she did not want to talk about it. She wanted to forget it.

Her old Smith-Corona seemed as sluggish as she. It was a struggle to make sense out of Paula's outline. She felt as if her brain was encased in thick layers of cotton batting.

Lauren stubbornly hung in and by noon the sun was shining and she began to feel awake. She stopped for a grilled cheese, and the rest of the script went much better. Finished, she edited the script. She was not satisfied, but she was not dissatisfied either. She allowed herself to call Kerry.

From the street Burning Embers, the private hospital where Alex had taken Sally, gave the appearance of being a private estate. A six-foot red brick fence protected the grounds. Wide wrought-iron gates were discreetly guarded.

Having refused a suite, Sally was in one of the small private rooms on the second flood. There were no wards, no double rooms. Alex LaBarre sat on the edge of Sally's bed. The sheets were silky soft and from Saks Fifth Avenue, as were the towels in the bathroom. Two walls were papered in soft green and powder blue. The oversized windows were hung in floor-length draperies of a matching blue.

Sally tucked her hand into Alex's. His fingers were broad and decorated with dark hairs, the nails professionally manicured. He lifted Sally's hands. "You've been biting your nails, baby girl," he remarked.

Sally grimaced. "I know." She gazed up at him with her dark cinnamon eyes. "I'm going to be okay, aren't I?"

"Of course you are," Alex said. "Dr. Bennett is the best. He only handles stars."

Her fingers tightened around his. "This is costing too much money."

"You aren't to worry," he said. "I thought we settled that before I brought you in."

"You have to keep count of everything," Sally insisted. "I'm going to pay you back."

"Of course you will," Alex said, noticing that she was staying rather still. "Are you in pain?" he asked.

She laid her head back on the raised bed. "Yes, a little," she conceded.

"A lot, I'd say."

"I—I think I'm better," she said, touching her breast lightly.

Alex didn't answer her obvious lie. He could see the angry redness above her breasts. She winced every time she moved and Dr. Bennett was worried. The infection was not responding to the medication he had pumped into her body.

"I'm getting better," she said again. Alex patted her hand. She was such a determined little mutt. He wished he could magically put her back on her feet intact.

"Did you call Morris before you went to Mexico?" he asked.

"For the California Girl Cosmetics thing? I was going to as soon as I got back. I thought he would like me better with a real bosom."

Alex looked at her intently. "It's your face, not your body he'll be interested it," he said.

"What about my hands?" she asked. "I'll fail if he wants hands."

"I'm sure he will be using hand models for fingernail

215

polish," Alex said, though he didn't know that at all. "And there're always procelain nails."

"Those things cost fifty dollars," Sally protested, her voice weak as she made the effort to keep up the conversation. "Are there really hand models?" she asked.

"Sure. There are girls who specialize. Girls with great hands or terrific legs. Some girls make a living just modeling shoes."

"I didn't know that," Sally said, her voice faint with fatigue now.

"Well, it's true."

She closed her eyes. She looked so drawn and pale, the dark circles under her eyes making her seem incredibly vulnerable. Her hand rested lightly in his; the skin was dry, and she was much too warm.

"Daddy?" she asked.

"What, baby?" He leaned closer to catch her soft words.

"How come you spend so much time with me?"

"I make time for you," he replied.

"What about your wife?"

"Oh." Alex cleared his throat. He did not discuss his wife with his girls. "She's in Europe. We have a villa in Italy."

"Are you, like, separated?"

"No, not necessarily. But my wife is Italian. She has a lot of family there. We—we never had children of our own and she lavishes a great deal of money and attention on her nieces and nephews."

Sally tried to lift herself, the effort making her cry out. "My God, what's wrong?" Alex said, gripping her hand tightly.

A wan grin passed over her face. "I moved too quick, that's all. Your wife—she's Italian, huh? She's Gina Beradino, isn't she?"

"Yes," Alex said. "My wife is Gina."

"She's beautiful!" Sally whispered. "I saw every movie she ever made. What do you see in me when you have someone like her?"

Alex sidestepped her question. "Gina was very beautiful. She still is, in an Italian way."

Sally nodded. "You mean she got fat?"

"Yes," he said. "She dieted severely while she was acting. She gave up both a few years ago." Alex stood abruptly. "Well." That was enough about Gina. They had been tied together for many years by a sort of love. Not an exciting romance now, but they still enjoyed each other. They were contemporaries and California was a community-property state There was no way he would let Gina walk off with half of his worldly possessions. And Gina tolerated his affairs as long as he was reasonably discreet. "I've got an appointment, honey."

Sally sighed disappointedly, "Oh."

"It's on *Rainbow*. We're trying to get Redford. He wants a million. Minimum."

"Wow!"

"You sleep now," he ordered. "I'll call you tomorrow."

He kissed her on the forehead and she nuzzled against him. "You're so good to me."

He ruffled her hair. She was such a funny little creature. Elfinlike one moment, a child the next. A hussy in bed. "Bye, baby."

Alex walked out of the room. He was calling Dick Morris himself in the morning and he was going to pitch Sally. If Sally ever found out this fancy hospital cost a thousand dollars a day she would freak out. Of course, he would see that a much smaller bill was made out for her eyes. The kid deserved something good in her life, and California Girl Cosmetics could be it.

Lauren spent an anxious Monday waiting for Paula to find time to read her script. She wished Germain would get in her version so she could compare them, but she knew it would be Thursday before Germain's could be picked up.

Lauren wondered why it took Germain and Mel nearly a week to do a script while Paula could knock

217

one out in a few hours. She hoped she would be like Paula.

At five o'clock Paula yelled from her office. "Let's lock it up, girls," she said. "It's been a long day."

Lauren stayed on in her office, finishing up a letter that needed to go out. When she took it in for Paula's signature, Jenny was gone and Paula was sitting at her desk with a glass of sherry.

She was wearing black pants and a gray sweater. She looked tired and somehow the severe haircut contrasted more sharply than usual with the aging face. Lauren laid the letter in front of Paula. "This needs your signature," she said.

"Okay." Paula bent over the letter. "I'll try to read your script tonight. I know you're eager for some comments."

Lauren smiled across at her. "Very!"

"How do you think it went?"

"I honestly don't know. I've been both up and down about it."

Lauren picked up the letter and started to leave. "By the way," Paula said, "how is our friend?"

"Sally? I don't know. They won't tell me anything when I phone. I'm going to the hospital from here and see her."

"Where is she?"

"Burning Embers," Lauren answered.

"Burning Embers!" Paula's eyes flashed. "How in the hell can she afford a place like that?"

Lauren hesitated. Every time she lied to Paula she got caught. "Sally has a friend, a man, who took her there."

"Who?"

"Alex LaBarre," Lauren said uneasily.

"How interesting." Paula tapped her nails on the desk. "Now, how in the world did she connect up with a man like LaBarre?"

"She met him at Spark's."

"A pickup! So, what else?" Paula leaned back. It

was the young ones with their willing bodies who got all the interesting men. "I hear he has a very jealous wife," she said, not acknowledging her own envy.

"I wouldn't know," Lauren said.

"Well, he does. I knew Gina a long time ago. I used to see her at parties around town. She was quite famous for a while. Well . . ." Paula stood. "LaBarre can do many good things for Sally. But I assume she is aware of that."

Lauren didn't comment, because she knew it was pointless to argue with Paula.

"So," Paula went on, "that means we could be losing Sally."

Lauren's heart caught in panic. "I don't think so." Sally needed this job and she was Kerry's love interest. This could put him in jeopardy, too.

"I always knew we couldn't keep Sally indefinitely."

Lauren was getting more uneasy by the moment. This was not going right at all. "She has no plans for leaving the show, Paula," Lauren insisted. Her throat had tightened to a dry cord and it was difficult to breath. "None."

"I'm sure LaBarre will change all that. You go along, Lauren. Tomorrow send flowers to Sally in my name. Jenny will tell you which florist to use."

"Yes, Paula," Lauren said automatically. "Good night." She hurried out, feeling absolutely sick. Damn Paula! There was no winning with her. Lauren did not know what to do now. Talk to Sally? Warn Kerry? Do nothing?

On the drive to Burning Embers she decided it would be best to say nothing to Sally or Kerry. There was no point in stirring up problems over something that could come to zero.

When she arrived at the gate to Burning Embers she braked halfway up the drive, certain this could not be correct. There was no sign, only the street number on the wall. She was searching through her purse for La-

219

Barre's card when a uniformed guard appeared at the gate.

"May I help you, ma'am?" he called.

She pulled the car up closer to him. He had a clipboard in his hand.

"I'm looking for Burning Embers," she explained. "The hospital."

"This is it."

"I want to visit a patient."

"The patient's name, and yours, please," he said.

Lauren gave him Sally's name, then her own. He scanned the page clipped to the clipboard and said, "You may go in."

"Thank you," Lauren said, awed by the elaborate security setup.

He let her through the gates and she followed a wide drive that circled around the brick building. There was no parking lot as such. An ambulance was parked near what was evidently an emergency entrance in back.

There were two Mercedeses and a Bentley parked at the edge of the driveway. Lauren pulled in behind the Bentley, careful not to get too close. One fender of a Bentley was probably worth more than her entire car.

She felt terribly out of place as she approached a middle-aged woman behind an antique desk in an elegant entryway.

"I'm Lauren Parrow," she announced. "May I see Sally Rook, please?"

The woman opened a drawer and took out a file card and consulted it. "Your name is on the list of approved visitors," she said. "But she hasn't been allowed any company."

"I know," Lauren said. "But I'm very concerned. I'm her roommate. She has no family here."

"I'll call up," the receptionist offered graciously.

Lauren waited uneasily as the call was made. The woman hung up the phone and turned to Lauren. "Take the staircase up to the second floor," she said. "You'll find Mrs. Rogers there."

"Thank you," Lauren said.

The dark oak staircase circled up to the second floor. And as promised, a woman waited at the top. The uniformed nurse moved toward Lauren. "You're a friend of Miss Rook?" Lauren nodded and Mrs. Rogers led her inside. "She's quite upset. We've given her a shot to calm her down, but it hasn't taken effect yet. Perhaps you can help her."

Mrs. Rogers pushed open a door. Lauren stepped in, momentarily taken aback by the surroundings. The only normal piece of hospital equipment in the room was the bed where Sally huddled. She was crying softly. Lauren moved to her.

"Sally, what's wrong?" Lauren asked gently, touching her arm.

"Oh, Lauren. You're here." Sally's eyes clung to Lauren's face, pulling Lauren closer.

"Yes, yes. I'm here." She bent over the girl, her heart catching. She did not look better; if anything she was thinner and paler than before. Sally's fingers plucked at her sleeve.

"Get me out of here, Lauren," Sally begged.

"Why?"

"Dr. Bennet. He—he says my implants have to come out. Don't let him, Lauren. Don't let him take my breasts away."

Lauren grasped the hot dry hand. She caught a glimpse of movement and looked up to see a man before her. She nodded to him and squeezed Sally's hand. "Honey, I'm sure Dr. Bennett knows best," she said.

"I certainly do," the man said and strode across the room. "The only way we can clear up this infection is to get the implants out. I don't think the damn things were sterile when they were put in."

"No!" Sally protested.

Lauren gasped at the girl's stupidity. "Shut up!" she yelled back. "Damn it, Sally. This doctor knows what he's talking about. Do you want to die?"

"I . . ." Sally's mouth closed. She finally whispered a small "No."

"All right then," Lauren said. "Straighten up. Stop acting like a child."

Sally nodded but did not look up.

"Look, I can do implants for you again," Dr. Bennett offered, his voice kind. "Better ones, too."

Sally raised her head. "You can?" she asked hopefully. "When?"

Dr. Bennett shrugged. "In a couple of months."

"Two months!" she wailed. Lauren glared at her, eyes snapping silently, until Sally settled down again.

"We have to give you time to heal," Dr. Bennett explained gently. "You wouldn't want your body to reject the implants, would you?"

"No," Sally conceded in a low tone.

"We'll be taking you into surgery in an hour. The nurse will be in with an injection."

The doctor left and Sally pulled Lauren closer to her. "I'm scared, Lauren," she whimpered.

"I'll be here," Lauren promised, glancing at her watch. She was supposed to meet Kerry in an hour. She would have to call him and tell him she would be late, if she made it at all. Disappointment mingled with quiet anguish. She didn't want to cancel out. She needed Kerry tonight.

Chapter Twenty-Three

It was Thursday night and Paula was furious. Twice a year she got together with Silverstein and Shepard to iron out problems. The meeting included detailed critiques of each actor and how well he or she was functioning in his part as well as the character's place in the overall story line.

Normally the meeting took place in Los Angeles. Six months ago Paula had hosted the meeting in her penthouse. She had liked that, liked having them come to her. She had been scheduled to act as hostess again this Friday. She had worked out an elegant luncheon menu with her housekeeper.

It was fine until Shepard managed to break a leg while climbing around over some boulders on that mountain where he lived.

She had gotten the word on Tuesday. Instead of delaying the meeting. Silverstein had turned highly solicitous of Shepard and insisted he and Paula could easily drive up to Shepard's place.

She had argued with Silverstein and it had proved useless. She had tried everything from ignoring him to being angry to being sticky-sweet. Nothing had worked. They were going.

"I do not want to go up there," Paula told Joe, who was sitting on the sofa reading the newspaper.

He glanced up. "Shepard's an old guy," he said. "It doesn't hurt to cater to him once in a while."

"It pains the hell out of me," Paula said. She smoked and paced back and forth in the living room.

"Don't you owe old Caleb something?" Joe asked. "He took you in, taught you—"

"I was a writer before I met him," Paula interrupted. "He used me for years. He used to take credit for everything I did."

"It was his show," Joe offered.

"Not any more. It's my baby now."

Joe gave her a curious look. "That's it, isn't it? *Dreams* is the child you never had."

Paula stopped pacing and ground out her cigarette. "I guess you could look at it that way."

"Possessive little mother, aren't you?"

"You're damn right I am!"

"You should remember that Caleb gave birth to it," Joe reminded her. "You didn't."

Paula shot him an angry look. "What in the hell are you getting at?" she demanded.

"Nothing." Joe shrugged and picked up the Los Angeles *Times*.

"Do you think I couldn't be a mother?" Paula went on. "That I couldn't have conceived a child?"

"It would have come out of a cold, cold womb."

"I don't know why I tolerate you," Paula replied in disgust.

"Because you're afraid of being alone," he suggested almost sadistically.

Hot tears nearly blinded her. Where had they come from? She never allowed herself the luxury of tears. Not since she had lost Naomi.

Joe looked up. His face registered immediate concern and she turned hurriedly away. He thrust the newspaper away in a rustle. "Hey, I'm sorry," he said, coming up behind and putting his arms around her. "I care about you, Paula. I don't want to be alone either."

"Does that make us two losers?" she asked.

"I hope not."

"So do I." She shook his hands loose and walked away. She almost turned around and invited him into her bed. She would have liked to have had his warmth next to her. She would have liked to have been held and cuddled. But that would not have satisfied Joe. He would want sex, too, and she could not tolerate that. It was better to sleep alone.

She arose at five the next morning. Silverstein was to pick her up at seven. It was a long drive to Shepard's little mountain retreat, a disgusting waste of time.

She dressed, had coffee and went to her office and typed up notes for Jenny and Lauren. She put her personal notes in her brief case and went back to the bedroom a little before seven and took out a full-length mink. It would be cold in the mountains. There was probably still snow on the ground.

Paula did not go downstairs to wait for Silverstein. She stayed in the living room until the doorman phoned up to say Silverstein was waiting for her. She picked up her briefcase, grabbed her mink and went to the elevator.

She found Silverstein in one of his boring jovial moods. He made meaningless chitchat for endless miles. Paula did not mind the drive so much until they left the freeway and picked up a secondary highway. She was a city girl, comfortable only in New York and Los Angeles. Country made her nervous.

Shepard could not live in one of the homes bordering the highway that ribboned up into the mountains. No, he had to live off the beaten track where the only road up was a narrow winding strip barely two cars wide.

Each curve Silverstein screeched around sent her stomach topsy-turvy. "Can't you please slow down?" she asked.

"I can handle this car."

"Well, I can't handle this—this terrain." She looked out the window. Only inches away was a sheer drop down into heavy undergrowth. All that separated the car and the drop was a dilapidated-looking guard rail. "Heights bother me," Paula complained.

"Come on, now. You live in a penthouse."

"That's different," Paula said. "It doesn't move." She pulled the mink collar around her face. "I think I'm going to throw up."

"Don't look out," Silverstein cautioned her.

She closed her eyes tightly and gripped the door handle with one hand and the seat with the other. She took slow, easy breaths until the queasiness subsided slightly, but nothing could stop her head from swimming.

The car bumped and Paula cried out. "What is it?"

"We're leaving the road. It will be easy now."

They followed a graveled path through giant overpowering trees that blocked out the sun. Wild shrubs brushed against the side of the car. They finally emerged in a small clearing. A brown shingled house, looking like something airlifted from Virginia Beach, sat squarely in the middle of the clearing.

Trust Shepard to be out of sync with his surroundings, she thought. But at least they were here. She got out of the car and shaded her eyes against the sun. Behind the house the edge of a mountain rose upward in a jumble of boulders, evoking visions of a glacier that must have once cut through the land with its mighty edge.

Above the boulders soared the biggest television antenna Paula had ever seen. It was monstrous and seemed to sway slightly. Her stomach tightened and she looked down to the solid earth beneath her feet.

The door open and Caleb Shepard swung out on the porch on crutches. "Welcome, welcome," he called. "Good of you to come up here. I appreciate it, I do."

Paula managed a smile. Old goat. Caleb had once been a handsome man, and some remnants remained. He was tall and thin and stood up straight. She looked

226

hopefully for a stoop to his shoulders and found none. His white hair was thin and receding, but his beard was full and well trimmed.

He wore a flannel shirt and a pair of old trousers split up the leg to accommodate his cast.

Inside an airy living room, a woman wearing a soiled print dress served coffee and rolls. "Does she live here?" Paula asked when the slovenly-looking woman was out of the room.

"No. No, not Goldie. She comes up from town twice a week and does it for me. Cleans the house and cooks up a batch of food."

"How nice. But aren't you lonely?" Paula asked, not really caring.

"No. No. I have three shows to worry about. I watch every one of them every day. You've been doing a fine job, Paula. A fine job."

He reached over and patted Paula on the shoulder. She swallowed a nasty reply.

"How's your leg?" Silverstein asked.

"Just cracked," he answered, then went into a long-drawn-out explanation of how he had broken his leg when he went up to tighten guide wires on the television antenna.

"You shouldn't be doing things like that," Silverstein said.

"Why not? My doctor says I'm in great shape. Got the heart and lungs of a thirty-year-old."

"Wish I could say the same," Silverstein muttered, patting his protruding stomach.

Paula grimaced. Shepard would probably live to be a hundred and three. He would be riding on her back until the day he died, unless she died first.

Silverstein pressed the edge of his digital watch, a signal for work to begin. "Well, we all know why we're here. So let's get to it. The ratings aren't looking good. Last week we dropped down to a twenty-seven-point-three share. The sponsors are screaming."

"Then we've got to pep the show up," Shepard said.

"Get something hot going. I've made some notes." He picked up a legal pad from the floor. "I think we should shift emphasis to Rose Jardine and explore new sides to her character of Helen."

Silverstein squirmed slightly in his chair. "We don't get good responses from older people's problems, Caleb. Sex and romance is what draws the viewers back."

"Well, I guess I know that!" Caleb retorted. "I've been at this longer than either one of you. That's why I've been thinking about Irene's daughter. What if Anne Voll accidentally kills her? We could have Anne arrested, have a trial. Once she is cleared, then Irene could set out to get revenge. She could try and take Lee Trent away from Anne."

Paula looked pointedly at Silverstein. The last time they had tried to have a TV trial, the ratings had fallen and the mail had been very negative. Nobody wanted trials anymore. They bored the viewers. But that was not the only factor. "We did that eight years ago with Belle," Paula said, none too gently, pleased to catch Caleb short.

"The viewers want Anne and Lee married," Silverstein offered, ignoring Paula's comment. At least Caleb had the grace to look embarrassed.

"I don't want them married," Paula said coldly.

The arguments went on and on, through what Paula considered a perfectly horrid lunch of thick heavy stew, and on into the late afternoon.

Paula was tired. "I'm beyond thinking," she complained.

Silverstein checked his watch. "So am I. We'd better start back. I wouldn't want to drive out of here in the dark."

It took them another half hour to escape from Shepard. Once in the car, Paula scooted down low and pulled the mink collar up around her face so she would not have to watch the road.

"I told you!" she hissed at Silverstein. "I told you. He's old!" His ideas are dated."

"Yes, he's old," Silverstein agreed. "But I'll never force him off the show, Paula. We'll work around him. He's always been fair to me. Better than most of the cutthroats in this town."

"You're crazy, Bob," she said. "He's going to get us in trouble one day."

Silverstein looked over at her. "Now, how could he do that?"

Paula looked straight ahead. "He'll surely find a way." Just by existing Caleb Shepard was trouble.

Chapter Twenty-Four

Once the implants were out, Sally's recovery was rapid. She telephoned Lauren Friday afternoon at the penthouse. "I'm getting out," she said, her voice high with excitement. "Alex will bring me home. He said he should be here by seven."

Lauren suppressed a surge of disappointment. She was supposed to go straight from work to Kerry's apartment. Now she would have to be home for Sally. "I'm glad for you," she said.

"Not nearly as glad as I am," Sally said.

"Are you feeling okay?" Lauren asked.

"I don't hurt any more. Just a little sore now."

"But how do you feel otherwise?" Lauren asked. She had watched Sally cry a lot of tears over her flat chest this week.

"I've stopped weeping," Sally answered. "I guess I did a dumb thing, huh? But I'll still get my breasts one day. Alex says they'll be better."

"Of course they will be," Lauren said. There was no way they could be worse, she thought.

"I can't wait to get home."

"I'll be there," Lauren promised, with some reluctance, then mentally chided herself for being selfish. She was happy for Sally.

They hung up, then Lauren dialed Kerry's number. There was no answer. She rubbed her temples and sighed, then went back to the sample script Paula had finally critiqued. Lauren was comparing her script scene by scene with Germain's.

Paula had not been kind with her red pencil. "Stilted" was scrawled over page after page. "Bill would never say that." "Rose is too kind to be hateful." "Irene would attack."

Lauren had fouled up a couple of times because she was not up on every minuscule piece of background. Her biggest problem was her own writing past. She kept treating scenes as though they were a short story or a chapter in a novel. She kept trying to wrap them up, instead of leaving them open-ended, with unanswered questions that would carry interest to the next scene or show.

She thought a couple of her fade-outs were good because they were unique. "But we don't want things that are too different," Paula had told her. "They jar the viewer."

The wrap-up was marked "Good," as was one other scene between Cobb Strong, as Ned, and Irene. Oddly enough she had found Ned the easiest character to write, perhaps because he was an uncomplicated and kind man, much like Cobb himself.

"Overall, I'm pleased," Paula told her. "There is usable material here. The next sample will have even more. You're coming along very fast."

But Lauren was disappointed and she could not help it. Deep inside, she had hoped it was so good that Paula would be overwhelmed, an unrealistic dream.

That did not happen, and she had to admit that Paula was right. Germain's script was professional. Her own was amateurish, which meant she had to put in more time and study.

Paula had written the Friday outlines yesterday. Before she delivered them to Germain and Mel, Lauren was going to make copies for herself. She could try scenes without telling Paula, then privately compare them to Germain's and Mel's scripts.

Lauren glanced at her watch. She had to get Mel's and Germain's scripts to the studio, then the outlines to the authors.

An hour later Lauren moved up the sidewalk to the small cluster of town houses in Westwood where Mel Lorenzen lived. She rang the doorbell and folded the outline in half and stuck it into the mailbox as usual.

Before she could turn away the door opened. Startled, she cried out, "Oh!"

"I didn't mean to scare you, but could you come in?" a man asked.

Lauren struggled to keep a straight face as a diminutive man held the door open for her. Six inches shorter and he would have qualified as a midget. He was wearing a silk dressing gown over maroon trousers. Embroidered bedroom slippers encased tiny feet. He bowed slightly as she passed inside to a room done in white wicker and bright floral patterns, white latticework dominating one wall. A greenhouse window extended the length of one wall. Plants hung from the ceiling and sat on every available surface. The warm humidity pressed around her.

She sat down on a low wicker sofa and smiled at Mel Lorenzen. "It's nice meeting you at last," she said pleasantly.

"I don't get out much," he lisped softly. He barely raised his eyes to meet hers. "I like it here." He made a limp-wristed gesture.

Why, you little swish, Lauren thought. You shy little leprechaun, you're adorable.

"I have heard Miss Rook is ill," he said.

Lauren nodded, fighting to keep a sober expression on her face. "Yes, she is. But she's being released from the hospital today."

"I have a gift for her," he announced solemnly. "Would you please see that she gets it?"

"Certainly."

"Excuse me." He left the room and returned in a few moments with a Boston fern. The fronds reached down to the floor though he carried it at almost shoulder level.

"It's beautiful!" Lauren said, taking the green and lush plant. "Did you grow it?"

He beamed with pride. "I did. Plants are my hobby, you know."

Lauren smiled. "I thought they might be," she said, looking around the room.

"Now be careful not to bruise it," he cautioned. "Water it daily, but don't make it soggy. Soggy is not happy. I have a special food for ferns. One I mix myself. This packet will last for a year. Mix a half teaspoon in a pint of water and feed it every two weeks."

Bemused, all Lauren could do was nod. He walked to the door and opened it for her. "Thank you," he said.

Dismissed, she walked past him and turned around, balancing the fern. "Thank you," she said. "You are very kind, and your place is beautiful." No wonder he never went out. He had built his own little private world of green in the middle of the city.

"I'm happy here," he conceded shyly, and for the briefest moment, blue eyes met hers.

He politely but firmly said good-bye and Lauren carried the fern out to her car. She arranged it as best she could in the front seat. She had the feeling that if she bruised it he would know.

She was touched by Mel's gesture. He was a very private little man and only his sincere concern and liking for Sally as an actress would have prompted him to let her inside his domain.

She delivered Germain's outline, stayed to chat a moment with the little lady who tried to feed her warm gingerbread. Lauren did not return to the office. Jenny had said there was no reason to come back and sit around and wait for five o'clock.

Lauren had not managed to reach Kerry by phone, so she swung her car in the direction of his apartment.

"You're early," he said when he opened the door for her.

"I'm glad I caught you." She waited for his touch, achingly aware of him.

"I was out auditioning," he said.

"Did you get a part?" she asked, immediately anxious.

"No," he answered, his face grim.

"I'm sorry." She kissed him, wishing she could make his world right. "Hmmm." She rejoiced for herself as he took her into his arms.

He needed her, too. He nuzzled her ear. "Nice kiss, lady." He wrapped his arms around her and swayed gently.

"I can't stay," she told him. "LaBarre is bringing Sally home tonight. I want to clean up the place."

He stepped back slightly, moving his hands to her waist. "LaBarre himself is bringing Sally home?"

"Yes. He's picking her up around seven."

"I see." Kerry ran a hand through his short-cropped hair. "I think we should have a little celebration for Sally," he said.

"Oh, not her first night home."

"Why not?"

"She'll be tired, Kerry."

"She'll be thrilled out of her silly little head. Look, you go on home. I'll stop at a deli and pick up some food and champagne."

Lauren hesitated. "I don't think we should, Kerry. LaBarre—he's not our kind."

"You let me make these decisions," he said firmly. "Okay?"

"But . . ."

"Hush." He pulled her close again. "Wear something sexy tonight."

She could not refuse him, but she did not feel right about it. Not that there was much time to think about it once she got home. She ripped through the apartment with a dustcloth, ran the vacuum, put fresh sheets on Sally's bed and scrubbed down the bathroom.

She was stepping out of the shower when Kerry knocked at the door. "Coming!" she yelled and wrapped a terry cloth robe around her damp body and rushed to open the door.

Kerry nearly fell into the room. Fresh-cut flowers protruded from the huge box in his arms. "Heavy!" He put the box down and handed Lauren the flowers. "Get these into water." He spied the fern she had hung in front of the single living room window. "My God! What's the droopy tree?"

Lauren smiled. "A gift from Mel Lorenzen to Sally," she explained. "King of overwhelming, isn't it?"

"Big, very big." He shook his head. "Well, you get dressed," he said, not really looking at her. "I'll take care of the food. Hey, do you have a cloth for this table? How about champagne glasses? Maybe some candles, too."

Disappointed that he had yet to kiss or touch her, she pulled out a cloth and candles and offered ordinary wine glasses that would have to do. She left Kerry to the food and slipped into a black-and-white jump suit that flowed softly over her body and ended in wide flare legs. She made her face up and pinned her hair back off her face.

Kerry rewarded her with a long wolf whistle that righted her world. She laughed and went into his arms. She was happy now, caught up in the festive mood. "Too bad Sally is coming home," she murmured. "We could do other things."

"Yeah." He barely seemed to hear her. "See what you think of the table," he said. "Do you have a silver tray for the sandwiches?"

"No, a plate is the best I can do. What size . . ." Her voice trailed off as she approached the table. Kerry had gone to more than the average deli. An elaborate spread included a whole cold fish elegantly decorated with black olives and pimento.

"Bagels and chopped liver would have been fine," she said. "This . . ." She waved a hand. "My God! Is that caviar?"

"It's not too good," he said. "But it's the best I could do on short notice."

She turned away, feeling off balance. She checked the refrigerator. She did not know much about wine, but the two bottles of champagne resting on their sides looked horribly expensive.

She was struck by a horrible thought. Kerry was not doing this for Sally! It was to impress LaBarre. But surely not. Kerry did love good food, and he was a better cook than most women. She turned to face him. "Honey?"

"What?"

"I . . . Nothing." She could not ask. "I'll get you a plate for the sandwiches."

When the door opened a few minutes later, Kerry beat Lauren to Sally's side. He cupped her shoulders. "Welcome home, Sally."

"Kerry! It's a party!"

"For you," he smiled.

"Look, Alex!" She tugged at his arm. "Look at this! There's flowers and candles. And food. Oh, Kerry!"

"Don't get too excited now," Alex warned with gruff affection.

"Oh, no. Don't do that." Kerry hovered too closely, his smile too eager. "Lauren, bring a blanket. We'll fix Sally a place here." He indicated the end of the sofa.

"Oh, I don't need a blanket," Sally said. "See?" She held up the skirt of a soft pink robe. "Alex got me this. Isn't it pretty?"

"Beautiful," Kerry enthused. "Oh, yes," he said then, as though it was an afterthought. He turned to Alex, "I'm Kerry Scott, Mr. LaBarre."

Alex held out his hand and the men shook. "Kerry's on *Dreams* with me," Sally explained.

"Great to meet you, sir," Kerry said with an eager little-boy look on his face that made Lauren cringe.

237

"We've missed Sally," he said. "Here, honey." He scurried around, making Sally comfortable. He snatched out the champagne and forced wine on everyone. He pressed at LaBarre to eat, but Alex said he and Sally had already eaten dinner. Lauren hung back, nibbling at a small plate of food and praying she was wrong about Kerry's actions.

"I hear you're doing *Rainbow*," Kerry said to LaBarre.

"Yes, I am," LaBarre answered, but his attention was focused on Sally. "Don't you think you should be in bed?" he asked her.

"Not yet," she said. "I'm okay."

Lauren thought she looked pale and tired. But at least those dark circles under her eyes were gone.

"Who's getting the lead in *Rainbow*?" Kerry pressed.

LaBarre's eyes flicked to Kerry, then slid away. "I don't know yet," he said. "It isn't settled."

"*Variety* says you've been talking to Redford," Kerry said.

"He has," Sally put in.

"We're talking to a lot of people," LaBarre said, his eyes studying Kerry's face. He seemed slightly amused by Kerry's eagerness. Humiliation washed over Lauren. "Well . . ." Alex LaBarre stood. "Time for all good little girls to be in bed," he said to Sally.

She held her arms up as Alex bent over her. She put her arms around his neck and he scooped her up and carried her back to the bedroom.

Kerry grabbed Lauren's hand and dragged her into the kitchen. "He liked me, didn't he? He liked me!" He pulled her closer to him and she hid her face against his chest, ashamed for him. "This could be it, Lauren. This could be my big break."

Lauren felt lost, as though a piece of her world had been destroyed. She had never seen Kerry like this. He was always laid back, always confident. Tonight he had all but licked Alex LaBarre's feet.

238

"Don't you want to eat?" she asked, gently pulling away.

"No, I can't. I'm too excited. How about you?"

"I can't eat either," she murmured, but it wasn't for the same reason. She was sick with the knowledge of an image demolished.

LaBarre came out of the bedroom. Kerry grabbed his own jacket and followed LaBarre out the door, leaving Lauren alone, her eyes glazed, her throat scratchy, her heart wounded.

Lauren slumped against the table. The beautiful food had barely been touched. She waited for Kerry to return. Finally she gave up and put the food in the refrigerator.

Chapter Twenty-Five

Sally was written out of *Dreams* for a total of three weeks instead of a month, but it still made for a tight money situation and Lauren had to carry all the rent and bills. Sally seemed to take it well enough once she had adjusted to the idea of losing work.

Kerry Scott was wildly upset because when Sally was written out of the show, so was he. Paula was making no effort to pick up on a relationship between him and the character of Irene.

"Can you push her a little?" Kerry asked Lauren on the telephone a couple of days after Sally was released from the hospital. "I need the work."

Lauren's hand tightened around the receiver. She could not help but feel that she was letting Kerry down. What she could not tell him was that he and Sally were lucky it was only for three weeks. Paula was so annoyed at Sally for doing something stupid that it was a wonder she had not written her out longer as punishment.

"I've already tried pushing Paula," Lauren told him. She had gotten her head snapped off for her efforts. "Paula says the time isn't right."

"Damn!"

"I'm trying to help you," Lauren whispered.

"Oh, I know you are, honey," Kerry soothed. "It's

241

just that I don't know what I'm going to do. The parts aren't coming down."

"But you're so good," she said. "They will."

"It's not just me. Things are tight all through the industry. Maybe LaBarre will come through with something in *Rainbow*."

"I hope so," Lauren said, even though the incident still bothered her.

"Any word yet on when he'll be casting?" Kerry asked hopefully.

"No, nothing," Lauren replied.

"Okay, honey. I'll see you. I've got to get back to my agent. There has to be something out there."

Lauren hung up slowly. She wasn't over the way Kerry had acted with LaBarre. She discussed it with Sally, and Sally had told Lauren she was crazy. "You strike when you can," Sally told her emphatically. "You never let an opportunity for a part go by. You use any ins you can get. Kerry saw a way to make an impression on Alex. And Alex will remember him. That's important."

"I suppose so," Lauren agreed with some reluctance. She supposed that Sally was right. It was the name of the game. It was just that it was a shock seeing Kerry as less than perfect. In her heart he was all-knowing, always confident. She had not liked seeing him demean himself to LaBarre, and destroy a bit of her by doing so.

Over the next couple of weeks Kerry's agent got him two small parts; then he and Sally were back on the show, and Lauren relaxed. She continued to write scenes on her own and compared them to the ones written by Mel and Germain. She knew she was getting closer. Soon she would be ready to try another sample script for Paula.

Lauren's mother was pressing her to come up north for a visit and had invited her and Sally for Easter. Of course that was impossible because Sally was still recovering. Lauren could not go off and leave her alone, even though Alex was more attentive than ever.

And the truth of it was that she had no desire to be away from Kerry, not even for a three-day weekend. So she put Mama off, telling her she had not been working for Paula long enough to ask for time off. Then she diverted her with some gossip about *Dreams*. Of course, she could not tell her what was going to happen on the show. That was absolutely forbidden. Soaps kept their secrets as well as the CIA.

When Kerry mentioned wanting to see the *Sherlock Holmes* production at the Shubert Theatre, Lauren bought orchestra seats for the two of them. She surprised him with them the same night over a supper of sandwiches at his apartment. They were seated at the small oak table in the old-fashioned kitchen with its deep graying sink and dark Spanish tile.

"I have something for you," she said.

"Oh?" Kerry glanced up from the sandwich he was carefully building of roast beef, cheese and lettuce.

She grinned impishly. She felt so close to him in moments like this. All he was wearing was a pair of jeans. His bare feet were hooked over the rungs of the chair. His chest was lightly sprinkled with dark curling hair.

"Here." She pulled the tickets out of the pocket of her gingham smock dress and laid the tiny envelope beside his plate.

"What is it?" he asked.

"Open it and find out."

She leaned forward eagerly as he opened the envelope and slid out the tickets. He stared at them, then at her. She waited for delight to leap into his eyes. Instead his face remained immobile. "Why did you do this?" he asked.

The joy died in her breast. "I . . ." She rubbed her fingers on the table top. Because I love you, she wanted to cry. Because I want to please you, because I'm so incredibly grateful for all you have given me and because I'll never be able to pay you back. "Because I wanted to," she said, her voice soft, almost pleading. "It's just a little surprise."

"Two fifteen-dollar tickets to the Shubert isn't little," he said.

"Kerry." She reached out and touched his hand. "I wanted to do something nice for you. Something we could share and remember. Don't you want to see the play?"

"Of course I want to see it. I want to see how Mr. Spock makes the transition from *Star Trek* to the Royal Shakespeare Company. But you should have let me buy the tickets for us. If and when I could afford them."

"Kerry Scott! You're being chauvinistic. Please don't act that way."

He lowered his long, thick eyelashes and a sheepish look spread over his face. "I guess I am being chauvinistic," he growled.

"You old bear!" She ruffled his hair and he grinned. Relief spread over her, making her limbs go weak.

"Come here," he said with a jerk of his head. "Let me give you a kiss."

She moved to him and he pulled her down on his lap. She offered her lips to him. He touched her lightly, then took her lower lip between his and nibbled gently. His mouth moved to her chin and down to the hollow of her throat. Her head went back and her breasts pressed against his chest.

Her body warmed with yearning. It was astounding how often she wanted sex with Kerry. She had avoided sex with Benji, was always careful not to do anything to turn him on. But with Kerry she could not get enough. She wanted him when she saw him, wanted him when she thought of him.

"Let's go to bed," she whispered as her hands moved through his hair.

She resented the time it took them to walk back to the bedroom. He stripped off his jeans in one long, fluid motion and moved to her, turning her around. She felt

244

him untie the belt in back, then his fingers moved to the zipper and opened it.

He peeled the dress from her shoulders and let it fall around her feet. She moaned softly as his hands cupped her breasts. The nipples hardened under his touch. She rolled her head against his shoulder and turned her face up for his kiss.

Both nude, they slipped into the bed and his mouth covered hers hungrily. Lauren rejoiced anew in the unique taste of him, in the firmness of his flesh under her hands, the lean hardness of his muscles.

She belonged to him, she gave herself up to his kisses, to the tongue that probed and searched; dizzy, intoxicated by him, she reveled in the sensitivity of her body.

She moaned as he moved down. He cupped her breasts and took first one, then the other into his mouth. Her body trembled with need. "Kerry, Kerry! Oh, God!" She was not aware of speaking, only of her need and of her love for him. He moved down again and she offered herself up to the exquisite sensations.

Afterward, she lay against him, her head on his shoulder, struck anew with a sense of awe. She had never dreamed sex could be like this. She played with the hair on his chest, letting it curl around her fingers. "I feel closer to you than I've ever felt to anyone in my life," she told him.

"Do you?" he asked.

"Yes." She rose up and rested on one elbow. "I guess we really don't know each other yet. But I want to know everything about you. Like how you grew up, what you looked like when you were ten years old."

He lay silently with his eyes closed. Her heartbeat picked up. Fearful, she kissed him. Had she gone too far? "What's wrong, Kerry?" she asked.

He didn't open his eyes. "I don't get close to people," he said.

"You mean I'm asking too much?"

"Yes," he said.

Her heart tightened painfully. "I know," she sighed. "Your career comes first."

He opened his eyes and sat up. "Always." He caught her eyes and held them, his face somber. "It has to be that way, Lauren. I can't let anything get in the way."

"Not even love?" she asked with hope.

He rolled off the bed and it rose and fell under her. She felt lost and desolate. "I'm sorry," she choked.

"Not even for love," he said. He pulled on his jeans and left the room.

Lauren lay very still until the bed stopped moving, conscious only of the abiding ache ripping her insides apart. He wouldn't make a commitment to her and she had to acknowledge that, had to find a way to live with it.

Yet she knew he cared. He couldn't want to be with her if he didn't care. And it wasn't as if he had said he didn't love her, he had only said he couldn't let love get in the way of his career. She took what comfort she could from that thought.

She got up and put on the smock dress. In the bathroom she combed her hair and touched up her makeup with the kit from her purse. She returned to the kitchen with a bright smile stiffly in place. "We'd better hurry," she said, "or we'll be late for the curtain."

They finished the sandwiches on bread that had dried, then drove to Century City in Kerry's Fiat. Century City had always fascinated Lauren. It was like something out of the future, all white and clean and sleek, plunked down in the middle of an old city, to be enjoyed by those wealthy enough to afford it. Adjoining Beverly Hills, Century City was a development of several skyscrapers catering to those matrons who could afford centuries-old antiques from China and furs from Dicker and Dicker of Beverly Hills. The food available ranged from continental cuisine to Japanese to corned beef sandwiches in the Entertainment Center deli, a place of leather booths, a discreet bronze bar and impeccable service.

Tonight as they drove up the Avenue of the Stars she was only vaguely aware of the fountain dancing in the center of the street, of the power of the buildings rising up to the sky.

Kerry guided the car down a ramp going under the ABC Entertainment Center and they disappeared into the bowels of the building. It was cold down below, well lighted, but giving the impression of darkness and shadows, for the sun never touched the concrete and cinder blocks.

They parked on the D level and took the escalator up to the luxurious theater with its carpeted aisles and velvet seats. Behind them soared the balconies, reaching up and back in a gigantic arch. After they were seated and the play began, Kerry immediately became lost in the play on stage. The London fog that was really some sort of foul-smelling smoke irritated Lauren's nostrils. Even though Leonard Nimoy was marvelous as Sherlock Holmes, Lauren found it difficult to maintain an interest in the slow-moving play.

After the final curtain call, Kerry offered to take Lauren to Harry's Bar for a drink.

"I don't think so," she said. "I'm tired."

He put his arm protectively around her waist. "Then we'd better get you home and into bed. Spend the night with me, Lauren?"

Her heart leaped with fresh hope, sweeping away the coldness of only moments before. "All right. Sally won't need a ride into the studio tomorrow."

She stepped ahead of him onto the escalator near the Playboy Club entrance. Asking her to spend the night was his way of making up to her. He did care. He did love her. All she could ask now was that he let her go on loving him and not send her back to be alone as she had been after leaving Benji. She could never tolerate that kind of loneliness again.

She awoke before the alarm went off the next morning. She leaned across Kerry, careful not to rock the waterbed too much, and turned off the clock. She watched Kerry sleep, memorizing the strong profile, the way the dark, thick lashes brushed his cheeks, and the firm lines of his mouth. He was beautiful. She wanted to wake him and tell him so. But if she did, if he rejected her words of praise, she could not bear it.

She eased out of the bed and got her oversized purse and carried it into the bathroom. She took the Pill, brushed her teeth and slipped into the shower. She had learned to keep a change of fresh clothes in her car at all times now. It was one of the unpleasant but necessary realities of an affair.

She rolled yesterday's dress and panties into a bundle and put on a pair of brown slacks and a blouse of a dark cream color. She tied a chiffon scarf in soft folds under the collar and stepped back. The outfit was plain, but it suited her lean form.

Satisfied, she went into the kitchen, made coffee and fixed a tray of toast and scrambled eggs, wanting to please him in all ways, desiring to make herself indispensable. She carried it all back to the bedroom.

"Kerry, wake up," she said.

He opened his eyes and blinked, then looked around the room as though to orient himself. Kerry was a slow starter in the morning. "Nice," he said under his breath. He scratched the whiskers on his chin and ran his hand up through his hair.

He yawned and stretched. She marveled at the lean hardness of his muscles again. He was beautiful. She put the breakfast tray on a small table and moved it beside the bed.

They drank their coffee and Lauren nibbled on a single piece of toast while Kerry wolfed down the eggs. "Delicious!" he said. "You're some special lady, Lauren."

"That's nice," she smiled, wishing he meant it.

"Come back to bed," he invited.

"I can't, Kerry," she whispered with regret. "I've got to go to work."

"Tease!"

248

"You're tempting," she said, leaning over for a kiss. He rubbed her back and she felt herself responding. She pulled away. "I've got to go," she sighed, not wanting to go at all, never wanting to leave him.

"So be it." He swung his legs over the side of the bed, completely naked. There was no self-consciousness about him.

"What are you going to do today?" Lauren asked.

"I guess I'll harangue my agent. I have an audition this afternoon."

"Anything exciting?"

He grimaced. "No."

"I'm sorry." She put her arms around his shoulders and he pressed his head against her midsection. He put his arms around her and they held on to each other until Lauren had to leave.

On the drive to work, Lauren realized Kerry had not mentioned her moving over the hills lately. She had held back before, too insecure in her relationship with Kerry to make the move totally for him.

It was something she wanted to consider now. In spite of last night, or perhaps because of it, she wanted to live closer to him. Whether he could admit it or not, she did not doubt that he loved her. How else could they have this type of relationship?

She swung her wheezing Chevrolet into a Von's parking lot and got out to get a copy of the Los Angeles *Times* from a sidewalk vending machine. Back in the car, she discarded everything but the classified section.

She checked carefully over the listings, her hopes sinking. There was not anything listed for less than three hundred and fifty dollars in the area she wanted. Rentals went up from there to seven fifty. She closed the paper, hoping the Sunday edition would offer more choices.

Chapter Twenty-Six

Alex sent his car and driver for Sally and she was delivered to a rented sound stage in Hollywood, where Dick Morris was auditioning for the California Girl. As she walked into the front offices, a busty girl came out of an inner office. The curly-haired young man who was seated at a desk nodded to Sally, then turned to the other girl.

"Thank you for coming, Miss Nichols," he said. "Mr. Morris wanted me to tell you he will be in touch if he needs you."

"Well, I guess I know what that means," she said. She shrugged and winked at Sally. "Better luck, honey."

Sally's spirits dipped. Miss Nichols was beautiful, and had a perfect hourglass figure. If they didn't want her, they surely wouldn't want Sally.

Envious of the generous breasts, Sally watched her walk away, then approached the young man. "I'm Sally Rook," she said.

"Ah, yes." His eyes studied her. "You're the chick LaBarre recommended. Come on in." He walked to a closed door and opened it. "Boss, LaBarre's girl is here," he announced. He stepped back and gestured for Sally to enter.

Nervous, she walked into the room. The curly-haired young man followed. "Sally, this is Dick Morris."

"Hello, Sally." Dick Morris stood and offered his hand. Sally took his hand, noticing he was younger than she had expected him to be. About thirty-five or so. He wasn't tall, maybe five foot eight. He had a pleasant face that somehow did not match the brilliant blue eyes.

He looked her up and down. "Well, at least you aren't another *Playboy* centerfold type. I put out a call for a California Girl and all I get is centerfold types."

Sally's hands moved automatically to her breasts. She had worn a loose-fitting blouse, hoping she wouldn't look completely flat. Her fingers plucked at the buttons. She did not know what to say.

She managed a smile for Dick Morris. Everything about him proclaimed New York, from the cut of his dark suit to his accent. Dick came from around his desk. "We'll want to get some stills of you, then some tape. Come with me. I'll turn you over to Lydia. She's our makeup gal."

They moved back through offices that looked like any other rented sound stage in Hollywood. The rooms were bare of any sort of decoration. Only the most basic furniture was scattered about. There were coffee, soft drink and candy machines in the hall that had bare cement floors. There was a cold and drafty feel about the building.

Dick ushered her around a corner and into a small room. He poked his head in and said, "This is our next girl, Lydia. Give her your best." His hand moved to Sally's back and with a slight pressure, he guided her into the room.

Dick's footsteps echoed back down the hall. Sally flashed a smile to Lydia. She was an older woman, maybe forty, wearing a smock over jeans. She sat Sally down in front of a well-lighted mirror. She tipped Sally's chin back and studied her face, moving it from one side to the other.

"I'm not sure I can improve on you," she said. "You're marvelously natural."

"Thank you," Sally said, waiting eagerly to see what would happen next. She had been made up many times before for the cameras, but this time was something special.

Lydia placed a cosmetic cape around her neck. "You're getting the full works," she announced. "We are going to start out with these beauty grains. They're mixed with honey. Then we'll do a facial mask. That'll tighten up the pores and get rid of any dead skin."

An hour and a half later, Sally gazed at herself in the mirror. "That's me?" she breathed. "My God!" Awed, she could only stare at herself, not daring to touch her face and move even a speck of the carefully applied makeup that caused her to shimmer.

"You have it all, honey," Lydia said. "The cheekbones, and those eyes—I've never worked with eyes that color before." Their color was deepened and heightened by shadow and the faintest touch of liner.

Lydia fluffed Sally's hair about her face. A curling iron had added soft waves to the lustrous hair. Sally knew she shimmered as she walked out in a white tennis dress provided by Lydia. The still photographer was waiting in another small room.

The photographer was female and young. She wore tight-legged jeans that disappeared into boots and she worked with an array of cameras. She introduced herself as Elaine. She placed Sally against a plain background and repositioned the lighting.

Sally stood very still and smiled as Elaine stood in front of her with the camera. "Too much teeth," Elaine said, taking the camera away from her face. "You aren't a professional model, are you?"

"No, I'm an actress," Sally answered.

"Okay, let's act then. Look at me like I'm one stoned fox, like you've got to have me." Sally closed her eyes a moment, envisioning Alex. As her eyes popped open the camera clicked.

Elaine circled. "That's the way. Smile! Pout! You're hurt, you're happy. Now move. Move. Move. Move. You've just come off the tennis court. Move, turn. Turn. Smile. Again. Again. Turn. Whirl. Throw back your head. Move. Move. Move!"

The camera clicked with lightning speed. It was replaced with a second one, then time out to reload them both. She put Sally on the floor. The girl twisted and turned and they finished off the roll with a series of mood shots. Sally with her head down and her face nearly hidden by her hair, then Sally staring off into some distant place and finally looking up, eyes full of hope.

"That's it," Elaine said. "I think we got some good ones. Go on over to the sound stage. You'll find everyone waiting for you."

"Was I okay?" Sally asked eagerly.

"You were terrific! Hey, drop back in on Lydia. You have a little perspiration on your upper lip."

"Thanks." Sally ducked out and back to Lydia, who blotted her face and retouched the makeup. She ran back down the hall to the sound stage and walked through the massive doors. A black man stood up. He handed Sally a one-page script and closed the doors behind her.

Sally nodded to a cameraman and to Dick Morris, who was seated back in the shadows. "I've never done a commercial," Sally said, looking from one to the other.

Morris didn't reply. The black man stepped up to Sally. "Timing is critical," he said. "Sometimes it takes us several days of shooting to get thirty seconds of air time. But we aren't going to worry about that today. We just want to get you on tape. We want to see you move, we want to hear you talk."

"Will I be holding something? Some cosmetics?" Sally asked.

"No, just a tennis racket." He reached behind him and came around with the racket. "Here you go. Come on over here. Let's let Willie get the lighting set up and I'll explain."

Sally moved in front of the camera. The background was plain. Nothing but an ugly wall. "Now you've just come off the courts, you're glowing with good health. And not one eyelash is out of place. California Girl Cosmetics are for the active woman. It stays with you, no matter what you're doing."

Sally stood still for the first lighting adjustments and then walked through the part several times with the script in her hand, reading the words.

Then they were ready for shooting. Morris stayed in the background, never speaking, never offering advice or making a comment. Yet Sally was more aware of him than of the two men working with her.

Two hours later the taping was finished and Sally was exhausted. It was hard, grueling work. The words had been spoken over and over so many times that they became hollow and wooden-sounding to her ears.

The lights went out and Sally sighed. The slender shoulders slumped. She looked to the back of the room. Morris was gone. Disappointedly, she turned to the black man. "Thank you, Eddie," she said. "You're magnificent."

His dark eyes glistened in appreciation. "You must be somebody special yourself," he said. "Nobody else has gotten this much attention."

"Really?" Sally came up on her toes, tingling. "Are you sure?"

"I'm sure," he said. "Good luck to you."

"Thank you!" She wanted to shout and hug someone. Bursting with hope and good feelings, Sally returned to Lydia, who provided cold cream to remove the heavy makeup. "Could I do street makeup?" Sally asked her. "I loved that base powder."

"Sure," the woman said and smiled. "Here, I'll do it for you. You just sit down."

It took only a few minutes to reapply the makeup, then Sally changed back into her street clothes. She walked up the cold corridor alone, wondering if she should speak to Morris again. At least she would tell his curly-haired assistant she was leaving.

She found Dick Morris instead of his assistant in the outer office. "You were good, Sally," he said to her. "Very good."

"Do I have a shot at the job?" she asked hopefully.

"Well, I think you do, yes. Of course, I don't have the final say. We're wrapping up here this week. I'm shipping all the stills and tapes back to New York. There will be conferences with the client. We'll make our decision with him."

Morris draped an arm across her shoulders. "I'll be seeing you later. I understand we've having dinner with Alex."

Sally shook her head. "We are?"

"Sure. He told me you would be there with a girl-friend for me."

Sally frowned. "I think I'd better call," she said. "I think he forgot to tell me."

"Okay. Just find me a girl, and make sure she's intelligent. I hate dumb broads. See you at the Polo Lounge. I'm cutting out."

He walked out. Sally picked up the telephone and put in a call for Alex at his studio office. His secretary put her straight through. "Alex," she said, "I think there's been some mix-up. Dick Morris just told me that—"

Alex cut her off in mid-sentence. "I know, baby. I talked to him while you were being photographed. I thought us having dinner with him might help. We'll show him a little of the town. You get your roommate for Dick."

"I'm not sure I can," Sally protested. She dates Kerry Scott, and . . ."

"It's only one night for dinner," Alex told her.

Sally squirmed. "But, will Morris expect her to go to bed with him?" she asked anxiously.

"No. If that's all he wanted I'm sure he has quite a choice of chicks walking in and out of his office."

Sally smiled. "Okay, that'll be all right then. It's just that Lauren is kind of straight."

"No problem. You keep the car, honey. Go on home and change and meet us at the Polo Lounge for drinks. We'll have dinner elsewhere."

"Okay," Sally agreed happily.

"How was the audition?" Alex asked.

"They were very good to me. The director told me no one else had gotten this much attention. That's because of you, Alex. You're so good to me, Daddy."

"It's easy to be good to you," he said. "See you tonight."

Pleased with herself and Alex, Sally pressed down the button to break the connection, then dialed Lauren at work. Lauren was hesitant. "I don't think so," she said.

"Oh, come on," Sally coaxed. "How often do you get a chance to go to the Polo Lounge?"

"Never."

"It'll be fun. And I already asked Alex, and you don't have to go to bed with Dick Morris."

Lauren gave a wry laugh. "Gee, thanks, kid," she said.

"Well, that's important to know. I wouldn't walk you into just anything. And besides, maybe you can get in some points for Kerry with Alex."

"Work the angles, huh?" Lauren asked.

"You don't have to sound so cynical about it," Sally said. "It's something we all have to do."

"I know," Lauren replied. "You keep telling me that. But it still bothers me just the same."

Sally pounced on the opening. "Then you'll go tonight? Please?"

"I guess," Lauren conceded.

"Great! See you at home."

Alex's chauffeur was an older man with iron-gray hair and a flat German accent. Sally chatted with him on the drive back to the Valley. She talked. He answered in polite tones, but never said much more than, "Yes, miss" and "No, miss."

At the apartment, Sally popped out too quickly for him to get out of the car and open the door. "We'll be ready at seven," Sally said, then hesitated. "Uh, you want to come in or something?" She did not quite know what to do with him.

"No, miss," he answered. "I have some errands to run."

"Oh, okay," she said brightly. "I don't want you just sitting here in the car alone."

"If I did, it would be my job," he pointed out politely.

"Okay."

Sally was just stepping out of the shower when Lauren came home. "In here!" Sally yelled, wrapping a towel around herself. She opened the door. "Isn't it exciting?" she asked Lauren.

Lauren wasn't excited. "I feel sort of funny about it," she answered slowly.

"Why?" Sally asked.

"Well, I've never been on a blind date," Lauren said.

"Don't look so glum," Sally told her. "It'll be real kicky. We'll see how the other half lives. It'll be fun, you'll see."

"It will certainly be something to write home about," Lauren agreed without enthusiasm.

"Sure it will," Sally said, refusing to be daunted by Lauren's uptight hesitance. A free meal in a glamour spot was not to be looked down on. "Now, hurry up! We've got to look great tonight."

At seven-thirty, the two girls were delivered to the pink castle on Sunset known as the Beverly Hills hotel. Lauren had to admit she felt terribly elegant and excited at the prospect of seeing the inside of the famed watering hole. She slid out of the car after the door was opened for her by a uniformed attendant.

The girls both wore long dresses. Lauren's was a halter dress she had bought a long time ago and never worn. A matching jacket hugged her body to the waist. Sally wore a wrinkled off-white cotton from Mexico. It was a simple dress, trimmed in heavy lace. She wore her multicolored shawl with the long fringe around the shoulders.

Nervous, Lauren eyed the long walk up a red carpet laid out under a wide canopy. Probably the most famous hotel in the world, the Beverly Hills was home and playground for kings and queens, presidents and Hollywood royalty like John Wayne, Barbra Streisand, Elizabeth Taylor, Paul Newman and Johnny Carson, and faces not recognizable to the public but powerful in their positions as heads of studios, directors and producers.

Situated in a sixteen-acre park, the pink stucco hotel offers its guest a turquoise pool and championship tennis courts, a few shops and a choice of places to eat and rub elbows with celebrities.

Sally, with the aplomb of one who knew her way around, led the way under the canopy, into a lobby dominated by a fireplace burning real logs, past the great front desk and into the Polo Lounge.

They paused in the open archway of the bar, searching for a glimpse of Alex. The host, a tall, thin man in a short black jacket and white shirt, came up to them and Sally told him they were meeting Alex LaBarre. He immediately came to attention. For a second, Lauren thought he was going to snap his heels together. "This way, please," he said.

They were escorted to one of the numerous little round tables clustered in wide banquettes. Introductions were made and Lauren managed a nervous smile and a handshake with Dick Morris. Drinks were ordered for the girls and Lauren was immediately aware of LaBarre's protective attitude toward Sally. He was there, adjusting her shawl, patting her hand, reaching across to make sure her drink was right.

Lauren hung back, being as unobtrusive as possible, and listened to the others talk. She felt ill at ease and completely out of it with this man and his hard and rather rushed New York accent. She supposed he was attractive in a mild way, but except for the deep blue eyes there was nothing exceptional about Dick Morris, especially in comparison with Kerry.

It was difficult to be casual and not gawk like any tourist at the sleek people around her, whose manner breathed money and position. Two men at the table next to them were discussing a new book and the possibilities of making a film. A tall, lushly built girl of twenty-one or so was batting double-thick false eyelashes and making soft cooing sounds at an older man. Lauren took her to be a starlet, or perhaps a hooker. She had never seen so much makeup piled onto one face.

She suppressed a cry of surprise at the sight of a familiar TV actor and lowered her face so she would not come off like a drooling fan.

Dick Morris turned to her, dropped his arm around her shoulder and asked how long she had been living in Los Angeles. Made intensely uncomfortable by his casualness, she managed a cool reply and he removed his arm.

When the subject of the theater came up, Lauren found she had something to add and began to relax a little as she told them about the *Sherlock Holmes* production.

After two drinks, they adjourned to the Habitat for dinner. On the sidewalk in front of the restaurant, Sally and Lauren both looked to the building next door and up to Joe Seals's offices. The windows were dark.

"That's my agent's office," Sally said. "I guess he's Lauren's agent, too."

"In that building?" Morris asked, looking skeptical. "It's not very, uh, prestigious."

"Joe's not the status type," Sally said. "He's real down to earth, huh, Lauren?"

"Yes. Yes, he is," Lauren agreed. "And he works very hard for Sally. He cares what happens to her."

"He'd better care," LaBarre muttered, and Lauren noticed how rigid he had turned. Why, he's jealous, she thought, he's jealous of Joe. She looked at him with new interest.

She had not liked or disliked Alex LaBarre. She simply considered him much too old for Sally. He was fifty and portly, famous and rich, and, worst of all, married. She had worried over Sally's being hurt by him, even though she was grateful for his getting Sally into a hospital.

Alex herded them inside the restaurant with its Western artifacts and saloon atmosphere. They were shown to one of the best tables by a girl in a rustling taffeta dress reminiscent of *Gunsmoke*'s Miss Kitty. Lauren passed up the offer of a drink and Morris asked her to dance.

She accepted. Still somewhat ill at ease with him, she went into his arms. She made an effort to smile as the music wafted gently around them. He held her closer than she would have liked. But he was a good dancer, easy even for her to follow. She had never been really comfortable on a dance floor.

"You fit nicely into my arms," he said against her hair. She did not know what to say to that. "But don't be so stiff. Relax a little," he coaxed.

She pulled back slightly. "I'm sorry," she said.

"Tell me about yourself?" he asked.

"Oh, there's not much to tell," she evaded.

"I don't believe that." His eyes moved over her face and she felt he was amused by her.

"I work for the head writer of a soap opera," she said, then briefly explained her job.

"That's interesting," he said. "We have some clients who advertise very heavily on the daytime dramas."

"That's nice," she murmured, searching frantically for something else to say.

He pulled her close again and she was aware of her breast pressing against his chest in an oddly exciting way. "I hope this evening doesn't end too early," he said, "because I like you."

"Thank you" was all the reply she could muster. The smoothness of his suit was silky under her hand on his shoulder. He smelled faintly of an aftershave she found pleasing. He was a good-looking man though his nose was a bit too large, but the jutting chin was good, evening out his features. He had compelling eyes and a strong sense of maleness, as though he had no doubts about his masculinity or his place in the world.

He brushed his face against her hair. "After dinner we can go on our own way," he whispered into her ear. Her body responded with a flash of heat, surprising her.

She stopped in the middle of the dance floor. "Mr. Morris," she said as evenly as she could manage, "I was told you would not expect me to go to bed with you."

He blinked in amazement, then grinned. "Well, a guy has to try," he said.

"Does he?" she came back, annoyed now. "Why?"

"Uh . . ." He was obviously taken aback. He rubbed an index finger against his chin. "I don't know," he said. "I suppose because it's expected."

"I have a steady guy, and I didn't expect it," she said.

"I see." He reached up and pushed her hair back from her face. "And you wish you were with him right now, don't you?"

"Yes," she answered honestly. "I do. But this was important to Sally, so I came." She faced him squarely, almost on eye level with him. If she had blown it, she had blown it; at least she was being honest with him.

He took her back in his arms, holding her loosely this time, and began to move again to the music. "I'll tell you a secret," he said. "I wish I was back home in bed with my wife."

Suddenly they were both laughing and Lauren felt the tension flowing out of her body. "I like you," she said, happy now.

"Come on, then. Let's go order something wildly extravagant and just stuff ourselves."

The menu was elaborate and the choices difficult to make. Lauren finally settled on the jumbo shrimp. It was butterflied and stuffed with bread dressing, secured with bacon. Dick ordered mushrooms stuffed with lobster. Alex chose steak for himself and Sally. Dessert was a chocolate mousse, chilled and airy, piled high with whipped cream and topped with a sprinkle of chocolate bits.

It was nearly midnight when they left the Habitat. There was an awkward moment as the four of them stood on the sidewalk waiting for the car to be brought. "You two take the car," Alex told Dick and Lauren. "Sally and I will get a taxi."

"That isn't necessary," Lauren said quickly. "Sally and I can—" She stopped as she realized she had put her foot in it. Alex wanted to take Sally to bed, and he was giving Dick the same option with Lauren.

Morris laid a comforting hand on Lauren's shoulder. "Lauren and I will take a taxi," he said. "I'll take her home."

She looked up at him, grateful for the smooth handling of the situation. LaBarre made polite sounds of refusal, but in the end he and Sally got into the limousine and Morris and Lauren slid into a yellow cab.

"You don't have to see me home," she told him. "I live way out in the Valley."

The cabby turned around. "Hey, I ain't going to the Valley," he said. "It don't pay."

"Then take us to the Beverly Hills Hotel," Dick Morris instructed him. He turned to Lauren. "I have a rental car there."

Lauren tried to protest, but he hushed her and they both leaned back as the cab took off. "You know," Morris said to her. "Los Angeles is barbaric. People out here should be born with wheels instead of legs."

"I guess it is bad," Lauren agreed. "I never really thought about it. You just have to have a car. And that's that."

They picked up his rental car at the hotel, then he

263

drove her to the Valley. Outside the apartment complex he helped her out of the car. It was quiet here, the streets empty. A small breeze rustled the leaves of a palm tree.

"It was a lovely evening," Lauren said. "Thank you."

"Thank you for coming." He leaned over and dropped a gentle kiss on her lips. Lauren was shocked to find herself liking the kiss. There was a sweetness in it. She could feel her breasts swelling inside the dress.

"Are you sure you won't change your mind?" he asked gently.

"I can't," she whispered. "But if I could, you'd be the man."

"Tell your guy he's a lucky man. He's got himself quite a girl."

"Thank you." She found herself reluctant to say good-bye. "Can you find your way back to the hotel?"

"I think so. This isn't my first trip to L.A."

"Good night, then," she said.

"Good night, Lauren." There was a faint wistfulness in his voice. He got back into his car and she moved to the gate at the front entrance. She paused there, her hand on the wrought-iron. She felt oddly disappointed and it puzzled her. Had she wanted to go to bed with him?

She waved to him and opened the gate and went inside. She liked him, but sleeping with him would have been pointless. She wasn't like Sally. She could not keep it friendly and light. She could not enter into any relationship without depth and purpose. Yet her body had responded to him.

The two-story complex was set in a U around the pool. A porch light glowed here and there. She walked around the pool and back to her door and inserted the key.

She wondered why men seemed to feel obligated to come on hard and fast to a woman. What had happened to romance? And to friendship? What was the rush, and why?

They were questions she couldn't answer. Perhaps neither could a man. Dick Morris had admitted to coming on because he thought she exepcted it. There was something wrong when people thought two bodies had to bump together before the minds could meet.

Chapter Twenty-Seven

One of the luxuries of time Paula allowed herself was an occasional half day at a beauty salon on Rodeo Drive. She worked in a frenzy all morning to finish a script so she could keep her appointment.

When she rolled the last sheet out of the typewriter, she felt the sudden urge to dump it all in the wastebasket. It wasn't good, it lacked sparkle. The characters were all full of gloom and despair. She shook her head. She did not have time to do another, and if she had, she did not know what new direction she could take. It was one thing to make the viewers cry, but quite another to depress them.

She desperately needed something to jolt the viewers, something that would keep them tuning in every day. The ratings were down again. The show's share of the audience wasn't good. It was holding for the moment, but if it fell again, Silverstein was going to have the advertisers down on his back.

The networks generally lost money on their prime-time shows, so they needed the daytime profits to finance the more expensive evening programs. It cost her network 170 thousand dollars a week to produce *Dreams*, but advertising revenues ran around 120 thousand dollars a day. But only as long as the ratings stayed up. Sponsors had a way of dropping like flies in the face of falling ratings, and if the axe fell it could be on her neck. Not that they could replace her, no one else in the world was as knowledgeable about *Dreams* as she, but they would give her plenty of hell because no one else carried as much responsibility either.

She shuffled the newly typed script together. There was nothing more she could do about it today, and sitting at her desk and agonizing was pointless. But walking away might help; sometimes a fresh view got her mind going in new direction.

The first thing was to relax. She turned the script over to Lauren and drove to her one o'clock appointment at the salon. The beauty palace always reminded her of a strawberry sundae, done up in gloriously rich pinks and splashes of white.

The girl who greeted her was young and fresh-faced. She wore a bright pink smock and looked as though she had never had a problem more serious than buying the right false eyelashes. "Miss Cavanaugh," she said, consulting her appointment book. "Max is waiting for you."

Max was the masseur. Back in a small dressing stall Paula stripped off her clothes and handed them to another female attendant. She wrapped herself in the crisp pink floral sheet provided.

Max, who worked out at Muscle Beach on his day off, helped Paula up onto the table. Max worked stripped to the waist and seldom missed an opportunity to flex a muscle here and there. He was as queer as a three-dollar bill, but Paula had it on good word that for a generous tip he could bring himself to enjoy a woman. His showing off always amused her.

"I haven't seen you in a long time, Miss Paula," he said, his voice deep, seeming to roll up out of his massive chest. "I've missed you."

"I've been working hard," Paula said.

"You shouldn't do that. Life is for enjoyment, too."

Paula did not answer. His hands were already moving over her body. She gave herself up to his touch as he probed the muscles from the small of her back up to her neck. Fingertips tested the tendons running from her neck to across her shoulders.

"My God, Miss Paula. You're been working too hard! These feel like steel bands. Breathe deeply for me. That's right. Let it out slowly. I want you in the whirlpool after this. You're a bundle of nerves."

"I know," she said, closing her eyes, giving herself up to his touch. His touch was soothing, relaxing. She felt herself begin to float under his ministrations. Her breathing became deep and regular. She kept her mind as clear of thoughts as possible, concentrating only on the experienced hands.

Slowly, without noticing at first, new feelings began to seep into her body, warming it. Normally she did not find a massage a sensuous experience. In fact, she had been known to fall asleep. But not today. Today her body was all up, reaching back to Max's touch. His hands were gentle, then insistent, demanding more mobility of the muscles.

When the strong fingers moved down to her buttocks she became aware of a warmth spreading, starting deep within her belly and down to the mound pressed against the table.

She opened her eyes and stared at a white wall painted to give the effect of a tropical jungle. She concentrated on dark green ferns in an attempt to will away the responses of her body.

I'm too old to feel this way, she thought. People are supposed to lose interest in sex when they're old. She felt her small breasts begin to tighten and the nipples harden.

"I—that's enough, Max," she blurted out in panic. She didn't want to be one of those love-starved bitches reduced to paying Max for his favors.

"Not yet," he protested. "I want to do the ultrasonic on your back today. It'll loosen up those muscles deep inside."

He smeared warm greasy stuff down each side of her spine and she felt the small metal orb moving up and down. There was no real sensation from it, yet she would almost feel the muscles spreading and flattening. The pulsating in her groin increased.

"That's enough." She sat up, forcing Max back. He pulled the sheet discreetly up over her and she grasped it together in front with shaking fingers. He took her arm to help her stand and she felt her inner thighs trembling.

Max made a final check of the bare shoulders and gave her a pat. "I'm proud of you, Miss Paula," he said. "There's not a spare pound on you. No fat."

"Fat has never been one of my problems," she informed him.

"But you keep up with the exercise, true?"

"Yes, Max. One hour every morning." She had always worked hard to keep her body in good shape. Her morning routine had not varied in years except for the occasional addition of a new exercise.

She felt safer standing on her own, back in control. Max pressed a button and the attendant appeared and led Paula into the next room where she stepped into a deep whirlpool bath.

The pink marble tub was empty and Paula appreciated the solitude. The water was kept at a constant 110 degrees. Paula moved down into it slowly until she was sitting on the ledge. She moved so that her back was in front of one of the high pressure outlets. She leaned her head back on the hard ledge and rolled it back and forth. The neck muscles were a little sore, but free.

She ran her hands down through the foaming swirling water and over her body. Her breasts were small and not so firm and not so high. One advantage to having never been large was to sag less as you got older.

Her hands moved over her stomach that was hard and lean; caressing herself lightly, she stroked the belly and watched the distorted underwater movements as her fingers found the pubic hair. She hadn't done herself in years. It had always seemed like such a childish, undisciplined thing to do.

The fingers moved deeper. Suddenly the door opened. Startled, Paula jerked involuntarily. "Hi." An overweight blonde plopped herself into the water. "Damn that Max! He's going to pound me to death. Nag, nag, nag. I mean, a girl is entitled to eat, isn't she? Who the hell does he think he is, telling me what to do? I pay him to keep this stuff off me."

"Excuse me," Paula said, getting out of the pool. She picked up one of the oversized pink towels stacked at the side and bound it around herself like a sarong.

Back in the dressing room, the attendant provided Paula with a soft white gown edged in pink. After a foul-smelling mud pack, a silky cream was massaged into Paula's face. Then it was a trip to the shampoo bowl. All the shampoo girls were experts at their job. No shampoo and rinse here, but an elaborate ritual of shampoo and scalp massage, then a protein conditioner, another shampoo and finally a color rinse of raven black.

Her hairdresser, Carl, fluff-dried her hair with a towel. "You're down for a cut," he said. "Shall I do something different today? Something softer?"

"No, Carl," Paula said. "I like this cut."

"But most of our ladies are going to the softer cut."

"You mean your ladies my age?"

"Well," Carl sniffed. "If you want to put it that way, yes! The Sassoon cut is too severe for you."

Annoyed, Paula glared at him in the mirror. "Carl, please. I like this cut. It's easy to take care of. I shampoo and I dry it and that's that."

"We could do a perm, and you'd still be able to blow-dry it."

She stared at herself. With wet hair and no makeup she looked like a scrawny chicken. Except in the salon and in the privacy of her own bedroom, she was never seen without makeup.

271

An odd sadness settled in her chest. "The Sassoon cut, Carl."

"Yes, madam," he muttered, his body stiff and his eyes not meeting hers.

After her hair was dried and cut, Paula moved to the makeup section where Hildy laid out her wares. Paula let herself be talked into buying several items, including a new eye cream costing fifty dollars an ounce.

She was out by four and went two doors down to the nail boutique. A couple of her porcelain nails needed replacing and she wanted a pedicure. By five she was out of the boutique. She knew she should rush back to the penthouse. She could catch Jenny and Lauren if she hurried.

But going back to the office depressed her. If any emergencies had come up, Jenny would have called her. To hell with it, Paula decided. She did not want to face Jenny's everlasting smile and good humor.

Paula wished, with a kind of desperation, for just one person to talk to. Not Jenny, who had no real understanding of what Paula went through. Certainly not Lauren, who was too new and awed by the glamour to understand.

There wasn't anyone. She had never developed close friendships, for she didn't have the time. She couldn't talk to Shepard; he was too old. And most certainly not Silverstein. You didn't confess doubts to your producer. Once, when they were first married, she would have talked to Joe, but whatever intimacy they had shared was gone now.

Unable to face the loneliness of going home, she headed across the street to a small bar with a canopy-covered entrance extending out over the sidewalk. The decision made, she moved swiftly and purposefully. She wore black Swedish knit slacks, a black-and-white striped blouse of soft polyester and a black blazer.

She opened a door of brass and stained glass and paused inside to let her eyes adjust to the dimly lit interior. The bar was nearly deserted. Two men sat at

272

one end, a cocktail waitress flirted with a man at a table and there were two Beverly Hills housewives sipping Gibsons at a table stacked high with packages bearing the Gucci trademark.

Paula moved to the empty end of the bar and took a stool. The bartender pushed himself away from the sink where he was leaning. "Good afternoon," he said pleasantly.

"A martini, please," Paula ordered. "On the rocks with a twist of lemon."

"Yes, madam."

The drink was placed before her in seconds. The bartender lit the cigarette she took out of her purse. She picked up the martini and sipped it carefully, savoring the first taste. "Nice," she murmured and toasted the bartender.

He nodded his thanks and moved away. She stared blindly down at the cocktail napkin. She had to find a way to get the ratings up. The romance between Kerry and Sally was going nowhere. Sally was gone too damned much, first with her stupid surgery and now with a movie. Paula did not have room to develop anything with Kerry and Sally.

She wondered if she should consider Lauren's suggestion of an affair between Kerry and the Irene character. The older woman–young man thing was good. It happened from time to time. But it did not particularly appeal to Paula. Her own complications were always better and easier to work with because they were hers.

There was the child, Timmy. A child stricken with a dread disease always made for a good tearjerker. She could see the bright little boy being hit with leukemia. Except she didn't want to kill Timmy off. His family situation was good for years and years of stories. She considered an accident.

"Madam?" The bartender interrupted her thoughts and placed a second drink in front of her.

Paula frowned at him. "I didn't order this," she said coldly.

"The gentleman at the end of the bar asked if you would accept it," he explained.

"Oh." Bemused, Paula looked down the bar. Only one man was there now; he held up his glass in a toasting gesture.

"Thank you," Paula said and toasted back. She was flattered and amused. She had not had a drink sent to her in a long, long time.

Her heart gave the oddest little flutter when she saw him get up and make his way to her side. "May I join you?" he asked politely.

"All right," she said with a faint smile. The bartender gracefully went back to the middle of the bar.

The man was good-looking, Paula decided. About forty, with a touch of gray at his temples. His face was broad and well defined. There was no real hint of jowls yet, but he was the kind who would have them as he got older.

"I'm Gil Richardson," he said.

"Paula Cavanaugh," she replied. She looked at him closely. The suit he wore was tailored well enough, but it hadn't come from one of the better stores. The fabric gave it away, as his eyes gave him away. They were bedroom eyes, the kind that say, "When, where and what time?" His kind showed up in all the bars. When she was young they would have called his sort a "rounder." She supposed he would be classified as a swinger now.

"Are you a Beverly Hills housewife out for an afternoon on the town?" he asked.

"No, I'm not," Paula said, not offering anything further.

"Not a wife?" He glanced at her left hand. She wore a small wedding band, but it was nearly obscured by a large oval opal.

"Yes, I'm a wife."

He leaned closer. "I'm not a husband."

"Good for you," she said, smiling to herself. God, she hadn't sparred with a man like this since—since she met

274

Joe. And she had had little use for men before that. There had been no one immediately after Naomi, not man or woman.

"Maybe it's good, maybe not." He looked down into his drink and she sensed the answer was not a ploy. There was an aura of loneliness about him, or perhaps of being alone. "Maybe if I had a home I wouldn't be sitting in a bar like this."

"What do you have?" she asked, with a nasty edge to her voice. "A hotel room?"

He did not take offense, choosing to ignore her tone. "No, I have an apartment in the Marina. Just off Admiralty Way."

"Nice area," Paula said, nicer this time, wishing she didn't have to be always on the defensive. It was a professional necessity she should not carry over into her social life. "Do you have a boat?"

"No," he said. "No yachts for me. I don't run in that class."

"Not even a sailboat?"

"No."

Paula found herself warming to him. Or maybe it was the drinks—she never had anything stronger than sherry. Or maybe it was Max's massage. She really didn't care; it was kind of nice being picked up.

They studied each other openly, Paula calculating. He was the kind of man who knew about women and sex. His sort almost made it a profession. It would be very important to him to satisfy a woman. He would pride himself on that, she was certain. And the knowledge sent a small thrill through her thin body.

She pushed her jacket sleeve back to check the time and he covered the watch with his hand. "Don't be in such a hurry to run off. I'd like to have dinner with you," he said.

"I couldn't."

"I know an Italian place on Santa Monica that lays out a mean spread."

"No," she repeated.

275

"Why not?" he persisted. "Jealous husband? I'll never tell him." His eyes were gray and teasing.

"I have commitments," Paula said.

"What kind that can't wait?" he asked.

Suddenly she realized what she was doing. She was leading him on, enjoying the attention. Heady, she raised her eyes to his. "I can't go out with you."

He stroked her hand on the bar. "Why not?"

"I'm older than you," she said. The words came out harshly, and she felt a certain irrational shame in having to say them.

"Are you?" He shook his head. "I don't think so."

"Oh, come on," Paula threw back. "Don't take me for a fool."

"Are you so sure you're older than I am? And even if you are, does it matter? Does it?" he pressed. It was the eyes more than the voice that would not be denied an honest answer.

"Oh, I suppose not," she murmured.

"Okay, then . . ."

Paula shook her head. "I really can't," she said, amazed at the undercurrent running between them. She was jittery, her heart was pumping far too fast.

"Another round before you go?"

"No more drinks," Paula pleaded.

"One more. And if you want to leave then, I won't try to stop you."

"That's hard to argue with," Paula said, not at all sure she wanted to argue with him on any point. It was a heady, exciting feeling to have a man look at her like this. She decided to enjoy it, and another drink would do no harm.

"What do you do, Gil?" she asked. "Besides hang around in bars and pick up strange women?"

"Lots of things. I'm a money manager, a financial adviser. It takes me into a lot of areas. I put together people who need each other. A couple of years back I put together a new pet-food company."

"That sounds good."

"It was, for a while. We had a movie name to promote it. Well-known actress. Then she got on her high horse and wanted control of it. She wasn't content enough to sit back and take the royalties we handed out to her. She wanted to run things. It all ended up in court and the company fell apart."

"Too bad," she said. He was a fringe operator. Making a living, but never making it big. "What are you into now?"

"A couple of things. I'm putting together backers for a Canadian movie. And there's a builder out in the Valley who wants me to find investors for a condo development he's putting together in Woodland Hills."

"Do you like your work?" Paula asked, curious.

"It's a way to make a buck and it keeps me hustling." He picked up his drink and studied her over the rim of the glass. "Paula Cavanaugh. Didn't I see your name somewhere recently? Maybe in one of the trade papers?"

"Not mine," she said and smiled. He was fishing, trying to find out if she was somebody or married to somebody.

He turned his barstool slightly and put his hand under the counter and laid it on her leg. "Let's go to dinner," he said. "And maybe we can find other things to do afterward."

He gripped her leg, letting the fingers dig in gently. She went weak and a stab darted through her stomach.

She pushed his hand away. "I've got to go."

"Don't." The gray eyes begged in a sweet way. "I like you, Paula Cavanaugh."

Puzzled, she drew back. What was his game? He couldn't know who she was. Could he really find her attractive enough to want to take to bed? "Why don't you try one of those girls?" Paula asked, nodding toward two younger women coming in the door. Didn't all men want firm young bodies and unlined faces?

He turned, looked and shrugged. He turned back to Paula. "I like you," he said.

Feeling girlishly flattered, she picked up her purse from the bar. "I really do have to leave now," she said.

He caught her by the arm. "Paula, would you give me your phone number?"

He was tempting. But no, she couldn't. She would not be a foolish old lady. Not that he was that young, of course. Not like some twenty-two-year-old gigolo, and he was graying at the temples.

"Please, Paula," he urged, his gray eyes intense, making him acutely tempting. "We'll have dinner sometime. Or a drink here again. We'll see if the attraction is still there."

He stood up and she felt very soft and feminine as he gazed down at her. "If you don't want me to call you at home," he said. "Then let's make a date now."

"I—I don't know." She dropped her eyes. "I don't do things like this."

"Then it's time you started. Tomorrow?"

"I can't," she protested weakly.

"Next week? You name it and I'll be there."

"I'm not sure." She wavered, without purpose or plan, conscious of the freshly awakened needs of her body.

"Let's set a date and time and if you don't show, I'll understand," he suggested.

"Friday," she said, the word slipping from her lips almost unbidden, with a sigh of relief at the decision made.

"Seven?"

"Seven," she confirmed, blood pulsing through her veins at a rapid rate.

He took her hand and pressed it to his lips. "Next Friday."

She walked out, heady with emotions and conscious of the warm tingling left by his simple kiss.

"Why not?" she asked herself with some belligerence. How many more times in her life would she have a chance to indulge herself? One day she would really be old. What then? Her body turned icy cold at the prospect of being old and alone. She had to take her chances and live now, then she would have memories to warm her nights.

Chapter Twenty-Eight

Head back, eyes closed and arms spread, Sally gave herself up to the tanning rays of the sun. Her hipbones jutted out above the brief bikini bottom. The sun was too bright, causing red spots to dance in front of her closed eyes.

She flopped over on the striped towel she had spread on the grassy area by the pool. She wished she could clear her mind as easily as she had cleared a spot to lie down on.

She could not stop worrying about Dick Morris. He had promised to call her in a week and he hadn't. Another week passed, and she found herself getting very edgy. Alex and Joe both told her to be patient; she tried, but it darn sure was not easy.

She had been so busy she should not have had time to worry. She did two shows for *Dreams* after her recovery, then she had to take off again for the part in *Slocum*. She was keeping up with her voice and dance lessons and really getting interested in tap dancing.

On top of that, Lauren was talking about moving to West Hollywood or West Los Angeles. Sally was agreeable enough to moving, but she didn't see how she could afford it. She had to pay back Joe, and the lessons were costly. Lauren had covered her rent last month and that was hanging over Sally's head. Joe could be put off; all she had to do was love him a little bit and tell him her troubles.

And there was still the hospital bill Alex had paid. Sally considered it thoughtfully. He had shown her a bill for just over a thousand dollars. She was not at all sure she was going to pay him back. He did not expect it and a small part of her mind kept nudging at her, asking why shouldn't Alex pay. He was the one who had made her check into the private hospital and he could afford it. Hell, he would never miss a thousand dollars, it was so much pocket money to a wealthy director like Alex.

Sally found leading a straight life was turning into a very complicated situation. With Jake she had never worried beyond the next day. Now she seemed to worry constantly. A heavy sigh slipped from her lips. She flipped over and faced up to the sun again.

Lauren had been distracted from moving for the moment because Paula had assigned her sample script number two. Lauren was deep into it this weekend and Sally was making an effort to keep out of her way.

Sally turned over again and riffled through the *Slocum* script she had brought along to study. The part was demanding, pushing her hard, forcing her to reach out for more depth, stretching both her mind and her talent.

She had spent the last week doing location shots, mostly scenes with the maniac stalking her from home to school. Friday they would shoot the grab scene, where the maniac dragged her into his car. Next week would be interior shots, including the rape. The final scene would be her dead, discarded at the bottom of a canyon in a garbage dump.

It was the biggest part she had ever had, a real supporting role. It was important to her career, and she could feel in her bones that it was good.

Restless, Sally got up and swam ten laps in the pool. Panting a little, she pulled herself out and sat on the edge. She considered calling Kerry to see if he wanted to do something. She immediately rejected the idea, not because Lauren would be jealous, but because Kerry was not pleased with her.

He was put out about her being off *Dreams* so much lately. She could not blame him and she wished good things were happening for him, too. His career seemed to be at one of those standstill points. He was moody and ready for a change. Sally wondered if Lauren was aware of it.

Sally made a mental note to mention Kerry to Alex again. He would be casting *Rainbow* soon. There would surely be a place in it for Kerry.

Bored with the pool, Sally returned to the apartment. The typewriter, set up on the kitchen table, was clattering away until she opened the door.

"Sorry," Sally called. "I'll go to my room."

"It's okay," Lauren said and immediately returned to the typewriter.

Sally showered and shampooed her hair and went into her room and closed the door. Lauren didn't know it, but Sally had a small stash of grass she had bought on the street.

She rolled a joint, overlapping two papers. She took the first long deep drag. It was harsh, certainly not the Colombian she had been told it was. It was not the greatest, but it would do to while away the afternoon. She wished Alex would call. It was better to get stoned with someone.

Tuesday morning Sally's telephone rang, jarring her out of a deep sleep. "Hey," she muttered into the receiver. "It's only dawn."

"Sorry. I was afraid I'd wake you, but I wanted to catch you before you left for the day."

"Dick Morris?" She came up out of the bed fast.

"Yes."

"I'm awake, I'm awake!" Goose bumps were breaking out of her arms, a band of hope tightened around her chest. Please, please, please, she prayed silently.

"How's life in California?" he asked.

"Mr. Morris, Dick," her voice shook. "Why did you call? Did I? Am I?"

Dick chuckled, the sounds rolling happily over the wires. "You're our California Girl," he announced.

"Oh, my God! My God!" She wrapped her arms around her head. "I don't believe it!" She laughed out loud. "I got it! I got it!" She bounced up and down on the bed, incapable of finding a way to express her soaring joy.

"Hey, there's a few things we have to iron out," he said. "I need to talk to your agent now. I'll call him this morning and we'll start working out the contracts."

"Okay, okay. Joe is going to flip. He'll be so proud of me."

"And we'll have to ask you go give up that part on the soap opera," he continued.

Sally stilled. "Why?" she asked suspiciously.

"For two reasons. You have to be available to us. This isn't a one-shot photo assignment. We're building an entire campaign around you. Just you. So we'll be making heavy demands on your time. Second, the soap isn't the image we want."

"It—it isn't going to hurt me, is it?" she asked cautiously.

"No. Your fans will hang in with you. People who don't watch soaps won't associate you with them."

"I—I guess I understand. It's just that *Dreams* gives me regular money."

Dick chuckled again. "Hey, don't you know this could make you rich? And famous? Don't you know that?"

"I . . ." It was too much to comprehend. She had not let herself think about it too much. Well, she had thought about it a lot and had kept telling herself she didn't have a chance at it, she admitted to herself.

"Well, I'm sure your agent knows exactly how much

this will mean to you. We'll need you in New York. How long will it take you to tie up things there?"

Her head spun. "I don't know," she answered. "There's *Dreams* and I've got another week on this movie I'm doing."

"I'll talk to your agent about that. And Sally, we'll need some background information on you."

"Background? What do you mean?"

"Do you remember the Ivory Snow scandal?" he asked.

"No, I don't think so," she answered, puzzled.

"The pure and lovely young mother type they were using on the boxes turned out to be a porno actress. It was quite a scandal, and it's made advertisers a little paranoid."

"Oh." Sally slumped on the bed.

"So you work up a résumé for us," he said. "List all your credits. Tell us where you were born, a little about your parents."

A dark pain shot through Sally. "My—my parents are dead," she said.

"Dead?" Dick's voice dropped. "But you're so young."

"Daddy died when I was a baby in—in a car wreck, and after I graduated from high school, my Mom . . ." Sally's voice broke.

"You poor kid. I didn't know. I'm sorry."

"I've survived," Sally whispered, fighting to control her panic. She had to talk with Joe. Oh, God! If Bunny and Patty ruined this for her . . .

"I'll be in touch, Sally," Dick said. "You're going to be terrific. Your tapes overwhelmed us all. Those eyes—they reach and grab."

"I'll work hard," Sally promised, gripping the phone so tightly her knuckles turned white.

"You'll be terrific," Dick said.

"Oh. Hey, say hello to your roommate for me, will you," Dick added.

"I will. And thanks, Dick."

They said good-bye and Sally sat on her bed, copper eyes alive with fire, feeling the wild excitement returning in a rush. She jumped out of bed and dashed across to Lauren's room, barging in without knocking.

She leaped onto the bed, her hair flying. "Lauren! Lauren, wake up!"

"Huh? What?" Lauren struggled up and blinked, then focused on Sally's face. "What is it, Sally?"

"I got it!" she cried out. "The California girl. Dick Morris just called. And he said to tell you hello." The words tumbled out on top of each other. "I'm it! I'm in!"

"Oh, Sally!" Lauren shook her hair back from her face. "That's wonderful."

Sally knelt on the bed, grinning widely. "We can move now. I can afford it soon."

Lauren laughed. "You'll be so rich you can keep me."

"Oh!" Sally hugged herself. "There's so much to do. I've got to talk to Joe. And to Alex. Hurry up and get dressed. I'm riding in with you."

"But it's not even six yet," Lauren complained.

"I don't care! Oh, I do care. Joe, I've got to talk to Joe." She pressed her hands together. "I'd better not call him at home, huh? Paula might be mad. Oh, I'll have to give up *Dreams*."

Lauren's green eyes widened. "Oh, no."

Sally nodded. "Dick said I would have to."

"Let's let Joe tell Paula," Lauren suggested as it hit her that she was stuck in the middle again. "No, I'll tell Paula," she said. She might as well get it over with.

"Will the Witch be mad?" Sally asked.

"Who knows? And who cares?" Lauren said, smiling at Sally. "She was hell on wheels last week. Maybe this week will be better."

Sally sobered. "Kerry isn't going to be very happy either, is he?"

Lauren shook her head. It had been her first thought.

286

"I guess he'll be knocked off the show until they replace you," she said.

Sally frowned. "I feel sad all of a sudden. It'll be like I'm breaking up a family to leave *Dreams*."

"But you're going on to better things," Lauren reminded her.

"It won't change for you and me, though. We'll always be friends, won't we, Lauren?"

"Of course we will," Lauren assured her. Sally reached out and they embraced.

Sally released her slowly. She loved Lauren, more than she had loved her own sister. She felt herself getting teary. None of that. This was a happy day. She slid off the bed. "Oh, I don't know what to do first," she cried.

"You can start with making me some coffee," Lauren said. "We'll celebrate with a real breakfast."

"Okay," Sally agreed. "You grab your shower." She tap danced out of the room and into the kitchen, singing "Everything's Coming Up Roses" at the top of her lungs.

She made Lauren a pot of real coffee instead of instant. She reached into the refrigerator for a Coke for herself and spotted the bottle of champagne left over from the night she was released from the hospital.

She maneuvered it around the milk and orange juice. She pressed the cold green bottle to her cheek. "You're next, baby," she said to the bottle.

She set out wineglasses and scurried around, setting the table with the green place mats. She melted butter in the skillet for scrambled eggs and dropped bread into the toaster.

When Lauren emerged wrapped in a robe, everything was ready. Lauren stopped and looked at the table. "Wow! Champagne yet."

Sally beamed. "It's a celebration, isn't it? I see all kinds of champagne breakfasts advertised in the newspaper."

"Well, let's do it then. Pop the cork," Lauren said.

Sally ripped off the foil and unfastened the twisted wire. She poked at the cork. "It's stuck."

"Push it out with both thumbs," Lauren said. "From the bottom."

Sally struggled with it, finally got the bottle down between her legs and gave the cork a powerful yank. It popped out, the foam spilling out.

"In the sink!" Lauren yelled and grabbed the glasses.

Giggling, Sally managed to salvage half the bottle. After mopping up the floor, she sat down at the table.

"A toast," Lauren offered. "To you, Sally, To a California Girl Extraordinaire!"

Sally's eyes misted. "I still don't believe it, Lauren." Apprehension overcame her. "What if something goes wrong?"

"What could go wrong?" Lauren asked.

Sally poked at her eggs with her fork. "Dick said they would have to have some background on me. You know, to make sure I've never done anything that would embarrass the client."

"Oh." Lauren looked at Sally with concern.

"Yeah. I'm not exactly a shining example of clean living," Sally said. "And there's my sister."

"But you don't even know where she lives," Lauren said. "Surely . . ."

"I know, but what if it comes out? That she's a hooker?"

"But that isn't you," Lauren said. "It can't reflect on you."

"I—I lied to Dick on the phone," Sally confessed. "I told him my parents were dead."

Lauren nodded slowly. "I guess I can't blame you for that."

Sally's face took on a look of deep intensity. "I want this." Every muscle in her body was taut. "I want this so bad!"

"I know you do, Sally."

"So . . ." Sally scooped up a forkful of eggs. "I guess I'd better come up with a nice sweet past."

"Talk to Joe," Lauren said. "He'll know what to do and say."

"I hope so," Sally said. "Oh, God, I hope so!"

Chapter Twenty-Nine

Lee Trent did not know why he had let Anne drag him to The Bistro for lunch. For serious eating he preferred The Cove or Scandia, but Anne never thought beyond The Bistro or the Beverly Hills Hotel dining room. Like most of the other customers, Anne came to be seen. The Bistro was considered by many to be *the* Los Angeles answer to New York's famed 21 Club.

Anne had insisted on being seated up front near the slightly curved bar with its brass railings, where she was assured of seeing and being seen. A potted fern grew out of the ledge behind Anne. Cheeks alive with color, Anne's violet eyes danced with excitement as she played with a ruffle that ran around her neck and dipped low in front over her small breasts.

They were barely seated when Anne spotted a woman director across the room. Anne waved gaily. "I'll be right back, honey. I have to talk to Margaret. After all, she's one of the few people doing women's stories. She's going to come up with a part for me one day," she said to Lee as she darted away.

Lee nodded and ordered a scotch and soda for each of them from the waiter who had been hovering at his side.

"Darling!" he could hear Anne cooing to Margaret.

291

He adjusted his jacket and leaned back in the chair. Voices carried at The Bistro and he considered that a problem. Everything could be heard. At peak serving hours the clatter of dishes and voices could become unbearable.

The waiter placed the drinks on the table. Lee downed his in two gulps and lit a rare cigarette. He had cut back on them because they affected his voice. He settled back to wait for Anne to return. She did not, but the waiter did.

"Another one, sir?" the waiter prompted.

"Yes," Lee agreed, handing him the glass.

He was halfway through the second drink when Anne flitted back to the table. Her eyes were wide, excited pools under thick dark lashes. "Margaret is working on a new project," she announced. "A women-to-women type thing for PBS. It will be a series."

"A women's-lib scene?" Lee asked, his tone sarcastic. Anne didn't seem to notice.

"Yes!" Anne said. "Isn't it marvelous? She wants to break through the barriers that keep women from achieving. She says her show will be a new kind of consciousness-raising program."

"Anne," Lee said. She kept rattling on. "Anne!"

She stopped. "What?"

"Do you know what you're talking about?" he asked.

She blinked rapidly. She looked at him in confusion. "I'm a career woman," she said, almost pouting.

"Yes. Yes, you are," he said and let it drop. She was also a dingbat. She would pick up on any cause and could mouth any line of rhetoric that was "in" at the moment. Lee doubted that she had ever had an original idea of her own.

"Oh, look!" Anne cried. "There's Elaine. You know, from Saks. I bet she can advise me on a wedding gown. You know I can't wear white again."

"Hey, Anne . . ." He reached across and covered her hand with his. "Let's not talk to outside people just

292

yet. We haven't set a date, we don't know where we want to live."

"Oh, in my house, of course," she said and made kissy sounds at him. "Don't be a bear, Lee. Elaine is discreet and she will know what is appropriate."

"Don't you know?" Lee asked. "You've been married three times already."

"Lee!" she wailed. "You're being mean. What's the matter with my guy, huh? Are you tired. Oh, I know what you need." She stood, pulling her hand free of his. "As soon as we finish lunch I'm taking you straight home and to bed."

"Anne!" Her name was a groan from Lee. She whirled off and across the room to whisper to Elaine of Saks. Lee felt sick. He finished his drink and traded glasses with her and nursed it for a while.

The waiter returned and Lee ordered a salad for Anne—she was back on another one of her diets—and eggs Benedict for himself. "And another scotch," he added. "These are awfully weak."

The waiter looked at him. "I'll speak to the bartender, sir," he said. "You'd like another?"

"Yes."

Lee finished Anne's drink. Normally he drank for the lift it gave him, and two would suffice. Booze had a marvelous way of brightening up the world, but not today.

Lee did not want to hurt Anne. She was so damned excited and pleased, like a kid. And that was the hangup. She was spoiled and childish. Lee got the feeling sometimes that Reenie was more adult than her mother. Now, Reenie was an odd one. He had avoided her at all cost since the night she crawled into bed with him.

That was one scary kid, and he was not about to get involved with that scene. He had told himself she was an innocent kid, but he was not certain that was true. She could be child one moment, begging her mother for extra money, and a woman the next, watching Lee with cool appraisal from across a room.

Lee wanted out, and he wondered how the other three husbands had managed their escape. Maybe he should call one of them and ask. The idea made him smile. He suspected they had simply fled, for it was impossible to sit Anne down for a serious discussion. She would toss it off with some insane statement or gloss it over and come up with her own brilliant solution, which was generally taking him to bed. That was supposed to solve everything. He did not know what this marriage was supposed to solve. He was not sure how it had come about. He damn sure had not proposed to her.

It was going to break her heart when he broke off with her. He cringed to think what it might do to their relationship on *Dreams*. They were billing and cooing all over each other now. It was all very sticky-sweet. It would not be easy to put on a convincing show like that with your ex-lover. He knew he could cope with it, but Anne could not. She would end up causing scenes and weeping on the set and gaining everyone's sympathy.

Lee was afraid of having it come down to the point where he and Anne would have to leave the show. He had been on *Dreams* for years, almost since it began, but Anne drew more fan mail than any of them.

He shifted uneasily in his chair. He had to bring the breakup about somehow, some way so that Anne would think it was all her idea. Then they could stay friends and she could be sweet and kind to her ex-lover.

To be an ex-lover meant there needed to be a new lover on the scene. The waiter returned with Lee's drink and a small dinner salad. Lee looked the waiter over. He appeared to be Italian, broad-shouldered with slim hips. Only Anne would not go for a waiter.

"Are you an actor?" Lee asked the waiter. That might appeal to Anne's mothering instincts. She would like seeing herself as the driving force in molding a new career.

"No, sir," he replied. "Just a waiter."

"Too bad."

"Yes, sir," he answered, making no attempt to conceal his disinterest.

Lee toyed with his salad. There ought to be some likely young stud out there who could entice Anne away from him. He ate the salad mechanically and mentally ran through his collection of male friends. He sighed. An appealing guy ripe for an affair just was not there. A new lover would have to be a guy who would shower Anne with attention, like constant telephoning and plenty of gifts. He would have to need Anne. Or make Anne think he needed her.

Now, just who in the hell, Lee asked himself, who was going to magically slip out of the woodwork and do all that?

Anne, lovely enough to make heads turn, slipped back to the table. "I ordered for you," he said. "A Caesar salad."

Anne smiled. "You're so sweet, Lee. Have I told you today that I love you?" Her misty violet eyes adored him. "Could we have some wine?"

He signaled the waiter and ordered a bottle of rosé.

The wineglass in Anne's hand completed a lovely picture of worshipful love. She toasted him. "To us and our wedding," she said. "Wherever and whenever it may be." She set the glass down untouched. "I guess we could go to Las Vegas. But that's so shabby." Her lips twisted in distaste.

"Very shabby," Lee muttered in agreement as the waiter placed his food in front of him. He cut into the yolk of the nearest egg and hungrily watched the yellow ooze out over the ham and muffin.

Anne dug into her salad with gusto. She did love good food and fought a constant weight problem because of it, always winning the battles, but never the war.

Lee had to be careful himself. Sometimes he wished he was an ordinary businessman. Then he could let himself grow round and paunchy and comfortable. At thirty-six, the struggle to maintain an appearance of twenty-nine was getting difficult.

Lee finished the bottle of wine, then out of habit ordered brandy with his coffee. He signed an American Express chit for the meal. It was not until he stood that he realized he was drunk.

"Oh, boy," he muttered under his breath and gripped the back of the chair for support.

Anne was immediately upon him. "Darling, what's wrong?"

"Uh . . ." He shook his head. Damn it, the room was beginning to spin. "I don't think those eggs agreed with me," he grumbled.

Anne put her arm around his waist. "I think my big old boy drank a tweeny-weeny bit too much."

"For God's sake, Anne!"

"Come on," she cooed. "I'll drive us home."

In her Encino house, Anne tucked Lee into bed. He did not argue. He was too grateful to have the world still at last. He lay nude under cool sheets and closed his eyes. Anne kissed his cheek and smoothed his hair. "I've got to run," she said. "Beauty shop appointment. I'll be back in a couple of hours."

"S—sure." He was having trouble with his tongue. "What time is it?"

"It doesn't matter," she said. "You go to sleep now."

"It doesn't matter," he repeated. He was asleep before she was out of the room.

The next thing he was aware of was the bed shifting slightly under added weight. He was still floating, half-asleep and half-awake, lost in that good place in between where you do not have to think.

He was on his side and he felt her slide up against his back and mold her naked body to his. It was a warm and cozy place to be. Her fingers moved lightly over his buttocks, then along his thigh and down to play delightfully over his stomach.

She stroked gently, fingertips running in small tantalizing circles over his flesh and finally downward where they found the tightly curled hair. She played with him, using fingers and palm, stroking upward and then down, not touching his manhood, but coming ever closer.

At the point where he thought he could not stand it another moment she darted under the sheet. Her body and hands pulled him over on his back and her hot wet mouth found him.

"My God, Anne!" he gasped. His head arched back, his eyes closed with delight. "Anne. Anne." He reached under the covers and fondled her body that was crouched over his from one side.

She had never felt so good. The body was so firm, the skin like velvet. His hand moved up to her shoulder and into her hair. Hair! He went cold. The hair was long and thick.

"Anne?" He threw back the sheet. Reenie turned wicked laughing eyes to him. Her tongue flicked over him.

"Reenie!" Horrified, he scrambled backward and with a thrust of his leg knocked her sideways. The brass bedstead was cold and hard against his back.

Reenie sprawled on the bed, her legs spread. She ran her hands over her stomach, then cupped her breasts suggestively. "I want you," she said.

Like a cat, she sprang up and crawled toward him on hands and knees. "I want you," she said again.

"No!" he tried to scoot back, but there was no place to go except off the bed. "No!" He teetered on the edge, lost his balance and fell to the floor.

She laughed and slid to the edge of the bed and peered over at him. Her eyes gleamed wildly through the hair that tumbled over her face. Without a word, she scrambled over the edge of the bed and fell on top of him. He tried to push her away but she wrapped herself around him with arms and legs. They rolled over and over on the floor. She bit and gasped at him and suddenly it was the most exotic carnal experience Lee

297

Trent had ever known. She was not a child, not a daughter now, but woman gone mad with eroticism.

He knew now what it could feel like to be raped. Willingly raped perhaps, but raped all the same. Fear and intense need mingled together. Somehow she got underneath him and his hands that had been pushing her away were now drawing her close. She arched up to him. "Do it!" she begged from deep in her throat. "Do it, do it, do it!"

She was no virgin. She took him inside with a soft moan of animal pleasure. Lee closed to everything but the pulsating need of his body and her insistent demands. Lost in the mindless rhythm of the ages, they coupled with total abandonment.

Afterward, he lay flat on his back on the floor, his mind grappling with the returning sense of reality. She had drained him of energy, leaving him limp and helpless. He was not certain he could even move. His breathing was rapid and shallow, his body beaded with moisture.

She came up over him on hands and knees, hair hanging down each side of her face, and kissed him on the mouth. "You're real good for an old guy," she said. She had the same violet eyes as her mother, but they were wiser and more worldly.

"Oh, God." He closed his eyes to the pleased expression on the young and flawless face. "Anne is going to kill me. She'll have me arrested."

"No, she won't," Reenie said, swinging herself over him and to the floor. "I'm not going to tell her."

"I—I've got to get out of here." He pushed himself up to a sitting position.

"Why?" Reenie asked blandly.

"I can't face Anne," he said, waves of aftershock still washing over him.

"Why not?"

"My God!" He covered his face with his hands.

"It was good, wasn't it?" she asked.

"No!" He flung the denial at her.

"Yes, it was. I bet I'm the best you've ever had."

His hands fell away from his face and he stared at her. "You're crazy!"

"No, I'm not," she retorted. "I'm perky and cute. I just wanted to do it with a man. All I've had is boys. You're much better."

"You're just a child," he whispered, more frightened of Reenie now than of Anne. "A child!"

She reached for him, her laughing eyes saying he was wrong.

Lee scrambled to his feet. His legs threatened to give way before he could make it to the bed.

She stayed on the floor, sitting cross-legged, gazing up at him. "You'd better get back in between the sheets, Lee," she said slyly. "Mommy will be home soon." She stood and stretched lazily, unashamed of her lush, nubile body. "We'll do it again sometime."

She looked down at him, a gleam of triumph in her eyes. "You're just going to enjoy, baby. Just enjoy." She leaned over and kissed his forehead, then walked out of the bedroom, her rounded buttocks twitching proudly.

Chapter Thirty

Lauren put off telling Paula about Sally leaving the show until just before five. She did not want to do it at all, and she kept hoping Joe would call the news in to Paula. He did not, so there was nothing she could do except tell Paula herself. She knocked on Paula's door, then opened it. "May I talk to you?" she asked, her heart beating erratically with apprehension.

"Sure." Paula had been in an oddly mellow mood all day. "Would you like a glass of sherry?"

"No, thank you." Full of trepidation, Lauren slid into the black-and-chrome chair by Paula's desk.

"Is that a new outfit?" Paula asked of the washed denim pants suit Lauren was wearing.

Surprised, Lauren blinked. "Why, yes, it is."

"I like it."

"Thank you." Lauren shifted nervously in her chair. She was not at all certain that she didn't prefer the scowling Paula to this friendly one. From the former she knew what to expect.

"I know you're anxious for a report on your script," Paula said.

"Yes, but . . ." That's not why I'm here, she wanted to say.

"Well, I'll have to tell you that it is quite good."

Paula paused to light one of the long cigarettes she preferred. "At least half of it is usable."

"Half?" Lauren kept her face bland, careful to hide her disappointment. She had given herself four months to make the writing staff. She had not made it.

"I'm pleased with you and your progress," Paula went on.

"Thank you," Lauren answered, grateful for that much.

"I'd like to go over it with you scene by scene and explain what's good and what isn't, and why. But there isn't time today."

"Yes." Lauren glanced down at her hands that were pressed together in her lap. "I worked very hard on the script. I had hoped it would be better."

"You'll get there," Paula assured her. "Don't be impatient."

"All right," Lauren had no choice but to agree. "But that isn't what I wanted to discuss with you. This is about Sally Rook."

"Oh?" Paula stiffened slightly. "What's she up to now?"

"Nothing bad, but I think she'll be leaving the show."

Paula tapped her cigarette on a crystal ashtray. "Why?" she asked. "Why would she leave the show?"

Lauren hurriedly explained about the California Girl cosmetics line.

"I see," said Paula, stubbing out her cigarette and looking straight at Lauren, her face unreadable. "How soon is all this going to take place?"

"Well, immediately I'd say, from the sound of things. They want her in New York as soon as possible."

"Okay." Paula picked up a pen and began doodling on a pad. "If we had the time we could kill her off with some horrid disease. However, I like the character and we've already hinted to the viewers that she may be Reese's illegitimate daughter. So . . ." Paula paused and nodded thoughtfully. "We'll replace her. It's the only thing to do. I want you to go back through the more recent scripts and see if there is anything we can use for an audition scene. And I'd better let Silverstein know what's coming up. And I'll have to cool it between Sally and Kerry on the show. I think we can just send the character off on a trip. That will give us time to find a replacement."

"That means Kerry won't be on so much, doesn't it?" Lauren asked with a sinking feeling in the pit of her stomach.

"Not much, I'm afraid," Paula replied. She looked up, her eyes all-knowing and somehow accusing. "Are you still seeing Kerry Scott?"

"Yes." Lauren fought to keep her voice at a normal level. God, this woman always made her feel as if she were on trial, and guilty at that. She had not realized Paula was aware of the continuing relationship between her and Kerry. "Yes, I am seeing Kerry."

"That gives you a vested interest in him and his career, doesn't it?"

Lauren could not help squirming slightly. "Yes, I suppose so," she replied as cooly as possible.

"Is that why you came up with the Irene thing—to give Kerry more air time?"

Lauren felt her cheeks warm. "I . . . It was something that occurred to me," she said, wishing she could vanish. Why had she let Kerry talk her into presenting the idea to Paula? She felt as if Paula could see straight into her mind. It was like being a kid and getting caught by the principal for playing hooky.

"You know that Kerry Scott isn't an outstanding actor, don't you? He can only play one kind of character—a somehow spoiled, good-looking man who is used to having his own way."

"I—I don't know," Lauren said in anguish. "He does a lot of other things on TV and the movies. He's had a lot of roles."

Paula was not impressed. "I'm sure none of them required much depth on his part," she said.

"I—I don't know."

Paula flipped her pen onto the desk. "Tell your boy-friend I'll use him as much as possible. I don't deliberately shaft anyone, Lauren. Unless they ask for it." Her voice held a dark warning. "Just remember this, though. The story comes first. The ratings are all-important."

"I understand," Lauren said with as much dignity as she could muster. She stood. "Is there anything else?"

"Not today," Paula replied, her voice cold and distant.

Lauren turned and walked out on stiff legs. She was trembling inside and felt horribly exposed and vulnerable. She wished she was harder, tougher, and most of all she wished she could stop finding herself constantly in the middle.

Jenny glanced up as Lauren closed the door behind her. "Joe called," she told Lauren. "For you."

"Oh. Thanks, Jenny." Lauren hurried back to her own cubbyhole and dialed Joe's number.

"Hi, baby," Joe said. "Can you come by the office after work? Sally is here, and we all need to talk."

Lauren's shoulders slumped. She was not sure she was up to another "talk" of any kind. "What's it about, Joe?" she asked, her head down and her fingers working futilely over pounding temples.

"Well, it's too involved to go into over the phone," he evaded.

"Joe! Is there a problem?"

"Nothing that can't be solved. Sally is here with me now. We'll see you in a bit."

Joe hung up before Lauren could reply. She replaced the receiver slowly. A small ache was beginning between her shoulders. She wished she could just go home and soak in a hot tub and then sleep for days. Instead she was going to have to break Sally's good news to Kerry. And it would be bad news for him.

Kerry was already annoyed with Sally. Now he would be angry, perhaps at both of them. Jenny appeared in the doorway. Today, like most days, she was wearing one of the generously cut dresses she favored. The frizzled hair leaped out in all directions. "Let's cut out of here before Paula remembers something," she suggested.

"Okay." Lauren stood slowly, wondering what Joe and Sally had cooked up.

She drove from Wilshire to Sunset and with every block the ache between her shoulders spread deeper into her bones and muscles. In Joe's office she found the pimply-faced secretary, Maggie, preparing to leave. She had her purse open on her desk and she was studying her face in a compact mirror, working futilely at covering the flaws on her face.

Lauren smiled. "Mr. Seals is expecting me," she said.

"Yeah." The girl snapped the compact closed, practically glaring at Lauren. "You know, some days I wonder why I bother. I spend half my life worrying about how to clear up my face and the other half applying assorted goos, and then you walk in with your green eyes and flawless skin. You give me the same kind of complex Sally Rook does. Remind me never to go boogying with either of you," she said, cheerfully now.

Lauren laughed for the first time that day. "I'll remember," she promised.

"The doctors keep telling me I'll outgrow it. But who knows? At twenty-six how much more growing can I do—besides out?" She waved toward Joe's door. "Go on in. They're waiting for you. See you," she said and began pushing assorted paraphernelia back into her purse.

Lauren tapped on Joe's door, then opened it. "Ah!" Joe popped up from behind his desk. "Lauren, you're here." He was beaming and much too jovial as he came around and held a chair for her.

Today he was wearing a green bow tie and a shirt with a slight green pattern. The suite was immaculate, and he wore the jacket even though it was hot in the room.

Sally was sprawled in the other office chair with her

305

jean-clad legs stretched out in front of her. She grinned broadly. "Hi, Aunt Lauren," she said.

Lauren stopped. "What?"

Joe patted her on the shoulder and dropped a kiss on the top of her head.

"What's up?" Lauren demanded as Joe returned to his chair. Sally just kept sitting there grinning with a mischievous look in her tawny eyes. "I think I'm about to be had," Lauren choked.

"Not that way, baby. No," Joe soothed. "We just need a little help, and you can provide it."

Sally came up straight in her chair and leaned forward. "It's the perfect solution, Lauren," she said.

"Let's hear the problem first," Lauren said, but she had already guessed.

Joe explained: "Well, let's put it this way. Our California Girl here has a past that isn't exactly chaste, shall we say. Not that Sally has done anything so far out, but there is her sister."

"I know," Lauren said.

"Sally has already told Dick Morris her parents are dead. And the most logical thing in the world would have been for her to move in with a relative after her last tragic loss. A dear aunt. You!"

Lauren shook her head. "I knew it! Now, you two just tell me what's going to happen if they check her out?"

Joe spread his hands. "What's to check? They aren't going to hire private detectives to dig into her past."

"But I've met Dick Morris," Lauren pointed out. "Won't he think it odd that we never mentioned this to him before?"

"Why should he?" Joe queried.

"It just seems like something that would have come up," Lauren replied.

"Well, don't worry about it," Joe advised. "Sally will handle Morris. Her résumé reads beautifully. She's never played any raunchy parts."

Lauren looked to Sally. "Come on, Lauren," Sally

pleaded. "It will be okay. It's the best answer we could find. Please, this is important to me. If this is blown because of my damn family, I'll—"

"It's not going to be blown," Joe interjected.

Tears filled Sally's eyes. "Please, Lauren. You're the only person in the world who can help me."

Lauren felt herself weakening. She cared about Sally and in a way felt responsible for her. "It does scare me," she said. "I'm an awful liar. What if someone calls up and starts asking a lot of questions?"

"Who's going to do that?" Joe asked. "Dick liked you. He knows you're a real lady." Then he added, "Dick Morris is also a realist, Lauren. Don't blow this thing all out of proportion."

"Please," Sally begged again. She was so appealing, so in need of Lauren. And this was all-important. It was her chance to be somebody.

With reluctance, Lauren agreed. "Meet Aunt Lauren," she whispered, defeated by the two of them.

Sally squealed with delight and jumped up and swooped down on Lauren. "You're the best friend anyone ever had!" she cried.

"I hope this is right," Lauren said softly, returning the enthusiastic hug.

"It is! Oh, it is, Lauren. You'll never regret it. I'll never forget it, I'll always be grateful."

Lauren laughed nervously. "Just don't let anyone question me. I'd blow it for sure."

"We'll protect you, Lauren," Joe promised.

Chapter Thirty-One

All day Paula found herself on a strange high. She could feel the excess adrenalin racing through her body, coursing just under the skin. A hyper personality at any time, her metabolism was running at double speed. She struggled all day with herself over whether or not to keep the date with Gil Richardson. She told herself she was being a foolish old lady, yet she knew she would not have many more opportunities like this. And she liked Gil; he excited her with his look of a man who enjoyed pleasing women. She had put herself to sleep every night since meeting him with fantasies about how it might be between them.

Fantasies were one thing. To go and be disappointed would be something else. She wavered back and forth and had almost talked herself out of going when Joe called shortly before five and made the decision for her.

"I'm going out of town," Joe told her. "I'll be gone all weekend."

Paula felt her body tightening. "To Palm Springs, I assume?" she said.

"Yes."

"I see." With Sue Bergman, of course. He had not bothered to curtail his affair with her since she had confronted him with her knowledge of it. If anything, he was seeing more of Sue and being quite open about it. So be it, she thought.

"It doesn't matter," Paula said. "I'll be having dinner out tonight."

"Have fun, Paula." He paused, as if he wanted to say more. "I'll see you Monday," he finally said before hanging up.

Paula turned back to her typewriter, but it was impossible to continue working now. The Friday outlines were completed and Lauren had left early to deliver them on her way home. She could hear Jenny still typing. She buzzed Jenny on the intercom.

"Time to go home, Jenny," Paula told her. "It's Friday."

"Trying to get rid of me, huh?" Jenny teased.

"It looks that way."

"I'm going in a minute."

"I'll see you Monday," Paula said.

"Have a good weekend, Paula."

"I'll try," she said faintly. She knew now she would not turn back. She was going to meet Gil Richardson. Whatever happened, happened.

She waited at her desk, sipping a final glass of sherry until she heard Jenny leave. Then she walked back to the living quarters. Margaret had left, leaving behind a note on the refrigerator. There was baked chicken and cole slaw for dinner. But not for tonight, Paula thought as she headed back to her bedroom.

Apprehensive yet exhilarated, Paula entered her bedroom and closed the door. It was the one area of the house that only she entered, with the exception of the housekeeper. It was Paula's sanctuary.

It was a quiet, soothing room, with walls and woodwork painted a gentle gray. Silver-and-gray wallpaper covered one wall and spread through the dressing room and bath. The bedspread was a darker gray velvet. There were blackout curtains underneath the gray-and-white floral draperies, so that Paula could sleep in after working all night.

310

The only other color was green. Clear, bright green pillows were placed decoratively against the headboard. The boudoir chaise was done in a muted green and gray stripe.

Two Boston ferns, gifts from Mel Lorenzen, hung in the bathroom, flourishing magnificently in the sunlight provided by floor to ceiling windows of one-way glass.

Paula turned on the hot water in the step-down square tub. She poured in bubble bath and went back into the dressing room where she slipped out of her clothes.

She took a satin robe of soft peach from the walk-in closet. She knew people found her hard and unbending. It was an image she purposely conveyed and she dressed to suit the image of competency and efficiency. She assumed people thought she took no nonsense showers and wore dowdy nightclothes.

It was not true. Beautiful lingerie and fabulous gowns and robes were her one weakness. A hot bubble bath was a reward for a hard day's work. Back in the bathroom she adjusted the water to cold and mixed it in with the hot. When the temperature was just bearable she sank through the iridescent bubbles. She closed her eyes, rested her neck against the rim of the tub and lay still, waiting for the tension to melt away.

Release did not come. She could not stay still, could not get her mind off Gil Richardson. She sat up and washed herself with lavander-scented soap and stepped out of the tub. Her stomach began to feel queasy, something that happened a lot lately. Tonight she blamed it on the bath water being too hot.

She opened a cupboard and took out a bottle of Maalox and drank it straight from the bottle. She almost gagged swallowing the horrible chalky stuff. She wiped her mouth with the back of her hand. It was bad, but it worked.

She brushed her teeth quickly to rid her mouth of the taste and grainy feel of the antacid. Wrapped in the satin robe, she settled herself in front of the makeup mirror. She carefully removed the day's makeup, working in upward swipes, then used a cream base and began to reapply the foundation.

She wore a lot of makeup, and felt naked and exposed without it. Tonight she added false eyelashes over heavily outlined lids. She reached for the brightest red lipstick, then changed her mind and chose a paler one.

She checked the time. It was passing much too slowly. If she was not careful, she could end up pacing around the empty apartment. She was not about to arrive early and be found waiting for Gil Richardson.

Still unable to quiet the excitement raging through her body, she chided herself for overreacting. But it had been a long time since she had done anything like this, since she had been in bed with anyone—man or woman.

Paula studied herself in the mirror. The harsh lights were not flattering. They showed every wrinkle and even hints of wrinkles yet to come. There was a sag under her jawline, though she exercised her face every day along with her body.

What if Gil took one long look at her and walked out? No, he would not be crude, but he might have second thoughts and gracefully disappear early. Doubts assailed her from every direction. Was she being foolish? It was the one thing she would not be able to tolerate of herself. Coming off foolish was the worst of all sins, the ultimate humiliation.

She shook her head, swallowing back a rush of salty-tasting bile. She was going to need another dose of Maalox before she left.

The walk-in closet was lined with her garments. One side for summer, the other for winter, with clothes that could go either way at the end. Down the center was a small row of clear plastic drawers stacked on top of each other. They contained shoes and scarves and handbags.

She moved to a long black dress that was high necked and long sleeved. It was one of her favorites,

312

but much too formal for tonight. She discarded the idea of a long dress. She checked through her clothes, hanger by hanger. The blacks and grays and whites all seemed to take on a sameness. And why not, she thought. They were all similar, with only cut and fabric distinguishing one from the other. She leafed through a collection of street dresses and chose an Italian silk with a tight-fitting bodice and flared skirt.

She took black high-heeled pumps from a drawer and black knit sweater with a silver fox collar from a zippered bag.

Dressed, she added a cameo brooch to the dress, sprayed on a mist of perfume and checked herself in the floor-length mirror. She twisted to the side. Not many women her age looked this good, not many at all. Satisfied, she checked the time again.

If she left now she would arrive on time. If she could wait, she would be fashionably late. Only it was never fashion that made Paula late. It was ego and power play. She made a practice of making others wait for her.

But not tonight. She went to the building phone and called down for her car to be delivered to the elevator door. She checked her handbag for door keys, took the elevator to the underground parking lot and headed for Rodeo Drive.

At the canopied door of the bar she almost turned and fled back to the penthouse. But to what? An empty apartment and a television set. And to the knowledge of her husband in a motel in Palm Springs with Sue Bergman.

She plunged through the door and passed inside. Immediately Gil Richardson stood up and came to her. "Paula." He took both her hands in his. "I'm glad you came."

Her stomach was quivering again, but she smiled. He was not as handsome as she remembered. But the eyes were the same, knowing, sensuous eyes. She smiled back at him.

"Here, this way," he said. He took her arm and

313

guided her back to the table where he held her chair and immediately signaled a waiter. "Martini?" he asked.

"No. Something icy cold." A martini was not going to help her stomach. Gil suggested a daiquiri and gave the order to the waiter.

The table was tiny and covered with hammered metal. The chairs were replicas of the ones from old-fashioned ice-cream parlors. He moved his chair close to hers and their thighs touched under the table. She did not move away.

Gil gazed at her, the gray eyes soft and pleased. "All women should wear furs," he said softly. "There's something very touching and vulnerable about a woman's face when it's surrounded by fur."

"Vulnerable?" She laughed and it was a harsh, brittle sound. "No one ever calls me that."

"Did I make a bad choice of words?" he asked solemnly.

"Perhaps not," she said softly. She toyed with the napkin the waiter had left on the table "Most of us are vulnerable at one time or another in our lives. But I haven't let myself be vulnerable in a long, long time." Not since she had lost Naomi. Before that she had let men hurt her, by being too soft, too loving and giving.

"Good for you," Gil said, but he sounded faintly skeptical.

"Don't you believe me?" she asked.

"I don't know you yet. I can't disbelieve anything you tell me." His smile was as warm as the touch of his hand on hers. "I've thought about you," he said.

"Have you?"

"I keep thinking of you as my mystery woman. But then that's the fun of any new relationship, isn't it? You discover each other. Now, you, Paula Cavanaugh, you're no ordinary woman."

"I suppose that would depend on your definition of ordinary," she countered.

"You're something special. Different. I don't think

you're an actress. If you were, I would remember having seen you. But I get creative vibes from you. Are you an artist?"

"Not the painting kind, no."

"A decorator?"

"No." She laughed softly, enjoying the conversation. The waiter returned with their drinks and Paula took a sip from hers. "Delicious. That was a good idea."

"Thank you. But now, tell me What are you?"

"A writer!"

The gray eyes darkened in triumph. "I knew it!" he laughed. It was a beautiful sound, very deep and full. "I knew you were something special. No, you have to tell me what you write."

"A soap opera," she answered. *"Dreams to Come."* She watched him, gauging his reaction. People's response to her profession usually put her off. Most immediately volunteered that their mothers watched the show. They never watched themselves, of course, seldom admitting their own addiction.

"I think that's wonderful," he said. "Terrific! I knew you were a creative person."

"Thank you," she said, finding herself highly pleased.

"It must be a fascinating business," he offered.

"Oh, a grueling one, at any rate."

"Yeah. It would be heavy. I can see that. No reruns, huh?"

"None."

"Do you carry this load all by yourself?"

"Mostly," she replied, then went on to explain briefly how the show was put together.

They had two drinks, then he suggested dinner at the Marina. She offered to drive her car out. "Then you won't have to come back into town," she told him.

"No way," he said, grasping her arm firmly. "I'm not taking any chances on you getting away from me."

His car was a slightly battered Eldorado, discolored and dull from sitting out in the sun and smog. He tossed a briefcase into the back seat and helped Paula inside.

All through dinner, Paula found herself watching Gil, waiting for him to start pulling away, waiting for his eyes to stray to one of the younger women. But he barely glanced at the waitress who wore a tiny ruffled skirt that did not hide her matching panties.

All his attention stayed riveted on Paula, so strongly that she could barely eat the steak and lobster on her plate.

When the plates were cleared away Gil ordered a White Russian for each of them. Paula sat back silently. A sense of panic rushed over her as she realized they had run out of conversation and the next step was approaching, the move to, or away from, bed.

Yet he seemed comfortable and relaxed, pleased with her and the meal. He offered her a second drink and she refused.

Back in the car she sat stiffly on her side, hands gripping her purse. He got in and slid over next to her. His arm went around her shoulders and he buried his face in the fox collar. "Pretty," he said. He raised his face and with his other hand cupped her chin. Her lips trembled as his came down to touch hers. She let her lips part and his tongue probed gently, sensuously.

Her chest swelled and she whimpered softly against the onslaught of emotions that threatened to engulf her.

"Wow." Gil pulled back and looked into her eyes. "You *are* something special. I want you, Paula. I want you tonight. Now! My apartment is near here."

"I . . ." She couldn't speak. She wanted him, needed the kind of release he offered. But she was so damned scared. "I—I'm not very good with men," she whispered in anguish.

"Maybe you haven't known the right men," he said, then kissed her again. Slowly they came apart. "I'm taking you home with me," he said. "And we're going to do it right."

He moved to start the car and Paula closed her eyes and sank down into the seat, remembering something Naomi had told her a long time ago. "You can't divide the world into men and women and decide to love only one sex. It can be good either way. You must be ready to accept love where you find it. Don't ever turn away from love. Human closeness is a very precious commodity."

Chapter Thirty-Two

Lauren was in a strange mood as she drove to work Monday morning. It was going to be one of those panic days. She could feel it getting ready to happen.

Paula had reacted well enough on Friday to the news about Sally leaving the show. Today they would start pulling scripts. Since they wrote a month ahead of the taping date, any show Kerry and Sally were in would have to be rewritten and any references to Sally made by other characters would have to be changed.

Lauren had been so concerned over Sally on Friday that she had barely reacted to Paula's critique of her sample script. It was only after she was alone on Saturday that the full force of it hit her. She went into an angry sort of depression. She had been so certain she could make the writing staff in four months and not the six to twelve Paula had warned her it would take.

Paula was right and she was wrong. Maybe if she had worked harder, or studied more, if she hadn't spent so much time with Kerry. She berated herself, playing the possibilities over and over in her head.

And Kerry. She went to him Saturday needing comfort, seeking solace. Instead she had found him in an odd frame of mind, withdrawn and moody, which did not make it any easier for her to tell him about Sally leaving. She searched her mind for how to do it, trying to foresee every possible reaction he might have.

When she finally told him she tried to be positive about it. "Sally has had a fantastic offer," she told Kerry after they had made love.

"Oh?" He didn't even raise his head from the pillow to look at her as she explained about the California Girl opportunity.

"So she will be leaving the show," Kerry said dryly.

"Yes. Paula says she will use you as much as she can. And they will replace Sally. I've already picked out an audition scene."

"Yeah, I'll just bet Paula is going to use me a lot." His tone was bitter. "I don't know what in the hell I ever did to make her dislike me."

"She doesn't dislike you," Lauren protested, aching for him as she remembered Paula's comment about Kerry not being a very good actor. "She doesn't have anything against you."

"Then why doesn't she make better use of me?" he demanded.

"You know how soaps are," Lauren soothed. "They focus heavily on one set of problems at a time. You and Sally were a developing subplot. The relationship will be a major focus soon."

"Not for months and months the way we're going now," he said.

He was so stiff and far away. She reached over and laid her hand on his chest, wanting to pull him back. He did not acknowledge her touch. "I've been thinking," he said. "Maybe I should get out of soaps. It can be a dead end for an actor. Look at Cobb Strong and Lee Trent. They'll never be anything more than they are today."

"They seem happy enough," Lauren offered.

"I'm not." Kerry pushed her hand aside and rolled off the bed. He grabbed his jeans and drew them on without bothering with underwear. "I'm going to have a drink. Do you want one?"

"Yes," she answered, uncertain and a little frightened

at his mood. She had never seen Kerry quite like this before. She could touch him physically, but she could not touch what was eating at his insides.

He stalked out of the room and she scrambled out of bed. She got dressed and followed him to the kitchen where he was mixing stiff gin and tonics.

He picked up the conversation again. "You know, I latched onto *Dreams* for the steady money. It was there and I needed some income I could depend on. But one day a week just isn't cutting it."

"I know, but it will get better," Lauren said, praying that Paula would come through for Kerry.

"I hope you're right," he grumbled. "I hope to hell you're right." He picked up his drink and walked off, leaving her to reach for her own. Dejected, she followed him to the living room. He arranged two logs in the fireplace and lit them even though it was a warm night, as if he had to have something to do with his nervous energy.

The logs had barely caught when he took the poker and shoved them over and back. "I think we should go out," he said. "I can't stand sitting around here."

"I'm ready," she offered gamely.

"Let's do something for fun. If I stay cooped up in this dump for one more day . . ."

"We could go to a movie," Lauren suggested, leaning forward.

"No!" He snapped out his refusal. "Let's hit some discos."

Lauren swallowed hard. "Okay." She tried to smile. "That should be fun. Let's do it."

It was not fun at all. He dragged her from one crowded disco to the next. They were all jammed with the Saturday night crowds of restless cruising singles. They had to squeeze between people to get to the bar for a drink, and half the time they could not find a table, so there was nothing to do but stand, shoulder to shoulder, back to back with strangers.

They would no more than finish a drink when Kerry

would be out the door again to the next place. The music in every sounded the same—loud, pounding out meaningless rhythms.

When they did manage to find a table, Lauren was usually left alone while Kerry danced with girl after girl. She could not believe how women came on to him. There was nothing backward about them, and they certainly were not shy. They came on with their eyes and mouths and swaying bodies.

When a man approached Lauren to dance, she would turn him down. She could not do the bump or the hustle, even with Kerry. She felt too awkward with the music to dance and she was not interested in the men anyway.

By two A.M. Kerry was drunk and she had to drive him home. "You're a great little mother," he kept mumbling as she undressed him. "Great little mother."

She got him into the waterbed. When he tried to pull her down beside him she sidestepped and his arm fell with a thud. He objected in a vague way and promptly fell asleep.

Torn, she stood over him. She wanted to stay and she wanted to go home and spend Sunday working on scenes. Finally she left because she was certain his mood would be no better the next day. Mostly she left because she had no idea of how to change his mood.

All she really wanted to do was hold him and tell him everything would be okay. She wanted to give him the solace she had needed so desperately from him tonight.

She almost turned back at the door of Kerry's apartment. Then she remembered how Kerry had accused her of wanting too much. He would hate it if she started making like a wife.

She told herself he would want that in time. It would come eventually when Kerry had learned to trust and share with her. It would come when he realized how much they needed each other.

Lauren knew she was to the point where she could not envision life without Kerry Scott. He had made her

322

a whole woman and she wanted that feeling to go on forever, this knowing she was complete.

If only . . . She shut it out of her mind. Kerry was not ready for marriage or any kind of permanent relationship. His career was not stable enough yet, and she was barely getting started on her own.

But hers was different. Once she made the writing staff she could stay home and write. She could be a full time housewife, even a mother, and still continue with her career.

We could have two beautiful children, she thought. Kerry and I could have such beautiful children. Her breast filled with soft yearnings. Once she had wanted children with Benji. She was glad now it had not happened. It would have only made for more heartache.

Meanwhile, she had to cope as best she could and wait for Kerry to realize how much they needed each other. Maybe it was time to start looking for an apartment near Kerry again. She had been sidetracked before. Maybe it was time to accept Kerry's offer to help her find a place.

She tried to cut off all personal thoughts as she left the freeway and picked up Wilshire. A professional did not carry problems into the office, and today was going to be heavy.

She found Jenny at her desk. There was a stack of scripts on the glass coffee table.

"I see you've already pulled the scripts," Lauren said.

Jenny shook her head. "Not me. Paula pulled them and rewrote them all over the weekend. That woman is an absolute dynamo." Jenny shook her head in awe. "She must have worked all weekend. And now they're all yours. Edit them, retype whatever is necessary and get the changes to the studio."

"Wow! And I was dreading today." Relieved, Lauren smiled. "Well, I'll do the coffee and sherry and get to the scripts first thing."

Lauren was placing the decanters on Paula's desk

when the woman walked in. "Good morning, Lauren." The voice was soft and light.

Lauren looked up in surprise. "Good morning." Paula was wearing a black pants suit with a vest that emphasized the thin, firm body. "You're looking lovely today."

"Why, thank you," Paula said. "I like this outfit."

How odd, Lauren thought. It wasn't just the clothes that made Paula seem different. Black was black. Paula was more relaxed. The lines in her face seemed less tense and she looked younger.

"Jenny tells me you've already rewritten the scripts," Lauren said.

"All done. It seemed impossible when I considered it, but once started it wasn't difficult at all. I want you to send flowers and a note to Sally. Tell her we've enjoyed having her on the show and congratulate her on her new job. Tell her I think she will go a long way."

"Yes, Paula," Lauren answered, hiding her surprise. The boss lady was in a rare mood. "I'll do it right away. Sally will be so pleased."

"She should be pleased. I don't want to be disturbed now. I've got a show to write."

Paula poured herself a cup of coffee and carried it to the window overlooking Wilshire Boulevard. Friday night had turned out better than she had dreamed possible.

If Gil Richardson was aware of her nervousness, of the apprehension gripping her depths, he was careful not to show it. He was casual yet attentive when he took her to his apartment.

It was not one of the better Marina apartments. It was on the wrong side of a small building away from the water, so that meant it was one of the cheapest.

Still, it met Marina del Rey standards. The pale shag carpeting was of good quality. The walls were done in burlap and grass paper. But the furniture was at odds with the room. "It's a nice apartment," Paula remarked.

"No," he corrected her. "It isn't particularly nice. But thank you for being so kind. I rent the furniture, as well as the rooms."

"Rent it?" she asked. "I didn't know anyone rented furniture."

"I do. That way I'm not tied down."

An unexpected surge of disappointment hit her. "Then you expect to be leaving the area soon?"

Gil shrugged and took off his jacket. "Who knows?" he said as he loosened his tie. "My work takes me to a lot of places. So I don't tie myself down with a lot of possessions. Not to mention the fact that my finances fluctuate." He moved behind a breakfast bar and took out the makings for a drink from the cupboard. "It gets hairy sometimes. But things are really going to be up if I can get the building thing going for Andrew Jones. I only need a couple more backers, then we can go to the bank or a savings and loan for the rest of the money. I just wish to hell I had more of my own money to put into this project. The way real estate sells in Los Angeles is phenomenal. Lotteries to buy houses, people standing in line, even camping out on building sites just to put down a deposit or to get their names on a reservation list."

Paula took one of the barstools and Gil handed her a drink. "Tell me about the project, Gil," she prompted.

"Oh, you don't want to listen to me discuss business, Paula. And frankly, I don't want to listen to me either. I don't even want to think about business tonight." He leaned over the bar and Paula stretched forward to meet his lips. It was meant to be a casual kiss, but the second their lips touched Paula went breathless. Desire coursed through her body and it was Gil who drew back first.

He set his glass down hard. "Do either of us really want this drink?" he asked.

"No," she answered honestly, trembling.

"Then come on." He came around the bar. There

325

was another kiss before he lifted her from the stool to the floor and led her back to the bedroom.

Paula stared down Wilshire Boulevard, not really seeing cars and buildings as she remembered Gil's love-making. He was good. No, not good. Superb. There didn't seem to be anything he didn't know about pleas-ing a woman.

There were few words spoken between them. The language of their bodies said it all. He undressed her, caressed her skin and slowly and sensuously took her to a shattering peak. Afterward, he held her in his arms and stroked her body and trailed kisses over her face, telling her she was a wonderful woman in bed.

She searched his gray eyes, looking for regret. She found none there. There was no rushing out of bed. He kept her there and made love to her again. The second time was slower and easier, and she responded to him with all her being, like dry earth opening up to drink quenching rain. She had not known how starved she was for affection and sexual release. It was so good just to be held in warm and loving arms.

It was after two when he returned her to her car on Rodeo Drive. They had found much to talk about. He showed more awareness than most people of the kinds of problems she dealt with on a day-to-day basis.

When they separated she gave him something no one else had except Joe, the telephone number of the pri-vate line in her bedroom. "I'll call," he promised with a final kiss. "You can be sure I'll call."

She drove home alone, content for the first time in years. She woke up early Saturday morning, and in spite of only having had a few hours sleep, she was bubbling with energy. She went through her exercises in double time, made coffee and tackled the rewrites to get Sally off the show.

Gil called Saturday about six. "I can't get you off my mind," he said. "Would it be too much to ask to see you again tonight?"

A delighted laugh spilled from her lips. "Come here,"

she said impulsively. "I'll make dinner for us." Joe would not be back until late Sunday.

She took great joy in the small task. She never cooked any more, though once she and Naomi had prided themselves on their home-cooked meals. She put the cold chicken in the oven with a barbeque sauce over it. The cole slaw was already made. She mashed potatoes and fixed buttered corn. It was a simple, ordinary meal, but the sort a man should like.

Gil seemed impressed with the penthouse and gave her many compliments as she showed him through the office and living area. But he was not overwhelmed by it, and she liked that. The man had class, and she liked that in men. Which made her wonder again why she had married Joe Seals. Class was certainly not Joe's high point; he was quite ordinary.

Gil ate with enthusiasm. "You don't know what a rare event this is in my life," he said. "I never get home-cooked meals. But . . ." He stopped and laid his fork down and picked up his wineglass. "But you—you're an even rarer event."

"Gil." She looked down. "Don't put me on. You're a handsome man and a bachelor. I know you have your pick of women."

Gil nodded. "There's a lot of women available. If you just want to go to bed with someone, anyone, then that's easy. But meeting a woman who is . . ." He paused and seemed to be searching for the right word.

"Mature," Paula said, embarrassed for herself.

"No," he said. "Not the way you mean, Paula. Age has nothing to do with it. Nothing. I mean a woman who is together. A woman who is bright and intelligent. Like you. That's the difficult part. Very few people face life head on and deal with it. I think you do, I think you are everything I've mentioned and probably more."

Flattered and confused by his direct gaze, she shook her head. "I don't know what to say." She could not remember the last time anyone had given her a real compliment.

"I just hope the people around you appreciate you for what you are," Gil added.

She did not reply. Appreciate? Ha! She might get a pat on the shoulder now and then, but appreciation was quite rare in this business. You made your own rewards and you fought for them. Otherwise you got walked on by people like Shepard who were quite willing to take credit for someone else's hard work and creative ideas. She had been his willing student in the beginning, grateful for a chance at a writing position on a soap.

A series of shows she had conceived and written won an Emmy the third year she was with *Dreams*. It was Shepard who accepted and took the credit and applause, beaming and gracious and never mentioning her name.

She had wanted so little, just a public acknowledgment of her talent. She never forgave Shepard, and the resentment toward him grew over the years, though she kept it hidden until her position as head writer was assured upon Shepard's retirement.

Silverstein was as bad in his position as producer and with his pipeline to the head of the network. When dealing with the network, Silverstein took full credit for any success and blamed Paula for any failures.

She worked hard, she earned her money, but little glory came with it. She shook her head, jerking herself out of her reverie. Today was another work day. She had a show to write.

Chapter Thirty-Three

Lauren took the script changes to the studio during lunch hour. They had to get the revisions into mimeo immediately so the actors would have time to learn their lines. Sally's sudden leaving was definitely causing a hassle. It affected every member of the show. New call sheets would have to go out because Paula had to shuffle some of the actors around to give her enough room to get Sally off.

At least it would mean Sally and Kerry would get three days' work this week. It would not please Sally, who was in a panic over what clothes to take to New York, but Kerry should be delighted. She had tried to reach him by phone all morning to give him the good news, but she had only gotten his answering service.

He still was not in that afternoon. She made one last try before she left at five. "Hey, look, honey," the girl at his service complained. "You've called several times now. We'll give him your message when he calls in. Okay?"

"I'm sorry," Lauren said and hung up. There was nothing left for her to do but go home. The traffic was bad and it seemed to take forever to get over the Santa Monica mountains. She could not help thinking that if she lived in West Hollywood it would be so much easier.

It was hot in the Valley for May. Lauren's Chevrolet had no air conditioning and she was damp and tired by the time she got home.

The apartment was empty and quiet. There was a note from Sally who said she she had gone shopping and had a dinner date with Alex. She watered the fern that still dominated the small living room.

After straightening the apartment, she stripped off her clothes and stepped under a cool shower. She was toweling herself when the telephone rang. She flew to answer it. Kerry's most welcome voice responded to her hello.

"Kerry!" She pulled the towel around her. "I've been trying to reach you all day. You're on the show three days this week!"

"Yeah, I already got the word," he said without emotion.

"Aren't you pleased?" she asked.

"For what? For three days when better things are happening? Lauren, I was called back to read for a second time today for a director."

"Oh, Kerry! That's wonderful."

"The part is mine!" he announced triumphantly.

Her heart soared. Good things were happening for her man. "I can't wait to hear all about it," she said. "Do you want to come over here? Sally is out for the evening. Or I can drive over there and—"

"No, I . . ."

"Then come over here," she said. "We'll celebrate."

"All right," he said. "I'll be there in an hour or so."

"Wonderful! Bye, darling." She hung up. "I love you," she said to the room, wishing he would let her say it to him.

She decided she would not dwell on that now. There was too much to do. She had to get dressed and find something to eat. She let his joy over the new part become hers. She wanted tonight to be a real celebration, in more than one way. Tonight she would ask Kerry to help her find an apartment.

She threw on jeans and a blouse and rummaged through the refrigerator. Neither it nor the kitchen cupboards yielded anything special. She grabbed her purse and drove to the nearest market where she prowled up and down the meat counter and deli section.

She wanted something quick and easy, but special. Steaks would be okay, but common. Her eyes fell on the jumbo shrimp laid out on ice. They were outrageously expensive, but Kerry adored shrimp. She closed her mind to the price and ordered them.

She picked up cocktail sauce, fresh spinach for a salad and chose a chocolate pie at the in-store bakery. Back home, she washed the spinach and fried bacon and boiled eggs to go with it. She cleaned the shrimp, so they would be ready to dump into boiling water.

By the time she had the table set an hour had passed. He should be here by now, she thought. Then she chided herself for wishing him here too quickly. He would surely want to shower and change clothes.

Well, since he was not there, she decided she would take the time and do something to herself. She changed out of jeans into the one hostess dress she owned, a summer print. She applied makeup, using extra shadow to emphasize her green eyes. Kerry still had not arrived so she touched up her hair with the curling iron and sparyed on cologne.

Growing tense and anxious, she opened a bottle of wine and poured herself a glass. When he finally knocked at the door, relief surged through her. "I was getting worried," she cried as she opened the door. "I was afraid you had been in an accident or something." She encircled him with her arms and hugged him. "I'm so glad you're here."

He patted her waist. "I had some phone calls to make."

"Oh?" She waited for him to explain. He did not. "Well, want some wine?" she asked brightly.

"Sure."

When she returned from getting the wine he was sprawled on the sofa, feet stretched out in front of him. He seemed lost in thought.

"Kerry?"

He looked up. "Oh, thank you, Lauren." He took the wine she offered.

"You don't look very smug," he said. "I thought this was to be a celebration."

"I'm pleased about the part," he replied, but she caught the cautious note in his voice.

"Good." She hesitated, watching his face, waiting again for him to tell her about it. When he said nothing, she curled up on the sofa beside him, bursting with her own plan. "Kerry, you told me once you'd help me find an apartment in West Hollywood," she began.

"I said that?" he asked.

"Yes, when we first started dating. Don't you remember?"

"Vaguely, I guess," he murmured.

She swallowed painfully. What was wrong? "You— you said you were an expert at finding cheap places with good addresses," she reminded him.

"Sure, yeah. I do remember now. I am good at that."

"Well, I'm ready to start looking. I'm tired of driving back and forth to the Valley. And I want to be closer to you."

Kerry drew his legs up and turned to face her. "Lauren, that might not be such a good idea right now," he said.

"Kerry?" Her stomach knotted up into a hard ball. She went cold all over. "Why not?" she asked tremulously.

"Well, you shouldn't move because of me, Lauren." His eyes seemed glued to the wineglass in his hand.

"Why not?" Was he trying to break it off? The thought made her ill.

"Because I won't be there, Lauren," he said evenly.

"That reading I did today—it wasn't for a movie. It was for a play."

"I—I don't understand," she whispered, trying to fight her way through the sudden bleakness his words had brought.

"A play back East. It will open on Broadway in a few months."

The relief hit her first, then panic followed. He was not pushing her away, but he was leaving her. She clutched his arm. "New York?"

"Yes. It's my big chance, Lauren. You have to understand that. If I make it big back there, it will give me the leverage I need out here."

"But you'll have to move," she choked through the ice forming around her heart.

"I know. That's necessary when you're in a New York play. They kind of expect you to live there." He tried to make his voice light and teasing, but she could not respond to that. "The parts aren't coming here, Lauren. You know that. It's all I can do to keep the bills paid."

"If it's just the money for now, I can . . ." She stared at him, not daring to look away.

"No!" he said emphatically. "Borrowing money won't solve anything. And it's not the money, Lauren. It's the recognition."

Hearing him say that triggered a memory of something Paula had said once. "What kind of part is it, Kerry?"

"It's a play about four Vietnam veterans and how they're dealing with life now. One is a paraplegic. One is a country boy, one a Bronx type, and the other is me, a guy out of a wealthy family."

"Spoiled and rich," she said with a sinking feeling.

"Yes. He has the most and yet he's having the hardest time coming to grips with life."

"I—I see." She was shaking, but she forced herself to stand. "I'm happy for you, Kerry. I really am. It's just that I'll miss you, and . . ." She flung back her head

333

and smiled. "And we're going to celebrate. I have shrimp and everything."

She ducked her head and fled to the kitchen. At the sink she stood, gripping the edge of the countertop, fighting back the tears. He had never lied to her. He had never committed himself. He had bluntly told her his career came first. So why hadn't she believed him?

Because she loved him too much, that's why. And nothing could stop the pain from encompassing her at the thought of losing him. She took several deep breaths and blinked her eyes until they were dry, then mechanically began to prepare dinner.

She heard Kerry turn on the radio to some soft music on an FM station. His footsteps moved to the kitchen and she had to prepare herself to turn and face him.

"I need some more wine," he said, holding his glass out.

"Here." She got the bottle out of the refrigerator and handed it to him. She did not trust herself to pour it.

"How soon will you be going back East?" she asked, fighting to keep her voice level and still the raging beat of her heart.

"Three weeks."

"All right. I'll tell Paula," she said. Her voice sounded dead, even to her.

Kerry sneered. "That bitch. If she had just given me a chance . . ."

Lauren's heart leaped with renewed hope. "You mean if you had gotten the three-day guarantee you would have stayed?" she asked.

"Yes, I would have stayed. But she's probably doing me a favor. I never wanted to spend my whole life doing a soap opera."

"No, I suppose not," Lauren said in soft despair. But only a short while ago the show had been all-important to him. Damn Paula! If she had only let Kerry have a bigger part, this would not be happening.

Lauren turned away from him and began dropping shrimp into the boiling water. He came up behind her,

334

lifted her hair and kissed the back of her neck. "Oh, God," she whimpered, loving him with everything in her. She turned and put her arms around him. She raised her face for a bittersweet kiss.

"Hey!" Kerry pulled away. "The shrimp is boiling over."

"Oh!" She jumped to turn down the burner.

Kerry moved away to the table. "The food looks terrific."

"Thank you," she replied automatically.

The meal was a disaster. The expensive shrimp was just so much mush in her mouth. She dipped and chewed and swallowed and picked at her salad. There was no joy in her, though she tried hard to be up and bright for Kerry.

It was not really so difficult. All she had to do was keep smiling and listening to him rave on and on about the director of the new play.

She did not know how he could be so excited when she felt as if all the props had been knocked out from under her, when everything she had come to depend on was going to disappear. But then he was going on, to new and better things in his career. She would be left behind to cheer from a distance.

Kerry ate the last shrimp and pushed back his chair. "Delicious, just delicious, Lauren."

Lauren shrugged. "It wasn't anything."

"I'll help with the dishes," he offered.

"All right." She stood and tried to smile. Then she was crying openly. She could not stop the tears from flowing down her cheeks, could not hold it back any longer.

Kerry reached for her. "Hey, Lauren, don't be like this."

"I—I can't help it," she sobbed. She tried to hide her face against his shoulder. He held her close and stroked her hair. "Kerry, take me to bed," she whispered.

He pulled back slightly. She swiped at her tear-streaked face with the back of her hand. He leaned over

335

and kissed her cheek, then her closed eyelids. When his mouth found hers, she could taste her own salty tears on his lips.

Their lovemaking was wild and grasping. It had never been so sweet, nor so sad as tonight. She could not get enough of him, could not hold him close enough or long enough.

Finally, Kerry disengaged himself from her. "I want some more wine," he said. "How about you?"

"All right. A little."

She turned over on her stomach and clutched the pillow to her breast. He still had not said it, not even tonight when it would have meant the most. He still could not say he loved her.

Chapter Thirty-Four

Sally was delivered back to the apartment in Alex's car shortly after midnight. There were so many packages stuffed into the car that the chauffeur had to help her carry them inside.

Sally tried to be quiet, but it was not easy. Sacks rattled and she dropped a box of shoes, then had to thank the driver for his assistance.

She locked the door behind the chauffeur and tiptoed back to Lauren's bedroom. The room was dark, but the door was open. "Lauren?" she called softly.

"I'm awake."

"Good! Get up and talk to me. I've got lots of new stuff."

"Okay." Lauren sounded distant.

"Is there something wrong?" Sally asked.

"I'll be out in a minute," Lauren replied.

"Okay." Sally withdrew to the living room. Lauren sounded weird. Sally began opening bags. There were purses and new shoes. She rubbed a gauze blouse against her cheek. Alex was so good to her. He had taken her shopping himself, giving up a whole afternoon of appointments so she could have the right clothes for New York. Not many men would do a thing like that.

She protested at first, of course, over the money involved, vowing to pay it all back. He told her not to be foolish and she surprised herself and nodded in acquiescence. She discovered she liked having a man like Alex to buy her clothes. There was a nice warm feeling about it, one of knowing he was concerned and cared enough to do this. And accepting gifts was certainly nothing like being a whore. There was no comparison at all.

Sally looked up as Lauren padded barefoot into the room. Lauren's eyes were red and puffy, her face splotchy. Her eyes were a dark and hurting emerald green.

"You've been crying!" Sally said, dropping the blouse and rushing over to her. "What's wrong?"

Lauren took a deep breath before she answered. "Kerry is leaving. He's got a part in a play in New York."

"Oh!" Sally hugged her. "But you two are still together, aren't you?"

"How can you be together when you're three thousand miles apart?"

"But you didn't break up or anything, did you?"

"No, but . . ."

"But what?"

"Nothing." Lauren brushed her hair back from her face with a listless hand. "I—I'm just having problems adjusting. I feel like I just found Kerry, and now I'm losing him."

"Hey, come on," Sally said, trying to cheer her. "Actors run back and forth between New York and Hollywood all the time. He'll fly back out, and there's letters and the telephone."

"I know, I know. I'll be okay." She waved Sally off, not looking okay at all.

"Come on," Sally repeated. "This will cheer you up. Alex helped me pick out a wardrobe appropriate for a California Girl."

Lauren's eyes widened as she noticed the names on the bags. "Saks and I. Magnin's! How could you afford those places?"

Sally laughed. "I couldn't. But Alex can. Look at this, a real leather suit. I'm going to wear it on the plane."

"It's beautiful, Sally."

"Alex had to pay for everything. See this dress? And it has its own sweater."

"They're all beautiful, Sally. You're going to knock them dead in New York."

"I hope so," Sally said, sinking down in the middle of the clothes. "I get scared about it sometimes. I'll have to remember not to cuss and not to invite some guy to bed. God, can I pull it off, Lauren?"

"Of course you can. With these clothes you can pull off anything. Use your part on *Dreams*. Janie is a demure young girl, a little wide-eyed but sports-minded," Lauren told her.

"Yeah! Hey, if I get stuck I'll just figure out how Janie would handle it and I'll do that." There was that one big problem though. "What if they start prying, you know, into my past?"

"Go teary-eyed on them," Lauren said. "After all, you lost both your parents."

Sally grinned across at Lauren, who was almost perky now. She was glad she had awakened her. "I think I'll sign you on as my coach."

"Sure." Lauren's smile faded and both the girls fell silent.

Sally cocked her head to one side. "I guess we won't be moving over the hill now, huh?"

Lauren shrugged. "What's the point? I was moving for Kerry. I told myself it was for you and me, too. So we would be closer in, but it was for Kerry."

"He's got such a super apartment," Sally said. "I wish we could get it."

Large tears formed in Lauren's eyes and Sally wanted

to bite her tongue. "Hey, I'm sorry, Lauren. I wasn't thinking. See what I mean? I have a way of sticking my foot in it. Oh, Lauren! What if I blow New York?"

"You won't. You can't." Lauren wiped at her tears. "You have Joe and me and Alex all rooting for you. And they're going to adore you. They're already in love with your pictures and your screen test."

"I just wish I didn't have to go alone."

"Oh, Sally!" Lauren laughed huskily. "You hitched to California when you were a lot younger. And now you're afraid to fly to New York?"

"But this is so—so real! So important."

"You'll shine," Lauren insisted.

Sally jumped up. "I'll do my damnedest. For you and Joe and for Alex."

"And do it for yourself, Sally," Lauren reminded her.

"And me, too. I guess we should go to bed, huh?"

Lauren forced a smile. "I think we should."

"You won't cry any more tonight, will you?"

"I don't think so," Lauren murmured. Sally hugged her and watched her pad back to her room.

Sally mentally shook her head. Lauren took men far too seriously. She should not have fallen in love with Kerry and she couldn't say Sally had not tried to warn her against making such a dumb mistake.

Sally had always envied Lauren her stability and conventional ways. Now she found it comforting in a strange way to know Lauren could make a grand mistake, too.

She was personally glad Kerry had something going for himself. It took some of the guilt off her shoulders, though she had not felt as bad as expected at cutting him off *Dreams*. Realistically, a girl had to look out for herself first, for no one else was going to do it.

Of course, she had approached Alex about a part in *Rainbow* for Kerry. Alex rejected her with one flat statement. "We don't have any roles for pretty boys." She was relieved not to have to report that to Lauren or Kerry.

Sally gathered her new clothes and carried them back to the bedroom. She hung each item carefully in her closet, pausing to caress a fabric or adjust a collar. Smug and pleased, she stepped back to admire it all.

She felt like a woman tonight and less of a little girl than ever before in her life. Damn it, she was going to be somebody! She was going to be a famous star and nothing or no one was going to stop her.

"Watch out, New York!" she cried aloud. "Here I come!"

Lauren sat at her small desk watching the lights on the phone. When Paula was finished with her conversation with Silverstein, Lauren was going to talk to her. She knew it was pointless to delay the inevitable. Paula had to be told Kerry was leaving the show and the sooner she got it over with the better.

An odd thought stirred in Lauren's mind. She had hated being stuck in the middle between Sally and Paula and Kerry and Paula. Now they would both be leaving the show and she would never be caught in the middle again. Some small favor, she thought somewhat bitterly.

She could not really blame Kerry for taking this new part. It could mean everything to a career that was stagnating in California. If only he had told her he was trying out for the New York part, then she would have had some warning, some time to adjust to the idea of his leaving. She had asked him why, and he had looked at her as though she were a child.

"You work for Paula, remember? I didn't want any of this leaked to her. I didn't know if I'd get the part or not. And you don't resign from one steady job until you have another."

"I wouldn't have told her," Lauren whispered, in anguish because he had not trusted her.

"Maybe it wasn't just that," he said, softer now. "I figured why get you upset or excited about something that might not ever happen."

"Oh, Kerry. Kerry." She had hidden in his arms then, not wanting to think, wishing hopelessly for a way to shut out the pain.

Lauren lifted her head and checked the phone lights. Paula's was out now; she should go in and talk to her. But Lauren did not move; she was locked tightly into depression.

She picked up a pencil and began to doodle on a pad. "Kerry. Kerry Scott." She penciled his name over and over. Abruptly she slashed an X across the page, tore it off, crumpled the paper and dropped it into the waste-basket. Sitting there wallowing in self-pity was not going to get her anywhere.

She silently damned Paula for not giving Kerry the three-day guarantee. If she had done that none of this would be happening now. Lauren shoved her chair back and walked into Jenny's office. "Do you think I could talk to Paula?" she asked.

"I suppose so," Jenny replied, studying Lauren. "I can't hear her typewriter going." Jenny's normally placid eyes filled with speculation. "Something up?" she asked. "A problem?"

Lauren nodded and ran her hands over arms that felt ice cold. "We're losing another actor," she said, hope-lessness reflected on her face. "Kerry Scott is . . ." She had to stop and swallow. "He's leaving the show for a Broadway play."

"Nice for him, but not for you, huh?" Jenny re-marked.

"Not very," Lauren admitted. She had tried to keep her dates with Kerry a private matter, but everyone knew. *Dreams* was like a small town and gossip traveled fast with Sue Bergman at the head of the pack.

"Well, just don't forget one thing—there are seven million people in Los Angeles. About half of them must be male."

"Oh, Jenny!" Touched, Lauren had to smile.

"That means you have three and a half million to choose from. Of course, you'll have to eliminate the married ones and the old ones and the too young ones and . . ." Jenny stopped and looked embarrassed. "Oh, dear. That narrows it way down, huh? Some help I am."

"Yeah, some help you are," Lauren teased. It was better when she smiled.

"Do I get an A for effort?"

"Well, it was a nice try," Lauren said. "Excuse me while I walk into the lion's den." Lauren knocked on Paula's door and opened it.

"Yes?" Paula looked up from a legal pad where she had evidently been making notes. "Oh, Lauren. Come on in. I was just talking to Bob Silverstein. They're having trouble casting a new Katherine. A hundred and fifty actresses have applied. They've got it down to twenty now. But Bob doesn't think any of them are right. I think he's trying too hard to find a woman who looks like the old Katherine. That could be a mistake. We need a warm and lovely woman. I don't care about hair color or features."

Lauren stood by the desk, her hands gripped together at her waist. "We'll have to be auditioning for an actor, too," she said.

"Oh?" Paula's mood changed immediately. The dark eyes narrowed under heavily mascaraed lashes.

"It's Kerry Scott," Lauren blurted. "He's leaving in three weeks for a part in a Broadway play."

Paula muttered a four-letter word and threw the pen across the table. "Nothing like having it all dropped at once, is there? Damn!" Paula stood. "It's tough enough to get the viewers to adjust to one change. We've brought back Belle with a new actress. Katherine will be coming back different. Maybe I should just write Sally's and Kerry's parts out completely for a while. I— damn it!"

A shiver passed over Lauren's body. "If . . ." She hesitated, afraid to go on, but more afraid of losing Kerry. She brought her chin up and took a deep breath. She would never know if she did not ask. "If Kerry

343

could be guaranteed three days a week, I think he might stay."

"I doubt that," Paula said.

"He would, I'm sure of it."

"Anyway, I don't have that kind of control," Paula said. "I'm the writer, not the producer."

"But you have the influence," Lauren responded, desperation making her voice rise. "If you felt it would hurt the ratings to lose Kerry, and if you pushed it with Silverstein . . ."

Paula snorted. "Kerry? Silverstein would laugh me out of his office. And even if I felt that way, which I don't, I wouldn't ask him to keep an actor who wants out." Paula brought both hands down flat on her desk, eyes sparkling. "We've been locked in with Kerry Scott, and frankly I've felt we made a mistake in choosing him. I've used him as best I could, but I think another actor would give the part more scope."

Lauren recoiled as if she had been slapped. "What do you have against Kerry?" she demanded.

"Very little, actually," Paula replied. "It's you that's biased, Lauren. You're standing on his side and can't see anything else."

Paula's hard stare pierced Lauren's carefully controlled shield. On the verge of crumbling, she reached for a chair back.

"Why are you really asking for this?" Paula demanded. "Is it for Kerry Scott? Or is it for you?"

"No. I . . ."

"Yes, for yourself," Paula said. "Because for some reason you're terrified of losing him. Well, you'll learn one day not to depend on men for your happiness. Because it doesn't work. You can only depend on yourself. No one else!"

Lauren gestured helplessly as hot tears filled her eyes. "It's just that . . ."

"I know. It's just that you love him and you don't want to lose him. Well, face facts, Lauren Parrow. He's leaving."

Lauren pressed one hand to her mouth to hold back a sob. But she could not stop the tears from flowing down her cheeks. "I'm sorry," she managed to choke.

"So am I," Paula said. "I gave you credit for being stronger than this. Go wash your face."

Devastated, Lauren fled to lock herself in the bathroom. She sank down to the carpeted floor and sobbed. It had all happened too suddenly for her to comprehend. Their love had not had a chance to grow.

There was a soft tap at the door. "Are you okay?" Jenny asked through the door.

"No," Lauren whispered, pressing her cheek against the coldness of the bathtub. "In a minute," she called to Jenny.

She could feel Jenny out there listening. Damn it all to hell! Paula was right. She was being weak. She had thought she was stronger, too, until she humiliated herself in front of Paula.

Lauren got up and washed her face and stared at herself in the mirror. She looked like hell. The green eyes were glazed and tired and red-rimmed. Her face was blotchy. She ran her fingers through her hair and pushed it back off her face. She would not cry again, she vowed. She would not cry again in front of anyone.

Lauren moved through the rest of the day like a zombie, performing her necessary duties while avoiding Jenny and Paula as much as possible.

Chapter Thirty-Five

The last three days of the week were ones of sheer misery for Lauren. The date of Kerry's leave-taking hung over her like a death sentence and she wanted to spend every available moment with him. Ironically, it was Sally who spent Tuesday, Wednesday and Thursday evening with Kerry. Paula had rewritten their parts to make Sally's disappearance from the show more dramatic and logical. Their extended roles on *Dreams* meant concentrated studying each night, and they chose to do it together.

Lauren had desperately wanted to be included, but neither of them invited her, so she simply stayed home, letting Sally take her car. At least, she told herself, she had stopped crying. Not that she didn't get teary from time to time, but she had not let herself break down again.

Unable to shake the desolate feelings that had wrapped her in a shroudlike haze, she spent her evenings alone writing scenes that refused to come to life. She drifted through the days, living for Friday night when she could have Kerry back, at least for the weekend. For the next week he would have to do three shows again before he left *Dreams,* too, sent off in search of Sally. It would be the last week for the character of Bill until he was recast and returned to the show with a new Janie.

Lauren wondered idly if the viewers guessed how often the story line was dictated by the circumstances of real life. And perhaps that was part of the charm of soaps; they were never predictable.

Lauren counted the days she had left with Kerry. This weekend and the next week and the next, then he would be leaving for New York. She was going to the airport with him, she had decided, even if it meant taking off work and incurring Paula's wrath.

She awoke Friday morning feeling more positive about the world and herself and Kerry. She dressed with care, in a shirt and blouse Kerry had complimented her on, a pale green print that made her eyes seem a darker green than usual. She went to work and waited for his call.

Lauren's heart jumped eagerly with every ring and sank with disappointment when it wasn't Kerry. At four, Sally called. "It's wrapped," she said. "I'm finished with the show."

"Congratulations," Lauren responded, trying to sound cheerful.

"I think Kerry and I did a hell of a job. I really got into the part, Lauren. I was leaving and nothing could stop me. Maybe because I really am leaving!"

"Sally," Lauren could not help asking. "Is Kerry . . ."

"Hey, don't pick me up. I'm meeting Alex later. So I'll just hang around until then."

"Okay," Lauren said impatiently. "But Kerry—he hasn't called me."

There was a pause. "Oh."

"Is something wrong?" Lauren asked, pouncing.

"Not that I know of. He left the studio. He seemed in a big hurry to get home."

"Didn't he say anything about me?"

"No, Lauren. Listen, are you all right?"

"Yes. No. Oh, I don't know." Lauren hung her head, ashamed.

"I'm sorry," Sally consoled. "I wish you could be as happy as I am. I wish you could be happy for Kerry." There was a hint of accusation in Sally's voice that jolted Lauren.

Her hand tightened on the receiver. "I—I guess you think I'm being selfish."

"A little," Sally agreed. "But maybe you don't understand what it means being in this business. What it's like for us."

"I thought I understood."

"You call Kerry at home," Sally advised. "You'll feel better after you talk to him."

"I don't know," Lauren murmured, knowing she sounded wishy-washy.

"Oh, for God's sake!" Sally came back. "Crawl out of that hole you've dug for yourself. Quit mooning around like a kid and call him!"

"You're right," Lauren choked. "You're right." She was full of self-pity and she was depressing herself.

"Damn right I'm right," Sally said firmly. "Take action, Lauren. It will be better than what you are doing to yourself."

"I'll call him," Lauren said, forcing a firmness into her voice she did not feel.

"Good. I'll see you tomorrow, and Sunday you're putting me on the plane to New York. Don't forget that."

"As if I could," Lauren said, then actually laughed.

"And you'll have to help me pack tomorrow. Alex is giving me a set of luggage. I get it tonight. It's a good-luck present."

"That's wonderful."

"Isn't it? I never even thought about luggage. Just clothes. Wouldn't it have been hysterical if I had arrived in New York with my beautiful new clothes in paper sacks clutched to my chest?"

Lauren had to smile at the image that formed in her mind. It was just the sort of thing she could see Sally doing.

"Now, you call Kerry," Sally told her again.

"All right, I will," she promised.

"Bye for now."

Lauren depressed the receiver buttons and hesitated. Why hadn't Kerry called her or sent a message through Sally?

No. Stop thinking, she ordered herself. You think too much. Remember what Benji said about you. For once in your life, react instead of thinking. Fresh determination washed over her. She released the button and purposely dialed Kerry's number, one more familiar to her than her own.

Rigid and anxious, she listened to the phone ring at the other end. Three, four, five, she counted to herself. Six. Maybe he was in the bathroom. Seven. Maybe he had not had enough time to get home. Eight. Hang up, she told herself. With a small sigh, she started to replace the receiver. Then she heard the breathless "Hello?"

"Kerry!" she cried. "Kerry, I didn't think you were at home."

"I wasn't," he said. "I was putting the key in the door and I could hear the ringing."

"Oh," she said and paused, not quite knowing what to say now that she had him on the phone. The truth, she supposed, was best. "I've missed you. I thought you would call me today," she began.

"Like I said, I just got in. "It's been hell this week. You know that, Lauren."

"I know. It's just . . ." She took a deep breath and plunged in. "I think we need to talk, Kerry. I'm taking this very badly. Sally chewed me out for not being happy for you. But I am, in a way. I—"

"Lauren, I'm running pretty close here." The impatience in his voice made her recoil, but she didn't give up.

"Can we talk later?" she asked. "I'll drive over." She was humbling herself, but she didn't care.

"No," he said abruptly. "Joyce and Mickey are getting married tonight."

"Oh." She felt confused. "I didn't know."

350

"Sure. I told you, didn't I?"

"No, you didn't," she choked, her voice scratchy with emotion. She could feel her throat constricting.

"Well, this is a big night," he said, "and I'm the best man, remember?"

"I remember that," she answered, but she had thought she would be invited to the wedding.

"Look," Kerry said. "I'll be back sometime tomorrow."

"Tomorrow?" she asked. "Where is the wedding?"

"Oh, down on the Peninsula. They're getting married at Wayfarer's Chapel. You know, the glass church down by Portuguese Bend. A bunch of us are spending the night there."

"I see," she said. A bunch that obviously did not include her.

"Hey, now," he said. "Come on, Lauren. It's only some old friends. It's a very small and private wedding. I would take you if I could."

Would you? she wondered. She had met Mickey and Joyce; they had seemed to like her. Surely they would not have minded if she came, too. "I understand," she whispered past her doubts. "At least I'm trying to understand. Sally thinks I don't understand actors at all."

"You'll get there," Kerry assured her.

"Tomorrow, then?" Lauren asked, humbling herself again.

"Tomorrow night, I guess. I should be back by late afternoon." The impatience was still there in his voice. She could tell he was eager to be on his way.

"I'll drive over," she offered again. "Whatever time you say, and I'll be there, I promise. I'm proud of you, Kerry."

"Ah, lovely lady," he whispered, and for a moment it was the way it used to be.

"I'm your biggest fan," she told him, trying to keep it light.

"You are certainly my sexiest fan. See you tomorrow night. Make it late, at least eight," he said, then he was gone. She hung up. Sexy. It had never been a word used by anyone else pertaining to her. You've come a long way, lady, she told herself. A long way.

Despite the disappointment over the night, Lauren felt stronger than she had in days. She attacked the dreaded guarantee count she had been putting off all day. The job would not be nearly so tough if there were a method to the madness. If they had a form, something that could be done up on a weekly basis by taping dates.

Lauren began to draw lines on a sheet of paper. She could devise a form herself and have it printed up. It was such a simple idea, she wondered no one had bothered to do it before.

Paula dressed in slacks and low-heeled shoes for her date with Gil Richardson. They were driving down to Fisherman's Wharf at Redondo Beach for dinner and she was looking forward to a walk along the beach. She had not seen or smelled the ocean in a long time.

From now on, Friday night was going to be her night out, whether Joe was in or out of town. She did not intend to flaunt her lover in front of him as he flaunted Sue. She had come up with polite lies, because she did not care to discuss Gil with Joe.

She took a gray flannel jacket from her closet and checked herself again in the mirror. She liked the glow in her eyes and the softening effect it had on her face. She was not foolish enough to call what she had found with Gil love, not in the purest sense. But she felt a great deal of warmth for him and he was certainly sexually exciting. Not love perhaps, but there was a special kind of caring between them. It was enough, more than she had expected to find at her age.

She walked out into the living room where Joe was sitting with the morning issue of the *Times* and a drink. His jacket was off, though the inevitable bow tie was still clasped under his chin.

He glanced up and set his drink on the end table. "Are you going out?" he asked.

"Yes, I am," she replied without elaborating.

"Did I forget something?" he asked, obviously puzzled.

"No, Joe. It's just that I've come to a decision. I keep myself locked up here too much. I'm getting dull-minded. So I've decided I need to get out more. In fact, I'm going to make myself go out at least once a week, and Friday night seems best."

"When did all this come about?" Joe asked, his forehead wrinkling below his bald head.

"It came about because of my writing. What else? I've been getting bogged down too often lately. So tonight I'm having dinner with Germain Gips."

Joe looked at her skeptically. "That's still business, you know."

"Oh, I suppose that's right." She gave a deliberately casual wave of her hand. "Germain can't talk about anything but soaps. But it does mean getting out of the house. I'll go to a play or something next Friday. You know . . ." She tried to appear thoughtful. "I never see Marie Hodges any more. She used to be such fun."

"You and Marie?" Joe asked. "You're always putting her down for being a social climber."

"But I liked her in a way. And who better to get me back into some social situations?"

"I'll take you out," Joe offered. "Any time. You know that." There was a sincerity in his voice that momentarily surprised and pleased Paula. Then she thought of Sue.

"Do I?" Paula asked, her eyes and voice turning hard. "Aren't some of your weekends committed to Sue Bergman and Palm Springs?"

He flinched, then picked up his drink and stared down into it. "You know why I have Sue. She gives me what I can't get at home."

"Don't wait up for me," Paula ordered, as if speaking to the housekeeper. She turned on her heel and walked

353

out the door without calling down for her car. A faint sense of loss rode with her in the elevator. She had been so wrong to marry Joe Seals and she supposed it would end in divorce one day. The thought did not upset her. Divorce seemed inevitable. She was certain he would never leave her. Never. If the break was made it would be her doing, not Joe's.

Paula met Gil at his apartment in the Marina. Though they made no pretense about why they were together, they did not go straight to bed. Gil had martinis ready when she arrived. She would have preferred wine or sherry, but she knew she was a martini drinker in Gil's eyes and it was his way of trying to please her.

There were nuts and cocktail sausages on the coffee table in an attempt at appetizers. Paula was touched by the small gesture and dutifully dipped the sausages into the hot sauce provided.

Gil did not rush her off to bed as some men would who were involved in a clandestine relationship. He made love to her first with his eyes and his touch, in small ways meant to please her. She felt indulged, wanted and highly flattered.

They talked and touched and let themselves move to a sexual high that carried them into the bedroom. She gloried in the attention given to her body, which had gone so long without pleasure.

She enjoyed him as a male, taking delight in giving as well as taking. When they were finished Paula reached for the sheet to cover herself.

"Don't do that," Gil said.

"What?" she asked.

"Don't cover yourself?"

"Gil, please," she whispered, somehow ashamed. "I'm not young any more."

"That doesn't mean you should cover your body. It's beautiful."

She followed his gaze down over her naked flesh. She was not beautiful. Oh, the muscles were firm enough, thanks to her daily ritual of exercises. She was slim through careful eating, but she was not beautiful. Her skin was etched with the lines of aging. Gil had one leg resting over hers and she felt a sting of envy. The contrast was startling. He was tan and she was pale. His skin held the look of youth while she had passed over the line into old age. He looked—she searched for the right word. He looked *healthy*.

Healthy. What an odd thing to come up with, she thought. A pinpoint of panic hit her. "Let me up, Gil," she said. "I have to go to the bathroom."

She fled, aware of him watching her walk away nude. She wanted to run, but forced herself to walk into the bathroom, then closed the door firmly behind her.

The flourescent lighting was not kind. It emphasized every shadow and wrinkle and gave her carefully made-up face a grayish cast. She stared at herself. Earlier she had thought her skin seemed softer, but now under the harsh, unforgiving lighting she saw something else.

Gil looked healthy. She did not. Her color reminded her of someone else, someone ill, like Naomi. The realization hit her hard and she almost went down to her knees. Naomi had been like this when she first became ill, rather gray and drawn. Later Naomi's skin had become tinged with yellow, then turned patchy and scaly. But in the beginning, before she even knew she had cancer, she began to lose her natural color.

As if on cue, Paula's stomach began to hurt. It was a localized but intense pain at the point where her rib cage curved inward. She pressed back against it with her fingertips harder and harder until she was doubled over the sink and the pain she inflicted upon herself was stronger than the pain coming from inside.

She rose slowly and the pain was gone. It was nothing, she told herself, a stomach upset. She was not really sick, she was getting old and not liking it. She had always had a sensitive stomach, that was all. Didn't she have a yearly checkup, didn't her doctor tell her she was incredibly healthy for her age?

She took a careful breath and let her chest and stomach expand out, then slowly back in. It was okay, the pain was gone. She ran fingers over her face, as though smoothing on foundation.

Composed, Paula returned to the bedroom and said, "Let's go eat. I'm starved."

Gil grinned wickedly up at her from the bed where he still sprawled naked and uncovered. "You want to eat so soon after that bout? I'm not sure I can stand up yet. You are one hell of a woman, Paula Cavanaugh."

She was good in bed, she knew that. "Hand me my clothes, Gil."

He did not move and Paula glanced at his face. For just a second there was a strange expression in his eyes. A glitter of disgust? Something. But as quickly as it came it was gone and he cheerfully got out of bed and handed her the clothes.

She dressed quickly and they drove to Redondo Beach in her car. They had cocktails before they ordered dinner and Paula cautiously asked for sherry this time. Her stomach stayed steady.

Gil seemed to grow quieter throughout the meal until she finally made mention of it. "I don't think you're here with me," she said. "Is something wrong, Gil?"

"Oh, I'm sorry," he said, his gray eyes lifting to hers. "I'm afraid I was letting business intrude on my thoughts."

"Problems?" she asked.

"I'm not sure. The backers for the Canadian film are all lined up. It's in the hands of the lawyers now. But I'm not so sure about the building project. It looks shaky. My biggest investor is starting to fishtail on me. But that isn't your problem, Paula. That's mine, and we aren't business partners."

"I don't mind listening, if it will help."

"No, that's okay."

Curious, she leaned forward. "I'm truly interested," she said.

"Nope." He closed the subject with a wide grin. "No business. I'll handle this. I always do."

356

Do you? she wondered. You aren't really as prosperous as you would like to be. But then you don't pretend to be something you aren't, either. You're a hustler. Or was he? Maybe he was just a hardworking guy who had not gotten the breaks he needed, or maybe he didn't have what it took to aim for the top. He didn't seem to want a great deal beyond life's necessities.

Paula wanted to hear more, for the insight it would give her into him, but Gil was adamant about not discussing business over dinner and she had to let it drop.

After dinner, she had to order a soda and bitters. Gil was immediately concerned. "Are you feeling ill?" he asked.

"A little queasy. Too much rich food, I suppose," she said, glossing it over, but she was delighted by his concern.

The soda and bitters was placed before her. "Drink up," Gil urged.

She drank it down quickly. The release was immediate. It was as she had said, the seafood was too rich. "Let's walk along the beach," she suggested. "I've been thinking about doing that all day."

When they were outside on the wharf boardwalk, Gil put his arm around her waist.

She resisted the urge to run her fingers through his crisp, graying hair. He was handsome in spite of his uneven features, she decided. And his eyes—she could lose herself in the depth of those gray eyes.

She was overwhelmed by gratitude that he could care for her. She went into his arms and pressed her body against his. She raised her face and he kissed her. The kiss deepened until she was again raging with desire for this man who had appeared in her life so unexpectedly.

Chapter Thirty-Six

Lauren's mood worked itself up and down her internal emotional ladder. All day Saturday she hovered between joy, knowing she would be seeing Kerry that night, and despair because he had gone to the wedding without her.

It was Kerry's casual attitude that hurt the most. She could feel him slipping away from her, emotionally as well as physically. He was facing up to the end of their relationship, preparing himself for the inevitable break, and all his energy was geared toward New York and the play.

She wished she could be as strong and logical as Kerry. This misery seemed worse than the dissolution of her marriage. That had happened gradually. She had fallen out of love with Benji, and she wanted out of the marriage once she faced the reality of their insoluble problem. But this—a delicate shudder ran over her body. She loved Kerry and did not want to lose him. Depression clawed at her insides until she no longer cared if she functioned or not.

Lauren arrived at Kerry's apartment at eight sharp. She was surprised to find a car in the spot where she usually parked. Resentment washed over her even though she had no right to feel that way. After all, it was only street parking, open to everyone. But how quick we are to form habits, she thought. She pressed down hard on the gas pedal.

She circled the block, finding the streets lined with cars. The only break she found was two blocks away. She maneuvered into the spot, missed it the first time in her nervousness and had to do it all over again. She hurried up the dark tree-lined street, heels clicking on the concrete sidewalk.

She was breathless and trembling slightly when she knocked at Kerry's second-floor door. She was both eager and frightened, but determined to keep it cool as Sally had advised. If not cool, then at least she would look to Kerry and follow his head.

Clutching her handbag, she waited what seemed an endless span of time until Kerry opened the door. "Hi," she murmured, then hesitated until he held out his hand and welcomed her with a light kiss on the cheek.

He was bare-chested and wearing jeans, so that meant they would be staying home tonight. She held on tightly to his hand and followed him into the living room.

His hand loosened on hers and she moved in front of him. She touched his chest lightly with her fingertips. He's beautiful, she thought with an ache. It seemed necessary to memorize the look and feel of him, so she would have it to hold tightly in her heart when he was gone.

She leaned back slightly. "Oh," she said. "You've had your hair restyled."

"Oh, just cut for the wedding is all. It is a little shorter."

She rubbed her palms across his chest and curled her fingers into the dark hair. "I've missed you terribly," she whispered, forgetting her promise to follow his lead.

He took her into his arms and she sensed a certain reluctance on his part, but she ignored it and nestled against his body, wanting to be held forever where she could feel and hear his heart beating so close to hers.

"Have you eaten?" he asked, pulling away from her.

"Have you?" she asked back, not wanting to force him into anything.

"Oh, I'm not hungry," he murmured.

"I could scramble some eggs," she volunteered, a bright, unhealthy smile on her lips. "That would be light, and quick."

"No." He was moving away from her and she felt cold and lost. She suppressed the desire to fling herself at him.

"Could we have Capuccino?" she asked.

A frown creased his forehead. "Why? It's too warm tonight for a hot drink."

"I don't know," she murmured huskily, unable to look at him directly. He had forgotten that the first night she came to his apartment they had shared cups of Capuccino in front of the fireplace.

"Well," he said, shrugging a bare shoulder. "If that's what you want, I'll make it for you. I want something cold. It's getting to be gin and tonic weather."

"Then I'll have that, too," she said too quickly, trying to be agreeable.

Kerry scowled at her. "You're sure in a strange place tonight. Don't you know what you want?"

"I'm sorry." Her lips ached with the smile she forced.

Kerry stalked out and she sank down on the ledge in front of the fireplace. A blackened chunk of wood lay half off the grate, very dead and cold looking. The fireplace was sooty and looked desolate, deserted for the summer. Kerry had not bothered to clean it. It was as though he had forgotten it was there, cast it aside because it was no longer of use. It would never burn for her and Kerry again.

She pulled her knees up, crossed her arms over them and rested her head. Darn it, she was not going to cry! Not in front of Kerry, never again.

She slowly raised her head. Her eyes moved around the room that felt empty and lonely. She frowned in astonishment at the empty walls. "Kerry," she called. "Your paintings are gone!"

"Oh, yeah." He padded back in with a drink in each hand. "Joyce and Mickey are keeping them for me. They needed something for their walls."

"Oh." She wished he had asked her to keep them. It would have meant so much, a commitment to the future. She took the glass he offered and moved over, motioning for him to sit down beside her. But he was already moving to the far end of the sofa. He crossed one leg over the other and moved back, but he did not look very relaxed. The muscles in his chest were tense and his eyes avoided hers.

Lauren sipped her drink as the desperate craving to be near him returned. She loved him and she did not give her love lightly. He had known that from the beginning.

"Are you shipping your furniture to New York?" she asked, since he was making no effort at conversation.

"No," he said. "I'm selling it."

"Even the waterbed? You love that bed."

"I can always buy another," he said. "It's just a bed. I'm going to start out with a furnished place in New York, if I can find one. I heard the apartment situation is hell. I may have to stay in a hotel for a long time."

"I see." It hurt to think of his furniture going off to strangers, but that was his choice and she had no say in it. Unless . . . No, she wiped the thought away, the one that kept coming back to her again and again. The one that tormented her with its possibilities, the one she dared not ask.

"How was the wedding, Kerry?"

"Oh, okay. Mickey and Joyce seemed pleased."

"That's good. Where are they going for their honeymoon?"

"They couldn't afford one," he answered, then abruptly stood up. "I'm having another drink."

She had barely touched her own and his glass was empty. She lifted the glass and drank it down quickly, feeling the cold liquid hit her stomach and gradually change to a spreading warmth.

She hurried after Kerry. "Make me another drink, too?"

"Okay." He kept his back to her, and his attitude kept her from touching him physically again. He's hurting, too, she thought. It was the only answer for his behavior, for the distance he had put between them. I am selfish, she decided. I haven't considered how Kerry felt about leaving me, that he might be throwing up shields to protect himself from pain.

He dropped ice into the glasses. "You know Paula is cutting me off the show early. I only get next week when I could have done two more weeks."

"I know," Lauren answered miserably.

"Do you know why?" he asked, turning around and facing her.

"No. She hasn't confided in me. I suspect she's annoyed at losing you and Sally so close together."

"I'll bet," he sneered. "She's probably glad to see me go."

"Kerry, that's not true. She thinks you're a wonderful actor." She felt her cheeks go pink at the lie.

"Oh, yeah? I never saw any sign of it." Lauren shrugged. What could she say when Kerry was speaking the truth? He went on. "Paula is punishing the bad little boy, isn't she?" His gaze was belligerent and accusing.

"I have no control over Paula," Lauren said stiffly.

"So I've noticed," he muttered and walked out of the room, leaving her freshly made drink on the counter. She picked it up, swallowed half of it down and replaced it with straight gin. She added just a splash more of tonic water.

Lauren trailed back into the living room and sat down on the opposite end of the sofa from Kerry. He drank silently, and so did she until her glass was empty and the silence unbearable.

"Are you angry with me?" she finally asked, trying to

be careful with her words, aching all the while because she needed him so.

"Not really," he replied, his face closed.

"Then what's wrong? I feel so far away from you and I want to be close, Kerry. As close as possible for as long as possible."

His dark eyes dropped away from hers. "I'm sorry, Lauren. I'm in a mood. Come here." He patted the back of the sofa.

She scooted down next to him and nestled against him, her breasts pressing against his chest, her lips eager for his kisses. He closed his eyes and kissed her gently. "Love me," she whispered intensely. "Please love me."

He smiled, his eyes flickering now. "Once you got turned on to sex you sure did take to it, huh?"

The remark was cold, almost cruel, but she ignored it, intent only on the nearness of him, on the deepening yearnings of her mind and body.

His lips sought hers again, hard and demanding this time in their force. She gasped as one hand clamped over her breast and squeezed too tightly.

"You're hurting me," she whimpered against his mouth.

"Don't pull away." He urged her back with his hands. She yielded and tightened her arms around him, letting her nails dig into his back.

"Stand up," he said suddenly and physically moved her with his hands. She stood and swayed slightly from the effects of the gin. Her head was spinning and her body was alive, vibrating with yearnings and love. She closed her eyes and he stripped her quickly and rudely out of her clothes.

His hands disappeared from her body and she opened her eyes. He was stepping out of his jeans, his back to her. She remembered that Sally thought he had a cute behind. He did, very firm and nicely rounded. She moved up behind him and went back into his arms as he turned.

"Come on down," he whispered and she dropped to

her knees. Then he pressed her backward onto the floor and entered her without gentleness. She whimpered and moaned underneath him, desperately wanting her own release, but deferring to him and the hard quick thrusts that pounded her against the floor.

Abruptly he stopped and she felt him start to move away. She locked her arms around him. Dizzy, she began to nibble at his ear and wished there was a way to bind him to her forever, to somehow always hold a little piece of each other.

"Kerry. Kerry," she moaned. "Take me with you."

He stilled, his body becoming rigid. "What?"

Her eyes popped open, her heart sinking. She had sworn to herself that she would never ask it. The idea had tormented her and she had thought she would overcome it until now. She looked up into his face and said it again. "Take me with you to New York."

He planted a hand on each side of her and came off her with a push up, landing lightly at her left side.

Cold air washed across her body. God, what had she done? She had wanted to ask, but she had never meant to say the words aloud. Never.

He stood over her, his feet planted wide apart, hands on his hips. His brown eyes narrowed into slits. "Just who in the hell do you think you are?" he asked harshly.

"Kerry." She tried to scramble up. Her head spun and she only made it to her knees. "I'm sorry," she said. "I'm drunk. I'm so sorry."

He was looking down at her as though she was the lowest creature on the face of the earth. "Kerry, I'm sorry. I didn't mean it. It just popped out. I . . ." She gestured wildly, knowing she was babbling, unable to control it.

"I think you'd better face some facts, Lauren. Ones you've conveniently ignored." He grabbed her arms, lifted her to her feet and deposited her on the sofa. She cowered, rubbing her hands across where he had held her too tightly.

He yanked on his jeans and all she could do was sit, pulling her feet under her and keeping her arms crossed over her breasts.

"I have never said I loved you," he spat at her as he zipped his jeans. "And I have avoided letting you say it to me."

"I know, your career," she said, her eyes burning with unshed tears. "But you do care for me. I know you do." He didn't respond. Her heart constricted into a hard lump. "You do love me!" she cried.

"Shit!" He ran his hand across his face, which was distorted into something or someone she did not know. "Shit!" he repeated, taking two steps away, then back to her. "Hey, I guess I care. I never wanted to hurt you, Lauren. And I've tried to let our affair, our relationship, taper off. But you wouldn't go away quietly."

"Is that what you've been doing to me?"

"Yeah. You're slow, but you catch on now, huh?" he asked, loathing making his voice thick and brutal.

She hung her head. She had no pride left now. It was pointless to pretend otherwise. "But I love you," she whispered. "I don't want to lose you."

"Tough." He was being cruel, but she did not care. It would not matter if he was cruel now if he would change his mind later. "Do you know why I started seeing you, why I came on to you?"

"No." She shook her head, instinctively drawing farther away from him.

"Because you and Sally led me to believe you had some influence with the Witch."

"Oh, no," she breathed, her mind flashing back. She had let that happen knowingly and it had seemed harmless enough at the time. It was Sally's doing, but she never denied any of it. "Was that so awful?" she asked. "Didn't we have something? Didn't what we found together erase that?"

His dark eyes raked over her face. "No, it doesn't erase it at all. But that wasn't all, either." There was a certain plea for understanding in his voice. "You're beautiful, Lauren. There's no denying that, and you were damn sure intriguing. There's not many women your age who are so naive, so unawakened. That was exciting."

Like a rag doll incapable of defense, she became smaller, drawing her arms tighter over her bare breasts, hunching her shoulders. "And that's all it was for you?"

"That's all," he said, with a certain amount of kindness now that she seemed to understand. "It was fun for a while, but it hasn't been lately. We would have broken up whether I left or not. I'd hoped that me going to New York would ease it off slowly."

"Go away," she begged. She wanted to cover herself, she wanted to hide. She held back a sob that made her chest ache. She had never felt so used, or so small in pride.

"Get dressed," he said. "I won't come back in here until you're gone."

He walked away down the hall, taking with him the last shreds of hope. Shaking violently, she dressed hurriedly, then picked up her shoes. She could not get a foot into either of them. With a sob she threw them aside, grabbed her purse and ran from the apartment.

She stumbled down the stairs, grasping the iron railing until she was on the street. Then she ran barefoot over the sidewalk until something, a branch or stick, caught her foot. She fell hard, landing on knees and palms. She sprawled, gulping in air, then got up and continued on to the car. She fumbled in her purse for the keys, somehow got them out and unlocked the door. She collapsed inside.

Lauren lay down across the seat, consumed with searing flames of pain. She cried helplessly, giving in to the great aching sobs that wrenched from her chest until there was nothing left but a dry barren emptiness. Still, she lay there. "What's wrong with me?" she asked aloud. She had thought she was a woman. "I'm not! I couldn't please Benji or Kerry."

Lauren remained in the car most of the night, occasionally dozing off only to awaken again and cry. Toward dawn, when the sky began to turn from black to gray, with what seemed like the last parcel of her energy, she searched for the keys and found them on the floor.

She drove back toward the Valley slowly.

Chapter Thirty-Seven

Sally awoke suddenly. She sat up and listened, but the apartment was silent. The room was filled with soft gray morning light. She checked the clock; it was shortly after six. Sally yawned and slid back under the covers, feeling warm and cuddly and deliciously excited. Her plane did not leave until two, so it was still eight hours until she would be flying to New York.

Another sound brought Sally rigidly alert. "Lauren?" she called softly and listened for an answer. None came. She pushed back the covers and tiptoed to the door. "Lauren?" she called again.

"I—I'm home," came a feeble reply.

Sally rushed down the short hallway to the living room. Lauren was huddled on the sofa. Scraped knees were exposed beneath a torn and dirty skirt. The matching blouse was buttoned crookedly and out of the skirt. Lauren's hair was a mess and there was a dull look to her features.

"My God!" Sally cried and rushed to her. "Did you have a wreck?"

"A wreck?" Lauren looked puzzled as Sally pushed the hair back from her face.

"You're hurt," Sally said, taking Lauren's hands. They were cut and torn. "What happened?"

Lauren's faded eyes moved from her hands to across the room. "I fell down."

"Oh," Sally cried with a sinking heart. "Did Kerry beat you up? If he did, I'll—"

"No, no. I fell down." She repeated the words like a small child. She raised red-rimmed and swollen eyes to Sally's face. "He doesn't love me."

Sally sucked in air between clenched teeth. She thought that had been obvious from the beginning. "Let's get you cleaned up," she said gently, with pity. "Come on."

Sally coaxed Lauren to her feet. She followed Sally docilely to the bathroom where Sally turned on the hot water full force. Lauren stood mute and let Sally undress her.

"You should have called me," Sally rebuked her. "How did you get home?"

"I—I just drove," Lauren answered vaguely. An ominous coldness ran down Sally's back. Lauren was being downright creepy. Sally turned off the hot water and switched on the cold, then mixed the water until the temperature was tolerable.

"Here." Sally helped Lauren into the tub. Lauren shuddered once at the first shock of the hot water, then slid dutifully down into the tub. Sally washed her knees and hands gently. With the blood and dirt gone, they were not so bad, just scraped.

Sally let her eyes roam over Lauren's body, inspecting her. "My God," she said. "Your arms are bruised."

Lauren's dull eyes looked from one arm to the other, then covered the bruises with her hands. "Kerry grabbed me," she explained. "He threw me on the sofa."

Angry, Sally gave a small cry. "Then he did beat you up, the no good son—"

"No! No, I fell, he, he . . ." Lauren's voice trailed off and silent tears slid down her cheeks.

"You poor kid," Sally murmured, hurting for

Lauren. She had warned her to play it cool; obviously she had not. Dumb, yes. But also sad.

Sally scrubbed Lauren's back because she thought it would make her feel better, then ordered Lauren to sink down into the tub to soak while she washed the splotchy face.

Sally helped Lauren out of the tub and dried the slumped body. For a moment, she felt envious of the full breasts that were beaded with water, while she was left with scars and sagging skin. She wrapped a towel around Lauren, then sat her down on the toilet lid. Sally found a brown bottle of peroxide and poured the liquid over Lauren's knees and hands. Lauren did not even flinch.

Instinctively knowing it was useless to try to pry any information out of Lauren, Sally got a warm gown on Lauren and tucked her into bed. "Sleep now," she whispered, tucking the covers up under the woman's chin.

"The plane, your flight," Lauren murmured with some resemblence of reality.

"That isn't for hours. You just sleep for a while. You'll feel all better when you wake up."

Lauren tossed her head restlessly back and forth over the pillow.

"Hush, now," Sally ordered. "Hush, and sleep. You'll be okay when you wake up. It will all be okay."

Sally stayed with Lauren until the woman fell into a fretful sleep. She was furious with Kerry, with Lauren and with herself. She threw the pillows on the bed and smacked them down hard with the palms of her hands, knowing she had to share some of the blame. Lauren had only done good for her, and she had encouraged Lauren to see Kerry. She had gotten Lauren mixed up with Kerry. She had known Kerry thought he was God's gift to women and had about as much depth as a rat. But she had still liked Kerry as a friend and coworker, she had enjoyed him and accepted him for what he was. So why couldn't Lauren do the same thing? Why did she have to get all mushy and moony about him? Why couldn't they all have gone on being friends? Why did life have to get so complicated, and why did you have to split your loyalties?

She nudged a platform shoe under the bed with her toe, calmer now. This was supposed to be a happy day, maybe the happiest of her life. She reached for the remains of last night's dope. About half of the flattened Zig-Zag rolled joint was left. She held it between her fingers over a match flame, rolling it back and forth until it caught.

She flopped back on the bed and brought the joint to her lips. She inhaled, sucking the smoke deeper and deeper into her lungs, then held it as long as she could. She let the smoke out slowly through her nose. It was good for three tokes. She saved the end, carefully extinguishing the fire. The last portion was good for putting into the end of a regular cigarette. Jake used to call them cocktails.

She lay back on the bed, letting the anger slowly seep away as the grass took effect. Gradually the world of slow motion took over, a nice world where nothing ever happened too fast.

Sally snuggled down, pulled the bedspread up over her and eventually dozed off. When she awoke she was still on a small high. She smoothed out the bedspread, then checked on Lauren, who was sleeping heavily. For the tenth time, Sally checked the contents of her packed bags. There was nothing left to do now but gather up the bathroom things and put them into the overnight bag. The leather suit with matching boots hung ready to wear in her closet.

With nothing better to do, Sally decided to clean the place. So for the next two hours, she devoted herself to dusting, sweeping, mopping and scrubbing down the bathroom.

At eleven-thirty, Sally leaned over Lauren, who was drawn up into a tight fetal position. "Time to get up," she whispered, "I want to leave for the airport in an hour."

"Get up?" Lauren stretched out full length. "Oh." Realization hit hard, turning the green eyes into pain-filled orbs. She moaned and turned over to hide her face in the pillow. "Oh, Sally!"

Sally touched her shoulder. "You okay now?" she asked.

"No," came the muffled reply.

"But you'll live," Sally said cheerfully. "Come on now. Sit up. Do you remember coming home?"

She turned slowly and faced Sally. "I remember." The green eyes were dull now, the lids swollen almost shut.

"Come on," Sally urged. "It's a beautiful day. Lots of sunshine."

"Is it?" Lauren, moving like a palsied old woman, got her feet off the side of the bed. "I ache all over," she complained vaguely.

"Why don't you have another hot bath?" Sally suggested. "And I'll make us some real coffee and maybe an omelette."

"Thanks." Lauren smiled weakly. She sank into a chair and slumped over the table.

Sally served the toast and eggs and pushed Lauren's plate in front of her. "Eat. You'll feel better."

Lauren played with the fork. "Why doesn't he love me?" she asked, childlike.

Sally shrugged. "Oh, I guess because Kerry isn't the type to love any woman."

"That's not the reason," Lauren said. "There's something wrong with me."

"No, there's not," Sally insisted. "That's not true at all."

Lauren stared at her fork. "It must be me. I failed Benji. Now I've failed Kerry."

"No," Sally corrected, though she did not believe Lauren was free of blame. "You managed to latch onto two losers. It's them, Lauren. Not you."

Lauren shook her head. "No, it's me," she said resolutely.

Sally had enough. "Okay, goddamn it!" she growled, making Lauren's head snap back in shock. "You weren't willing to settle for what Kerry offered, which was friendship and fun and games. You wanted too much from him, you wanted more than he could give!"

"I—I don't know how to . . ." Lauren groped for words that refused to come.

"Well, you are damn well going to have to learn how to play for fun. Sex is great, but it's not . . ." Sally's young face formed a grimace as she searched for an explanation. "Look, it's like this. Just because a guy sleeps with you doesn't mean he's going to marry you, or even love you. You're still living in the dark ages. You've got to get out in the light and get over this peculiar hang-up of yours!"

"Peculiar?" Lauren laughed hollowly. "Peculiar. Oh, Sally, am I peculiar?"

"Yes!" Sally answered emphatically. "Yes, you sure are!"

"Then I'll have to learn to do it your way," Lauren said.

Sally didn't think she meant it; those green eyes were still filled with self-doubt. Sally leaned over and touched Lauren's hand. "Hey, you're a beautiful woman, Lauren. Very warm and very loving. One day you'll find the right kind of man for you, a guy like you want. Maybe my way isn't so great. It's okay for me, but maybe it isn't for you."

"I'm going to figure life out one day," Lauren said. "And maybe myself."

"Sure you will. Now eat."

Sally cleaned her plate, then finished off Lauren's as well. She dumped the dirty dishes in the sink and hurried them both around. This was one time she was not going to be late. Planes did not wait.

All effects of the grass were gone now. Sally's excitement, mixed with apprehension, grew until she was

374

ready to burst with it. "What's it like on a plane?" she asked Lauren as they moved toward the TWA gate.

"I don't know," Lauren admitted. "I've never flown."

Sally giggled nervously. "Really modern and with it, aren't we?"

"I guess it's just like in the movies," Lauren said.

"Oh, Lauren!" Sally squeezed her hands together. "I wish you were going with me. I'm going to blow it, I just know I am."

"No, you're not," Lauren said, more of her old self now. "Think before you act. Think!"

"I'll try." They were at the gate. Sally threw her arms around Lauren in a tight hug. "Take care of yourself, Lauren. Don't be so hard on yourself. I'll call you, and I'll be home Friday."

"I know," Lauren said. "I have the time and the flight written down, and I'll be here."

They hugged again, then Sally broke the embrace and walked away, feeling Lauren's eyes on her. She paused at the entrance to the tunnel. Lauren was turning away, one hand up to shield her face. She's crying again, Sally thought. She's frightened, and I shouldn't be leaving her. She hesitated. She had to go; this was her point of no return.

"Here I come," she whispered, then disappeared from view down the tunnel, her eyes darting ahead to take in this new adventure.

Chapter Thirty-Eight

Lee Trent clutched a glass of straight scotch. It was his second of the afternoon, because the first had not dulled the gnawing ache in his guts. He glanced at the antique clock over the built-in bar. It was approaching two-thirty. If Reenie was going to appear today she would be arriving soon. He never knew when she would choose to show up without warning on the days he was not taping.

Every time it happened with her he swore he would throw her out on her nicely rounded ass the next time. Only they always ended up in bed or on the floor or sofa, any place she could take him.

He knew he was the one being taken; there was no kidding himself about that. Reenie was an aggressive, demanding and stubborn pursuer, a witch who mesmerized him, who made him lose all sense of right and wrong.

He paced uneasily through the two-story town house he had bought three years before. The place was meant for a family, not a bachelor, and he had bought it as an investment. Three of the four bedrooms were closed off and empty. He had meant to hold the unit for a couple of years and sell it, but it was a comfortable place and it was so easy to pay the monthly maintenance fee and not be bothered with such things as yard work and repairs. The kidney-shaped pool was always clean and warm. There was a gym where he worked out a couple of times a week as well as a Jacuzzi and sauna. Trapped by his own comfort, he stayed on, though he could have taken an easy twenty-thousand-dollar profit and bought a smaller place.

He should sell now, he though, and move as far away from Encino and Anne and Reenie as possible. He could live in an apartment in West Hollywood or buy out in Upland, which was supposed to be a booming area. It would be a logical investment, but he would have a hell of a time explaining to Anne, who was still living with the illusion of an upcoming wedding.

It was not going to happen; it was just that he had not figured out a way around it yet. If only they weren't on *Dreams* together, if only Anne wasn't the most popular character on the show. If she would find someone else. If, if . . . He had played all the ifs over a dozen times in his mind, until he felt as though he was going crazy.

All he could do for now was keep it drifting until Anne began to lose interest. And there had not been one single sign of that yet.

There was another alternative—he could leave the show. He might *have* to leave the show if he broke it off with Anne. The thought made sweat pop out on his forehead. It was downright terrifying to consider, for he liked being Dr. John Reese, liked being set in a very safe and secure job.

Lee Trent did not want to go back to nagging his agent for parts, back to pounding the sidewalks for work, prostituting himself by being nice to every casting director in town. He was making seventy-five thousand dollars a year on *Dreams,* a very comfortable amount of money that gave him just about everything he wanted.

Lee did not consider himself a man who wanted a lot out of life. He enjoyed the usual amenities, like having a nice place to live and being able to buy good clothes.

Though Lee seldom admitted it to himself, he was a man who followed the line of least resistance, and mostly he just wanted to be left alone. He did not want his life messed up with a lot of complications.

He finished his drink and glanced at the clock again. It was a beauty, and he had had to pay top dollar for it, but it was worth it, as were the other antiques he had spent so many hours collecting.

It was getting late. Reenie must not be coming, thank God. Yet there was the faintest little twinge of disappointment. He set his glass down on the bar and went back to the bedroom where he changed into a black swimsuit.

He stood in front of the full-length mirrors that covered the sliding closet doors. His tummy was getting bigger. He could not deny that any longer. It was the booze, damn it. He was not eating any more than usual; well, maybe a little. He had been so jittery lately with Anne and Reenie both springing on him at the most unexpected times.

He studied his body. He was tanned and virile still, the face was good, except for . . . He leaned in closer. Except for the hint of a sag under the jawline. He was buying too much of his food at the nearby deli and that had to stop. It was time to get back to steak and fresh vegetables again. No more hard rolls, no more garlic toast, no bagels and cream cheese. And definitely no more hot flour tortillas dripping with butter and stuffed with Monterey Jack cheese.

Saliva filled his mouth and his stomach growled. No, he could not be hungry; he had had lunch, breakfast. He patted his stomach into silence, then went to get a towel from the bathroom.

He was in the hall when the doorbell chimed. He stiffened, trying to ignore it. She would go away, he told himself, but he knew she would not. Once Reenie camped on his doorstep for an hour, until he was certain all the neighbors were aware of her presence.

She would stay out there and ring the doorbell with

her school books clutched to that magnificent firm chest. He crept silently over the dark shag carpeting and into the living room. The drapes were open, Reenie was peering in. He jumped back, but it was too late. She had seen him and she was waving coy fingers at him.

He threw the towel onto the bar beside the next day's script and went angrily to the door. He opened the door and glared at her. "What are you doing here?" he demanded.

She ignored the question and walked on in, saying, "Hi, lover." She dropped her school books on the entry table, smiled lazily up at him and said, "Aren't you glad to see me?"

He tore his eyes off her chest. She was wearing a thin white T-shirt and no bra; her hardened nipples poked provocatively against the fabric, causing a reaction in his groin. Young girls should not be allowed to dress like that. They were asking for it. Such sights had a way of turning a man's mind into mush. It made it damned hard for a guy to think.

She started toward him and he turned away. She came on, hurrying behind him and putting her arms around his waist. He ordered his heartbeat to slow, commanded the warmth in his groin to grow cold.

"Reenie." He pushed futilely against her arms, aware of the smoothness of her skin, of her breasts pressing against his back.

She dug her clenched hands into his belly. "I love you, Lee Trent," she whispered, her breath warm on his flesh.

"Reenie!" His heart pounded like a jack hammer. "Go away, damn it. I don't want this."

She rubbed her cheeks against his bare back. "I do love you."

"You're a fourteen-year-old kid," he snorted. "You don't know about love."

"I know plenty!" she said, laughing deep in her throat. "Don't I, lover?"

Lee got both hands around her wrists and forced her

arms away. "You know about sex," he muttered, breathing a little too hard.

"I surely do," she taunted, swaying gently back and forth in front of him. "I've been thinking about you all day long." She ran her tongue over her lips.

He turned away and headed for the bar. Reenie followed him, asking, "Can I have a drink, too?"

"No," he snapped. "You're too young to drink."

"But you're practically my father. Kids can have drinks if their fathers give it to them."

"I am *not* your father!" he insisted.

"Please," she begged, pouting prettily, more child than woman now, a kid. The abrupt changes she made back and forth kept him constantly off balance.

"No."

"Oh, be that way then!" She ran silky fingertips over the flesh just above the waistband of his low-cut trunks.

"Stay away from me," he growled.

She tossed her head. "No! You can't tell me everything to do."

"Reenie."

"Reenie!" she mimicked and formed her lips into a pucker. "You like it, you want it as bad as I do."

Lee threw up his hands. "You're too young, you're Anne's daughter."

"Oh, pooh!" Childlike again, she stamped her foot. "You say the same things every time. Why don't you come up with a new argument?"

"Reenie. Oh, God!" He was choking, his temples pounding. She took a step back, reached down with both hands and gripped her T-shirt, then stripped it quickly up over the top of her head.

"Put it back on!" he gasped, sweat beading on his forehead as the warmth in his loins grew.

"No!"

His eyes riveted on the lush globes, the hard pink nipples surrounded by a brown areola.

She cupped one breast and jiggled it. "Want a taste?"

"No!" He yanked his eyes off her breast, wishing the

tempest would leave him in peace. "Put your shirt back on."

Instead, her hands moved to the front closure of the thirty-dollar French jeans Anne had supplied for her.

"Don't!" He grabbed her arm. She stood still, gazing up at him with the magnetic violet eyes of her mother, eyes that drew him in. With her free hand she rubbed the front of his trunks.

"The evidence is in," she said with a smug pleased smile. "You want me, don't you?"

"Reenie," he begged. "Please don't."

She pressed her bare breasts up against his chest, matching her strength against his, never taking her eyes off him.

"Reenie," he whimpered in the back of his throat. "Reenie."

"Lee!" She parted her lips and held her face up to his, her eyes daring him.

"Oh, damn," he groaned. His hand released her arm and encircled her waist. Their lips met in a fiery kiss and he felt Reenie's hands working under the band of his trunks.

Reenie sagged to the floor, whispering his name over and over and pulling him down on top of her. Her lips found his and her tongue darted into his mouth. Lee was lost completely by then. Nothing mattered but the pulsating need that blocked out all reality. There was only this moment in time, only this young, sensuous, demanding body under his.

An hour later, Reenie was gone and Lee was soaking in the Jacuzzi by the pool, damning himself for his weakness. Next time, he vowed, next time I just won't let her in.

He was not a man to examine himself or his motives. He considered himself an easygoing fellow, a good Joe who worked hard and did not fight life, but flowed with it. He generally got on well enough with whatever people were around.

What he could not figure out was how or why his life

382

had gotten so complicated. Becoming Anne's lover on *Dreams* had flowed naturally enough into a real affair that had nicely satisfied his needs. Somehow it had gotten all messed up, and now mother and daughter seemed determined to take over his life, to possess him, to swallow him whole into their own plans.

Behind closed eyes, Lee tried to fathom what had happened to his well-ordered life. It was that damned show, of course. He wished the Witch would start throwing rocks into the love affair. Or better yet, let Anne's character fall in love with someone else. But that was not going to happen. It was essential to keep a set of star-crossed lovers on the show. It was part of the unwritten Bible of every soap; one set of star-crossed lovers was the number-one requirement.

Lee adjusted his back against the hard-gushing water and lifted his face up to the sun. It would not do to have an uneven tan, certainly not one with white crevices in the wrinkle lines.

Lee was hungry again, but too exhausted from the session with Reenie to worry much about it. She had drained him, taking every ounce of strength he had to give. He did not need to eat again anyway, he had to get back on his diet. Even Bob Silverstein, who certainly did not worry about his own waistline, had dropped a gentle hint that Lee should watch it.

"Yoo hoo," came a female voice calling.

"Oh, damn!" Lee kept still, not opening his eyes. It was Anne. Nobody else in the world called "yoo hoo." "Goddamn it," he muttered. He was going to be in trouble if Anne was looking for a roll in the hay. There was no way he would be able to perform again so soon.

He opened his eyes as Anne's footsteps neared. He raised himself up out of the Jacuzzi and sat on the edge, dripping. "Darling!" Out of guilt, he greeted her profusely, accepting a kiss and apologizing for being wet.

"I just had to come straight over," she gushed. "I know how you feel about people not calling you first, but then I'm not people, am I, Lee?"

"No, darling." The thought of her showing up unannounced when Reenie was there made him feel as though he were turning a sickish green.

"Lee, I have such a marvelous idea!" She smiled happily at him. He knew the violet eyes were glowing behind the oversized sunglasses. Tiny diamond chips spelled out her initials in one corner. He hated those sunglasses; they looked gaudy and cheap.

"Oh." She looked up at the sun. "It's so hot out here. Let's go inside. My, do you realize it's almost July? Where has the time gone?"

"I don't know," Lee said dryly. He stood on legs that still felt a little shaky.

She walked in front of him toward his town house. She was wearing a pale blue T-shirt and patchwork jeans that would have been better suited to Reenie. A floppy white hat hid her hair.

She glanced back at him. "I just can't wait to tell you, Lee. I'm about to bust."

"Don't bust yet," he said. "I'm freezing." The wind was cold against his body after being in the overheated water. He toweled himself dry as they walked down the path beside a pump-fed stream strewn with fake boulders and rocks. The two-story Spanish buildings rose up on both sides of them, creating a canyon dotted with hanging pots and manicured shrubs. Sometimes the place reminded Lee of Disneyland or a movie set; all they needed was a carousel to go with the redwood gazebo and maybe an ice-cream stand by the pool.

They moved up a short stretch of steps, across his private patio and into the house. "Drink?" Lee asked. He had a feeling he was going to need one.

"No, yes. Maybe some wine." She discarded her hat and glasses and gazed at him lovingly, as though for a camera take. She ruffled her hair. "I have just the most perfect answer to our problem, Lee."

"Problem?" His eyes avoided hers and he busied himself at the bar. "Have you studied the script for tomorrow? I don't like that last scene. It's awkward. I think the Witch is losing her touch."

"Oh, I don't want to talk about that," she cried, making Lee realize for the first time what it was about her that irritated him most. She had a slight tendency to lisp her words when excited. "I mean, I do," she rushed on. "I do want to talk about Paula and the show, but not about tomorrow's script. It's really the most marvelous idea I have, and we'll be the most talked about couple of daytime television."

Lee gave up, knowing he might as well hear it. "And just how are we going to accomplish this magnificent feat?" he asked.

"Well . . ." She repositioned herself prettily on the sofa. "I know Bob is going to love it. "He'll just love it! You know the ratings are getting worse. At least they're not rising. The show needs a jolt."

Lee carried the scotch and wine over to the low-slung sofa. He sank down on the floor, not wanting to get a wet spot on the fabric. "What in the hell are you talking about?"

"Our wedding! What else?" She blinked at him. "Lee, what else could I possibly be this excited about?"

There was a sinking feeling in the pit of his stomach. "Not much else, I guess." He stared gloomily into his drink.

She sipped primly at the wine and plunged the glass down on the table. Lee flinched as the wine sloshed over on the delicate rosewood. He reached over and set her glass on a coaster.

"Now, Lee."

"Yes?" He reached across her and mopped up the wine with his towel.

"Lee, are you listening?" she demanded.

"Sure I am." The plumeria-blossom perfume she wore assailed his nostrils. How could she stand smelling so sweet? How had he tolerated her this long?

"Then look at me, pay attention," she said. "This is going to knock your socks off."

"I'm barefooted."

"Oh, you're being silly now," she giggled. It was a high, rasping sound that grated on his nerves. "It's an expression."

"No kidding," he said dryly.

She giggled again. "Lee, you're so silly. Well, now . . ." She paused to reposition herself again. "I've decided we will get married on the show!"

A swallow of scotch hung in Lee's throat. He nearly choked. "The show!" he finally gasped. "You mean you want our characters married?"

"Yes, and us, too. See, we'll use a real minister and we'll have our license. It will be a legal ceremony and I guess we'll have to use our real names, but the viewers will understand that."

Lee stared at her. "You're out of your mind," he said.

"Lee, I'm not! Bob will go for it. I just know he will."

"But—but we're the show's star-crossed lovers."

"Well, they can develop somebody else for that."

"The Witch will never stand for it. You know how protective she is and how she feels about actors."

"Oh, fah on Paula Cavanaugh. Bob can make her do anything he likes, and he'll like this. It will yank the ratings sky high."

"Darling," Lee hedged. "I think we should think this through."

She fluttered long black lashes at him. "I already have. I've got an appointment with Bob on Tuesday."

Lee stared at her. He had underestimated Anne Voll after all. She *was* capable of an original idea.

386

Chapter Thirty-Nine

Lee Trent was miserable. He had taken Anne away from the studio for lunch, hoping to talk her out of the absurd wedding idea she planned to discuss with Silverstein the next day.

He did not feel he could declare outright his refusal to marry her, so he took the angle that marriage was sacred and to do it on nationwide TV would turn it into a mockery.

Anne gazed at him sweetly over her salad. "Why, Lee," she said. "How sweet and old-fashioned you are."

She was touched, Lee thought, and he groaned. "Anne, please listen to me."

She didn't listen, she was too intent on her own motives. She wanted all the attention the publicity would bring, she wanted a shining moment when she could be the center of *Dreams*. The only promise Lee could extract from her was to keep it between the two of them until she talked to Bob Silverstein. He hoped Bob would shoot the idea down.

Lee returned to the studio, feeling sluggish from gulping down too much food and drink. Dress rehearsal went badly for him; he fluffed his lines twice and was relying heavily on the TelePrompTer.

Normally at dress rehearsal the show magically came

together. The sound effects, doorbells and ringing of telephones and such, were in use for the first time. The performers gave their lines without referring to scripts. By dress rehearsal the cameras were positioned and there were no more screams to raise and lower booms.

Lee glanced toward the control booth where today's director, Sid, was monitoring the show. Lee could see Sid's assistant taking notes, all meant for him, Lee was certain.

Lee adjusted his tie and buttoned the white medical jacket, readying himself mentally for the next scene. His eyes strayed back to Sid in the booth. Sid had a stopwatch in his hand. Every second was critical now, and they had to watch for signals to stretch or chop their scenes.

The scene on the next set was drawing to a close. Lee moved to the center of his "office" in the Maple Falls Hospital. A camera moved in on him, its red light out. Lee dropped his head and closed his eyes to ready himself. It was a method he had taken to using many years ago and it seldom failed him. He tried to envision the lines, but they were not there. Panicked, he searched frantically. Where was the TelePrompTer? There!

"Fade out," came Sid's voice and the light on Lee's camera went on, moving in on him, nearer and nearer until the merciless camera was in for a relentless close-up a bare foot away from his face as he studied a patient's chart.

He couldn't let anything on his face show except concern for his patient. Worried concern. Lee worried; it was not a difficult feat for him today. There was a knock at his office door and Lee looked up. "Come in," he said.

Anne, as an overdressed Lily, came in slowly. They were supposed to be ill at ease with each other because of a misunderstanding from last Thursday's show. He wanted to smack her or shake some sense into her, but the script called for him to take her hands in his and apologize. The words nearly gagged him and he fluffed the third line. Anne's eyes widened for just a moment, then she picked up and quickly glossed it over. He knew Sid was going crazy in the control booth. He could all but see Sid waving his hands in wild exasperation. Sid was always overreacting about something.

When the second dress rehearsal was over, Sid herded them all into the makeup room for a conference. "What in hell is wrong with you?" he demanded of Lee. "Your timing is crummy and you're throwing everyone else off. My God, man, didn't you read your script last night?"

"Sorry," Lee murmured. "I'll be all right."

"You damned well better be all right!" Sid turned on Cobb Strong. "Let's get some more emotion into your first scene. You're underplaying."

"You're right," Cobb said and nodded. Lee ground his teeth. Cobb was always so damned agreeable, never causing any trouble, always easygoing and affable. Normally it was a trait Lee admired, but today it annoyed the hell out of him.

"Rose." Sid turned to Rose Jardine. "You're off your mark in the hospital corridor scene. You're blocking the camera view of Maurice when the elevator opens. Move to the right."

The rest of the conference was quiet and friendly enough. Rose would not deliberately block out Maurice. No one on the show would sink to such juvenile tricks. For all of them it was the total show that counted.

Lee reminded himself that he was a professional, and being a pro was all that counted here. He wiped everything from his mind but the show and his lines and movements. Somehow the taping came off without a hitch on his part.

Lee wanted to go straight home, fix himself a scotch and relax in the Jacuzzi, but that was impossible. He had driven Anne in this morning so he could keep an eye on her. Now he had to drive her back home and find a way out of this insanity.

They were barely in the car when Anne brought the

subject up again. "What do you think I should wear tomorrow for my appointment with Bob?" she asked. "Would a white dress be too obvious?"

"A bit," he answered sourly.

"I guess so." Anne examined perfectly manicured nails. "But this white dress I bought is just perfect. It's eyelet. I feel about sixteen in it. Lee, why don't you go with me tomorrow?"

"No."

"Lee." She scooted over next to him as he braked for a traffic light. "Please go with me."

"No." He wanted to push her away. Her fingertips were like the cups on an octopus leg, sucking at his flesh. Or was it octopus arms? Or neither? A shudder ran over his body. "Come on, honey," he said impatiently. "I'm driving."

"Oh, pooh," she said, sounding like Reenie. She slid away from him. A car honked behind them and Lee threw the car into gear and took off with a jerk. "Lee, why are you being so mean to me?"

"Because you pushed me into it."

"Lee!" she whined. "Lee, it will be so nice. You'll see."

"It'll be a carnival sideshow."

"It won't!"

"We'll be laughed at by every serious actor in town."

"Who cares if they laugh? And if they do, it will be because they are jealous and envious. Lee, it will be a true happening!"

"Happenings went out of style many years ago," he reminded her.

"It will be an event, then. Nothing like this has ever been done before."

"It's been done," Lee said grimly. "Tiny Tim and what's her name, Miss Vickie, did it a long time ago on the Carson show."

"Oh, pooh! We aren't like that."

"We will be, if Bob lets us do it. Which he won't," Lee said with more hope than conviction.

"Bob is going to love it," Anne said for the hundredth time. Lee was afraid she was right.

"It's absurd," he murmured, his body heavy with dread.

They argued all the way back to Encino. By the time they pulled into her driveway, Anne was in tears. She was out of the car and running before Lee was completely stopped.

He sat for a moment, banging his head against the padded steering wheel, soft, helpless little bumps that solved absolutely nothing. She was not leaving him any recourse. He had hoped to get out of this without hurting anyone, not Anne, not his own career. But she had backed him into a corner, leaving him no choice but to refuse to marry her at all.

Marshaling his courage, what there was of it, Lee got out of the car, slammed the door and walked up to Anne's house. She had left the door open. How convenient. She wanted to be chased after.

He stepped inside. "Anne!" he bellowed. She did not answer. He stomped into the living room. Anne was on the floral sofa, legs drawn up under her, sniffling prettily and turning her face away from him.

He longed to ram his hands into that curly black hair, yank her to her feet and shake the living daylights out of her. The swinging doors between the kitchen and dining room opened with a squeak, making Lee glance around quickly.

Reenie was lounging by the door, her ripe body clad in the briefest halter and shorts he had ever seen. She winked at Lee. "I'm fixing dinner for you and Mommy," she purred.

Lee swallowed back a rush of moisture. "We don't want to eat now," he snapped. "Your mother and I have to talk—in private."

"Oh?" Reenie's knowing eyes moved from him to her huddled mother and back again, questioning Lee silently. He glared at Reenie. "Oh, okay," she sulked and withdrew, much to Lee's relief. It was sheer hell to have

391

both of them in the same room, because Reenie constantly tormented him with small suggestive gestures behind her mother's back.

"Anne." Lee took her shoulders and forced her around to face him. "You know I've had doubts about this wedding all along."

Her violet eyes glistened. She was the only woman Lee had ever met who could cry buckets but never smear her mascara or get red and ugly. "But Bob will—"

"I don't care what Bob will love, and I'm not talking about the show. I'm talking about us. I told you that I felt like we were letting the characters take over our real lives."

"That's so silly. Lily and John aren't us."

"Yes they are. And we are them."

"Lee . . ." Her fingers toyed with the buttons on his shirt. "Don't be like this. You're scaring me."

"I don't want to hurt you, Anne. I care too much about you. But marriage is a big step. We don't want to rush into something we'll regret."

"Regret?" She drew back in horror. "Regret?" Her voice rose shrilly. "I love you!"

"I'm sure you loved your other three husbands when you married them, too."

"Well, I did! And I don't regret any of them."

Lee shook his head. She was crazy. He tried another approach. "Anne, if we marry, I want it to be forever. I don't want to be one of your ex-husbands."

"Is that what's bothering you? Oh, my poor darling. I didn't realize. Oh, Lee! You think I discard men when I get tired of them, don't you. My poor baby. I'm not like that."

"Anne!" he wailed. She twisted everything.

"I never had anything in common with my other husbands," she continued. "That was what was wrong. Reenie's father was an oil man. He's off in Arabia or some such place now. He wouldn't stay here for my career. And Sam was a banker who got very dull and boring. Roger was . . ." She flushed and let her voice trail

392

off. "Well, Roger preferred men to women, though he felt he could change for me. But he couldn't, and . . ." She looked up at Lee, all helpless and female. "I always thought I failed poor Roger, but I won't fail you, Lee."

"Honey, I didn't think you would. It's just . . ."

"We have everything in common. The show, and this town, and we like the same foods, and, why, there must be a million things we have in common!"

Just the show, Lee thought, just the show and nothing else. She sees me as John Reese, not as Lee Trent. She doesn't know me at all. Lee ran a hand over his face in exasperation. Anne loved herself and was in love with love. "You don't know me," he offered lamely.

"Don't know you?" she laughed. "I've known you for three years now."

"Anne, you have illusions about us."

For the first time, he saw the fear in her eyes. It came and went so fleetingly he almost missed it. "Anne . . ." He reached for her.

She jumped back. "Illusions? What are you saying to me? Saying about me?" She sprang to her feet. Lee reached for her again. "Don't touch me!" she yelled and put the coffee table between them. "Oh, Lee, I love you!" She broke into sobs and ran from the room.

Lee sat still, knowing that if he stopped now, he would be lost. He had to calm her down, convince her that he cared and find some way to get out of the relationship without making her hate him. But by damn, he was not going to marry her!

Proud of his resolution, his own determination, Lee stood, tucked his shirt in deeper and adjusted his trousers around his waist. He was going to march into her bedroom and shake some sense into her.

The swinging doors squeaked again, announcing Reenie's return. "You made Mommy cry," she accused.

"I know," he said, using his newfound confidence. "There's not going to be a wedding."

Reenie moved toward him, her plump breasts almost popping out of the red-checkered halter. The white shorts were cut so high and tight she might as well have been nude. Stray pubic hairs had escaped from her panties, if she was wearing any. "Why isn't there going to be a wedding?" she demanded.

Lee was taken aback. "My God, Reenie. How can you ask? How can I marry your mother when you and I are . . ."

"Making it," she said for him. "What does that have to do with it?"

"Everything!"

She moved closer, her eyes focusing unwaveringly on his face. "Mommy loves you; she has her heart set on this wedding."

"Now, Reenie." In gestures that duplicated her mother's, she began to toy with the buttons on his shirt. She smelled faintly of musk and it was getting hard for him to breathe. What in the hell was the kid up to now?

"You don't really think I can marry Anne, and you and I go on together, do you?" he asked.

She tossed her hair. "Why not?"

He pushed her hands away. "You're a sick little kid, did you know that? A sick kid!"

"I'm not sick, Lee. Just realistic, and terribly advanced for my age. Just ask my teachers."

Lee's stomach turned over. "You should see a doctor."

"And . . ." She pouted sweetly. "And what would I tell him? About how you were going to be my daddy and how you let me get in bed with you and Mommy? How you let me sit on your lap and how you started touching me and making me feel all warm and funny, or maybe how one day you were baby-sitting with me and you let me drink some wine? And well, then I just couldn't stop from liking all those warm funny feelings, and you were almost my daddy, so . . ."

Lee's terror had grown with every word she said. "Reenie!" He stepped back, his leg catching on the coffee table. Arms flailing wildly, he heaved forward and righted himself. Breathing heavily, he edged around the table. "You wouldn't do anything like that!"

"Wouldn't I?" She challenged him openly, her eyes blazing. "Try me, Lee Trent, you just try me. You go to Mommy right now and tell her you were wrong. You tell her you love her and that you'll marry her. Because if you don't I'm going to call the police. Or better yet, I'll go to my counselor at school and she'll call the police for me. I'm going to cry and tell them how you got me drunk and raped me. I'll tell them how you keep after me all the time. My mommy is going to be very upset, and the newspapers will hear about it, and the magazines, and you'll lose your job and they'll probably put you in jail."

"My God!" Spittle formed in the corners of his mouth. She *was* sick. "Reenie, you wouldn't."

"I would. I will, Lee."

He groped for the arm of a satin-covered chair and sank down into it, too weak to stand. Reenie came to him and touched his hair. "I like you," she said and plopped herself on his lap. "I like you better than any of my other daddies. They all left me, but you won't ever leave me, Lee. Never, ever."

Dazed, he let her pat his face. He was trapped. Trapped! The meaning rushed over and over through his head.

"Come on," Reenie urged, tugging at Lee's hand. "You go and talk to Mommy now. I'll make you a drink and we'll have a family dinner. I want to hear all about the wedding."

"Reenie," he begged.

"Be nice to her, Lee," she said firmly. "Or I'll tell, I swear I will."

The scandal would destroy him and his career. The public accepted almost anything from their Hollywood heros now, drugs, adultery, homosexuality, but not child molesting.

He could wind up in jail, because who would ever believe a fourteen-year-old had seduced him; a grown

395

man in his mid-thirties. He would be the dirty old man. The courtroom scene unreeled before his eyes like a movie film. He could see Reenie, her hair caught back with a ribbon, dressed in a demure little schoolgirl dress as she cried softly on the stand. He could see Anne, indignant and angry, protective of Reenie. He could see the snickering, smirking reporters.

"Don't look so miserable, Lee," Reenie told him. "We'll be very happy together, the three of us. My, most men would consider this a dream come true."

"Dreams," Lee choked, his eyes burning. *Dreams to Come.* For the first time he understood the meaning of the show's title. But this wasn't a dream; it was a nightmare.

He held out both hands, palms up in appeal. "Reenie, you have to be rational about this."

The violet eyes were clear and unwavering. "Oh, I think I'm very rational and together and up front. It's blackmail, Lee, pure and simple. I thought you understood that."

"I guess I do," he whispered hollowly. They both wanted him and now they had him. There was no escaping.

Moving like a man on the way to his own execution, Lee went to Anne.

Chapter Forty

On her fifth night in New York, Sally was seated in an elegant French restaurant with Dick Morris, his wife, Kitty, and Johnny Fargo, who was the son of the president of the cosmetics company.

Sally would have preferred the father to the son. She was certain the older man letched after her, but she did not dare give him any kind of encouragement. There was the morals clause in her contract, and she had started out being demure and shy. She knew she had better stay that way for the duration of her New York stay.

Johnny was not a handsome man. At twenty-five, he looked and acted more like a spoiled sixteen-year-old. A few stray pimples still dotted his face, and he had no neck at all. He just went straight from head to shoulders. In one word, Johnny was a creep.

His leg moved to rest against Sally's. She carefully withdrew her leg, studiously keeping her eyes on the salad.

"A toast is overdue, I think," Dick said, picking up his glass. "To Sally Rook, our California Girl."

"Thank you," Sally breathed, basking for a moment in the admiration of the three sets of eyes turned on her.

"Congratulations," Kitty murmured as the glasses

clinked together. Kitty was a charming woman of about forty with casually styled red hair. But strictly a housewife who lived through her husband and children as near as Sally could tell, the kind of mother she had once dreamed of having.

Johnny and Dick were talking and Sally quietly tuned them out. Joe had approved the contracts and today Sally had signed all the copies in Dick's office. She was in. Nothing could stop her now.

She wanted to leap up on the table and announce her newly won position to the entire restaurant. Maybe kick her legs up as high as they would go and start dancing around the room. Instead, she accepted Kitty's quiet smile of approval.

The salad plates were removed by an overly solicitous waiter. When he was gone, Johnny turned to Sally. "I wish you would reconsider flying back to L.A. tomorrow. If you'd stay over the weekend we could run out to my father's Connecticut place."

"I can't." Sally made her voice regretful. "I have commitments in Los Angeles." She didn't, except to Lauren. She had telephoned Lauren twice. Each time Lauren had sounded worse. She was functioning, going to work and coming home, but the listlessness in her voice was frightening.

Sally wished Lauren would get angry, wished she would yell, wished she would hate Kerry. Anything but this desolation that seemed to hold her in an unrelenting grip.

"Or I could get Broadway tickets, if you'd stay," Johnny tempted her.

"I can't stay. I wish I could," Sally said. And in a way she did, but not with Johnny. She had already been through one groping match with him and she was not looking forward to another.

If she stayed in New York she wanted to be totally on her own. She wanted to visit Greenwich Village and ride the Staten Island Ferry and go to the top of the Empire State Building like any other tourist. She wanted to walk the streets and meet people in out-of-the-way bars. New York was very sensible about some things. She could drink here, no one ever asked for identification.

She had not been able to do any of those things. Instead she had spent hours and hours on another screen test. She had been photographed and had met what seemed like every employee of the Fargo Cosmetics Company. She had been made up by three experts who had argued over what powders and lip glosses and eye shadows would be exactly right for her. She had her hair trimmed and curled in four different styles, and they finally settled on the one she liked best, where her long hair hung loose in the softest of curls and waves.

The actual shooting of the ads and commercials would be done on location in California. Dick would fly out and personally oversee most of the work. Sally hoped that bit of news would perk Lauren up. The two of them had seemed to like each other. It could be fun for them if Lauren would handle it properly.

She was very grateful to Dick for not mentioning her affair with Alex to anyone at the advertising agency or the cosmetics company. Once in a while, during an interview with the company officials, he would catch her eyes and wink, or a conspiratorial look would pass between them, and she would know that he was seeing through the shy routine.

God, it would be good to be back in L.A. where she could sprawl out and be herself. She had been more Janie this week than she had ever been on the show.

After dinner, the two couples separated at the entrance, with Dick and Kitty taking a taxi home and Johnny escorting Sally back to her hotel. She ditched him nicely in the lobby. There was no way she would bed down this jerk, nor any man she cared nothing for. She had let men maneuver her into bed in the past, gone because they expected it, because she was too eager to please or did not know how to say no.

Such times always ended badly, left her unsatisfied and feeling used.

Those days were over and done with. The men she bedded down now were her choice, and if she deliberately chose a lousy lay like Joe Seals, she knew how to accept the consequences. She did it because she cared for reasons other than sex.

Sally returned to her room. She started to go to the telephone to call Lauren, then decided against it. She would see her tomorrow, anyway.

Sally stripped off her clothes, stretched out like a panther, let out a yell and leaped onto the bed. She was asleep within seconds.

Lauren left work a half hour early in order to meet Sally's five-o'clock flight. She ached with an overwhelming weariness that refused to leave her body. She was tired constantly and emotionally drained. It took all the effort she could dredge up to force herself out of bed each morning and get off to work. She kept up a false front as best she could with Paula and Jenny, but even that was a costly effort. She was not at all certain how or why her mind continued to function.

Lauren went straight to the baggage pickup area and found Sally and her three pieces of red luggage waiting.

"Lauren!" Sally greeted her with an exuberant hug. "I'm so glad to be home.

"I'm glad you're back," Lauren said. And she was; she didn't want to be alone again ever.

"You look like hell," Sally said bluntly.

Lauren flinched, a weak smile wavering on her lips. "That's how I feel, too. But let's not talk about me. I want to hear every word about New York."

"It was scary and wonderful," Sally said, nodding toward the exit. "How are you really feeling?" she asked as they walked toward the terminal exit.

"Like someone died."

"Maybe that's how it is when you break up with a

special person. Maybe you have to grieve for him for a while."

"I think it was me that died," Lauren said.

Sally's face reflected her shock. "Lauren, don't talk like that! You scare me."

Lauren nodded. She had scared herself last night. For the first time in her life she had considered suicide. It was a solution to a problem and there were many ways to accomplish it. Sticking her head in an oven would be one way. She had checked the house over and had been unable to find enough pills of any kind to do the job. She had considered the car. She could take a hose and run it from the exhaust pipe through a window. A gun was another possibility, but that would have required going out and buying one.

She was not sure why she had not tried the gas oven. Perhaps because she knew it would be Sally who would find her. Or that she would not do it properly, and then things would be worse than ever. The idea of not committing a successful suicide was abhorrent. Some sense of sanity had returned toward dawn and she had slept until the alarm went off.

"Look, I've got an idea, Lauren. Why don't you get out of town? You know, go somewhere different. It would help."

"Like where?" Lauren asked skeptically.

"I don't know. A resort, or home. Maybe you should go home and let your mother look after you for a few days. You could sleep in every morning."

Lauren gazed upward, letting the though sift through her head. It was a long time since she'd been home. Maybe she would not dare brood if she were home.

Lauren spent the weekend visiting her family and came home depressed and bewildered, upset over the unlikely discoveries she'd made in the small farming town. She returned to Los Angeles on Monday and on Tuesday went to work early. Sally was sticking close to home, studying for her part in *Rainbow* and waiting for Dick

Morris to arrange the shooting of the commercials. Morris was due out at the end of the month to oversee it all. He planned to start hitting with the commercials in September, using Los Angeles and Chicago as test areas. If the cosmetics sold in those two locations, they would then go nationwide with the products. If they didn't go nationwide, Sally would be out of work, but Lauren did not expect that to happen.

Sally had hinted that Dick Morris wanted to see Lauren while he was working in Los Angeles. "See me?" Lauren asked.

"Yes, he liked you," Sally said. "Didn't you like him?"

"He's a nice enough man, I suppose. But very, very married," Lauren added.

"But you two got along well."

That was true. She had liked Dick Morris and she had even wondered what it would be like to go to bed with him. But that was a fleeting thing, and it had happened in another time—in Kerry's time.

She had not quit thinking about Kerry yet. She was not certain she could ever rid herself of the memories of him. She felt now that she had done everything wrong, ignored all the warnings from people who knew Kerry did not take women seriously, ignored the signs he threw up, ignored it all and groveled at his feet, begging for his love. No wonder he had been sickened by her, no wonder he had fled. She had tried to smother him by wanting too much too soon. That's how it was, wasn't it, she asked herself. Her certainty wavered. There was no clear-cut answer, least of all about men in general.

The weekend at home had thrown her right back where she had been after leaving Benji. She did not understand men or their attitude toward sex. The weekend hung over her, clinging like a black nightmare to be sorted out and worried over.

She was left feeling as though there was nothing to believe in. She had learned that her father had betrayed her mother. Buddy, her sister's husband, had made a corny pass, a trite happening when she looked at it in retrospect; but it had happened, had been real and horrifying. Maybe one day she would be able to laugh about it, but now she didn't think so.

Daddy hurt her worse of all. He was her beloved father, a man she had trusted above all others for her entire life. Why had Mama told her? Why? But Lauren knew why. Mama had thought it might help, might somehow get her and Benji back together.

Damn Benji! She was angry with him for involving her parents with friendly phone calls. She wanted to call him and scream and yell and demand to know what kind of stupid game he was playing. He surely did not want her back. Or maybe he did, maybe his ego was smarting because she had left him. Women did not walk out on Benji Parrow, he cast them aside. Maybe he needed to prove he could get her back, then he would drop her. Or imprison her? What was he doing?

She did not know, and she would not find out because she refused to call him. It would simply make things more complicated and she could not tolerate another hassle in her life now. Her hold on reality was very fragile. She felt as if she had moved up maybe two feet from the bottom of the black pit Kerry had cast her into. Up two feet, only to sink back down to the bottom this weekend. She was climbing up again, but it was going to take time, healing time. She wanted to be alone, she wanted to pour herself into her work and not have time to think of anything beyond *Dreams*.

Lauren entered the office section of the penthouse using her own key. She slipped quietly down the hall and was startled by the sound of voices. Had someone left the television set on?

She opened the door to the TV room. Paula was at the set. "You're up early," Lauren said.

"So are you." Paula flipped a switch and rewound a tape. "I've been watching these audition tapes for Katherine. Come join me. Silverstein has it down to three women for the part. I've settled on Gloria Winston.

She's Bob's favorite, too, but one of the other girls is interesting."

Paula pressed buttons and the TV screen filled with color. Paula took her usual place in one chair and Lauren seated herself behind her on the sofa.

Paula lit a cigarette and stared intensely at the screen. The audition scene involved Katherine and her doctor at the mental hospital, and then a touching scene with Cobb Strong as Ned, her husband, who was currently involved with bitch Irene. They spoke of Timmy and the people back in Maple Falls.

Gloria Winston was good, portraying just the right amount of eagerness and apprehension at facing the world again. The second actress was warm enough, but she did not click with Cobb at all. She was too—Lauren searched for the right word—too garish for Cobb as Ned. Cobb would have a sweet, loving woman as his wife.

"He's such a nice person," Lauren said softly.

"What?"

"Cobb Strong—he seems like a nice person."

"Well, he never gives me any trouble, that's for sure. Not like some of them," Paula muttered pointedly.

Lauren's chin quivered. She clamped her teeth together and refused to respond.

The third actress was Claudia Renfro, who looked familiar. The same scene was replayed again, this time with different emphasis in timing. "She's good," Lauren remarked.

"She's an outstanding actress," Paula agreed. "Better than Gloria Winston. I could do things with her, but you know what's wrong with her?" She answered her own question before Lauren had a chance to respond. "She's not pretty."

"Well, she's not exactly ugly either," Lauren said.

"No, but she's a character actress, not a good lead. Look, her nose is too big and her chin juts too much. Her face isn't soft, and it's too bad. I have to go with Gloria."

"Maybe we could use the Renfro woman some day," Lauren suggested. "A homely woman who falls in love with a handsome man. Maybe she's a doctor who devotes herself to her career and hides from emotional involvement. I think women could identify with that."

"No," Paula replied, rejecting Lauren's suggestion. "No one wants to identify with an ugly person."

"But she wouldn't be ugly inside," Lauren protested.

Paula turned on her. "Who runs this show, you or me?"

"I'm sorry," Lauren murmured, ducking her head to hide the anger in her face. She wanted to scream back at Paula, but you did not argue with Paula Cavanaugh. Knuckling under, Lauren silently got up and turned off the recording machine and television set.

Paula swept out of the room, her black skirt rustling around her legs. I won't have to put up with this forever, Lauren reminded herself. One day I'll be writing on the staff and I can work at home. One day, maybe, she would even be completely free of Paula, maybe she would have her own show, a soap or a nighttime series. Other women writers made it big in all aspects of TV writing, which was wide open if you had the nerve to enter it.

Lauren began to contemplate seriously a career she would have given up for Kerry. She looked ahead, beyond being a dialogue writer to the endless possibilities available. She stretched her mind forward. Success was all around her and it could be hers, too.

Sally Rook placed the thick *Rainbow* script on the coffee table. The words were easy enough to memorize and the part should have been a piece of cake for her since it was the role of a young and eager actress. But it was not a simple part, because it required her to act out a bizarre audition in which she ran through a gamut of roles from little girl to brassy waitress to dowdy housewife to seductive vamp—all to be done with a sense of desperation because it was the character's last chance at success.

Sally knew that if she could bring it off, Alex would be very proud of her. If she didn't, if she wasn't talented enough, if she betrayed his faith in her, she would not be able to bear it.

All Alex had talked about was how good the part would be for her, how it would show off her ability to play a number of roles. A showcase role, he had called it. Alex would direct the scene, and that was the scariest of all, for if she failed it would be immediately apparent. If she failed she would never be able to face Alex again.

Sally found herself wishing she were back on *Dreams to Come*. She missed the cast and crew, and the role she had played with ease compared to what would be asked of her next.

Sally stood and checked the fern Mel Lorenzen had sent her. The tips of the fronds were burning brown. Sally didn't know if she was under- or over-watering. She only knew she would feel like a murderess if the plant died. "Come on, plant," she coaxed. "Be pretty!"

"Damn!" She twisted her hair up off her neck. It was hot, the air conditioner in the window doing little to dispel the heat. If she didn't get out of the apartment she was going to go stir crazy.

It was too bad all of life could not be like the weekend at Big Sur with Alex. She had been so happy up there with him. There were no decisions to be made, no problems to be faced, noting to do but enjoy each other. It was the most perfect weekend of her whole life.

She shook her hair down. Maybe she should take the script to her voice teacher, maybe she could help. But probably not. A voice teacher was not an acting coach. Alex would go over it with her, of course, before they did it on the set. But she wanted to be good for Alex from the beginning. Sally sighed. She should have kept up with the acting lessons or done a stage play as Joe

406

had wanted. Then she would have more experience and confidence.

She supposed she should go shopping, except there was nothing in particular she wanted. She had more clothes than she could wear now. The refrigerator was stuffed, so there was no need to buy groceries. It was too hot to cook anyway. They would probably have sandwiches and salad for dinner.

So what to do? Sally sank down on the floor in the lotus position. But she was not in the right mood for yoga. She needed to move, but she could not call Alex since he was busy with the film. They were doing location shots down at San Pedro.

Maybe she would just go into town and say hello to Joe. Then she could have Lauren pick her up and they could ride home together. She slid her feet into sandals, took time to brush her hair, found her purse under the sofa and left. She caught a bus to Ventura Boulevard, transferred to another that would take her to Coldwater Canyon where she could hitch it over the hills.

She took a window seat on the bus and focused her attention on the seemingly endless variety of shops and restaurants that lined Ventura Boulevard.

She promised herself that some day she would take an entire day and explore the area. Suddenly a name leaped off a small marquee in front of a shabby club. "Joshua."

Sally grabbed the overhead cord and hurried to the rear exit. She ran back down the block and stopped in front of a faded yellow building. She had not misread the marquee. "Featuring Joshua on the Guitar." It was a name Jake Sheeney had discussed using. Her heart pounding in a peculiar way, she tried to peek into the windows, but they were blacked out. She tried the door handle and it opened. She peered into a gloomy interior where chairs were stacked over tables. At one table a man in shirtsleeves leaned over paperwork, a cigar dangling from his mouth.

"Hey, lady, we're closed," he yelled at Sally.

"I don't want anything, except to ask a question," she said, easing inside. "Is Joshua—is he Jake Sheeney?"

"Yeah, he's been here a week or so."

"Is he doing okay?" She inched closer to the forbidding-looking man. He shifted his cigar to the opposite side of his mouth.

"Well, he shows up on time. And he plays a fair guitar."

"I think he's really good," Sally offered.

"You do, huh? You heard him play somewhere else?"

"Yes."

"You want to meet him?"

"No. No." She moved toward the door.

"Well, come in one night. Bring your friends. We need the business."

"I'll do that," Sally lied. "Will he be here long?"

The man shrugged. "Who knows? I'll keep him as long as he stays straight."

Sally backed out the door and closed it behind her, her heart pounding hard and fast. She was genuinely glad Jake had a job, but it gave her an odd feeling to know he was so near.

She walked slowly down Ventura past antique shops and a small cafe. Jake was not really a bad person, just a little mixed-up about what was important. He was a moody sort, all long hair and beard and jeans. But most talented people were moody, especially musicians with all their drugs. He could swing from high to low and back again for no apparent reason. He could be violent, too. Not that he had ever hit her, except that last night. But he had threatened her at times.

I was really dumb to stay with him as long as I did, she decided. Dumb. To heck with seeing Joe today. She would explore all the neat shops spread out before her.

In Bob Silverstein's office, Anne Voll sat perched on the side of her chair. Yesterday she had just been ready to die. Lee had been in such a mood, so disagreeable.

Sometimes she didn't understand that man at all. But everything was fabulously wonderful now and Anne smiled sweetly across at Bob. Lee had begged her to forgive him and declared his love so beautifully.

Anne had driven in this afternoon in her new dress of white eyelet. She felt her floppy-brimmed hat completed the promise of a bride to be. After all, a little costuming never hurt an audition and that was what this interview was in a way.

She had laid out her plans to Bob. He had asked a few questions and now he was leaning back in his chair, obviously mulling over the idea.

"Well, Anne . . ." Bob rolled his chair forward until his vest-clad belly touched the desk. "I can't give you an answer right now. This is quite overwhelming."

"But think of all the wonderful possibilities."

"Yes," Bob commented. "We could give it quite a buildup."

"I knew you would love the idea, Bob. That's what I told Lee, Bob will love it." Anne fluttered thick black lashes.

"And Lee?" Bob looked at her quizzically. "Why isn't he here?"

Anne fluffed the ruffle around the neck of the dress. "Lee thinks it's a terrific thing, completely in favor of it. And we're getting married anyway, you know. So why not make something grand out of it?"

Anne was certain the wedding would rock the town on its heels, it would be the sensation of the year. Newspapers would cover it, magazines would interview her, Silver Productions would buy her the most beautiful wedding gown in the world, perhaps have one designed just for her.

Bob shifted in his chair. "I like it, Anne. I like it a lot."

She clapped her hands together and squealed. "I knew you would!"

"But I don't have final authority on something this big. "I'll have to go to the head of the network. And if we go, we might get in touch with our sponsors. They may want to run with it."

"You mean like magazine ads? Oh, Bob! I'd *love* to do some product ads."

"Maybe. And I'll have to consult with Caleb Shepard. And, of course, with Paula."

"Oh, pooh on Paula!" Anne muttered as Bob looked grim. "She's so—so possessive, or something. She always acts like we're trying to interfere if we change a single line of dialogue."

"Paula is protective of the show and of her position, Anne. But she'll go for this," Bob said. His tone said she would go for it, or else.

Anne suppressed a feeling of glee. "You're a darling, Bob."

"And you may be the first daytime superstar—if we do this. And if we do, we'll want to get you and Lee on some talk shows. Maybe Dinah, and Merv's."

"Maybe Johnny Carson, too?" Anne asked hopefully.

Bob shook his head. "No, I don't think so. His audience isn't ours."

"Oh." Anne was disappointed. She had always wanted to be on the Carson show.

"Now, Anne . . ." Bob came around his desk and took her hand to help her to her feet. "Let's keep this between ourselves for a week or so. Until I've cleared it upstairs. Understand?"

She understood. It was Paula he was worried about. Anne let Bob escort her to the door, feeling totally self-satisfied. She was going to be responsible for putting over a big one on the self-righteous Paula Cavanaugh.

At the door, Anne and Bob exchanged kisses and conspiratorial smiles.

Chapter Forty-One

It was Friday, thank God! Paula lit a cigarette and poured a glass of Bristol Cream. She held the delicate stemmed glass up to the light and admired the amber color. It was beautiful, and she liked having beautiful things around her. The penthouse could not have been done better, which was only right, after what she had paid the Beverly Hills decorator. She loved the elegant, quiet rooms and liked leaving the clutter of her work behind here.

She glanced around at the accumulated litter of scripts and mimeos. It was time for Lauren to file it all away again, though half of it would be dragged out again next week to be checked for continuity.

It was of vital importance that they never erred, for the viewers caught the slightest inconsistency. Paula was careful never to create doubt over the reality of her characters.

She knew any writer who underestimated the viewers was headed for disaster. People did not watch soaps because they were an art form, nor for entertainment as they would a play or movie. Viewers reacted to soaps as they did to real life; they lived the stories being pumped into their living rooms.

The serials involved their viewers because they presented life as uncertain. Misfortune could strike anyone and everyone, just as fate struck out at random in day-to-day living. It was the uncertainty of tomorrow that kept people tuning in week after week, that and the compassion and caring that existed between the characters on the screen. To watch a soap was to be drawn into a small, enclosed world where the only motivation was love and the future was determined by fate.

Paula stubbed out her cigarette and returned to the small desk and typewriter. She liked Fridays when all she had to do was write the outlines for Mel and Germain and make a few notes on the next week's scripts.

She typed NEW DAY at the top of Mel's outline. Sometimes one day lasted through two, three or even four days of air time. So it was critical to note SAME DAY or NEW DAY so wardrobe would know when they could change costumes.

The words flowed quickly until Paula realized the Ned-Irene scene was almost identical to one she had done earlier in the week. Brought up short, she gazed in puzzlement at the pages before her. What in the world was wrong with her? She ripped the pages out, crumpled them and tossed them in the general direction of the wastebasket.

She knew what was wrong. Only half her mind was on the outline; the rest kept drifting off to Gil Richardson and their date tonight. She rolled fresh paper into the typewriter and began Act Four again. It wasn't brilliant when she finished, but it would do.

As she typed the final page there was a knock on the door. Annoyed, she stopped. "Yes?"

Lauren slipped inside. She had a script in her hand. "Paula, Sue just called. You've used too many sets in the script for Monday."

"My script?" Paula frowned. She never made stupid mistakes like that.

Lauren hovered nervously near the door. "I've gone over the script. I'm sorry to disturb you, but Sue is waiting for an answer, and . . ."

Paula tapped her nails impatiently on the typewriter. "Get on with it, Lauren."

"I've gone over the script," she repeated. "We can eliminate Rose's kitchen and Anne's front porch."

"I like the front porch scene. Let me see it." Paula held out her hand.

Lauren crossed the room. Paula snatched the script out of her hand. She scanned the second page that listed the sets. "There are ten," she acknowledged. "Why didn't you catch this before it went to the studio?"

"Me?" Lauren paled. "I—I really don't know. I never thought about how many sets we could use."

"Haven't you? That's not very bright on your part. You've been to the studio, you've seen the space available and you've been editing scripts now for six months. I would have thought you would have noticed *something* by now." Paula shoved the script back into Lauren's hand.

For a moment, Lauren's eyes flared and Paula thought she was going to throw the script back in her face. The eyes turned opaque and Lauren ducked her head. "I won't forget it again," she murmured.

"I'm sure you won't," Paula said, glancing at her watch. She was meeting Gil early tonight. "You fix it, Lauren. It will be good practice for you."

"And the porch scene?"

"If you can't keep it, you can't keep it."

"All right." Lauren walked stiffly out of the room. Paula assumed her feelings were hurt. Well, tough. It was a hard, cruel world, and Lauren should pay a little more attention to what was going on in it.

The door closed and Paula turned back to her typewriter. Hitting the keys too hard with her red-tipped nails, she banged out the last lines. She yanked the paper out and stacked it for Lauren. She carried the outlines to Jenny. "Lauren can deliver these now," she said. "I'm quitting."

"Yes, Paula." Jenny glanced down at her notepad.

413

"Did you realize Bob Silverstein has called three times. He wants to have lunch with you."

"I don't feel like talking to Bob now. I'll call him on Monday." She started to walk away.

"Paula?"

"What is it?" she said impatiently. She wanted to get out of there.

"Well, it's just that Bob doesn't like to be ignored," Jenny said.

Paula's eyes flickered over Jenny's round face. "It's good for him. It reminds him that the whole world doesn't cater to Bob Silverstein."

"Yes."

"You go home now, too," Paula offered, suddenly feeling generous. She shouldn't take her frustration with Bob out on Jenny.

"It's too early," Jenny protested.

"So take off early. Give yourself a break."

"I really can't, Paula. I still have several things to do."

"They'll wait."

Jenny's lips tightened. "And give you reason to yell at me on Monday? No thanks."

"Oh, really?" Paula scoffed, somewhat taken aback by Jenny.

Jenny smiled tentatively. "I'll leave as soon as I can."

Paula smiled back. "Okay." How odd for Jenny to talk back. That was not like her, and certainly her yelling had never seemed to ruffle the placid Jenny in the past. It was the one thing that Paula had appreciated about Jenny the most. Jenny never got uptight or held grudges. In fact, Jenny had always been quiet and appreciative of her position. Paula mentally shrugged. Well, even Jenny could have an off day, she conceded.

As was her custom, Paula made a short tour of the penthouse. She liked to make sure the housekeeper was doing her job. Everything seemed to be in its place and she found the housekeeper in the kitchen. "Margaret, is everything under control?" she asked.

"Yes, ma'am."

That done, Paula drifted to the bar, where she poured herself another sherry to carry to her room. She luxuriated in the ritual of a long hot bath, then slipped into a silk robe and removed her old makeup and re-made her face for the evening. She dabbed a Jean Patou fragrance along her throat and between her small breasts. Gil especially liked this perfume, had compli-mented her lavishly the last time she had worn it.

The man was truly incredible. He noticed everything, no matter how small. She liked that, liked it very much. She opened the bottom drawer of her dresser and took out a jewelry box. She slipped on a ring of pink coral, held out her hand to examine the ring and changed her mind. She owned very little jewelry, but what she had was good. She put the coral back in the box and substi-tuted a fiery opal. That was better. Her nails needed to be a paler color for the coral.

Paula slipped into a light summer print of green and white. She had bought the dress on impulse last week when she had gone to Saks for shoes. The dress was not her at all, yet the green and white pattern had en-chanted her. She smoothed it around her waist. She never wore colors, never looked at clothes that were not black or gray. But she had seen this on a black-haired mannequin and found herself inexplicably drawn to it.

Paula twisted in front of the full-length mirror, feel-ing decidedly unlike herself and liking it. She took a pair of white sandals and a matching bag from a drawer. She transferred her belongings from a black purse to the white and got a sweater in case the evening turned cool. The temperature dropped at night, even in mid-summer.

She called for her car and left the now empty apart-ment. The girls were gone and Joe had not returned, for which she was grateful. She did not have to explain the dress.

She met Gil at Monte's in Westwood where they were having a drink before making plans for the evening. She glimpsed Gil at a small table in the crowded bar. He stood and waved. She waved back, then started toward him, squeezing between two couples standing and talking with their drinks.

"I didn't dare leave the table," he told her, taking her hand. "Someone would have grabbed it."

"I don't wonder," she said, looking around. "Is it always this crowded here?"

"I don't know," he replied. "I've never been here before."

She liked that about Gil; he wasn't pretentious, never put on airs, never pretended to know about all the "in" places—not that they would dare frequent them together anyway.

Gil reached for her chair, then stopped. "Paula, you have a new dress," he said. "It's beautiful, you're beautiful." He took her hands and held her back, gazing at her fondly, then lifted one hand to his lips and kissed it.

"Gil," she whispered, both embarrassed and pleased.

"Have't you ever had your hand kissed before?"

"Only once. By a French actor, and he didn't do it nearly as well as you."

He held the chair for her and signaled for a waiter before he sat down. "What would you like to do tonight?" he asked.

Paula shrugged. "What would you like?"

Gil grinned crookedly. "What do you think? I'm wondering why we bothered to meet here instead of my apartment. You look so enticing."

"It's the dress," she said, loving every word that came out of his mouth, even when it was laid on too thickly.

He brushed her chin with his fingertips and was about to speak when the waiter appeared. Gil ordered for both, then turned back to Paula. "Now, isn't there anything special you'd like to do this evening?"

"Only whatever you want."

"Good." Gil clasped her hands in his. "You know what I want, besides you, that is?"

"What?"

"A hamburger, an old fashioned grease-dripping hamburger."

Paula laughed. "You're crazy, but Hamburger Hamlet is around here somewhere. They're all over."

"No," he said. "That's too fancy. Could you stand it if I took you to this drive-in I've found? They make chili burgers, too."

"I'd love it," she replied. God, he made her feel young, and, yes, adventurous again.

They did not linger over their drinks, but left soon and Gil drove straight to a hamburger stand on Washington Boulevard in Venice. It was shabby and the outdoor tables were dirty, but it did not matter. They ate huge messy burgers, full of onions and dripping with grease and cheese and mustard.

Laughing like two teen-agers at the looks they were getting from the other customers, they hurried to Gil's car and went straight to his apartment and to bed.

They made love, showered together and got back in bed. With the sheet pulled up over them and pillows stacked at their backs, they watched an old Bogart movie on channel thirteen.

At the end, Paula wiped away a hint of tears. Drowsy and happy, she nestled against Gil. She felt so good, her stomach had not acted up all day. There had been no big hassles with the show, and Joe was keeping out of her way. "I wish I could stay here all night," she murmured.

"Then do it."

"I don't dare." She reluctantly checked the time. She started to move away and Gil pulled her back.

"Paula, there's something I have to ask you," he said.

"Oh?" He seemed so ill at ease suddenly, somehow embarrassed. "What is it, Gil?"

"Well . . ." He licked his lips. "Oh, damn!"

"You can ask," Paula said. "You can ask me anything."

"I need a loan," he blurted out quickly.

"A—a loan?" All of Paula's built-in warning devices hit red alert.

"The rent is overdue, and I'm about broke. That's why we had hamburgers," he confessed, making Paula's heart constrict with pity. "I'm having money transferred from Canada, but it's taking a lot longer than I planned. A couple of thousand would tide me over. Damn it, I feel like a louse. I never asked a woman for money before."

Confused, Paula plucked at the sheet. "I—I don't know, Gil. I . . ."

"Oh, hell! Just forget it, Paula. I shouldn't have asked you anyway. I'll think of something."

"No," she murmured. Poor darling, he was genuinely embarrassed.

"I'll pay you back," he said. "Within fourteen days, with interest, I promise."

"Two thousand?" she asked.

"If you have it, Paula. I don't want to cause you any trouble."

"I think there's that much in my personal account." She got up and found her purse and took out the checkbook. The warning bells clanging inside her head had dulled to a faint ding. She wrote out the check and handed it to him.

He took it without looking at her, laid it aside and took her in his arms. "You're quite a woman, Paula Cavanaugh."

She brushed the graying hair at his temples. "And you're quite a man." She let him kiss her and only part of her responded. She would find out soon enough if Gil was being honest with her. She would find out if he was making a fool of her when he either paid back the money or hit her for another loan. God, how she wanted him to pay her back, to smother her doubts.

The penthouse was quiet when she got home. She knew Joe was there because his car was downstairs. She went straight to her room, closed the door. After undressing she moved to the dressing table and reached for a pot of cream. She stopped, staring at her hand. The opal was gone from her finger!

Jarred, she went straight to the telephone and called Gil. "I've lost my ring," she said when he answered.

"Ring?" He hesitated. "I don't remember a ring, Paula."

"It's an opal," she said, "a rather large one. Maybe I took it off when I washed my hands, or maybe it fell off in the shower.

"Hang on, honey," he said. "I'll check."

He was gone a long time. She heard his sigh as he came back on, "I can't find it. I checked the shower and the sink. Look, tomorrow I'll get someone up to take the sink apart. Maybe it's in the drainpipe. I've crawled over every inch of the floor. Was the ring loose?"

"A little," she answered. "But not much."

"Oh, God! What if it came off when we were eating those hamburgers? With all that grease and stuff when you wiped your hands, it could have. Damn it, Paula! I feel like hell about this."

"Hey, don't blame yourself, Gil," she said. "The ring is insured."

"If I don't find it tomorrow, I'll buy you another. Just tell me what it cost, and you can pick out a new one."

"Gil, don't be silly. I told you, it's insured."

"Well, is it insured for enough?"

"I think so, three thousand. It didn't have any diamonds, just the opal."

"I'll keep looking for it," Gil promised.

"Gil, don't let it worry you, please. It's not the end of the world."

"But I feel responsible," he insisted.

"Well, you weren't," she assured him. "Now, go back to bed and don't worry."

"I'll try. Sleep good, and dream of me," he whispered huskily.

"Good night," she murmured. Thoughtful, she

walked back to the dressing table. Poor darling, he was really concerned. Reassured, she sat down and dabbed cleansing cream on her face.

It was odd that Gil had not noticed the ring at Monte's. He never missed anything different about her. Perhaps she had lost it in her apartment, or in the car before meeting Gil. She would look tomorrow.

She turned back the gray velvet spread and got into bed. She was tired, and she thought she would fall asleep immediately, but it was difficult to relax, despite Gil's reassurances over the ring and the money.

Joe Seals lay in bed smoking one of his rare cigarettes. Joe was more than a little drunk. In fact, he was certain he would fall down if he tried to get out of the bed.

Paula had taken a lover, he was certain of that. Male or female, he didn't know, and it didn't matter. Either way, Paula still found Joe inadequate.

He silently damned Paula. He loved her, he cared and he hurt, because she didn't need him. Paula didn't need anyone; she was complete unto herself.

Chapter Forty-Two

Bob Silverstein was annoyed. He had called Paula's office the week before and invited her to lunch so he could broach the subject of Lee and Anne's marriage in a personal way so she would feel she was included in on the decision. He had dealt with creative neurotics most of his life and he generally prided himself on his ability to handle them.

But as a woman and a writer, Paula was fast making her way to the top of the list of the most difficult. She was ornery, contrary and, as far as Bob was concerned, she was a borderline paranoid. She was a good writer, or had been, until she got it into her head that she was the most important member of the show. She did not like interference of any kind, especially from Caleb, who was a fine old gentleman who understood the politics of TV. Caleb had never let success go to his head, had not turned into a complete tyrant like Paula Cavanaugh.

Well, she had not bothered to return his phone calls, so to hell with her. He would let it ride while touching base with all the other people concerned. Caleb liked it and gave his hearty approval. The network president asked for a couple of days to think about it, talked with both Anne and Lee, then got back to Bob with an affirmative answer.

So now the wedding to be was an accomplished fact. It would take place, and all that was left to do was break the news to Paula and map out a campaign with the publicity department.

Bob consulted his desk calendar. It was Thursday and Paula had let a full week go by without returning his calls. Bob buzzed Sue. "Get me Paula," he said. "And don't accept any excuses. I want to speak with her personally, now!"

"Yes, boss," Sue replied, and Bob knew she was smiling. Frankly, Bob was amazed Sue had managed to keep her mouth shut, but then, no love was lost between Sue and Paula.

Bob waited patiently, studying his newly manicured nails until Sue buzzed back. "Paula is on line three."

"Thanks." He picked up the phone, depressed the hold button for line three. "Paula, Bob here."

"So I've been told," she replied, sounding faintly annoyed. So be it, he thought. I'm annoyed too.

"We are having dinner tonight, Paula," he announced.

"Bob, I can't! I've got deadlines to meet."

"Paula!" His voice held a warning. "Consider this a command performance."

During the long silence that followed, Bob imagined the glints of fury that must have been reflected in Paula's eyes. "A command performance? Really, Bob!"

"Yes, Paula."

"The reason?" she asked. He could tell she was getting angry.

"The show, of course. There are several things to discuss, Paula. Things that will boost the ratings."

"I see. Where are we having dinner?"

"Is Scandia all right with you?"

"It will do," she murmured.

Do! Bob nearly gagged. Dinner would cost him at

least a hundred dollars tonight. "I'll make reservations for eight, then."

"Is there everything else for now?" she asked.

"Until tonight, love."

She hung up without saying good-bye. Up yours, too, Bob thought.

More nervous than she cared to admit, Paula arrived by taxi at Scandia on Sunset Boulevard a deliberate ten minutes late. She was greeted by the maître d' and escorted past the bar and into the dining room where Bob was at a table backed by latticework and plants.

"Bob," she said, giving him a controlled smile as he stood to hold the chair upholstered in a heavy floral print, her eyes not missing the champagne sitting in a bucket of ice. A glistening chandelier of beaded glass hung over the table.

"Paula, you're looking exceptionally elegant tonight," Bob said.

"This old shmatte," she said purposely, eyebrows raised.

"No, no, Paula, that's my game," Bob reminded her. Tension rode just beneath the surface of the polite bantering. Paula let him seat her. "It's good to see you socially like this," Bob said. "We've been friends a long time."

"So we have." There had been good times and some bad, but there was no love lost between them, not even for the short-lived affair.

There used to be a feeling of mutual respect, but this year Paula found it missing. Bob was determined to ally himself with Caleb against her. She was certain this dinner had to do with Caleb and some wild scheme he had contrived for Bob to present to her. Well, an expensive meal was not going to persuade her.

She scrutinized Bob Silverstein as he poured champagne into her glass, his face betraying nothing, though he was a bit more jovial than usual. If only the ratings were not down. Paula rubbed her cold hands together

423

under the table. If it ever came down to him or her, she knew the axe would fall on her neck.

Paula felt her only recourse in light of this was to present a solid front of confidence and control. Because whether Bob admitted it or not, she *was Dreams to Come*. It was her baby, and without her the show would crumble. No one else had her perception of the characters nor of their intricate past.

Bob lifted his glass. "L'chayim."

"To life," Paula acknowledged.

She sipped the bubbly wine and set her glass down on the table. "Why are we here, Bob?" she asked.

"First things first," Bob said and signaled for their waiter. "Let's order."

She took the menu and scanned it quickly and ordered the most expensive dish, having the pleasure of seeing Bob flinch. Tightwad, she thought, and added two appetizers. "And we'll need another bottle of champagne," she told the waiter. "Won't we, Bob?"

"Might as well," Bob agreed too quickly. "How's Joe?"

"Fine. And your wife?" God, how she hated enduring such pointless amenities.

"Sheila is busy. She's heading up a new Save Our Animals league."

"It's a worthy endeavor."

"I suppose, but it always ends up costing me money. I think we must support half the dogs and cats in Los Angeles County now."

Paula shrugged. Bob was chronic when it came to poor-mouthing. It had taken something unusual to get him into Scandia.

Over appetizers, Bob began to talk about the show in general and the fan mail over the main course. "They are going to get violent out there in TV land if we don't let John and Lily marry."

"No," Paula said flatly. "I thought we settled that a long time ago."

"Not quite. Something new has come up."

"Oh?" Paula's fork stopped in mid-air. "What could it possibly be?"

"Lee and Anne are getting married."

"No, Bob."

"I mean, *they're* really getting married. They will be Mr. and Mrs. Lee Trent."

"So I'll send a gift," Paula murmured.

"Do that. But send it to the studio. We're having the wedding there."

"Are they crazy?"

"A little, but it's a hell of an idea, Paula." Bob leaned forward. "Anne came to me with it. They want John and Lily married, too. Sort of a double wedding."

Paula looked at him coldly. "You aren't making a lot of sense, Bob."

"I mean, John and Lily's wedding ceremony will also be Lee and Anne's. They will be legally married—on the air!"

Paula laid down her knife and fork with a clatter. "This is the most absurd thing I've ever heard! Anne can't be serious."

"She's serious," Bob assured her.

The food in Paula's stomach lumped together. "She can't be. Why, why . . ." Paula had never been at such a loss for words before. "We'll be laughed right out of the industry."

"I don't think so."

"The network will never go for it."

"They like it, Paula. I'm seeing the people in the publicity department next week. We're going to promote the hell out of it."

Paula breathed in through her nose. Her face was turning dark red. "Are you trying to tell me you have gone behind my back on story line?" she demanded.

"I called you several times last week. You never returned my calls."

Bastard, she thought. "No one said your call was important."

"I don't call without reason, Paula. *All* my calls are important."

Paula's fingers rolled into tight fists, her nails digging painfully into her palms. "I'm the head writer. I make the story line decisions," she said.

"Caleb is agreeable."

"Of course he would be, the old goat!" Her stomach turned sour and she pushed the plate away and picked up the champagne to give herself time to think. She was shaking with rage. How dare he? How dare he do this? To go behind her back was unpardonable. "I won't do it!" she declared.

"Yes, you will. It's all settled. We're going to have a November wedding. We'll shoot it live."

"*Live?*" Paula almost choked on the wine.

"That's correct. Live! It hasn't been done in years. That alone will get us plenty of free publicity."

"I will not write it!" she announced, bringing each word out separately and distinctly.

Bob shrugged. "If you don't, someone else will."

"They can't. I have a contract."

"Contracts were made to be broken, Paula. Besides, Caleb has story control, not you."

Her throat constricted and she could feel the muscles in her throat bulging. "I'll quit," she threatened, certain he would never let her leave.

"Would you, Paula?" Bob leaned back in his chair, his food forgotten. "Would you quit?"

Panic ripped through her at Bob's challenge. A sharp pain hit in the pit of her stomach. She had gone too far. *Dreams* was her child, her baby. She had written the show out of dumb situations before, she could do it again.

"I'll honor my contract," she said, her voice dry. "I wouldn't walk out on you at a critical time."

She waited for his expected smile, his old enthusiasm. It didn't come. "All right, Paula. Let's be sure we understand each other. The wedding gets a big buildup.

We'll want a solid week of wedding on air. We'll need a reception, the whole schmeer."

"Have you decided how this miracle wedding is going to come about? How we swing Belle out of the picture?"

"No, but you can consult with Caleb. I'm sure he has some thoughts on this."

She bit back a sharp protest. "Bob, these contrived events never play as well as the story that evolves naturally out of past story and characters."

"So write it so it doesn't seem contrived," he said. "We'll want something dramatic to happen, so Lily and John will realize they can't live apart any longer."

"All my shows are dramatic!"

"But the ratings are down," he reminded her smoothly, making her swallow back her pain. "This will yank the ratings sky high. Paula . . ." He leaned toward her again. "The show is in trouble. We all have to face it. If the ratings don't change soon, we're going to find ourselves canceled."

"If it wasn't for Caleb's old ideas, I—"

"Paula!" Bob cut her off. "You have to take some responsibility for the ratings. You are the head writer."

"Yes, of course." He was treating her like a grip. She dropped her eyes to hide her growing rage. She wanted to hit Bob Silverstein, longed to slap his smug face, and she was very close to doing just that. If she had been given a free hand *Dreams* would not be in trouble now. If they had let her run the show, she would have shown them what good writing was all about.

Lee and Anne legally married on air! It was silly and stupid. But it was going to attract attention and Bob was obviously running scared. That thought made her feel a little better. If he weren't scared, he wouldn't be latching onto this wild scheme.

Bob cleared his throat. "We are auditioning now for the spot Kerry Scott vacated. I'll have some tapes sent over for you soon."

"Why bother to consult me?" she taunted.

"Paula," he cautioned, "let's not make it tough. We've been friends too long."

Have we? Paula wondered. Have we ever been friends? Not really. Any fondness she had ever felt for Bob was gone now. He was like Caleb, only interested in how he could use her for his own gain, all of it monetary.

Lonely in the empty apartment, Joe Seals reached for the phone and punched out Sue Bergman's home number.

"Oh, Joe," she cried when he identified himself, "I was hoping you would call."

"Were you?" His mood lifted and he sat up straighter and ran a hand over his balding head. "Sue, let's not go to Palm Springs this weekend. It's too hot in the desert. Let's just get in the car and start driving up the coast north. We'll find us a beach motel and just lay in the sun, maybe Pismo Beach."

"Oh," Sue said and paused. "Joe, I can't make it this weekend. That was why I was hoping you'd call. Some things have come up."

"Such as?" he asked, even though he suddenly did not want to hear the answer.

"It's my mother. You know how she is when she gets her heart set on something. A cousin's daughter is getting married and Mother wants to attend the wedding, and—"

"Sue," Joe cut her off. "Is it your mother?"

"Of course, what else?"

She was lying. "What else, Sue? I know you're seeing another man."

"Oh, Joe! I could cry. Who told you?"

"Word gets around," he muttered, but it wasn't true. He had seen them together when he stopped by the studio. He had seen the two of them walking through the parking lot together, seen the way she clung to the young man's arm and the way she flirted with him.

He had pushed it to the back of his mind, hoping it

was nothing or that it would make no difference for them. Sue was all he had now.

"Joe, you have to understand. You and I, we were always hiding. We never go out here. Joe, please talk to me. He's a nice Jewish boy. Mother likes him. You have to understand."

"I guess I do," he answered bleakly. "You deserve someone who can give you more than I can, who can offer you a future." A someone who was young and tall and liked to dance and whatever else young people were doing now.

"Joe, I care. I've loved you."

"Loved. Past tense, Sue."

"I'm sorry, Joe. I—I guess we just outgrew each other."

"You mean you outgrew me. You don't need me," he said. "Good-bye, Sue. No grudges."

"No grudges, Joe," she whispered wistfully.

He hung up. The bottle of bourbon he had left on the bar beckoned.

Chapter Forty-Three

Lauren held the official-looking envelope from the state of California. She had expected the document, but not this sobering sensation of finality. She picked up a fingernail file from the coffee table and slit the envelope open. She took out the notarized copy of the divorce papers.

The marriage of Benji and Lauren Parrow was ended, legally and forever. An odd sadness wrapped shroudlike around her. It was not supposed to have worked out this way. They had loved each other, were supposed to have had children and lived happily ever after.

So were Lila and Buddy, who had even had their two children, but they were not happy. Lauren stared off into nothingness, unable to think of a couple who were happy. Even her parent's marriage was marred by her father's long ago affair.

She put the carefully folded paper back in the envelope. Lauren wished for something as tangible as the Seal of California to finalize her affair with Kerry Scott. He was still there in her mind, embedded so deeply she was certain she would never be free of the memory of him.

An occasional fantasy would creep into her head.

They were a form of self-torture, yet she could not stop them. They were always similar. Somewhere, at office or home, late at night or early in the morning, Kerry would suddenly appear, his head cocked to one side and an embarrassed grin on his face. He would ask to talk to her, then they would silently go into each others arms and kiss hungrily, kiss as though they could never get enough and he would whisper that he could not live without her.

Her eyes filled with burning tears. "No!" She stood up and hurried to the kitchen. She was not going back into that pit of desperation because of an official document. This was going to be like any other night.

She opened the refrigerator and took out a pitcher of iced tea and poured a tall glass. There was cheese and ham. She debated between a sandwich or a salad, knowing it made no difference what she ate, only that it was important to make choices.

She could treat herself to a cooling shower which would make the evening more pleasant, she decided, then she could have her dinner in front of the television set.

She let the refrigerator door close and started undressing as she walked back to the bathroom. In the shower she let the water beat down on her body, switching from cold to hot and back again until she was gasping from the shock. She toweled her body, sprinkled herself with baby powder, ran a brush through her glossy dark hair that was trying to curl around her face.

She slipped into a thin pink gown and carried the matching robe into the living room. She felt better with the day's grime washed away.

Refreshed, she chopped ham and cheese over a bed of lettuce. Carrying tea and salad, she returned to the living room and was searching for the ever elusive *TV Guide* when a knock sounded at her door. She pulled her robe on and moved to the door. "Who is it?" she called.

"Lauren, it's Benji." Benji! Her eyes flew to the divorce papers on the coffee table. "Lauren, I want to talk to you."

Her throat dried and she could not speak. What did he want? Why was he here?

"Lauren, let me in, please!"

She flipped the bolt and opened the door. All the anger she had felt toward him since the Fourth of July weekend fled when she saw her own sadness reflected in his dark, beseeching eyes.

"We blew it, didn't we?" he asked softly.

"Come in, Benji," she murmured, finding her voice again. She stepped back, one hand gripping the door too tightly.

He entered and for a long moment Lauren was lost in the depths of his eyes, could feel his pain mingling with her own. His hand came out and gently brushed against her hair, pushing it back from her face in a familiar gesture.

She felt herself drawn to him, wanted to go into his arms and comfort him. She was shocked at herself. She closed the door and moved away, not looking at him. "I'm just having dinner," she said. "Would you like to join me for a salad? Or I could make you a sandwich." He used to love grilled ham and cheese sandwiches with mustard.

"I've eaten, went to a coffee shop when I got off work. Then I was driving around . . ." He shrugged. "I guess you got the papers today, too, huh?"

"Yes." Her heart was quivering. It was not a sexual feeling, but one of revived memories, her mind assaulted by things she had thought she had forgotten.

"Go ahead and eat," Benji urged.

She sank down to the floor beside the coffee table, poking at a chunk of ham with a fork. "I don't think I can," she said.

"I know. I've got a lump in my throat that won't go away. I couldn't eat when I ordered either. I didn't go to a coffee shop, Lauren. I went to Antonio's."

"The best plate of two-dollar spaghetti in town," she said, repeating an old phrase.

"The best," he said. He had taken the overstuffed chair in the corner next to the fern. He pressed the tips of spread fingers together and slowly raised his eyes to hers. "I miss you, Lauren. It's bad, coming home to an empty apartment every night."

Her body stiffened. "You didn't ever come home every night," she reminded him deliberately, some part of her wanting to get even for all the evenings she had spent alone while he chased other women.

"Lauren." He came to her and knelt on the floor. "We could try again, we could both give a little."

"No." Lauren scooted backward, suddenly aware of the thin gown and robe she wore.

"Lauren."

"What would I have to give, Benji?" she flung at him, her voice rough. "How far would I have to go? Would I have to tolerate your affairs, would I have to join one of those horrid sex clubs?"

"I stay away from those places now. The people—it was all a lot of people groping for sick kicks. Last time I went, I was . . ." He flushed and let his voice trail off.

"You were what?"

"Impotent," he choked.

"Oh." Momentarily subdued, she sank back. She was beginning to understand. His lifestyle was not working, and he was scared. "You will find someone else," she said as firmly as she could and pulled herself up on the sofa so he would be farther away.

His hand lashed out and grabbed an ankle, startling her. She suppressed a scream. "I want you, Lauren." His dark eyes begged for understanding. His hand loosened and he began to stroke her leg. "I want you."

"No!" She scrambled away but he came after her. "Benji!" she begged. "It's over. We can't go back."

"For old time's sake," he said, his mouth moving toward hers. She slid backward and hit the arm of the sofa. He moved over her.

434

"Benji, no!" She planted both hands on his chest and pushed. Somehow he flung her arms aside and his body pressed down on hers. "No," she whimpered.

"One kiss, Lauren. I won't hurt you. One kiss."

His lips assaulted hers roughly, his probing tongue invading her mouth. She wanted to scream, but she held herself rigid. She did not fight and she did not respond. Finally, he drew back. "Lauren, don't be this way."

"How else am I supposed to be?" she asked. She would never allow him to use and abuse her again.

"We meant something to each other."

"Let me up, Benji." Thankfully, he obeyed. Drawing the robe back across her breasts, she put the coffee table between them. She could hear herself breathing, conscious of the heavy rise and fall of her chest.

"You used to be warm," he said. "You didn't push me away."

"I tried for you, Benji. I really tried." She shook her head. "But it was never enough."

His eyes narrowed suddenly. "But you know more now. When I was here before, you were seeing some guy."

"No, you said I had a boyfriend. You made a lot of accusations," she remained him.

"Yeah, like you were giving out plenty to him and nothing to your husband."

"You aren't my husband," she said, fear slicing through her. He was turning mean.

His face went sullen. "I was. I still got rights, because I still care about you."

"Benji, please."

"Okay." His face changed abruptly and he flashed an open smile. "I'll keep my hands off you. You can eat. I'll go sit over there." He motioned toward the chair.

"I think you should just leave, Benji. Please?"

"No, I want to talk, Lauren." He sat down in the chair.

Lauren picked nervously at her salad, aware of his eyes boring into her relentlessly. She was not going to encourage him to stay any longer. But she could not stop the feelings of pity she felt about him. No matter what else happened, they were both now dealing with the same sense of failure, a knowledge of destruction. It was not a nice feeling, especially when you had to deal with loneliness, too.

"Remember that Sunday we had a picnic in Griffith Park? That was a good day."

"A good day?" she echoed hollowly. "You only went because I begged you. You said it was a stupid childish thing to do."

"But I liked it once I got there."

That was not the way she remembered it. He had sulked half the day and refused to touch the potato salad she had made. His mood changed only because he got to talking and drinking beer with a couple of guys who were waxing a car.

"We fed the squirrels," he offered.

"I guess we did," Lauren murmured. They had been close for a while, had lain together on a blanket and watched the park gradually empty itself of people. Then Benji had ruined it by wanting to make love with the blanket wrapped around them. She had not been able to do it, could not face the possibility of being observed.

"Lauren." Benji held out his arms. "Let me hold you. Be sweet to me, be my woman."

"No, Benji. It's over."

"Please," he begged. "I need you."

For the briefest moment, she wavered. He was suffering and it would not be so bad to let him have her, to give him some comfort. Only it would never end there. He would be back again and again, claiming her as his property.

"Let's not start something neither of us really wants," Lauren said.

"I want it."

"I don't!"

He came to his feet. "I could just take you."

436

"You've threatened me before," she said, suddenly feeling very tired of all this.

"I could take you," he repeated.

"I suppose you could. But what would it prove?"

His upper lip curled into a sneer. "You're a cold one, Lauren. A real frigid bitch." He towered over her, his face dark with anger. "A real bitch," he muttered again.

His hand lashed out, and even as she recoiled he caught the side of her face with his open palm. She fell sideways and cried out, but she knew to be still and not fight him. She huddled on the floor, waiting.

"I won't be around again, Lauren," he said. "This was your last chance."

She made no answer and Benji spun on his heel. She closed her eyes until the door slammed behind him, jarring the room. She scrambled up and locked the door.

Breathing heavily, she stood with her back to the door, her mind clearer now than it had been recently. Benji was selfish, never saw beyond his own desires, his own wants and needs.

Something clicked in her mind. When she had first met Kerry Scott there was something familiar about him. She knew now what it was. Benji and Kerry were alike, and it went beyond the fact that both of them had dark hair and brown eyes. They were out to gratify themselves first, last and always. And God help any woman who did not want to do it their way.

It wasn't just me, she realized. It wasn't my fault alone. No woman who had any sense of self, who had any needs of her own, could satisfy either of them. And such a woman does not exist. She felt sorry for them, for the lack in their souls.

She silently vowed to be more careful next time with a man. She was certain that from now on she would be able to recognize the self-centered man. And one day she would find a man who could love her back as freely as she loved him. Meanwhile she had her career, not something to hang onto for the sake of her sanity, but a real career she could pursue with joy.

Quiet happiness lifted her heart. She was free. Free of the black despair, free of the self-doubts of the past. "I'm not perfect," she said. "Not me. But I'm not so bad after all."

Chapter Forty-Four

Gil and Paula leaned against a railing overlooking a Marina canal. Below them was an assorted lot of boats and yachts bobbing gently in their slips.

"Would you like to own a boat?" Gil asked her.

"No. I like being near the water, but not on it or in it."

"Not even as a child?"

"I can swim," she said with a shrug. "But a pool is nicer. No salt, no sand. And no riptides."

"No secret longings for adventure?" he teased.

Paula turned to him. "I guess not."

"No secret dreams?"

"No, and that's terrible," she whispered. "I guess I never think beyond my job."

"And a demanding one it is. Is it worth it?"

"It's everything," she admitted to Gil, and to herself. "Writing has always been everything."

"Whatever makes you happy," Gil murmured.

Happy. It wasn't a word she dealt with in terms of herself, not since the loss of Naomi. Oh, she had been happy with Joe for a while. She had visions of building his small agency into one of the most elite, had been prepared to pour her money into better offices and to hiring the class of people who would attract clients. She had wanted to be involved with Joe in his agency.

But Joe, always cautious, refused to give up the crummy offices on Sunset. He refused to go after the big names, choosing to settle for the unattached writers and actors.

The truth was, Joe was not very ambitious and was happy to settle for simply making a living.

Gil slipped his arm around her waist. "You seem rather sad and preoccupied tonight."

"Preoccupied," she said. "There are some problems with *Dreams*. I'm getting some stuff I don't want to use pushed right down my throat."

"I'm sorry."

"I've been through it before."

"Hey, maybe I have something that will cheer you up," he said.

"What?"

"Money." He pulled back and took his wallet out. "Hold out your hands." He laid a stack of bills in her cupped hands. "There are twenty of them—one-hundred-dollar bills."

Paula felt the faintest sting of tears in her eyes, and tremendous relief. He had passed the test. "Gil, thank you," she said.

"As promised," he said with a smile.

"And on time." She returned the smile. She had been foolish to mistrust him, to deny herself their mutual attraction.

She put the money inside her checkbook and tucked it into the bottom of her purse.

"Let's walk," Paula suggested. Arms around each other, they strolled toward his apartment. Gil was good for her. She was not sure how she would be surviving right now without him, for there was no one else to turn to. She silently damned Silverstein and his veiled threats. Well, she knew the ropes. She would pull *Dreams* back up to the top.

Late afternoon sun filtered through the drapes and across the bed where Sally nestled against Alex La-Barre's substantial body. Sally thought of the Beverly Hills Hotel bungalow as their place now. She did not have her own key, but the people in the hotel knew her.

Sally ran playful fingers through the graying hair on Alex's chest. She thumped his belly. "You sound like a watermelon," she said.

"I'm fat."

"You're big, but solid. You're just my big old cuddly teddy bear."

Alex laughed out loud. "Oh, baby girl. Don't you know I'm considered a tyrant, a demanding, unreasonable director who reduces little girls like you to a puddle of tears?"

Sally rose up and rested on one elbow. "Did you do that to somebody today?"

"Yes, a young actress. She wasn't giving enough. She was holding back her emotions and I yelled at her."

"Sally stilled. "Alex, are you going to yell at me when we shoot my scenes?"

"I will, if you're not good enough," he replied.

"Will you hate me?"

He pulled her closer to him. "Sally, how could I hate you?"

"I'm scared, Alex. Can we take an evening and rehearse before we get on the set?"

"Of course." He patted her bottom.

She lay against him, her eyes closed. "Alex, you're been awfully quiet today," she said.

"I have a lot on my mind."

"Like what?"

"*Rainbow*."

"And what else?" Sally coaxed.

"You little imp! Have you taken up mind reading now? Or do you just know me all that well?"

"Then there is something else?"

"Yes." Alex untangled himself from Sally and sat up. "It's Gina. She's making noises about coming home."

441

Sally stilled, feeling her blood turn to ice. "Is—is she coming back?" she asked fearfully.

Alex shrugged. "I told her not to. With *Rainbow* I don't have time for the social stuff she likes."

"But when she comes back—will she stay?"

Alex shrugged again. "With Gina, who knows?"

"Alex, I don't mean to pry. But you two, you know? Are you like separated?"

"I guess you could call it that. Let's say that the less we see of each other, the better our marriage is."

"That's sad."

"Not particularly. It's how it worked out. My life is here. Hers is in Italy. Gina has never quite adjusted to no longer being a young sexpot. She can't bring herself to do character roles. If she can't be the romantic lead, she doesn't want anything."

As curious as she was about Gina Beradino LaBarre, it made Sally uncomfortable to talk about the woman. She didn't like to think about how it would be if and when she returned. Sally jumped up. "Is the shooting schedule completed?" she asked Alex.

"Yes. We'll do your scenes in September. Does that fit your schedule?"

"Yes. Dick Morris will be out the first of next week. I'll be tied up with him most of August. Then September is all yours." Sally shrugged her shoulders. "And then, I don't know."

"You'd better start auditioning again."

"You're right. I will, I'll talk to Joe." Sally put both hands on her breasts. "I still want breasts," she said.

"Hey, baby girl, you don't need them. Good things have been happening to you without them."

"I still want them."

"We'll see," Alex promised. "Just don't do anything foolish. Next time, I pick the doctor. Understand?"

"Oh, Alex." She was filled with soft, bubbly feelings. No one else had ever cared as much about her as Alex, no one else made her feel so protected.

442

"Sally, I've got to go now," Alex said. "I shouldn't be here at all, if the truth be known."

"Just couldn't stay away from me, huh?" Pleased, she rubbed her hands and face across his broad back.

"That's right." He pulled her around for a kiss. "Now get dressed. I'll have to send you home in a taxi."

"I don't want to go home."

"Oh?"

"There's nothing to do there. God, everything with California Girl was hurry, hurry, hurry. I quit *Dreams* and rushed off to New York. And now I just sit around with nothing to do."

"The action will start again next week," he reminded her.

"I know, but I still don't want to go home. Maybe I'll visit Joe. Tell him to find something for me."

"Okay," Alex agreed.

They dressed in silence and he was already lost to her, his mind back to the multitude of problems facing him.

Half an hour later, Sally popped into Joe Seal's outer office. "Hi," she said to the secretary, Maggie, who was in the process of polishing her nails. "Joe here?"

"Well, that's a matter of opinion, I guess. He's holding office hours next door."

"Next door?" Sally asked in bewilderment. "You mean he moved?"

"No, next door is the Habitat bar."

Sally was still puzzled. "Is there something going on around here that I don't know about?" she asked.

"Joe is drinking. A lot."

"Why?"

"I don't know," Maggie said with a shrug. "He doesn't tell me anything."

"All right," Sally said. "Thanks. I'll find him."

Concerned, Sally hurried downstairs and into the Habitat. The place was nearly deserted this time of day. Joe was alone at the far end of the oak bar.

He did not see her until she was standing next to him.

"Sally," he grinned broadly, his eyes bleary. "My favorite client. What are you doing here?" He patted the stool next to him.

"Looking for you, what else?" she said. He was drunk all right.

"Good girl." He was slurring his words. "Barkeep, get this little girl a drink."

"The little girl looks like a little girl," the bartender replied.

"A Coke," Sally muttered. Man, some day she was going to be twenty-one and have breasts, and no one would take her for a kid again. "Joe?"

"Huh?" Joe flung an arm around her. "Did you know this is a genuine antique bar? Right out of a saloon in Dodge City, Kansas. Kansas! Hey, ain't that right, barkeep? Everything in here is a genuine antique. Saloon Antique, right out of the Old West."

"I believe you, Joe, Sally said.

"Good!" He squinted at her. "Hey, you're from Kansas!"

"Not any more, remember? I'm a California girl living with my aunt."

"Yeah, I remember. They swallowed it, didn't they?"

"They believed me in New York."

"Yeah." Joe looked away and then back to her. "What were we talking about?" he asked.

"Not much, Joe. Have you got anything I should know about? After September, I'm going to be free."

"I had a rush call for a small part today. Just a walk-on with a couple of lines, a TV movie."

"I'll take it!" she said eagerly.

"No, you won't! No more walk-ons and two-liners for you. Not any more. Not after *Rainbow* and cos—cosm—the makeup thing."

"Oh, Joe! Come on, I want to take anything I can get."

"We're going to hold off. You're going to be big stuff after *California Girl*."

"Sure, Joe." She patted his shoulder. There was no

444

point in arguing with him now. "Let's go back to the office so we can talk," she urged.

"What are we going to talk about?"

"We'll think of something. Come on."

He got halfway up, then sank back down. "Got to pay the tab. Barkeep!" Joe fumbled around in his wallet until he found enough money to pay for his bill. Leaning heavily on Sally's thin shoulders, Joe shuffled out of the Habitat and they made their way up the stairs and into Joe's office.

"You go home now," he told Maggie.

"But there are some calls," she protested.

"You go home. I don't—I'll take calls tomorrow."

"You might as well go," Sally told Maggie. "I'll get him home."

"All right, he's all yours."

Sally guided Joe into the office. He collapsed on the shabby sofa. "Woe! I had a lot to drink," he said.

"Too much," Sally replied. She knelt in front of him and took his hand. "Why are you drinking, Joe?"

"I was thirsty," he said. "I was thirsty!"

"Nope. That's not an answer, Joe. It hurts me to see you like this."

"Oh." He patted her face. "You care about old Joe, don't you? You care. Paula doesn't care and Sue doesn't care."

"Sue?" Sally cried. "It's Sue!"

"Sue, she . . ." he choked.

"Did you two break up?"

"Aw, Sue got herself a young stud. A nice Jewish boy her mother will like. She don't have time for an old man any more."

"You're not old, Joe." Sally stroked his thin hair.

"Old, over the hill. And going down fast. Nobody wants an old man."

"Oh, you're not old, Joe," she insisted, her eyes glistening with tears. Poor Joe. She took him in her arms. "I care about you, Joe. You're good people, the best."

445

"Nice, Sally. Nice." He slid his hand under her blouse. "You're good to Joe."

"No, Joe. Not that." She could not go from Alex to Joe in the same day.

"You—you don't want me either," he mumbled.

"I'll hold you, Joe. You're drunk, you can't do anything now."

"Sure I can!"

"Joe, Joe. Hush, baby, hush," she crooned to him and kissed the top of his head as he relaxed against her. "Good, Joe. Just be still."

"Want you," he slurred, then his hand stilled on her thigh. His body went limp against her, relaxing until he was dead weight. She slid away from him and rested his head on the sofa arm. She looked around for something to use as a pillow but could find nothing.

She sat down in a chair and watched Joe sleep. Poor darling man, life had not treated Joe well. He went around being a nice guy and all it got him was a kick in the face.

That miserable Sue Bergman. And Paula Cavanaugh. The Witch treated Joe like dirt. Fuming, Sally considered calling both of them, telling them exactly what she thought of how they treated Joe. Or better yet, get the both of them over here at once. God, that would be funny, having Paula and Sue face each other across Joe's prone body. Or would it be?

Not very, she decided. Joe would be humiliated. She tiptoed to the other office and dialed Paula's office number and asked for Lauren.

"Sally here," she said. "I'm at Joe's office. He's drunk on his ass. He's passed out and I don't know what to do with him."

"Joe's drunk?" Lauren sounded surprised. "I've never seen him take more than a glass of wine."

"His secretary says he's drinking a lot. I guess he and and Sue broke up."

"I didn't know."

"Me neither. What am I going to do, Lauren?"

446

"Let him sleep it off, I suppose. I can pick you up in about an hour."

"I don't want him to wake up alone. I think he would just start drinking again."

"Do you think you could get him over here?" Lauren asked.

"Paula will blame me."

"That's probably true," Lauren agreed dryly.

"But who cares? She's nothing to me now. Don't leave without me, Lauren. And you don't know anything about this. There's no point in you getting in trouble with the Witch."

"Thanks, Sally."

Getting Joe awake, down the stairs and into his Mercedes was not easy, but they made it. Sally fished his keys out of his pocket and ran back up and locked the office.

In the car again, she studied the interior. "You better tell me how to drive this fancy contraption, Joe," she said.

"It's a car, just a car."

"Sure. Well, here goes." She stalled the car once and almost threw them through the windshield when she hit the brakes too hard. But after a few nervous blocks she felt reasonably secure behind the wheel. She supposed that one of these days she ought to get a driver's license.

The parking lot attendant helped Sally pour Joe into the elevator and took the car away to park it. Upstairs, Sally pressed the doorbell. The housekeeper opened the door.

"Hiya, Margaret," Joe grinned and almost fell down.

Margaret, startled out of her primness, jumped back. "Oh, Mr. Seals!" She was obviously appalled.

"Just point us in the direction of the bedroom," Sally told her.

"Oh, yes, miss. And I'll get Mrs. Seals."

"You do that," Sally said. "But let's get him to bed first."

447

"Yes, miss." Margaret scurried ahead, opened a door and turned back the bed.

Sally maneuvered Joe onto the bed. "Good girl," Joe mumbled and then suddenly turned white. "Oh, my God!" he cried.

He bolted for the bathroom. Margaret hurried from the room as Joe began throwing up violently. Sally went into the bathroom. "Poor Joe," she whispered, holding onto him as he retched repeatedly.

She got a washcloth, ran cold water over it and wiped his face. The rustle of Paula's skirt announced her arrival. "Margaret said Joe was ill."

Joe flipped down the corner of the washcloth that covered his face. "Drunk," he said.

"And sick!" Paula wrinkled her nose in disgust. "Really, Joe. I thought you were cured of the habit."

"I slid back," he slurred. "Backslid, backslider."

"I suppose you were around for all of this?" Paula asked Sally.

Sally shrugged. "Does it matter?"

"It does to me."

Sally ignored the comment. "Help me get him back to bed."

Avoiding touching or looking at each other, the two women undressed Joe and put him to bed in his underwear.

Paula covered Joe, and there was no gentleness in the motion. Sally wanted to slap the contemptuous expression off Paula's face. Instead, she followed Paula out of the room. "I found him like that," Sally explained. "His secretary says he's drinking a lot now."

"I hadn't noticed," Paula replied.

"Isn't that sort of thing kind of hard to miss?" Sally asked. "When the man is your husband?"

"Really, Sally," Paula said coldly, "I don't think this is any of your business."

"Joe is my friend," Sally retorted. "So it's my business."

Paula's eyes flared, making Sally cringe. If looks

could kill, I'd be dead, Sally thought. She lifted her chin. "I care about Joe."

"Do you?"

"Yes. He's suffering. He and Sue have broken up."

"Sue!" Paula's composure wavered.

"You did know about Sue, didn't you?"

"Yes," Paula answered stiffly. "You may go now. I'll look after Joe."

"Dismissed, huh?" Sally said. "Well, I'll let myself out."

That cold-hearted bitch, Sally thought as she stepped into the elevator. She would wait for Lauren in her car. Some day Paula was going to get hers and Sally hoped she would be around to see it happen.

Chapter Forty-Five

August was normally not the best month to find yourself living in Los Angeles and this year was no exception. The city was clogged with tourists and conventioners. The relentless desert heat kept the basin and valleys shrouded in yellowish-brown smog.

Lauren's eyes burned and she was sweaty and sticky. But nothing, not even the smog, could destroy her good mood as she walked toward her apartment.

"Sally," she called as she opened the door. "Guess what? Paula . . ." Her announcement died on her lips.

"Look who's here!" Sally said from the kitchen door. "Dick and I knocked off early today and I brought him home for dinner."

"Dick." Lauren recovered graciously and held out her hand to him. "How good it is to see you."

"And you." He clasped both his hands around hers. "I hope you don't mind me being here." He admired her openly with his eyes.

"No, of course not." She flashed him a smile and withdrew her hands, feeling her face growing warm, wishing Sally had warned her. It would only have taken a phone call.

Uncertain of exactly how she felt about Dick's being present, Lauren sank down on the opposite end of the sofa from him. He was better looking than she remembered, his eyes even more intense than before, their direct gaze making her self-conscious.

"Dick and I are doing dinner for us," Sally explained. "We went to the grocery store, and he made these yummy drinks, strawberry daiquiris." She held out a glass of pink liquid and pressed it into Lauren's hand. "Drink up," she urged.

Lauren sipped. "Delicious. How's the work going, Dick?" she asked, aware of the flow moving between them, the intangible attraction touched upon before.

Dick glanced over at Sally. "What can I say? Our girl here is beautiful. She works hard, never complains."

"Complain?" Sally almost choked. "They make me feel like a star. All those people just for me, hairdresser, makeup man, electricians, the photographer. Why should I complain?"

"Because your neck hurts from doing the same pose fifteen times, because your lips must get stiff from smiling so much."

"Oh, Dick!" Sally waved away his comment.

"She loves it," Lauren laughed. "Sally likes to work."

"I can tell," Dick replied with a fond smile.

They fell silent. Lauren was aware of the smug, pleased look on Sally's face. Dick had been in Los Angeles for ten days and Sally had tried to talk Lauren into seeing him again. She had badgered Lauren to drop in on them at work, but Lauren had refused. Dick was married, and she was not about to go out looking for him, even though she was curious.

Lauren was also aware of the flush in her cheeks and how pleased she felt about Dick's being here now. He was an easy man to like. "Oh," Lauren remembered. "I had something to tell you. I did my third sample script for Paula and she didn't cut me to shreds."

"She liked it?"

"Well, she didn't exactly say she liked it. She said it was better and that I should be ready for the real thing soon." She felt Dick watching her covertly.

452

"That's so exciting!" Sally cried. "Isn't she wonderful, Dick?"

"Wonderful," he agreed, his twinkling eyes catching Lauren's. He held up his glass. "To your writing success."

A ripple of pleasure moved through her body. "Thank you," she said, lowering her eyes from his and sipping her drink.

"We're having fruit salad for dinner," Sally told Lauren. "With fresh melons, and pineapple and strawberries and everything. I dripped honey over it and tossed it with coconut. Dick helped me."

Lauren laughed. "Would you believe she couldn't boil water when she met me? Now she's the one coming up with new recipes."

"Lauren taught me how to cook," Sally said emphatically.

"Your aunt here, huh?" Dick said. "She taught you how to cook?"

"Yes, my aunt," Sally giggled and stuck out her tongue at Dick.

"Dick, I . . ." Lauren began.

"Not a word," he said, holding up his hands. "I don't want to know anything more than Sally told the company."

Lauren glanced at Sally, who was grinning broadly. "Refill?" Sally asked. She darted back to the kitchen and returned with a blender half full.

"We're going to have to do something about the crystal if we keep indulging in these fancy drinks," Lauren remarked as Sally filled her glass.

Dick held out his glass for a refill, too. "This is a wineglass," he said. "It's fine."

"I'll get you a whole set of everything for your birthday," Sally promised. "Then we can serve in style."

"My birthday?" Lauren asked. She had kept the upcoming date to herself because she did not want a fuss made.

"It is Saturday, isn't it?" Sally asked.

"How did you know?"

"I'm sneaky. I checked your driver's license one time."

"You *are* sneaky."

"That's me," Sally said, grinning wickedly. "Let's eat. I'm famished."

The fruit salad was huge, but the level of the bowl dropped rapidly; the slices of corned beef wrapped around pickles disappeared along with the rye bread with mustard.

After dinner, Sally excused herself. "I'm taking a shower and going to bed."

"Bed?" Lauren cried, experiencing a moment of panic. "It's not even dark."

"I'm tired," Sally said, yawning elaborately. "I'll see you two tomorrow." She disappeared.

Lauren moved to the sink with a stack of plates. "I'm sorry," she apologized to Dick, embarrassed. "Sally is being a little obvious."

"Well, I don't mind," he said. "I've wanted to see you."

His direct honesty caused her to catch her breath. She turned around slowly, her heart racing. Their eyes met and held, igniting a flame. Dick watched her, a quizzical, hopeful look in his eyes.

"You have?" she said the words slowly.

"I kept hoping you'd show up one day. I thought about calling you."

"Why didn't you?" she asked, a little surprised at her boldness.

"I wasn't sure you would see me again." He shrugged and smiled in a shy, endearing manner.

"Because you're married?" she said more than asked.

He hesitated for a few moments. "Yes, because all we could be is friends."

Caught up in the depth of his eyes, she stood there, locked in suspended time, her mind racing, considering the opportunity he offered, the chance of knowing a man sexually with no strings attached, an affair for here

454

and now with no tomorrows. Sally and other women managed such things, enjoyed them, rejoiced in them. Lauren knew that for herself it would be a test.

Slowly she breathed out. "Then let's be friends, Dick."

He came to her and she stood very still as he took her face between his hands. Conscious of the commitment she was making, she closed her eyes and gave herself up to the quiet attraction she felt for him. His lips touched hers, tentatively, gently, moving away and coming back again as though he were savoring the first taste of her mouth. She accepted the kiss without moving and when they came apart they were both breathing fast.

"Nice," he whispered and dropped his face to nuzzle her cheek.

"Yes, nice." She was quivering, her body limp as she rested against him, inhaling the solid male smell.

They finished the dishes and went out to sit beside the pool. They held hands and talked for a while in a quiet, friendly way. Then Dick pulled her into a chaise lounge with him in a natural and undemanding way.

Half sitting, half lying, they stretched out on their sides. Dick held her, one hand moving in small circles over her back, sending wave after wave of sweet pleasure through her body.

She answered his kisses with enthusiasm, enjoyed his touch and the sense of rising desire, but another part of her watched and kept score on this new game. A piece of her calculated the chance of pain against the liberated attitude she had assumed. They petted and gently explored each other's bodies through their clothes. It was Lauren, flushed and growing uncertain, who pulled away first. "I think we had better stop," she murmured.

She could see him smiling in the darkness. "But I could keep this up all night long. My God, I haven't necked in years." He paused and dropped a gentle kiss on her forehead. "But I want more, Lauren."

"I know." She hid her face against his chest, her tongue a numb and twisted thing in her mouth. She wanted more, too, and it shocked her to some extent, surprised her that she could seriously be doing this. "But I can't. Not here with Sally home." She was not so liberated that she could lay a guy while her roommate was in the next room.

"I understand." He stroked her hair with broad strong fingers. "Lauren, let's spend the weekend together. Sally and the crew and I will be moving to Santa Barbara tomorrow. We're shooting beach scenes there. Why don't you fly up on Friday and I'll drive you back Sunday."

"I—I don't know," she whispered, doubt suddenly assailing her. She didn't know if she could go through with it.

"Please. Let's just enjoy each other for here and now. Can you do that?"

"I don't know," she answered honestly.

"I won't push you into anything you don't want."

Lauren shivered. Kerry Scott had said almost those exact words. "Can I think about it?" she asked.

"I'll call you from Santa Barbara."

"All right." They got out of the lounge chair, both reluctant to part. Lauren walked Dick out to his rented car and they said good night.

Lauren walked slowly back past the pool. She liked Dick Morris. He was older and considerate. She did not think he would lie to her, and this time she would not be fooling herself.

In the end, Lauren decided such opportunities did not present themselves every day. And she did want to be with Dick. He made her feel warm and safe. And for once in her life she was going to enjoy a man for the pleasure of the moment, with no commitments made on either side.

It was shortly after seven when Lauren stepped off the plane at Santa Barbara. She saw Sally first. She was waving wildly and clinging to the arm of a tall skinny man.

456

Then she saw Dick striding toward her. He was not very tall, and his shoulders were too narrow. His face was too flat for his nose, yet it all managed to come together very nicely. He was smiling as he took her hands in his. "I'm glad you came," he said sincerely.

"So am I," she murmured and lifted her face for his kiss. She could feel the pulse in her throat throbbing. He kissed her lightly, then took the small suitcase from her hands.

"Come on," he said. "Sally has all sorts of plans made. She's asked her director, Andy, to join us. She's determined to make this your most memorable birthday. So you had better enjoy every minute of it or you'll disappoint her. I don't want to see that smile fade a single time."

Friends. Lauren had promised Dick they would be friends. Could she go through with it? Could she be friends sexually with a man?

They lingered over dinner, savoring every last morsel of lobster dipped in butter and lemon. They treated themselves to brandy and coffee afterward.

Sally ended the meal. "Andy and I have to go," she announced. "We want to catch a movie and the last show starts in twenty minutes."

"Take the car," Dick said, handing his keys to Andy.

"Thanks. Now all we need is someone to point us in the right direction."

"Come on," Sally urged, tugging at Andy's arm. "I know the way. I don't want to miss the credits. You guys have fun," she said and whisked Andy away.

"Sally is being obvious again," Dick said. "She left us alone."

"Yes." Lauren fumbled for her purse, wishing for some glib words to cover her nervousness. "Andy is nice."

"He has a sense of humor and that makes him easy to work with."

Outside the restaurant, they stood for a moment.

457

Dick's arm dropped over her shoulders. She stiffened involuntarily.

"Lauren?" he asked.

"I'm sorry," she said, hating her nervousness and the necessity of apologizing.

"Are you sorry you came?"

"No, I—I wanted to come. I just feel so—so awkward. I'm not very good at this."

"Would you like for me to get a room for you, all your own?"

She wanted to cry. She had it all planned out in her head. It was just going to be fun, and she was going to be very sophisticated about sleeping with Dick, and now she was falling to pieces.

"Let's walk awhile," he said. "Our hotel is up the beach."

"We have to walk, don't we? They took the car. And, oh, my bag is in the car!"

"I'll get it for you as soon as they return."

She shivered. "I'm overreacting."

"It's okay," he assured her.

"Oh, Dick!" She turned to him and he opened his arms. She went into them and pressed her face down into the hollow of his neck. He held her tightly, murmuring soft, soothing words. Touched by his tenderness, she felt tears in her eyes. She clung to him.

When she pulled away she tried to hide her tears. She laughed shakily. "Sorry for being so silly."

"It's not silly at all. It just means you're a very thoughtful and sensitive girl who takes life very seriously."

"That's always been one of my problems," she agreed, letting out a deep breath. "Come on." She grabbed his hand and turned to face the ocean. "Let's walk now. It's nice here." She threw back her head and let the breeze lift her hair, determined not to fall apart again.

The street stretched out like a gray ribbon into the night. The beach to their left was wide and sandy.

There was a great strip of grass separating the beach from the street, making it all seem like one huge park. They strolled along on the sidewalk and Dick talked about the filming they had just completed. "I'm sure the beach scene will be the first commercial. We'll hit with it as soon as we have the products in the local stores, which looks to be the first of September. For once, everything seems to be happening on schedule." He squeezed her hand. "Am I boring you?"

"No." It was soothing, and she was beginning to relax.

"There's our hotel," Dick said, pointing ahead. It was too soon. Her hand tightened. "There, on the opposite side of the street."

As they stepped off the curb, Dick's arm came around her waist. "Would you like to go dancing?" he asked.

"Our kind of music?" she said, reaching back to the one other date they had shared.

"Yes. I checked that out." She was flattered by the thoughtfulness and felt herself relax a little.

He was smoother on the dance floor than she remembered. The soft lights and the easy music as well as a couple of drinks chased away her fears and doubts. She relaxed against him, liking the feel of the length of his body against hers. She savored the touch of his hands and felt the desire growing in her body.

"Let's go neck," he whispered against her hair. "Either that, or I'm going to kiss you right here."

She raised her lips to him and they kissed, swaying gently to the music. She grew warm and weak with desire. "Necking isn't going to be enough," she whispered, her voice husky.

"Not nearly enough." Holding her hand, he led her from the dance floor and out into the lobby. He kissed her again in the elevator.

In the room she hesitated and he noticed. "You take the bathroom first," he offered. "Or better yet, let's shower together. Would you like that?"

She swallowed. "I think I'd like anything you like," she said and knew it was true.

What awkward feelings they felt as they undressed passed quickly. Dick made everything easier because of his casual yet concerned attitude. It made Lauren feel safe enough to be free with him.

In bed, they came together slowly and conveniently. She matched his rhythm, wanting it to be good for him. For a brief time, she thought she would make it, too, but the rhythm changed and she lost the feeling. But it was all right. She did not mind. She had not really expected fireworks with Dick.

He lay next to her with his arms around her. "I'm sorry," he said. "It wasn't good for you."

"Good? It was very pleasurable," she said. "I don't have to climax every time." There! She had said another forbidden word to a man. She was learning. Kerry had taught her a few things.

"I'll make it up to you," he promised, but he fell asleep a few moments later. She eased away from him, needing a small space of privacy for herself. She felt faintly sad for reasons she could not identify and she was too sleepy to dwell on it.

Dick awakened first the next morning and she opened her eyes to find him leaning over her on one elbow. "You're awake," she whispered and stretched out, then molded herself against him.

"I want you," he said, kissing her cheek. "Let's shower."

It was only after teeth had been brushed and they had showered that he kissed her again. "Happy birthday," he said and drew her down into the bed. He laid her on her back and his hands cupped her breasts. He kissed her nipples, drawing them into his mouth and tonguing them until she was withering.

"Oh, please," she said. "Now!" He slid down over her body. This time the fireworks happened. She exploded, her fingers entwining themselves in his hair. "Wonderful!" she breathed.

"Was it?" He came up over her.

The question surprised her. She gazed up into his eyes that were only inches away. "Yes, it was beautiful."

"It's very important to me that it be good for you, too. I felt like a cad last night. I was in too much of a hurry. I wanted you so badly."

"Dick," she said, drawing him over her. "You're fantastic."

"It was good, you weren't faking?"

"Dick!" She held his head back and looked into his eyes to see if he was being truthful.

"Hey, don't you know men worry about this sort of thing?"

"You're crazy!" She hugged him. God, she liked this man.

It was a good day. Her day, a birthday to be remembered. They met Sally and Andy for breakfast, then were off on a fishing boat Dick had chartered. They caught very little, but they had a great deal of fun.

They returned to the hotel, swam, then separated for naps. They made love again, but only after a shower, and Lauren realized it was a quirk with him. They both had to be clean before sex.

They slept, showered again, made love and rushed to meet Andy and Sally for dinner and the final celebration of the day. Sally gave Lauren a card. Inside was a note promising Monday delivery of new stemware. Andy gave her a conch shell she had admired in the gift shop. Dick took a small package from his jacket pocket.

Lauren's heart caught as she opened the velvet-lined box. A slender gold chain lay glistening against the red velvet.

"It's beautiful, and it's too much," she cried. "I can't accept this."

"You most certainly will accept it," Dick insisted. "It was chosen just for you. I got it in Los Angeles."

She could not help but wonder what he would have done with the necklace if there had been no weekend

461

date. Would he have given it to his wife or daughter? She thrust the thought out of her mind and obediently bent her head so he could clasp the chain around her neck.

Lauren looked at Dick. He was a good man, a nice man, and she had gone to bed with him without loving him, without expecting anything beyond the moment. She tucked her hand into his. But she knew it only worked because he would be leaving. If she saw too much of him she would come to care a great deal. He would be easy to love. She would want more and more of him and he would never stand for it. He was committed to his wife. Once again, she felt sad. But she knew she had learned something. She had shed a bit more of her butterfly cocoon. No matter how hard she tried she could never enjoy sex casually as Sally did. She knew she must always be careful about the men. It was easy to want too much and get hurt.

Chapter Forty-Six

Sally and Joe Seals shared a small sofa in the green room of *Chit-Chat* at KKTV, a local Los Angeles station. Sally tucked her hand into Joe's and squeezed. "I'm scared," she said. "My hands are cold."

"Put your coat back on."

"I can't. I have to be ready to go on."

"Here." Joe reached across her and pulled the black leather coat over her lap.

"Isn't it pretty?" she whispered, running fingers over the silver fox collar. "I never thought I'd own anything so beautiful. Joe, do I look okay?"

"Yes," Joe shook his head. She was gorgeous. "You'll do." He patted her knee through the coat.

The transformation Sally had undergone since August was phenomenal. He never saw her in jeans now, seldom in pants. The hippie look was out and the fashion world was in for Sally and everyone else. It was now fashionable to be fashionable, and Dick Morris had seen to it that Sally was outfitted in the most stylish of junior clothes for her personal appearances.

Today she wore a three-piece suit of burnt orange, chocolate brown and cream plaid with a cream blouse. Her slender legs were clad in silky nylons and her hair was drawn upward on the sides and fell into a soft cascade down her back.

She slid her hand back into Joe's. "I'm so cold. Why do I always get cold when I'm nervous? And why do my armpits sweat when I'm cold? I'll go out there stinking."

"The viewers won't be able to smell you," Joe teased. "Now stop worrying!" Joe was glad she hadn't changed too much. She was still his Sally. There was a warm ache in his heart for this crazy kid. He squeezed her hand and something cut into his palm. He lifted her hand up and gulped at the sight of a small opal ring set in a high dome. "Sally, where did you get this?" he demanded.

"I bought it. Isn't it pretty?"

"Sally," Joe moaned. "Honey, you're supposed to consult me before you spend that kind of money."

"It only cost five hundred dollars," she protested.

"Sally, let me get you a business manager. He'll invest your money and put you on an allowance and take care of your taxes for you."

"No. I don't want to be put on an allowance, and you can take care of my taxes, Joe. I never had any money before and I want to enjoy it."

"That coat, the ring and that damned car. Honey, you aren't that rich. Not yet."

"I feel rich. I think I'm going to be. There will be lots more money when California Girl goes nationwide. Dick told me it would go in January."

"Dick said *maybe* in January," he reminded her.

"A maybe is as good as yes. The products are selling, aren't they?"

Joe had to admit that was true. Los Angeles was blitzed with ads, Sally's face jumped off billboards. There were four-color ads in every local magazine. She was pictured in newspaper layouts for all the major department stores. The personal appearances at the department stores were bringing in a nice bundle. Dick had managed to make Sally into a minor celebrity in a city of celebrities.

Slocum had not hurt either. When the TV movie was premiered in October, Sally was singled out in the review in the *Los Angeles Times*. She was mentioned in *Variety* and even in a gossip column:

> *What aging director is seeing what new young thing? And how does his wife in Italy feel about these blatant goings on?*

Joe was waiting to see if that was going to stir up some trouble. Gina Beradino had a reputation for being fiery. Like many Hollywood couples, it was known they tolerated each other's affairs, but only as long as they were discreet.

The only good thing going now was that Sally was not as available to Alex LaBarre as she had been in the past. She had her own commitments.

There was already mention of Sally in the trade papers for her part in *Rainbow*, which was still in the editing stage. Sally was suddenly a very hot commodity. Half the telephone calls coming into Joe's office were in reference to Sally, most of them easy enough to dismiss. He would not consider an offer for a low-budget film, nor, so far, for television. It was vitally important to Sally's career right now that he guide her in the right direction. He wanted to establish an image that was lasting and stable.

Sally was being difficult about it. She wanted to grab everything, wanted to take all the parts she could fit into her schedule and could not seem to understand the value of being discriminating. They had fought about it twice. Joe could not get it through her head that she could burn herself out and disappear as rapidly as she had appeared in the public eye.

It was of paramount importance that she be selective in the parts she accepted. Joe was grateful Sally still had Lauren, the one stabilizing force in the girl's life.

The door at the end of the small narrow room

opened. "You're next, Miss Rook," a young man told her.

"Oh, God!" Sally stood up and Joe gave her a reassuring pat on the behind.

"Do me proud, kid," he said.

"I—I'll try," she choked. Then with her quivering chin held high, she followed the young man out of the green room, which was actually painted white and held a selection of chairs that appeared to be discards from other offices.

Joe flipped on a television set that was already dialed to KKTV. He leaned back on the sofa and wished for a drink. It was impossible to get through the days without liquor. Of course, he had it under control now. He had a few bad times after Sue, but that was over with. And it was not as though he was really an alcoholic. He did not have to get bombed out of his mind, just needed enough booze to keep him mellowed out, enough to put him to sleep at night.

Joe picked up Sally's coat and absently began to stroke the fox collar as his mind slipped back to Sally. He did not admit it to himself, but Sally, her career and her problems, was the stablizing force in his life now. She needed him and he would never let the kid down.

His eyes moved to the television set as the commercial ended and the host of *Chit-Chat* smiled into the camera.

Lauren switched off the TV as *Chit-Chat* ended on a commercial. She felt very proud of Sally today. Lauren could tell Sally was nervous, but she carried off the interview beautifully.

It was short, but good. Sally was questioned about how she dealt with instant success and Sally pointed out that she had been around for four years. Lauren had to laugh when Sally said money had not really changed her life. It had changed her life and her. Money always had an effect.

Lauren sank back down on the floor of the penthouse television room where she had spread out Paula's latest script to edit. She had slipped in here so she could watch Sally and she was glad Paula had not caught her. With the mood Paula was in there was no telling how she might have reacted.

Lauren had kept the door closed and was enjoying the feeling of at least temporary isolation. Life with Paula had not been easy lately, not since the Anne and Lee wedding plot materialized.

The wedding was airing next week, and live, much to Paula's chagrin. When Lauren first heard about the so called "double" wedding she thought it was just plain silly. But when the ratings started climbing, Lauren changed her mind.

First Anne (as Lily) was hurt in a dramatic fall down a staircase, done by a stunt girl, of course. Lily struck her head and the injury was so bad that she was not expected to live. Jarred to his senses, John made a deathbed proposal. Lo and behold, Lily's will to live returned and she survived.

The publicity department immediately released the announcement that Lee Trent and Anne Voll would marry on the show along with John and Lily. Of course, it drew some snide comments from reviewers as well as some barbed remarks about the desperate measures a failing show would take to prop up its rating. But it was working. The viewers were ecstatic; favorable mail was pouring in, especially to Anne Voll. There was a fresh sense of excitement in all the people involved. It was reflected in the writing as well as the acting.

Lauren just wished Paula did not find it necessary to be so gloomy and dour about it. Yet even while Paula hated it, she was turning out good scripts. There was so much more drama to deal with now.

Lauren finished the last page of editing and began to gather up the scripts. She paused. This show would be aired in early December. There was something odd about that last Lily and John scene. Lauren picked up a script and thumbed back through it. She read it again.

Lily was depressed, and there was no explanation for it. Where was Paula heading with this? It made no sense.

Well, that's not my problem, she decided. She carried the stack of scripts back to her regular office. She was tired. Between Sally and Paula she had been running hard lately.

Yet she was filled with an underlying sense of restlessness. She knew she was ready to do a script. It had been August when Paula had approved her last sample script, and not a word from the woman since.

Paula had been in such vile moods that Lauren did not dare bring it up herself, but she knew she must soon.

Lauren fingered the slender gold chain around her neck. She wore it often and it always reminded her of Dick. There had been more dates after the Santa Barbara weekend, then he had returned to New York. He sent flowers back immediately and there had been no contact since then. And that was how it should be. She found it comforting to have good memories of a man, pleasant ones instead of the painful kind.

Sally and Lauren arrived home within fifteen minutes of each other. They had moved, at Sally's insistence, to West Hollywood, for far different reasons than Lauren had once envisioned.

Lauren had gone along with the move because she was certain she would go on the writing staff; otherwise she could not really afford the new place. Sally had offered to carry the larger share of the rent, but Lauren would not let her do that.

The new building was beautiful, five stories of apartments with underground parking, all fully secured, requiring either cards or keys at every entrance. There were two master-sized bedrooms, each with private bath. The drapes were new and the shag carpeting was thick and plush. The kitchen was compact and complete.

The day the furniture was moved into the new place

Lauren was appalled. It looked so old and shabby in the new apartment surroundings, and it did not begin to fill the large rooms.

Sally's room was the only one complete. She had bought a new oak bedroom suite and Lauren sold the old one, glad to be rid of another reminder of the past.

Dick had sent out a multitude of glossy prints of Sally, many of them four-color ad copy. Framed in chrome, the prints dominated one wall of the bedroom. Sally had replaced the plain white drapes with a yellow-and-white floral of the same fabric as the bedspread.

Glad to be home, the girls kicked off their shoes, settled down with drinks to discuss Sally's appearance on *Chit-Chat*.

"Did I look scared?" Sally asked. "I was petrified."

"You looked beautiful," Lauren replied.

"My hands were shaking."

"I couldn't see them."

"I thought I would just die when she asked me about men and sex. I almost blew it. Then I remembered who I was representing, California Girl and God. Was I obviously lying?"

"You looked taken aback, very properly naive."

Sally snorted. "I hope so." She rolled her eyes. "It was hairy. Hey, what do you want to do about dinner? Open some soup, or go out?"

"Oh, I don't care. I'm sort of tired. I think soup . . ."

The ringing of Sally's phone interrupted Lauren. Sally jumped up. "I'll be right back." She could not stand to let the phone ring until the answering service picked it up. Even when she did, she immediately called the service to find out who had called.

She picked up the receiver. "Hello."

"Miss Rook? This is William Akron."

"William Akron! Wow!" She sank down on the edge of the bed. "Really? *The* William Akron?" she questioned, skeptical.

"Well, I'm William Akron," the male voice laughed. "Of some television fame, if I may be immodest."

469

"Some!" Sally laughed in delight. Akron was a hot TV producer. He had at least two shows on the air now that never dropped out of the top ten and he was calling her!

"I've telephoned and written your agent," he said. "But I haven't been able to get any satisfaction, so I took a chance on your number being listed, then decided to call you direct."

"I see," Sally murmured. What was wrong with Joe? William Akron was somebody. Joe acted like he was trying to hold her back.

"We have a pilot that we think you might be interested in. I'd like to send you the script and talk to you about terms."

"Terms? What sort of terms?" She felt like she had learned enough to know to ask about money right away.

"We were thinking in terms of three thousand a week for thirteen weeks. And if the show goes, then we'll renegotiate."

Sally barely heard the rest of the conversation. Three thousand a week. It was a fortune. Of course, she had heard that Farrah Fawcett-Majors was getting five or more, but she had been around longer. The important thing was that it could make her a star. She would have her own series.

"I want to see the script," Sally told him. "As soon as possible."

"I'll have it sent over by messenger in the morning. And I'd like to have dinner with you tomorrow night."

"You're on!"

Dazed, her heart pounding, Sally ran back into the living room. "You aren't going to believe this, Lauren . . ."

Chapter Forty-Seven

"Damn!" Sally slammed down the telephone. She had called Alex three times today and each time she had reached his secretary who said he was out. This time there was no missing the impatience in the woman's voice.

"Miss, I *will* give Mr. LaBarre his messages when he returns to the office or when he calls in."

Old biddy! Sally grumbled and threw herself across the yellow-and-white bedspread. She snatched the television script and began to read again. She was so excited when it was delivered at noon that she could barely make sense of the first two readings.

It finally got through her delighted mind that the new show was sort of a combination of *Wonder Woman* and *The Bionic Woman*. Sally flipped over onto her back and stared at the ceiling. She needed to talk to Alex bad, he could tell her what to do and how to fight Joe, who had obviously kept this offer hidden from her. Joe had no right to do that. He was wrong.

Darn it! She was too restless and excited to hang around the apartment until it was time to meet Akron at the Polo Lounge. Alex was not ever going to call her back, so that left her with one choice. She would go in and tackle Joe.

471

She changed quickly, from jeans into a simple dress in an amber color that set off her hair and eyes. She gathered her purse and headed for the door. She stopped when she realized she wasn't wearing any makeup.

Sally darted into the bathroom and yanked open a drawer that was overflowing with an assortment of California Girl products. She took a deep breath to calm herself and began applying the makeup. The new image was a lot of trouble, she thought, but she had become so recognizable that she did not dare go out without looking her best. In her purse was a complete set of makeup she could use for touch ups when she was out.

In the underground parking area Sally popped into her Datsun 280Z. She loved the shiny red car. She had a driver's license now, and car payments, just like any other citizen.

She took the quickest route down Sunset to Joe's office. By the time she arrived she had worked herself into a righteous anger.

She burst into his office. "Joe! You've been keeping things from me!"

"Who, me?" Joe gave her one of his guileless smiles and adjusted his bow tie.

"Yes, you!" She planted her feet wide apart and stood with her hands on her hips. "William Akron called me last night. I read the pilot script this afternoon, and I want to do the show."

"Sally, honey." Joe came around his desk and put his arm around her rigid shoulders. "It's one of those comic strip shows."

"Joe, it pays three thousand a week. And it would be my show. I'd be somebody."

"You're somebody now. You're the California Girl. And that was a nice piece of acting you did in Devores' new flick."

"I didn't like that part," Sally sulked. "He made me look stupid. He yelled at me."

472

"He's a good director. It means something to work with him."

"I want this TV show, Joe."

"Sure, kid. You'll be a name then," Joe sneered. "To a lot of eight-year-olds. It's a family hour show. None of them last."

"*The Waltons* lasted."

"This is hardly of the same quality."

"Joe." She moved away from him, angered at having to plead. "This is prime time TV."

"It'll last a season or two, maybe half of one. That's all."

"I'll be a name," she insisted.

"Not for long."

"Damn you!" Sally stomped her foot and shook her head, sending her hair flying wildly about her face.

"Sally, sit down!" Joe commanded. He tried to push her toward the sofa but she shrugged off his hands.

"No!"

"Sally, think! Think ahead. What will you do after the series is canceled?"

"Get another one."

"Sure," he muttered, his tone skeptical. "You'll be another Mary Tyler Moore."

"And movies."

"Hey, little girl!" Joe's voice rose. "Look around. Nobody makes a good transition from television star to movie star."

"That's not true!" Frustrated beyond words, she stomped her foot again. She frantically ran a list of actresses through her mind. "*Sybil!*" she shrieked. "That girl, what's her name, that did *The Flying Nun*. Sally Fields. She made it in movies."

"She made a TV movie, and she was good. But she wasn't seen around much for at least three years. What happened to the woman on *Bewitched*? And how about the gal in *Gilligan's Island*? Huh?" Joe demanded. "And Barbara Eden? And Lorne Greene? My God,

473

girl, the list is endless. It takes years to shake the old image, and some never make it."

"Joe," Sally whimpered, not believing him.

"You know how snobbish the movie people are about television actors. They don't think they have it. The television screen is small, and it makes you into a small actor."

"That's all a lot of crap," Sally spat at him.

"Maybe, maybe not. But this is a snob world out here and they have their own measures for glory. You become a television star and the movies won't touch you. You'll have to start all over, back to small parts again. To character roles again."

"You!" Sally screamed. Too angry to put her feelings into words, she spun and hurried out of the office.

She got into her car and drove, mindlessly at first, just following Sunset. In time she came to Pacific Palisades and finally she found the ocean. She got out and walked a while along the broad expanse of sand.

If she had a big hit on TV she wouldn't have to work for a while afterward. She would have enough money to make it however she wanted to. Joe was wrong. Akron was offering her something right now. She could be a star in less than a year, not in the five or ten Joe wanted her to take. You have to grab the opportunities when they came along, or they might not ever appear again. She shivered in the early chill. It was getting late.

Sally got back into her red Datsun and drove back up Sunset to the Beverly Hills Hotel where she was meeting Akron. She left her car in the hands of a parking attendant and walked up the long canopied and carpeted entryway to the hotel.

Sally wrinkled her nose. The hotel kept so many flowers in the lobby the place smelled like a funeral parlor. She turned right and went back to the Polo Lounge. It was jammed and there was no way she could recognize Akron.

She was about to return to the desk to have him

paged when she felt a hand on her elbow. "Miss Rook?"

"That's me." She turned to face him, smiling broadly. This was *the* William Akron, this little pip-squeak of a man with his dark beady eyes and scraggly Vandyke beard?

"I'm so glad you could make it. Come, I have a table. Let's just slide between these people." They inched their way back to a table. "God, this mob," he muttered as he was seating her. "I don't know why I came here. There has to be quieter places."

"I love it here," Sally enthused. She was tingling with excitement. She knew marvelous wonderful things happened in the Polo Lounge. More deals were supposedly made here than in all the hollywood offices.

Sally looked around. The lounge was predominantly green. Green upholstery, green carpeting, even the huge round support pillars were wallpapered in green and white. The truth was, the place was rather ugly, but that didn't matter. Good things happened here.

Akron ordered a fresh drink for himself and one for her. There were no questions about her age this time, which pleased Sally to no end. Some places knew how to treat a lady.

"Now." Akron pushed a tray of pretzels toward her. "Did you like the script?"

"I adored it."

"Terrific." Eyes gleaming, he leaned closer. "Then we'll set up a screen test for you."

"A screen test?" Sally drew back. "I didn't know I'd have to test for it."

"It's just a formality." He picked up her hand and began to stroke it gently. It made her feel crawly. He went on: "The show will be used as a replacement in January, for the second season as they're calling it now. It's turning into quite a good time to be introduced."

"Is it?" The drinks arrived and she was grateful for a reason to withdraw her hand. She really didn't know if January was a good time or not, or if it even mattered.

"So we're all set then. I'll arrange for the screen test, and . . ."

"Not yet," she said, hesitating. "I have to talk to my agent again."

"Oh." Arkon drew back, an expression of distaste on his slim face. "That man is impossible to deal with. He ignores me."

"Joe's kind of funny," Sally said with a small shrug.

"Honey, I can get you into one of the really good agencies. Neither of us has to deal with a man like Seals."

Sally drew back again into the circular booth. "But, Joe, he's my friend. I've been with him for a long time."

"Sometimes we outgrow our friends," Arkon suggested.

Sally shook her head. "No." She felt confused now that her anger had faded away. And she didn't like William Arkon. What if Joe was right? What if she was only a star for half a season and then a nobody? "I have to think about this," she said, uncertain.

Akron's small eyes seemed to grow even smaller. "Sweetie," he pointed out. "You're somebody now. Just for now, this month. Maybe this year. But you'd better grab the gold ring while you can. You won't be the California Girl forever."

Startled by his words, her heart picked up its beat. No, it would not last forever, of course. She knew that. But her career would continue, she would always be an actress. Even Paula had said she would be a star.

"Come on," Akron coaxed. "Let me set up a screen test for you."

"All right," she agreed, dubious, but afraid not to do it. He wrote a time and place on a card and gave it to her.

"You be there Monday," he said.

Akron raised his arm and pressed the side of a digital watch. "Look, I know I asked you to dinner, but something has come up. Let's have another drink and then I'll run. If you want to eat here I'll pick up the tab."

"I don't want to eat and I don't want another drink," Sally said. She felt sick and a little scared, as though she might cry at any moment. "Excuse me, please."

"Hey, don't run off."

"I have to go, too." She fumbled with her purse and muttered a good-bye without looking at Akron.

She retrieved the car, but could think of no place to go. Not home. Lauren would be no help. She would be concerned and she would care, but she would have no answers. She needed Alex, needed him desperately. He would know what was right and wrong. He could tell her what to do. God, where was he?

She pulled into a service station and parked beside a phone booth. There was no point in calling his studio office. "Damn," she muttered. She was at the hotel just a little while ago, and it had not occurred to her to check and see if Alex was in his bungalow.

She dialed the Beverly Hills Hotel. Mr. LaBarre was not using his bungalow this week, which struck her as odd. He was in town and the film was being edited. He normally stayed at the bungalow. He hated being at his mansion alone.

There was one more number she could call that would get her Alex's answering service. "This is Sally Rook," she told the operator. "I need to get in touch with Mr. LaBarre."

"He's out for the evening. I'm sure he'll be calling in later if you'd like to leave a number."

"Listen, this is an emergency. I have to get in touch with him immediately. It's about *Rainbow*. Some film has been destroyed in a fire."

"Oh, that's awful! Goodness, Mr. LaBarre is having dinner at the Habitat. I'll reach him there immediately."

"Don't bother," Sally put in quickly. "I'm only a couple of blocks away. I'll find him. I think the news should be broken to him gently, don't you?"

"Oh, yes," the operator agreed, relieved of the responsibility. "This is just awful."

"Thanks," Sally said and hung up quickly. She hated lying, but what else could she do?

She whipped the car around and headed back up Sunset to the Habitat. Everything would be okay as soon as she found Alex. Parking was impossible. Sally was frantic by the time she jerked the little car into a space. She ran the two blocks to the Habitat, the amber skirt whipping around her legs unnoticed.

Panting, she scooted inside, then hesitated. The entrance to the restaurant section was blocked by a red cord. A hostess in a saloon-girl outfit stood behind a small podium.

"Yes, Miss?"

"Mr. LaBarre, please," Sally breathed.

The red-haired girl glanced down at a list. "Are you meeting him for dinner?" she asked.

"No—yes!" Sally shrugged helplessly. She had forgotten how protective they were of their customers at night.

"There was a table for two reserved."

Sally pleaded with her cinnamon eyes. "Please, I have to talk to him. It's an emergency."

"I'll see if he can be disturbed. Your name?"

"It's Sally Rook, but if you'll just point me in the right direction, I will find him."

"I'll see if he's available."

"Please!" Sally begged, frantic now.

"Let me get him for you," the redhead said, flashing Sally a phony smile.

The woman disappeared in a rustle of shimmering taffeta. Mumbling under her breath, Sally waited. Dumb girl. Didn't she recognize her? Didn't she know who she was? She wasn't some damn groupie to be fended off.

The hostess returned. "Mr. LaBarre is on his way," she announced.

"Thanks," Sally said, breathing a shaky sigh of relief.

"Here he is."

"Alex!" Sally cried, taking quick steps toward him.

478

He was scowling. "What are you doing here?" he demanded.

Sally grabbed his arm and tried to lean against him. "I have to talk to you. I'm so confused."

Alex glanced around. "I don't think this is the time or the place to talk." He pulled slightly away from her and removed her hand from his arm. "I'll call you tomorrow."

She whimpered, not understanding. "What's wrong?" He was so distant. Puzzlement pulled her forehead into a frown. "Is there a problem with *Rainbow*? Alex, if—if you hear some weird news about some film burning up, it was me. I had to lie to your answering service to find you."

"What in the hell are you talking about?"

"I'm sorry, Daddy."

"Daddy?" A woman's harsh voice ripped between Sally and Alex. His face tightened and his lips silently formed a four-letter word.

Confused, Sally glanced from Alex to the woman who was stepping to Alex's side and taking his arm possessively. Oversized breasts threatened to spill out of the tight confines of a black dress. A roll of fat nearly obscured a gold belt and wide hips ballooned out over short, thick legs.

Sally raised her eyes to the plump face and dyed red hair. "Oh, my God!" she gasped as realization paralyzed her, numbing her mind and body. "Gina Beradino!"

"Yes." She looked up at her husband. "Who is your little friend, darling? Who is so important that she could take you away from me during dinner?" She spoke with a faint Italian accent.

"Gina." Alex ran a hand over his pained expression. "This is Miss Sally Rook. She had a small part in *Rainbow*."

"Oh." The suspicious smile stayed in place.

"Let me walk Miss Rook to her car. She seems to have a problem."

"That's all right," Sally said, ducking her head, wanting to escape the dark, probing Italian eyes. "I don't mean to intrude."

"But what was so important?" Gina asked, her tone insistent.

"I haven't found out yet," Alex said. "Now, let me take her to her car."

"Nonsense." A pudgy hand lashed out and grabbed Sally's wrist. "You must join us," she told Sally.

"No, thank you." Sally tried to pull her arm away but Gina's nails dug in.

"I insist," Gina said.

Sally looked hurriedly to Alex. His face was turning an angry red.

"Please, Mrs. LaBarre," Sally said. "I can't stay."

"You can stay. You said it was important. Now . . ." Keeping a painful grip on Sally's arm, Gina pulled her deeper into the restaurant.

Trapped, Sally followed after Gina. She looked back to Alex and her purse caught on a chair. She stumbled, nearly fell and almost knocked a surprised diner to the floor.

Gina's grip finally loosened and it was Alex who steadied Sally from behind and apologized to the diner. "Be cool," he said under his breath.

She knows, Sally thought. She knows who I am and she hates me. Oh, God. How was she going to get out of this? There was a flurry of activity after Gina summoned another costumed girl to make room at the table for Sally.

Gina snatched a menu from another passing waitress and plunked it in front of Sally. "Order," she said with authority.

"I—I've eaten," Sally protested, her shattered nerves making her stammer.

"Ah, but you are so thin, so petite." She said it as though it was a disease. "You can eat a little something more."

"I can't, honest." Sally tried to smile but it came off

sickly. She swallowed and looked across to Alex. Get me out of this, she wanted to scream. Why did she come back? You're mine!

Gina forked a large chunk of bloody rare steak. "What is so important now, Miss Rook?" She asked.

Sally sucked in air between her teeth. "I—I've had an offer. For a TV show. It would be my show." Telling the truth was all she could do now. "It's from William Akron. Joe says it's a comic strip for kids and he doesn't want me to take it."

"Listen to Joe," Alex advised her. "He knows what he's doing."

She choked back a protest. "Thank you," she said. "I'll go now." She tried to stand but Gina's hand grabbed her wrist again.

"Oh, no. Don't leave. Come to the ladies' room with me and you can tell me all about this comic-strip thing."

"No, I'll go now," Sally said, trying to pull away. "I have another appointment."

"Just a moment," Gina insisted, digging her nails into Sally's skin. "I always like to get to know Alex's little protégés." Gina was up and using her large body to herd Sally toward the rest room. Sally couldn't escape without creating a scene, so she went along, hoping desperately she could allay the woman's suspicions.

They stepped into a garish powder room done in red velvet. Gina closed the door behind her and faced Sally. "Now, what you do with my Alex?" she demanded.

Sally flung her head back. "Nothing. I was in his movie and he was the director. I thought he could advise me."

Gina's dark eyes narrowed and she spat out stream of words in Italian.

Sally shrugged. "I don't understand what you said."

"Whore!"

"Whore?" The word and all its implications turned Sally's mind into a cauldron of bubbling anger. "You fat bitch!" Sally hissed. "Don't you call me names!"

481

"Whore!" Gina repeated.

"You—you fat greasy pig!"

"Alex is mine, my husband. You keep your filthy hands off him, whore!"

"Husband?" Sally screeched. "You don't even live with him."

Gina's dark eyes glistened with hate, but when she spoke the voice was low and controlled. "We like our marriage. I do not say no to his little affairs of the body. He—he has flaunted you. I have had letters from my friends. They tell me. Everyone knows."

"So that's what you can't take?" Sally cried triumphantly. "You can't stand people knowing he prefers me to you. Look at you! How could any man love you?"

"If you ask, then you do not understand men. You are young and stupid. I spit on you!" She spat and Sally jumped aside, horrified. Gina took a step closer.

Sally backed away. "You stay away from me!"

"You will not see him again."

"I will!"

"You will not! I tell him no!"

Sally said, "You get out of my way. I'm leaving." She tried to brush past Gina and dodged when she saw a movement. For an instant their eyes locked. Gina's were dark with naked hatred. Then her hand caught Sally's hair and yanked. Sally almost dropped to her knees. Then the pain was gone. Sally whirled away from Gina and planted her feet wide apart, a slow smile spread over her lips. "Okay, fat pig bitch," she muttered. "Come on!" Sally had not lived on the streets for nothing. She knew that women, like men, were particularly vulnerable in one spot.

Gina's hand flashed toward Sally's face. Sally ducked, took the blow with her shoulder and at the same time leaped into the middle of Gina. She grabbed the broad shoulders and brought her knee up sharply into Gina's groin.

Gina screamed and wrapped her arms around Sally

and squeezed. Sally hammered at her head until the hold loosened.

Sally tried to spin out of the way but Gina grabbed her hair again. "I tear it all out!" she gasped.

The door opened and two women entered. One woman screamed, but Sally was not aware of the sound. All she could feel and hear was the hair being ripped from her scalp. She clawed at Gina's face until she brought blood.

They rolled over on the floor and Gina's weight came down hard on Sally's thin body, knocking all the air out of her. She tried to scream but her throat was clogged. Then suddenly there were hands grabbing Gina's shoulders.

Gina fought them wildly, but two men finally pulled her to her feet and shoved her into the toilet area.

A waitress lifted Sally to her feet. "Are you okay?" she asked.

Sally was shaking from head to toe, her breath coming in small gasps. She reached for her mane of hair, pulled it around over one shoulder and ran her fingers through it. Great masses came out in her hand, making her stomach turn over. "Get me out of here," she moaned. Alex would be furious.

Half supporting Sally, the waitress got her out the door. "There's another rest room in back," she offered.

"My purse, my car keys," Sally murmured.

"I'll get them." She left Sally leaning against the wall. Sally could hear Gina's muffled yelling, all in Italian now as she harangued the two men.

"Sally?"

"Alex!" Shame and despair took over as she saw him approaching her.

He gripped her arm. "Get out of here, Sally. I just hope to hell I can keep this out of the papers." Disgust was reflected in his voice, his eyes.

Sally was crushed. "Alex, don't look at me like that," she pleaded. "Please."

"Get out," he said.

"Daddy?"

"Don't call me that! Gina is my wife." He pushed past Sally and disappeared into the ladies room, going to Gina.

"Alex," she whimpered. "Alex." But he had gone to his wife. Sally slumped against the wall, her heart a cold, dead thing in her chest.

The waitress reappeared. "Here's your purse. Let's go out this way."

"This way?" Sally raised her stricken eyes to the girl's face.

"Out the back. People are staring."

"Oh." She could hear them now, feel them gawking at her. She wanted to shoot them the finger, the whole crummy bunch.

"Come on," the waitress insisted. "This way."

Hot tears of anger and humiliation nearly blinding her, Sally stumbled after the waitress. Alex hated her and she did not know how to cope with that knowledge.

Chapter Forty-Eight

Paula nursed her sherry. It was not helping today. If anything, it was making the gnawing in her stomach worse. Reluctantly she opened a bottom drawer and pulled out a bottle of Maalox. She was living off the damned stuff. Just looking at it nearly made her gag. She uncapped the brown bottle and tilted it to her lips and swallowed as much as she could stand.

She was going to have to have a checkup. But not until things settled down on *Dreams*. Of course, there was nothing wrong with her. She was not like Naomi. Paula shoved the thought away. It was the tension getting to her. She would be fine once *Dreams* was running the way she wanted it to.

Paula flipped through the Rolodex file on her desk until she came to Germain Gips's name. She picked up the phone and dialed.

"Germain? Paula here."

"Paula!" Germain's voice expressed delight at the unexpected call. "How nice to hear directly from you. Aren't you excited? Tomorrow is the wedding. I'm going in, of course. Not that Mel will, but I am and I know you'll be there."

Paula grimaced. "No, I'm sending Lauren in my place," she said.

485

"But Paula, you just have to be there. Bob expects you."

"I think you know how I feel about this, Germain."

"I know," Germain murmured, subdued now. "You aren't angry with me, are you? I can't help being excited. It's a wedding!"

"Germain, I'm not angry," Paula assured her patiently.

"Oh, good!" Germain's mood perked back up immediately.

"I'm calling because I need your help," Paula explained. "Do you remember a few years back—one of the soaps let their star-crossed lovers marry when the couple involved were also married to each other?"

"Now, let me think," Germain said. Now, Vicky married Joe on *One Life to Live*, but they aren't really married to each other. They made him disappear. He was declared dead and then he reappeared and they got married again."

"No, that's not it. It was an older show, I think. They were husband and wife, on and off the air, Germain." God, that woman could be dense sometimes.

"I can't think right now, Paula. What are you up to, where is the story line going?"

Paula was not about to tell Germain any more than necessary. "Oh, I have this vague idea in mind right now. It hasn't been worked out. That's why I called you, Germain. I need to know what other shows have done when this situation came up."

"Well," Germain declared brightly. "We can't let them live happily ever after."

"That's been my point with Silverstein. We'll have to do something drastic."

"I know. I've worried about this."

"You see what you can come up with, Germain."

"Yes. And I'll call some friends," she promised.

"Do that. And thanks, Germain. I need all the help I can get on this." Paula hung up. Ammunition was what she needed, something she could use against Anne Voll

486

with Silverstein. She was certain this sort of situation had been dealt with before, and if she was not mistaken it was exactly the same solution she was going to use.

It was really quite simple. You killed off one of the newlyweds and in this case it would most certainly be Anne Voll. That would take the show's very own little mischievous troublemaker down a notch or two.

Paula smiled broadly. It was going to be sweet, and Anne Voll would come absolutely unglued. She would be wailing and moaning and there would not be a single thing she could do about it. Nobody, but nobody, could go up against Paula Cavanaugh and win. She would get Anne and one day Caleb and one day Silverstein.

The gnawing pain worsened. She gulped down another slug of Maalox and tried to will the ache away by filling her mind with other things. She glanced at her watch.

She was meeting Gil tonight instead of Friday because he had a business appointment he could not break. Gil had looked awfully gloomy last week. But she would make it such a good night that he could forget all his problems and she could forget hers.

Paula was not one to thank God for anything, but she was damned glad Gil was around. She was not certain she could have gotten through these last months without him. He had been a rock, always there to comfort her, always there when she needed him. He was the only one who understood and stayed solidly in her corner.

Thinking about Gil's support made her feel better. But it did not reduce her work load. She was tired all the time, never had enough energy. She rubbed her fingers absently over her stomach. Maybe it was time to let Lauren do a script.

And if Lauren could cut it, if Paula didn't have to do too much rewriting, maybe they could actually get ahead. Maybe she could take a vacation. She closed her eyes. Mexico was nice in the winter, she and Gil could have a wonderful time in some out-of-the-way place.

Paula rummaged through her desk, searching for

Lauren's last sample script. She could not find it, but she remembered it as being fair. She really should have assigned her another one and she should have spent more time with the girl, but . . . .

"Oh, hell!" Paula said and buzzed for Jenny, then asked her to step in. The door opened almost instantly. "Sit down," Paula ordered. "We need to talk."

Jenny's smile faded. "Oh?"

"It's about Lauren."

"Hey, she's marvelous. The best we've ever had."

"I'm glad you think so. How would you feel about losing her?"

Jenny hesitated, then said, "Well, if you're thinking about firing her, I would be very upset. If you're talking about putting her on the writing staff, then I'd like to see if we can work something out so that she can spend two or three days a week here until we have someone else trained."

"It's the latter," Paula said.

Jenny rolled her eyes. "Lauren is going to be so stoked!"

"Let's hope she's ready. You go find a contract. I'm sure there are some around. And send Lauren in."

Lauren was barely aware of the traffic as she drove home. That Paula was sending her to the studio for the wedding and reception for cast and crew was exciting enough in itself. It would have been plenty for one day. But on top of that, she was doing a script, her first one. Her hand had shaken as she signed the contract guaranteeing her the right to write one script a week at five hundred dollars a script, the Writers Guild minimum for an hour-long daytime show. Twenty-six thousand dollars a year was more money than Lauren knew how to handle, but she was looking forward to learning.

Paula and Jenny toasted her with sherry and Paula came as close to hugging her as she could. She placed both her hands on Lauren's shoulder and pressed her cheek to Lauren's.

Lauren hummed, then laughed out loud. At a traffic light she smiled at the man in the next car. He grinned back and winked. She wanted to invite the whole world in to share her happiness, to know the pleasure of reaching a goal. She sat at the light, smiling at the man and for a moment he was her friend. The light changed and in seconds he was lost in the traffic, the contact broken.

Lauren called out to Sally as soon as she stepped into the new apartment. There was no answer, and she called a second time. Lauren spotted Sally's purse tossed on the sofa and a pair of shoes that had been kicked off on the floor.

"Sally?" She walked down to the hall toward the bedroom, her nose picking up the unmistakable scent of marijuana. Though Sally smoked seldom, it still made Lauren uneasy. However, she did not have the right to forbid it.

Sally's door was open and she was sprawled across the unmade bed. Her head hung off one side and she stared up at the ceiling through glazed eyes.

"Sally!" Lauren moved to the bed.

"Lauren." Sally stretched languidly. "I was trying to sleep. I—" She stopped in mid-sentence. Lauren found it disconcerting when Sally was spaced out like this. Her mind would drift off and the conversations would get a little strange.

Disappointed, Lauren patted Sally's hand. She would share her news later. "You sleep."

"No, I can't," Sally said, sitting up slowly. "I can't sleep. Not even at night."

"Oh, Sally," Lauren murmured as the girl's eyes filled with tears.

"He never called me again. Why doesn't Alex call me, Lauren? Does he hate me?"

"No, he doesn't hate you, Sally. But his wife is back."

"Wife." A single tear slid down Sally's cheek.

"Sally, this isn't like you. You've never had any trou-

489

ble walking away from men. You knew he was married all along."

"It was different," Sally said. "So different."

Lauren caught her lower lip between her teeth, feeling totally helpless. She knew how Sally felt, she had been there herself. But she knew of no way to help Sally besides offering moral support. Somehow you lived with the pain and hopefully you learned something about yourself, and you went on from there.

"Hey, don't you have a personal appearance tomorrow?" Lauren asked.

"Oh, I guess," Sally answered vaguely.

Lauren knew Sally had gone for a screen test earlier in the week. Sally would not talk about it much, except to say Joe was against it. All she had volunteered was that it was some sort of TV show.

"Where's the appearance?" Lauren asked, trying to pull Sally back to reality, although she was not sure that was the right thing to do. Reality was not always so pleasant.

"At a Bullocks, in the Valley. Hey—" She suddenly came to life. "I've got the munchies. Let's eat."

"I thought you were going to sleep."

"Naw, later." Sally stood, swayed slightly, then wafted down the hall. Lauren followed after her, worried. Sally was awfully pale. She doubted that Sally would eat. In her condition she would lose interest in the food before it finished cooking.

Lauren wished there was someone else to call, someone who could help. But there was no one, no family, no other friends besides Joe, and something bad was going on between Sally and Joe.

"Wine!" Sally declared from the kitchen. "I want some wine." She opened the refrigerator.

"Not wine on top of grass," Lauren pleaded. "Come on, Sally!"

Sally shrugged. "It makes the high higher."

"I thought a high was supposed to be a happy place," Lauren said.

490

"Oh, it is," Sally said, her head moving like a puppet.

"Well, you don't seem very happy to me."

Sally pulled herself out of the refrigerator. "Are you trying to tell me how to live? Everybody keeps telling me how to live. What I can, what I can't . . ." Her voice faded, then picked up again. "Just me," she said and took two steps, then stopped. "Jesus, am I ripped!"

Cradling the wine bottle like a baby in her arms, she headed back toward her bedroom.

Paula was slipping into a mink jacket when Margaret knocked at the bedroom door. "Mrs. Seals?"

"Yes?"

"Miss Gips is on the phone."

"Thank you. I'll take it in here." Paula pushed the private phone aside and picked up the receiver of what she thought of as the house phone. With four private lines running into the house, along with all the extensions, she sometimes felt she was supporting the entire Bell system all by herself.

"Germain."

"I have the information for you. I called my friend, Hilda. You know she used to write soaps, too. And she thought it was *Love of Life* and she knew an assistant producer who was there about that time, so I called her."

"Yes, yes." Paula didn't care how she got the information. Just so she had it. "*Love of Life*."

"Yes. The couple was Gene Bua and Toni Bull. They were married in real life and on the show. They killed off Gene Bua."

"Ah!" Paula smiled in Triumph. A precedent had been established.

"Are we going to kill off Lee Trent?" Germain asked.

"Never. He's part of the Reese family. Anne Voll will have to be the one to go." Paula had to conceal her glee. "Just think how good it will be. We can exploit

Lee's grief to the nth degree. Now tell me, what was their rationalization for killing off Gene Bua?"

"Because of the viewers. They knew the couple were really married. The marriage was getting all intertwined with the characters on the show. People couldn't tell what was real and what wasn't. Plus, they were dealing with sagging ratings. The death brought them up, and they stayed up."

"You're a doll, Germain," Paula said happily. "Listen, type all this up for me, along with any thoughts you might have on our situation. I need all the solid information you can get, too."

"I'll get it to you next week."

"Thanks again." Paula breathed and made a mental note to have Jenny send flowers to Germain. It was going to work. And it would be so simple. Lily had already had her little accident, been near death and recovered. The head injury would start bothering her again. This time it would be a tumor. Paula would be generous on one point. Anne Voll could take a long time dying, but die she would.

Paula arrived at Gil's apartment half an hour late. He greeted her with a kiss, a drink and a gift. "I happened to see this," he said. "And it looked like you."

Touched, she opened the box and lifted out a crystal paperweight. Inside was a rose-pink orchid. "It's beautiful," she whispered.

"It just looked like something you should own."

"Gil." He saw her so differently from everyone else. She kissed him. "You're incredible. Thank you."

"Do you like it?" he asked eagerly.

"Like it? I love it!"

"I'm glad. It's okay, isn't it? I mean, you could take it home. I want it on your desk, so you'll be reminded of me."

He was so eager, so concerned. "I'll treasure it," she promised and patted his smooth-shaven cheek.

They went to bed and then to dinner at Gil's favorite Italian place. Paula studied him across the table. He was down again tonight, withdrawn from her, and a little edgy. It wasn't the first time he had been like this and it was always a business problem.

"Gil, are you having trouble?" she asked.

"Oh, I don't think I want to talk about it."

"You can tell me," she urged.

"No, you have problems of your own."

"And you always listen," she reminded him gently. "Come on, give!"

"It's the building project," he said reluctantly. "One of my backers pulled out on me yesterday."

"Oh, no!"

"Oh, no! is right. It was all ready to go. We had the bank loan lined up. It was all set and this bastard is destroying me. We were to get the loan Monday."

"How much?"

"A lousy fifty thousand. You wouldn't want to invest, would you?" he asked wryly.

"I might."

"Hey, no! Be serious, Paula. I was only kidding."

"I am serious," she insisted. "I might be interested. I'd get a good write-off. Epstein is big on real estate. I think he might go for it."

"No, I don't have time to deal with business managers. They're all right, but they're overly cautious—as well they should be with other people's money. But he would want to investigate—which is good, but it takes too much time. I've got to have the money by Monday or I can kiss the whole project good-bye."

"Do you think you will have it by then?" she asked.

"No," he answered bleakly. His eyes met hers, then he lowered them to his spaghetti. He dropped his fork. "Damn it! Six months of work down the drain!"

She reached for his hand. "Gil, I'll give you the money," she offered.

"Don't be foolish, Paula."

"I will. It's easy, and you've told me before that it's a good investment. You even said you wished you had more of your own to put into it."

"I damned sure wish that now. But I can't let you bail me out, Paula."

"Why not?" she asked. He didn't answer. "It's settled," she declared. "I'll call Epstein tomorrow."

His smile of relief was her reward. His hand covered hers in gratitude. "What can I say, Paula? Except thanks. Oh, by the way, get a cashier's check. I'm meeting with Andrew Jones and the bank people Monday. So it'll have to be a cashier's check, otherwise the bank might back out on us, too."

"I'll get it," she promised. "You can pick it up."

Gil raised both hands. "Oh, no, Paula. I don't think that's wise. Your husband—"

"He won't be around, and so what if he is? This is business, and it's my money anyway."

"You are some kind of lady, Paula. You're really something else."

Her eyes moistened with tears. Maybe, just maybe she had found someone she could live with. Someone she could love, not just for now, but always. Joe would never contest a divorce.

Chapter Forty-Nine

"Wait until you see Anne's gown," Sue Bergman whispered to Lauren as they stood at the edge of a specially constructed chapel set. "It's incredible. It's worth five thousand dollars. The gal from Saks is rustling around Anne like she was guarding the royal jewels."

The sense of excitement ran high through the sound stage as the last touches were added to the sets. They were only using four sets today: the chapel, Rose Jardine's living room where the reception would take place, Anne's bedroom and Lee's bedroom.

"Paula really isn't coming, huh?" Sue asked.

"She's not," Lauren answered carefully, aware that this was Paula's way of insulting everyone involved. "The work is stacked up."

"Behind again, huh?"

Lauren did not like Sue's eyes; they were too inquisitive, and not in a kind way. "Paula will be caught up next week." She cast a curious look at Sue. Why hadn't Sue congratulated her? "You know, don't you, that I'm on the writing staff now? I get my first outline today."

Sue's dark eyes widened. "You're kidding!"

Oh, no! She had done it again. Lauren closed her eyes briefly and silently damned Paula. "It is all right, isn't it?"

"Well, it had been discussed," Sue murmured loftily. "But really, she shouldn't have signed you without informing Bob."

Lauren mentally shook her head and wondered how she could escape from Sue. Her good excitement was gone. No, darn it! She was not going to let this day or her mood be ruined, not by anything, not even the vivid remembrance of Kerry Scott that the sound stage evoked.

Visitors were filing onto the set. Sue pointed out a darling young girl in a demure white dress as Anne's daughter. Bob was on hand, of course, and Germain Gips. Mel Lorenzen had declined, but had sent flowers and a silver water pitcher. Jenny had told her that the only time Mel visited the studio was for the anniversary parties that were held some years. There would be a big party this coming year in January for the twentieth anniversary of *Dreams*.

"Look!" Sue poked Lauren in the side. "There's Caleb. Have you met him?"

"No, but I want to."

"Come on, then."

Lauren studied the tall, thin man. He was not the ogre Paula had presented. His graying beard gave him a saintly look. He was elderly, yes, but he stood so straight and seemed to be a kind man. Sue made the introduction and Caleb took Lauren's hands. "How lovely you are," he said.

"Paula has put her on the writing staff," Sue confided.

"Oh?" Caleb raised thick white brows. His eyes moved over her again and back to Sue. Lauren could feel the unasked questions in the air. "Welcome, my dear. I'll be anxious to see your first show."

"So will I," she said as he patted her hand.

"If you need any help, feel free to call me," Caleb offered.

Lauren nodded, but she knew she would not dare, because it would make Paula furious.

496

"I think we'd better sit down," Sue murmured, checking her watch. "It's almost air time. Better say a prayer. This is live!"

Almost the entire cast was on hand for the wedding. They would squeeze themselves into the church pews. Lauren followed Sue to the small section of raised bleacher-type seats that had been rolled in for visitors. They were set up well out of the way of the cameras and technicians.

Lauren took the last empty chair, next to Germain Gips. She looked like a fat tulip in a pink satin dress. A perky hat was perched on graying hair and her cheeks were glowing. "Isn't it exciting?" she asked Lauren, her eyes darting, trying to take in everything at once.

"Yes," Lauren answered, deciding she might as well tell Germain her news too. "I'm going on the writing staff."

"When?"

"Today. Paula is home doing three outlines."

Germain's eyes widened. "Paula didn't tell me."

"I guess she didn't tell anyone," Lauren sighed.

"Not even Bob?"

"No."

"Goodness," Germain murmured, almost to herself. "Sometimes I think Paula just likes to stir up trouble. I do wish she would quit fighting with Bob. She always loses."

"Loses?" Lauren blinked.

"Every time, but she never gives up. As soon as one thing is settled, she finds something else."

"Has Paula always been like this?" Lauren asked hesitantly.

Germain dropped her eyes. "No. No, she hasn't. Paula had a great tragedy in her life once. It really changed her."

Lauren waited, eager to hear more, but Germain's lips tightened in a way that said further questioning was forbidden.

"Oh, it's time," Germain said. She fluttered her fingers at the actors who were making their way to their places. Silence fell over the group, who remained that way throughout the show.

It was a beautiful show. Lee looked properly nervous, maybe even too nervous, Lauren thought. Anne was a glowing bride who never stopped smiling except during the solemn exchange of vows read by a minister who did not seem to mind having a camera trained on his face.

The actors were sometimes misty eyed, and the actresses shed pretty tears for the camera. But Lauren suspected their tears were real as her own and Germain's, who pressed a lace handkerchief into Lauren's hands.

After a commercial break, the bride and groom were showered with rice, they they faded into the Rose Jardine living room for the reception where the show ended with a close-up of Lee and Anne kissing.

No one moved immediately. Then came a sigh from somewhere and looks were exchanged. The reality of the wedding, mingled with the *Dreams* story line had left everyone present touched.

"We did it!" Anne cried, breaking the silence. "We did it!" She grabbed Lee in a big hug.

"Oh!" There was a cry and a rustle behind Lauren. "She's crushing the veil!" Elaine, the girl from Saks wailed, her voice carrying throughout the gigantic room.

Lee and Anne jumped apart and laughter rippled through the room. People began to move. Anne was herded off to the dressing room before she could further damage the expensive gown.

Germain nudged Lauren toward the champagne fountain. The entire reception was set up in an exact replica that would be seen on TV Monday. Of course, that had been shot almost a month ago. Only the wedding day was shown live. Additional food was being carted into the studio by caterers.

"This is better than the anniversary parties," Germain told Lauren. "Look at the food. Hmmm, shrimp!"

"No dinner tonight," Lauren laughed.

Cobb Strong walked up behind Lauren and Germain. "Hello, ladies," he said.

"Cobb!" Lauren cried, genuinely pleased. "It's so good to see you."

"And so good to see you both. You both look beautiful."

"You're kind of pretty yourself, in that tux," Germain told him, flirting impishly.

Cobb smiled broadly. "Thank you. Now, let me get you girls some champagne. I don't care for the stuff myself."

"I adore bubbly," Germain giggled, making her hat dance.

Cobb caught a glass for each of them. Germain murmured a thank you and excused herself to find Anne Voll. "It was so beautiful," Germain said, wiping at her eyes. "Bye, you two."

Cobb focused his attention on Lauren. "Is there anyone you haven't met?" Cobb asked politely. "I'll be glad to make the introductions."

"I think I know them all now. How's the new Katherine fitting in?"

"Like she's been here always."

"Good." Lauren glanced up at Cobb over the top of her glass. He did look nice today. His hair was newly styled and the tux showed off his rugged build.

"Let's fix a plate and find a place to sit down," Cobb suggested.

They juggled plates around the table, pausing to chat with various people. When their plates were heaped Cobb signaled and they found chairs to one side. They were barely seated when Bob Silverstein called the group together.

Leaving their plates on the chairs, they joined the group gathering around Bob. "Hear, hear," Bob cried out and raised his glass. "Our bride and groom!"

Anne, dressed in a silky pale pink gown, clung prettily to Lee Trent's arm.

"May they live happily ever after, on the show and off!"

Anne glowed, accepting the tribute with a gracious nod of her head. Lee stood stiffly beside her, handsome in his tux, his face somber.

There were more toasts proposed and glasses were hurriedly refilled by the waiters. The cake was cut to the accompaniment of the electronic flashes of several cameras, then the scene was restaged twice for the benefit of the photographers.

The official bridal pictures had been taken earlier and were already distributed to various magazines and newspapers by the PR department. Lauren was certain Anne would make the cover of most of the dozen or so daytime TV magazines.

Cobb and Lauren fell in at the end of an informal reception line. The cameras seemed to flash endlessly and Lauren wondered if she would end up in one of the magazines. Probably not, she decided, except in a group picture, but even that pleased her. Occasional calls came in to Paula's office from one of the magazines and Lauren knew a couple of the editors by phone, though neither of them seemed to be on hand.

Lauren found herself in front of Anne. They touched cheeks. "You are beautiful," Lauren whispered.

"Thank you, dear," Anne said, already distracted. Her eyes were darting around. Cobb caught Anne in a hug and a reporter plowed through. "Can we get a picture of you two?" he asked.

Lauren was left alone with Lee Trent. She smiled hesitantly at him. She had never said much more than hello to Lee.

"Quite a crowd," Lauren murmured. The sound stage was cramed with people and more kept squeezing in from various offices and other sound stages.

"It's growing," Lee said and tugged at his collar. "I'm

500

choking," he muttered. "Wardrobe sent over a shirt with a collar a half inch too small. And they've got me wrapped in a damned corset that's cutting my gut in half!"

"Why don't you go change?"

"I wouldn't dare. Not yet." Lauren caught the strong smell of liquor on his breath. "Anne would have my head," he confided, "if I stepped out of line." He tugged at the collar again. "Paula didn't come?"

"No. She sends her apologies and her congratulations," Lauren fibbed.

"I'll bet! She didn't want this damned wedding any more—" He stopped abruptly.

"Any more than what?" Lauren asked, interested and curious now.

"Nothing. Excuse me. I've got to find a drink." He left and Lauren stood alone until Cobb returned.

"Where are we?" he asked.

"Well, we had a plate of food and we were . . . somewhere!"

They both laughed. The chairs and their plates were gone. "Want to try the tables again?" he asked.

"Sure."

Cobb nudged her. "Wonder what Bob and Sue are in such a huddle about?" he wondered.

Lauren looked around and flinched. They were looking at her. "Get me out of here, Cobb," she said. "I think it's me they're huddling about."

"Why?"

"Just get me out. Then I'll explain."

He took her hand. "This way." They edged sideways between chattering people stacked in shoulder to shoulder. The noise level was fast approaching the ear-shattering level. Food and drink were being gulped, sipped, munched and chewed.

Safe in an empty and silent corridor, Lauren let out a breath. "We made it," she said, smiling at Cobb. "Thank you. I can find my own way out of here now."

"Wait. You aren't escaping that easily. You owe me

an explanation. And we are still entitled to some food and drink."

"No, I couldn't impose on you," she protested.

"Of course you can. You wait here. I'll change and we'll go out."

"You don't have to take me anywhere."

"Hey, I want to take you out. Understand?"

Lauren nodded in acceptance. Half an hour later they sat opposite each other in a small restaurant near the studio. Gin and tonics rested on the dark oak table.

"So tell me," Cobb prompted. "Why did you have to do the disappearing act?"

"Paula signed me on the writing staff yesterday. Only she didn't consult with Silverstein or Shepard. And I told Sue, and Sue told them, and I didn't want to have to explain Paula's actions to Bob. You know Paula was conspicuous by her absence today."

"I don't blame you for fleeing. It never pays to end up in the middle."

"Don't I know that?" Lauren said, thinking of Kerry and Sally.

"But congratulations, anyway. I'm sure you'll be a very good writer."

"Oh, I hope so. I've got to go back to Paula's and pick up my outline, and deliver Germain's and Mel's." She checked her watch. "I'm going to have to leave."

"Not yet," Cobb protested.

"But I have to, Cobb."

"Then let me drive you. We can have dinner afterward."

"Cobb . . ." She felt confused, uncertain of what he wanted and of how much he knew about her and Kerry.

"Lauren, I've wanted to get to know you better. I had good feelings about you from the first time we met. A feeling of—how to put it—a kind of kinship with you. As though you were someone I'd known before. I wanted to ask you out, but Kerry . . ." He stopped and shrugged.

"Kerry moved in," she said for him. "And I couldn't see anyone else."

"Yes." His hazel eyes were deep and serious as he studied her. "I worried about you after he left for New York. When you came to the studio you were like a shadow of yourself. You looked so lost."

"I made a lot of mistakes with Kerry," Lauren said, taking a deep breath and deciding to be honest. "I was suffering a great deal over my divorce, I think more than I realized at the time. Kerry offered me renewal and excitement. He was different and I fell too hard and too fast. I hurt for a long time after he left, but I'm over that now."

"I can tell," he agreed. "You're different, you know, from when I first met you."

"I hope so," she said with a small, wry laugh. She had learned a few things.

"You are. You're more confident, and it becomes you."

"I think I'm finally a woman. I thought of myself as a girl for too long."

"Well, we all grow up eventually. It took me quite a while myself."

She had the feeling he was about to tell her more, but a waitress appeared before them, pushing her wares. "Would you like another drink?" she asked.

"I can't," Lauren replied. "I really have to go now."

"I'm going to drive you," Cobb said. "No arguments."

"I'm not arguing," she replied with a smile. He was easy to be with. She felt no need to pretend or cover up anything with Cobb Strong. Nor did she feel a need for any long explanations to justify her past. Cobb made her feel totally accepted.

She watched him from underneath her lashes as he paid the bill. He was about forty, with small lines running from the corners of his eyes and deeper ones across his forehead and under his cheekbones. The aging lines looked good on him, added character and maturity to his face. He was not handsome, not a pretty man like Kerry; instead he was rugged in his looks and dress.

Before they left, Cobb excused himself to make a telephone call. Returning, he said, "I talked to my housekeeper and my daughter."

"Oh, I didn't know you had a daughter."

Then it came again. The odd, closed smile she had caught before, a smile that told her absolutely nothing. "Yes, I have a daughter," he said.

He did not offer any more explanation and Lauren felt she should not pry. They swung by Paula's and Lauren went up alone. Jenny had left and Paula's office was dark. Lauren could hear soft music coming from the living quarters.

Lauren picked up the outlines from Jenny's desk. Hers was on top. Her heart speeded up as she looked at the outline. She had made it! Nothing would ever be the same again. She was somebody, someone unique. A writer. She pressed the outlines to her breast. Lauren Parrow was a writer!

Heady with happiness, Lauren scribbled a note to Paula that she had taken the outlines, then slipped away without seeing anyone.

She and Cobb delivered the other outlines to Mel and Germain. Cobb turned to Lauren. "Now, where would you like to eat?" he asked.

"I don't know," she said. "It doesn't matter."

"Japanese?" he suggested.

Lauren shook her head. Japanese food was Kerry's specialty. Too many places, like the Aware Inn, still reminded her of Kerry, still made her ache, and forced her to admit that maybe she was not yet completely over him. But the ache was lessening with each passing day.

"Chinese then?" Cobb asked. "Italian? Russian? Lebanese? You name it and we can find it in this town. Greek?"

"No, Mexican!"

Cobb laughed. "I missed that one. Any place in particular?"

"No."

"Okay. We'll drive and stop at the first one we find. How's that?"

"Easy. I like it when things are decided easily."

"Me, too. There's no point in making life more complicated than it already is."

They found a small place, evidently run by a family, for the dark-eyed boy who seated them could have been no more than fourteen. They ordered and sat sipping red wine and dipping fried tortilla chips into a red salsa so hot it brought tears to their eyes. Soon heaping plates of beans and fried rice and steak strips done in a sauce were placed before them.

"My daughter loves Mexican food," Cobb said.

"Oh? Then we should have picked her up and brought her along."

Cobb shook his head. "No, she doesn't go out very much. Our housekeeper is Mexican. She fixes all of Martha's favorites."

"How old is Martha?"

"Sixteen," Cobb said, surprising Lauren, who had assumed the girl was a small child.

"Then she must be a high school junior," Lauren ventured.

For the briefest moment, Lauren caught a look of sadness in Cobb's eyes, then it was gone. "No, Martha doesn't go to high school. There's a special school she attends. And she paints and she plays the piano and guitar."

"A very talented young lady then?"

"In her way. Martha was born with Down's syndrome."

"Down's?" Lauren shook her head, not understanding.

"She's what a lot of people incorrectly refer to as a mongoloid," he explained.

"I'm sorry."

"Don't be. She's very precious to me, and she's taught me a great deal about life."

"And her mother?" Lauren asked.

Cobb laid down his fork. "It's quite a long story. Are you sure you want to hear it?"

"Only if you want to tell me," Lauren replied.

"Her mother is Samantha McCall."

"You're kidding! Sally met her once. She's famous and beautiful, and . . ."

"And selfish and vain, and being famous and beautiful is all that matters to her," Cobb said. There was no trace of bitterness in his voice.

"That's awful," Lauren whispered.

"Not really. You have to be selfish to succeed. And I wasn't so different. Not from her, or Sally or Kerry. I wanted it all, too. And I was willing to do whatever it took to make it. I changed my name—or my agent did."

"From what?" Lauren asked.

"Ralph Zimmerman."

"You'd don't look like a Ralph," Lauren observed, studying him openly now. He was a more complex man than she had imagined.

"I didn't think so either. Back then. Samantha and I were quite a couple. Two rising young stars, two of the beautiful people. We had quite a romance and wedding, all guided by our press agents."

"No love?" Lauren asked.

"We thought we were in love. It could have all been taken care of in a short affair. Only we got married and Samantha got pregnant. For a while we were close, until she got big. She hated that. She retained water and looked bloated and fat. She wanted an abortion, but by then it was too late."

"That's sad," Lauren whispered, aching with sympathy for Cobb.

"I thought everything would be better, you know, after the baby was born. But Martha wasn't normal and Samantha wouldn't hold her or even look at her after we got home. The doctors wanted us to put Martha in an institution. I almost went along. Maybe I would have if we hadn't brought her home. But we did, and I held her. She was so tiny and so in need of protection. I fell in love with my daughter. Still, I was only going to keep her for a while, until she was old enough to go to a special school." He paused and a bleakness flickered once. "Samantha divorced me, and she's never seen Martha again."

"But her own child . . ."

"A retarded child was not in Samantha's order of things. She didn't want the world to know she'd given birth to anything less than perfect."

"Oh, Cobb."

"It's the way it was. And I couldn't give Martha up. The rest is unimportant now. I'm not bitter. I feel sorry for Samantha. Martha is a very happy person. She's very tender and loving. She's simple and in that simplicity is a rare beauty. She loves with no strings attached. There is no cruelty in her, no hatred, no bitterness. And nothing and no one will ever hurt her. I'll see to that."

Soft tears blurred Lauren's vision. "You're an incredible man, Cobb Strong."

"I'm not. Martha is the incredible one. She's taught me what's important and what's not."

"That's beautiful. But what about you? Hasn't there been anyone else for you?"

"No, not really. I've dated some. But I have my work and my daughter and my house and the land around it. It keeps me busy." Cobb's eyes roamed over her face. "Would you like to meet Martha? She'd like you."

"Yes, I think I would like that very much," Lauren answered sincerely.

"Tomorrow night?"

"I can't. I have the script to write. I want it to be as good as I can make it. I'll still be working for Paula three days a week, until we can hire someone else."

"Isn't that a bit too much?" he asked.

"It won't last very long. And I can use the extra money. I want new furniture for my apartment, and my

507

car is old. I need to think about getting a newer one."

"Maybe I can help you there," he offered. "I tinker around with cars some."

"I would like that, too," Lauren said. Benji could undoubtedly get her a deal but she did not want any involvement with him. She wanted nothing from Benji. "But I can manage on my own," she told Cobb.

"I'll bet you can." He gazed at her in frank admiration. "I think you're a woman who has her life well in hand."

"Well, let's just say I'm heading in the right direction," she said.

"Good enough."

They smiled across at each other and Lauren was content.

Chapter Fifty

A brisk wind whipped down Sunset Boulevard, stirring up leaves and other assorted trash. Sally sat alone in the dark at a small sidewalk cafe. She was back against a wall, a shadowy figure in a suede hat and dark suit. She was coming down off the small cache of Quaaludes she had bought on the street. Jake had introduced her to the joy of "ludes." They calmed her and made her feel good, not like Librium, which threw her into deep depression.

Sally sipped unhappily at a Coke and wished it was liquor, any kind, anything that would help. She rubbed her hands together and shifted uneasily, feeling itchy and restless.

It had been a rotten weekend. Lauren had her script to write and stayed holed up in her bedroom. What time they did spend together Lauren nagged her about smoking too much. Like what else in hell was she supposed to do besides smoke? Nothing was happening; smoking was better than crying.

Lauren was right about one thing. She had never reacted like this over a man before. She had never felt so betrayed, never so lost. Except, maybe one time, when she was a kid and Mr. Stillman was taken to the VA hospital and Donny was put in a foster home.

She had called Alex LaBarre, but the woman at the answering service and especially his secretary at the studio office were cold. The people at the Beverly Hills Hotel said he had given up the bungalow. Alex never returned her calls.

Sally did not care about his fat, stupid wife. He could keep her. She did not want to marry Alex, she just wanted to be with him, to be allowed to love him. She needed him, as she had never needed another man. Sally scratched at her body and tugged at the clothes that seemed to suffocate her. She had spent Monday and today doing personal appearances. She was sick of makeup, tired of smiling, bored with being a clothes horse.

She shifted in the hard metal chair. It was cold, but there was no place else to go. She needed more pills. She had not been able to find any on the streets today. The people she had approached wouldn't even talk to her, and she knew why. She didn't look like one of them in the getup she was wearing.

There was nothing at home, except Lauren. And she knew Lauren didn't want Sally around while she was writing.

"Miss?" A waitress came to the door of the cafe. "Aren't you cold out here?"

"Yes," Sally answered truthfully.

"Would you like to come inside?"

"No."

"Can I get you something hot to drink?"

"No, I'm going." Sally put a dollar bill underneath her Coke glass and walked to her car. There was one place she could get pills, one source who would not turn her down. Jake Sheeney.

She took off her hat and shook her hair free. Why not see Jake? It might even be good, and it would do no harm.

She switched on the headlights and pulled away from the curb. On Ventura Boulevard she drove slowly until she sighted the small, dingy club. "Joshua" was still featured on the marquee. She parked in the first available spot and walked back toward the club.

She stood just inside the door. The tiny stage was deserted, except for a chair and a guitar. Anxious, Sally scanned the faces at the tables, then at the bar. Jake was not there, but she spotted the man she had talked to before. He was at the end of the bar, chewing a cigar and thumping a man on the chest as he talked.

Sally moved to him. "Excuse me," she said. "Isn't Jake Sheeney here tonight?"

"Back in the dressing room, kid," he said, jerking a thumb over his shoulder. "Say, are you old enough to be in here?"

"I'm old enough for about anything," she said with a flirty smile and got away quickly. She went down a dark smelly hall, past rest rooms, and opened a door that led into a stock room. There was a curtained off section at one end.

"Jake?" she called tentatively.

"Yeah," he yelled back. She edged between stacked cases of beer and wine.

She hesitated outside the faded curtain, her throat so dry she could hardly swallow. The sudden and furious pounding of her heart made her more anxious than before. With a trembling hand, she pulled the curtain back. "Jake." He was standing in front of a cracked mirror, combing his hair.

His mouth opened and he peered into the mirror, then turned around quick. "Sally! Is that you?"

"It's me," she replied with a nervous giggle.

His eyes roamed over her face and down her body. "What in the hell are you doing here?"

"Oh, I saw the name on the marquee. Joshua, you know. And I remembered you were talking about using it, and I just kind of dropped in to see you."

"You don't look like yourself," he said.

"Neither do you." His dark beard was neatly trimmed and his hair was cut fairly short.

511

"Yeah," he grimaced. "Straight is in now. Hey, come here."

"Jake." She didn't want to go into his open arms, didn't want that scene again. But his eyes—they were as hypnotic as ever, and the need to be close to a warm body was strong.

"Oh, Jake!" she cried and went to him. He caught her tightly and pressed his lips down hard on hers. His tongue forced her lips apart and she gave in, letting him kiss her deeper as she relaxed against him. Suddenly he caught her lower lip between his teeth and bit hard.

"Jake!" She tried to jerk away. His powerful arms held her. She could taste blood, her lip throbbed painfully. "Why did you hurt me?" she whimpered.

"You were my old lady. You ran out on me."

"You burned my clothes, and you hit me!"

"I tried to find you," he said, pulling her close again, patting her back gently.

"Did you?" she asked. She felt weak and so tired, she wanted to believe him, but she didn't. "No, you could have reached me at the studio."

"Well, maybe I didn't look very hard. Another chick came along. You know Jake doesn't like to stay alone." His lips moved across her face. "A real kiss," he promised.

He lowered his face over hers and this time the kiss was sweet and tender, though the blood taste mingled with the taste of his mouth. Jake could be a sweet guy when he wanted to be. It was mostly the drugs that made him cruel sometimes.

She wrapped her arms around him and held on to him. By nature, Sally was a sexual being and her body responded to Jake's growing excitement, to his maleness, to the memories of shared experiences.

Jake pulled back away from her. He grinned broadly. "Now, that was my old lady."

"I thought you found someone else."

"She split for Mexico."

"I see." Sally gripped her arms. She was starting to shake again.

"Hey, you got troubles?" Jake asked suddenly.

"I'm coming down. Bad. I need something."

"Yeah." His expression changed. "So that's why you're really here?"

"Aw, Jake," she said. "I . . ." She had to stop and swallow a rush of saliva. "I'd had some bad things come down on me. If I could get some ludes or maybe some Miltowns, I—I'd be all right."

"I might have something."

"Please, Jake! I can't even get a stupid drink. And I can pay."

"Want a joint?" he offered.

"Sure." She nodded eagerly, wanting to please him so he would give her some pills, too.

He shook some cigarettes out of a Salem pack, fished out an expertly rolled joint and returned the cigarettes. He lit it and sucked in slowly.

She watched, her eyes burning. She could almost taste it. But he didn't hand it over, he let it hang out of one corner of his mouth.

"Please, Jake," she begged. "I'm in bad shape."

"I can tell," he said, his eyes studying her intently. "This isn't like you, Sally. You didn't pop a lot of pills, you wouldn't do coke. But you could sure suck up on all my grass."

"I paid for plenty of it," she reminded him.

He shrugged and inhaled again. He held it in and spoke in hollow tones without breathing. "Can you pay now?"

"I told you I could. I'm making plenty." She stopped and frowned. "Don't you know, Jake?"

"Know what?"

"That I'm the exclusive model for California Girl Cosmetics. I'm in ads, on TV. I do personal appearances."

"No shit!" He handed over the joint and exhaled a thin blue ribbon of smoke.

Sally took a deep hit. The grass was good; Jake always had the best. Her chest swelled as she filled it to capacity with smoke. "I've done some movies, too," she added without exhaling. Her voice cracked. "Good parts, Jake." She let out the smoke and sucked in deeply again. "And I'm sharing a groovy apartment with another woman."

His dark eyes widened with new interest. "What kind of money are you talking about?"

"A lot," she said, feeling the need to impress him. "Three thousand a week if I do this TV show that's come up."

"Jesus!" His teeth flashed white between beard and mustache.

She exhaled. "My own nighttime show."

Jake whistled. "You've been doing some high traveling since we split. I'm impressed, baby. And proud of you, real proud."

He opened a guitar case and took out a Band-Aid box. He shook out a handful of pills. "Take your choice," he said.

Sally took a five-hundred-milligram Quaalude. "Will you sell me some more?" she asked.

"Sure, Sally. You were my old lady, weren't you? I wouldn't turn my back on you."

Her shaking hand brought the pill to her mouth. She swallowed it dry. "I need lots, Jake. I got to keep myself together. Bad stuff keeps coming down on me."

"I'll help you," he promised and folded her into his arms. She rested lightly against his chest. He kissed her and she liked the feel of his beard against her face. It felt familiar, and right. It was terrible to be alone.

"Love me, Jake," she said.

He groaned and rubbed his face against hers. "Not now, Sally girl. Not now. I've got to go on. But I'll get you a table and a drink, and I'll sing for you. Like I used to, remember? And then we'll go home."

The pill was already taking effect. She felt all soft and floaty. Life was good again, everything was right.

It was a dreamy evening. She sat at a dark corner table alone and let Jake's songs drift around in her mind. His voice was husky and sexy, more polished than she remembered. He sang all her favorites, like Bob Dylan's "Lay, Lady, Lay" and some sad old country music that made her feel weepy.

During the midnight intermission Jake slipped her another Quaalude. Pills on top of grass on top of wine laid her back and nearly out. Jake half carried her to the car she pointed out to him.

"Hey, a 'Z'—nice piece of machinery," Jake enthused. He started the engine with a roar and sat revving the engine. "You weren't putting me on, were you, Sally? You're making good bread."

Sally giggled. She was flying. "I wouldn't ever put you on."

He patted her knee. "I guess you wouldn't."

He took her to his apartment, a slightly better dump than the last. This one had furniture. They collapsed on a creaking bed. Sally was only barely aware of his manipulations of her body. She drifted on the edge of unconsciousness, peacefully happy at being warm and being held closely.

It was afternoon when Jake woke her. His hands were working their way methodically over her body. She slid up against his lanky form. They were alike in a lot of ways, she decided. She lifted her face for his kiss. His mouth was warm and soft and the beard scratched her face lightly. He was all male. She felt his excitement and her growing response. A warmth ran through her, culminating in a flush of heat in her pubes. Her small nipples were hard, her tiny breasts supersensitive to touch. The ache in her grew and grew and she urged Jake over on her with her hand.

She gave herself up to the rhythm of his body and the touch of her own hand on her clitoris so they could make it together. The heat in all the muscles in her groin expanded, then contracted into an exquisite rush of fire. She cried out as he joined her.

515

They stayed in bed all afternoon, sharing icy glasses of Coke and grass and finally some wine with crackers and cheese. They talked endlessly, catching each other up on the events of their lives. Sally told him about Lauren, New York, the movie parts, even her aborted attempt at breast implants. She told him about everything except Alex.

Jake's moods still changed suddenly, as they had before. He had been up about his career, which included the possibility of getting a recording audition. Then abruptly his eyes darkened again. "But I guess I'm not so hot," he said. "I can't compare to you."

"I got some breaks, Jake," she said, rubbing her cheek against his bare shoulder.

"And I'm still living in garbage heaps and you got a nice place. You got a car. I walk. I have nothing to offer you, Sally."

"Offer me?" She sat up straight. "You don't have to offer me anything."

"Yes, I do. Because I don't want to lose you again, Sally."

She sat back on her heels, uncertain of how to respond, of how she wanted this to go.

Chapter Fifty-One

Paula finished reading Lauren's script and laid it thoughtfully on her desk. She ran the tips of her polished nails over her straight-cut bangs. She leaned back in the chair. There was not much wrong with the script; on the other hand, it was not brilliant. It was merely adequate.

She picked it up again and flipped through the pages and decided the second scene in Act IV was stilted. She scribbled in new lines, buzzed Jenny, and asked her to send Lauren in.

A few minutes later, Lauren seated herself on the opposite side of the desk. She flashed a nervous smile at Paula.

"I've read it," Paula said deliberately, feeling vaguely annoyed with Lauren. There was something about the eager attitude of her body and the wide green eyes and flawless complexion that grated on Paula's nerves. Youth, Paula realized. And she was jealous. No one had handed her this kind of break when she was in her twenties. She had scrambled and fought for every break, every opportunity. And here she was, handing Lauren a television writing career.

Paula cleared her throat. "The script is quite good."

Lauren's body relaxed.

"For a first script," Paula added.

"Oh," Lauren said, taken aback.

"Don't expect too much of yourself too soon," Paula cautioned. "It is thoroughly usable. I think perhaps you should rewrite this one scene. I've made some notes." She handed the script to Lauren, who read the new lines silently, frowned, then read again.

Lauren raised her head. "I don't understand the difference between your lines and mine," she said.

"It is more emotional my way," Paula replied.

Lauren dropped her eyes. "Yes, Paula."

"You don't agree with me?" Paula asked, her tone challenging.

"It isn't that I don't agree; it's that I don't understand," Lauren explained.

"You go and retype it my way, using my lines," Paula said. "Then you will see."

"All right." Lauren stood slowly, her slumped shoulders reflecting her disappointment.

Almost ashamed of herself, Paula forced her lips into a bright red lipstick smile. "I am pleased, Lauren. It is quite good."

"For a first script," Lauren murmured and smiled weakly. "I'll see what I can do with it."

"You do that," Paula said in dismissal.

The door closed behind Lauren. Paula picked up the rating sheet Bob had sent over earlier, after he had called her, wildly ecstatic, and full of "I told you so." The gloating old bastard!

He was so damned busy crowing he forgot to say much about her adding Lauren to the writing staff. Or maybe he didn't want to acknowledge Paula's successful coup. After all, she had the option of hiring anyone she wanted. Consulting with Shepard and Silverstein was only a courtesy, one she had chosen not to exercise. Naturally, he had sarcastically mentioned "missing" her at the wedding.

Well, she would score it two points for her side and one for his. Naturally, the ratings were phenomenal.

They had blitzed the air with promos for *Dreams*. The PR department had outdone themselves on getting coverage.

They had pulled a 44.8 rating with a 68 share. *Dreams* had just made daytime history. So the network, Bob and the advertisers were walking around patting themselves on the back.

But so what? The ratings would fall against next week. Anything following the wedding had to be anticlimactic. Unless, of course, Anne Voll died. Which she would.

The script Paula had completed this morning was the Christmas show. In the final scene, Anne fainted. It would take another week to get her into the hospital for a checkup and then they could begin Anne's long and painful dying. With any luck, the twentieth-anniversary party would also be Anne's going-away party.

The minute the script went into the studio, questions would start flying back. It was time to gird herself for battle again.

Not that she wasn't always having to fight someone on one level or another. Epstein had given her a lot of static over the fifty thousand dollars for Gil. Paula thought she had made a simple enough request when she telephoned Epstein. "I want a cashier's check for fifty thousand on my desk Monday morning," she had told him.

"No way!" he all but screamed.

"Yes."

"Why?"

"An investment opportunity has come up."

"I make your investments, Paula. That's what you pay me for."

"I'm making this one," she muttered, angered at his possessive attitude toward her money.

"What kind of investment?" he questioned.

"Look, it's my money, isn't it?"

"Sure, but fifty grand. I . . ."

"Sell something if you have to."

"Even if I did, I couldn't get the money by Monday," he protested.

"I have certificates of deposit," she reminded him.

"Paula, those are locked in. There's a stiff penalty for early withdrawal."

"Get it!" she ordered.

"No, not unless you tell me why you want it."

"You bastard!" Paula shrieked. "It's my money and I want it!"

She had hung up, trembling. Damn him! She had been willing enough to explain it all to Epstein and let him check out the builder, Andrew Jones. But Epstein had gotten on his high horse. Epstein, like Bob, seemed to have trouble remembering who counted. Somebody was always there trying to tell her what to do.

Everyone except Gil, bless his heart. He was such a darling when he showed up for the check. He had even given her the opportunity to change her mind. He was a dear, dear man, not at all the way she had perceived him to be when they first met. He was basically a very lonely guy, a man who needed the kind of stability she could give to his life.

She and Joe should not continue together. They never spent any meaningful time with each other, even though Joe had been staying closer to home than usual.

Well, she would worry about that later. She felt good today. Her stomach had settled down and she was treating herself to an afternoon at the beauty salon. She was going to let Max and Carl pamper her until she purred.

Paula picked up her bag and jacket, then after covering a couple of items with Jenny, went to the living quarters and called down for her car on the intercom. The attendant did not answer. She took the elevator down. The attendant still was nowhere to be seen. She suspected the aging ex-security guard kept a bottle hidden.

Annoyed, she headed back through the rather dark and dank garage. She had never liked underground places, any more than she liked narrow mountain roads.

The concrete floor was damp and she was certain all sorts of crawly things lived in the dirty cracks and crevices.

She fished her key out of her bag and opened the door to the Mercedes. She got inside and remembered her checkbook was still on her desk. She double-checked the shoulder bag, but it was not there. "Damn!" she said. She got out, locked the door from the inside, and unthinkingly in her rush, grasped the top of the door and slammed hard. Her fingers caught between the door and the car. Astonishment hit her first, then the pain started ripping through her hand. She swayed against the door, wanting to faint and not daring to do so.

The shoulder bag swung under her trapped left arm. Half in shock, red swirls blurring her vision, she got the purse open. "Don't faint," she told herself. "You'll make it worse, you'll tear your fingers off. God, where is that key? Where?"

Her fingers frantically dug through her purse, searching for the feel of metal. Her head was roaring. She wanted to scream, but there was no one around.

The key! Her fingers locked around it. She pulled it out and jammed the key into the lock. It wouldn't turn. She jerked the key out and looked at it. It was to Joe's Mercedes! Breathing hard, she fished for the right key and nearly dropped them all. Her heart almost stopped beating.

Her right hand was slick with sweat. She maneuvered the key with great care between thumb and index finger and inserted it. It slid in and turned and popped the door lock up.

She opened the door and freed her hand. For a moment, there was only relief, then the pain hit again and flashed up her arm. She sank to her knees, the throbbing hand cradled against her breast.

Mesmerized by her own injury, she stared at the hand. There was bone protruding from the middle finger and blood was seeping onto her jacket.

She tried to stand, scraping her knees on the hard concrete. Easy, easy. She stood more slowly. Each step she took jarred the hand, increasing the insistent throbbing. She made it to the small attendant's booth. Inside was the phone for the building intercom system. She eased her right hand down and turned the knob, then cradled the left again and pushed the door open with her right shoulder.

She reached up and pulled the receiver down. Unsupported, the hand hurt worse. God, the penthouse button was so high! She pressed it long and hard, let up, then pressed again.

After what seemed like an hour, Margaret answered. "Get Jenny down here!" she ordered. "I've hurt my hand and I have to go to the hospital!"

"Yes, ma'am."

Paula dropped the receiver. Heat flashed through her body. This was so foolish, such a stupid thing to have happen. She cradled the arm against her like a baby. She heard footsteps and looked up. The attendant was strolling back, zipping faded black trousers as he walked.

"Damn you!" she choked, darkness shadowing her vision. This wouldn't have happened if he had stayed on duty. What would happen to *Dreams*? She couldn't type. Paula slid slowly into oblivion.

"Mrs. Seals?" the attendant cried. He threw open the door and knelt over the body. Her skirt was hiked up over her thighs. Bony knees protruded out of the torn nylons. He tenderly touched the bloody hand. His fingers came away sticky.

It was after seven and Lauren was still at her desk. Jenny appeared in the doorway, her broad face creased with concern. "Paula is sleeping now."

"Good."

"She's exhausted. She should have stayed in the hospital overnight. But you know Paula, she insisted on coming home."

"There's work still to be done here," Lauren murmured. "What should I do about these scripts? Mine and Paula's? Hold them or take them in tomorrow."

"Hold them until we can talk to Paula. She plans on being in the office as usual tomorrow," Jenny answered. "You should have seen her hand. So much blood, and there was a bone sticking out!"

Lauren nodded in grim sympathy. Jenny had called her back in from the hospital. Three of Paula's fingers were broken.

"Paula is frantic about the show," Jenny remarked.

Lauren nodded. Paula's small accident had jolted her into realizing the importance of the head writer. The loss of any actor, director or writer could be worked around, but not the loss of the head writer.

"You called the studio, didn't you?" Jenny asked.

"Yes. I talked to Sue and Bob Silverstein," Lauren said.

"Everything cool there?"

"Seems to be."

"Let's lock it up. I have a husband and kids waiting."

"You go ahead. Paula wanted the viewer letters read and categorized."

"Why?" Jenny asked in puzzlement.

"I don't know. She wants their opinions, I guess. I'm supposed to do it from now on."

"So be it. Oh, we have two girls coming in tomorrow, to interview for your job. But I don't think Paula will be up to seeing them."

"You'd better reschedule them," Lauren murmured wearily.

"Okay. Good night."

"Night."

Lauren slumped in her chair and closed her lids over dulled green eyes. She was so tired, and she knew it was more emotional then physical. She had been so certain her script was right and good. Paula had not liked it at all and Lauren still did not understand why she had to rewrite that one scene. Paula had only shuffled some of

523

the dialogue around. Was it really better this way? Or did Paula simply have to find something wrong to keep Lauren humble?

Sally was a real concern now, too. The girl had stayed out all night, which was not all that unusual. Lauren had never worried when she had been with Alex. But she had no idea what had happened to Sally last night.

Sally's moods were becoming unbearable. They were going up and down like a yo-yo, and she cried at night. That got to Lauren more than anything. Sally didn't scream or sob; it was more of a whimpering, a small, hopeless sound.

Lauren pushed the fan mail back into its packet. She could do no more tonight; her mind was overloaded and beyond functioning. She was going home.

The minute Lauren stepped off the elevator into her own apartment building she could hear rock music blasting. Sally was home, her car was parked below.

Lauren hurried to the door and inserted the key. She stepped inside. The place was dark except for candles glowing on the kitchen table that sat in a small alcove to the left. The smell of marijuana nearly gagged her.

Lauren groped for the light switch, found it and flooded the room with light. Sally and a man jumped apart on the sofa. Startled, Lauren cried out.

"Hi!" Sally yelled. "Come join us."

Annoyed, Lauren marched to the radio and switched it off. "You want to get us thrown out?" she demanded of Sally.

"Aw, come on," Sally giggled. Her pupils were dilated, giving her face a vacant look. "This is Jake, my Jake." Sally cuddled up against the bearded man who wore nothing but a pair of faded jeans.

Lauren nodded and Jake nudged Sally. "I don't think your roomie is pleased," he said.

"Lauren is my best friend. Come on, Lauren. For once in your life have a toke. It's good for you."

"No, thank you," Lauren declined, her eyes studying

524

Jake. He looked back with a challenging macho gaze. He grinned as he took in her sweater-covered breasts. Then his eyes moved up to her face, meeting her gaze directly and insolently.

"Join us," Jake invited, patting the sofa. "There's room for three."

"No," Lauren said. "I have a headache. I want to take a bath, have some dinner and go to bed."

"Oh, you're no fun!" Sally pouted. "Come on, Lauren. I feel so good."

"You're stoned," Lauren muttered in disgust.

"Look, baby," Jake said as he disentangled himself from Sally's arms. "I think I'd better split. I'm not wanted here."

"Jake!" Sally whined.

"You going to drive me home, or can I take your car?"

"Oh, you can take it." Sally shook back her long silky hair. "You pick me up tomorrow and we'll do something."

"Don't you have to work tomorrow?" Lauren asked.

"Nope. I don't have to do nothing."

Lauren's lips tightened. She walked back to her room and closed the door. A few moments later she heard the front door close, then Sally came back and knocked on her door.

"Come in," Lauren murmured.

"Lauren, are you mad at me?" Sally asked, gliding into the room.

"I suppose I am. Where in the hell did you find Jake?"

"Hey, he's nothing like he used to be. He's changed. Honest! He has a steady job now."

"That's all well and good, but I thought you had outgrown people like him, Sally."

"He's not so bad, Lauren, honest."

"Are you sure?"

"Yes."

"You're still hurting over Alex. Don't rush too quickly to another man."

"Jake's my friend, an old friend."

"He's into drugs."

"So what?"

Lauren shook her head. It was pointless talking to Sally now. "Don't do anything foolish, Sally. You're into so many good things now. Don't screw it up with Dick, or with Joe."

"Oh, Joe!" Sally tossed herself across Lauren's bed. "He makes me so mad."

"You two still fighting over the television show?"

"Yes, Jake thinks I should take it."

"Jake isn't an agent, Sally."

"Jake's not stupid," Sally retorted.

Lauren was not so sure about that. He had never looked very bright to her. Street-wise, maybe. Woman-wise, definitely. But he was not intelligent. "Listen to Joe," she pleaded.

"It probably doesn't matter anyway," Sally said with a shrug. "Akron hasn't called me back."

"See, you may not even get the part in the pilot. Or if you do, the pilot might not be bought."

"It will go," Sally muttered, but she didn't sound very sure.

"Think, Sally, think!" Lauren cried, desperate for a way to pull Sally back where she belonged. "It's your career that's important, isn't it? Isn't that what you told me—the career always comes first?"

Sally shrugged her slender shoulders. Lauren could not read the cinnamon-colored eyes.

Chapter Fifty-Two

Paula yanked open her office door. "I can't do it," she announced to Jenny and Lauren, who were huddled over a paper on Jenny's desk.

Startled, they both straightened up. "Do you need another pain pill?" Jenny asked.

"No, they make me drowsy," Paula answered shortly. "I need another hand." She put her right hand protectively over the left arm that was supported by a sling of black silk. Her bandaged and splinted fingers protruded out the end.

"I can't write. Not in long hand. My mind goes too much faster than my fingers. And I can't read my chicken scratches. Lauren, you come in here. We'll try dictation."

"I—I can't take shorthand," Lauren said.

"Damn! Neither does Jenny. Well, we'll do it on the typewriter."

"We can try," Lauren said, uncertain but willing.

"Something has to work. I don't want to hire a professional steno. By the time I get her broken in, I'll be healed."

Paula strode back to her desk, poured a glass of Bristol Cream and lit a menthol cigarette. She was shakier than she cared to admit. She felt weak and her stomach was cramping, a reaction to the pills possibly.

Lauren seated herself at the electric typewriter and rolled in a set of multicarbons.

Paula emptied her glass, then poured a second while Lauren typed in the heading for the first outline. "Same day," Paula began. "Christmas day. Begin with the tag from the last episode of Anne Voll fainting."

"Paula," Lauren interrupted. "This is my outline. Why does Anne faint?"

"Oh, it's vary simple," Paula answered. "Anne is going to die."

"*Die?*" Lauren whirled around in her chair.

"Type!" Paula ordered, wondering why Bob had not called yet. Surely by now someone had read the script sent in on Wednesday. So far all she had received was flowers from Bob and other members of the cast.

Still, something was wrong. Someone should have asked about Anne's fainting spell by now. Not Anne. She seldom read more than a day ahead of taping. But Sue read the scripts as they arrived. Was she up to something?

Paula pulled her mind back to the outline and began dictating. After the first awkward hour, she and Lauren established a rhythm, and by the end of the day Paula was enormously pleased with the two outlines completed. Lauren had reminded her of a couple of loose ends, which irritated Paula at the time. However, it did show that Lauren was paying attention.

"We'll have to do the third outline Monday," Paula said. "It will throw Mel behind, but he'll understand."

Lauren turned around. "Monday? Paula, I don't come in on Mondays and Tuesdays now. I have my own scripts to write."

"Damn!" Paula tapped her nails on the desk. "I have to have you here. It went so well today. What are we going to do?"

"Hire another girl?"

"For Jenny, yes. But not for this. You've done sample scripts over a weekend, haven't you?"

"Yes, but . . ."

"Don't look so scared," Paula said. "You can do it, can't you? Or should I take you back off the writing staff until I've recovered?"

"No, please." Lauren's green eyes pleaded with the woman.

"Good. Look, I'll add another hundred dollars a week to your salary," Paula offered in a rare burst of generosity. "It won't make up for working seven days a week, but it won't last long either."

"Paula, if I could just have three days for my script. If I could come in on Tuesdays . . ."

Paula's lips tightened. "I suppose by Monday I'll be able to tap out an outline with one hand. But I can't do a script alone."

"Thank you, Paula."

"Well . . ." Paula cleared her throat. "You and Jenny get someone hired immediately.

"We've rescheduled two interviews for Monday," Lauren said.

"Good. You go home now." Paula wanted to be alone.

Anne Voll stepped out of her studio dressing room. She had changed back into her own clothes, a pair of tight-fitting French jeans and a white turtleneck sweater. The fine lines around her eyes made her look every day of her thirty-five years, but she didn't feel thirty-five. She felt bright and perky. It was such fun being married, both on and off the show. Actually, the show was more exciting. Lily and John had a romantic honeymoon in Mexico with plenty of tender, loving scenes. Anne and Lee did not have time for a honeymoon trip. Lily and John were making plans to build their own house. Lee had simply moved in with her and Reenie.

Maybe she and Lee should buy another house. Lee

could afford it, especially after he sold his town house. Then she could rent out her house for a hefty fee. And if she could talk Lee into selling all his antiques, then she would have a marvelous amount of money with which to furnish a new house. With a tennis court, she decided. A tennis court would be nice, and just *everyone* had one now.

Where was Lee? Dawdling again, she assumed. He was the slowest man in the world. Well, she would wait outside. She could use some fresh air. It was a wonder every actor in Hollywood didn't suffer from claustrophobia from being shut up in windowless rooms for half their lives.

Anne started down the corridor. Someone called her name and she turned around. It was Sue Bergman running toward her with dark hair bouncing and legs pumping. Sue slid to a stop in front of Anne, her breasts heaving under a dark sweater and blue blazer.

"I thought you should see this script before I sent it to mimeo," she said, gasping for breath.

"Why?" Anne asked, puzzled.

"It's the Christmas show, and you faint in the last scene," Sue answered, barely able to conceal her glee at being the bearer of possible trouble.

"Faint?" Anne took the script from Sue. "Why?"

Sue shook her head. "I don't know. There's nothing in the projected story line about Lily being ill again."

"Does she have me pregnant already?" Anne wondered.

"I should hope not. It's a little soon."

"What should I do?" Anne asked.

"Well, if I were you, I'd check it out," Sue advised, eyes gleaming with some malice. "I'd say Paula is up to something."

"Then I'd better talk to Bob," Anne said.

"I agree. He's still in his office."

"Thank you, Sue. You're a real friend," Anne said.

Sue smiled in triumph. Gripping the script, Anne headed toward Bob Silverstein's office.

After Anne had pointed out the surprise scene to Bob, he read it over, then leaned back in his chair.

"Well?" Anne demanded.

"I don't know," Bob said, toying with the buttons on his vest.

"You—you don't know what Paula is doing?"

"No," he admitted. "I don't."

"Well, she's up to something. I should have known she would do something. She planted a couple of headaches on the honeymoon," Anne muttered and plucked at an imagined piece of lint on her jeans. "I thought the headaches seemed so silly at the time. Bob, I felt very stupid saying such a corny line to my new bridegroom."

"Don't you worry yourself about it," Bob said. "I'll check this out with Paula."

"Call her," Anne urged. "Call her now." She dropped her voice and turned violet eyes on Bob's face. "Please?"

"All right," he agreed gruffly.

Anne sat back, feeling very smug and safe. She was the undisputed star of *Dreams*. Bob would make sure no one crossed her or walked on her, and that included Paula Cavanaugh. Paula's not showing up for the wedding had been bad enough, a direct slap in the face.

There were more interview requests coming in for Anne than she could handle. The fan mail was tremendous. The network was having the bridal photograph printed up by the thousands, so that ever fan who wrote in could receive one. Anne was considering having an oil of the same photo done. Of course, she would have to find someone really good and it would cost a fortune, but it would be a lovely gift for Lee to make to her.

"Paula," Bob was saying into the phone. "I was just going over the Christmas show. Why does Anne faint?"

He listened, sober faced. "Yes, yes. A tumor?" He frowned.

Anne wrinkled her nose. She did not like hospital

scenes when she was the one confined to bed. She needed to move in order to perform.

"Goddamn!" Bob suddenly roared, scaring Anne into jumping to her feet. "You can't make decisions like that without consulting me!"

"What? What?" Anne cried, but Bob showed no awareness of her presence.

Bob listened again, his face turning bright red. "No!" he thundered. "No!"

Bob held the receiver out in front of him. "She hung up," he said. "That bitch said she would talk to me when I'd calmed down, then she hung up on me!"

His face was a darker red now. He slammed the receiver down and yanked a handkerchief out of his pocket and wiped his face.

Anne's throat constricted. "Bob, what is it?" she asked. His eyes were bulging as he wiped his face again. "You had better sit down before you have a heart attack," she said, coming around his desk and coaxing him back into his chair. "There now. Tell me."

"Paula has taken it on herself to kill off Lily?"

"Me?" Anne choked, blinking her violet eyes in disbelief. "Me?" she cried louder. "Me?" she screeched.

"Yes," Bob said, wiping his face again. "I think Paula has flipped."

"Me? I . . ." Anne swung around, furious, incredulous. "I'm the star! I get more fan mail than—than all the rest put together. I'm the one who pulled this show up. I saved everyone!"

"Anne, Anne." Bob grabbed her hand. "I'll talk to Paula."

Anne yanked away. "You're damned right you'll talk to her! This, this is insanity. She can't do it to me."

"Of course she can't," Bob soothed. "I'm the producer. I'll handle it."

"That bitch!" Anne stormed. "What did I ever do to her?"

"You know what," Bob answered.

"The wedding!" Anne gasped, calming slightly.

"Yes, we pushed it right down her throat," Bob reminded her.

"But it worked! Look at the ratings!"

"But we still forced her to do it."

Anne's eyes narrowed, the pupils turning from violet to black. "You wouldn't go along with her, would you? Because you think you owe her one for the wedding?"

"Anne, I'll handle Paula," Bob said.

"You'd better," she warned.

Joe turned his car into the Bistro parking lot. The young attendant opened Paula's door. "Be careful with her," Joe cautioned.

Paula looked over at Joe. "Maybe we should go home," she said. "I don't think I'm up to this, Joe."

"Some food will do you good," he said. "You haven't eaten all day."

What the hell was with Joe, she wondered. He had been incredibly solicitous of her since the accident. Not that she didn't appreciate it. But she suspected she would be better off at home in bed. Or with Gil, who had been so sweet when she told him about her hand. He had insisted on canceling their regular Friday night date and told her to get some rest and take care of herself.

She was still feeling shaky from Bob's telephone call. She knew he would be angry, but his reaction was worse than she had expected. At least she had kept herself calm. The only reason she had let Joe talk her into going out to dinner was to be unavailable in case Bob called again.

Paula got out of the Mercedes carefully, brushing aside the parking valet who tried to help her. The car was whisked away and Joe and Paula stepped into the noisy Bistro where the maître d' greeted them. "Seals, reservations for two," Joe told him.

"Yes, upstairs. Madame." He bowed ever so slightly. They were escorted upstairs. Paula paused until the double doors were opened for her. She took one step inside and stopped as her eyes fell on Gil Richardson's face. Her first thought was of Joe, then she saw the woman across the table from Gil. She was sixty if she was a day, maybe more. Her face was heavily lined and rouge was smeared garishly over her cheeks. Lipstick streaked upward in the small lines above her lips.

Gil's eyes were intent on the woman's face. He was smiling and his hand covered the woman's in the same way he had so often reached across and done with Paula.

"Paula?" Joe questioned.

"Joe." She turned around and let the doors close. "I'm sick."

"Here, baby," Joe said, his arms coming around her tiny waist.

"Madame," the maître d' asked. "Would you like someone to escort you to the powder room?"

"No. I—I want to go home," she choked.

"Come on, then." Joe's voice was soft. She let him support her, knowing she could not make it without his help. The car was brought around quickly and she got in.

Paula slid down low, cradling her arm under her breast. It had been a few short hours since she had talked to Gil. He had canceled out, not she. Hot tears threatened underneath her closed eyelids.

Why would Gil be out with an old bat like that? It was absurd. He couldn't be on a date. Of course not! She was a client, and Gil was being his charming self. He had mentioned something about a new project, something to do with a medical center that would involve millions and millions of dollars.

Joe touched her shoulder gently. "Paula, how are you feeling?"

"Better," she whispered.

Gil had not called over the weekend, and for reasons Paula could not quite define, she had not telephoned him either. Of course, Gil never called on weekends anyway. Only on week nights, and late then, so she would be in her bedroom alone. Maybe he would call tonight and she could present the idea about Mexico to him. And she would just casually mention seeing him in the Bistro Friday night. Of course, the woman was a client, there was no other explanation.

Paula strode into Jenny's reception area. "I don't want to be disturbed," she said. "I'm going to type one-handed and you know how nervous that makes me." Paula kept going toward her office.

"Paula!" Jenny cried.

"Help me with my coat," Paula said. "Every time I take off something, I drop it."

"Paula!" Jenny hurried around her desk. "Bob Silverstein is in your office!"

"Bob!" A swift dart of triumph shot through Paula. So he had come to her. "Keep him waiting a few minutes more," she told Jenny. "I'll be right back."

Pleased, she hurried to the living quarters. "Margaret," she called. "Prepare a tray of coffee. Use the silver. And some of those little pastries if we have any."

"In the freezer, ma'am. I'll pop them in the microwave."

"Good. Bring it back to my office immediately." She walked to her bedroom and retouched her makeup and ran a comb through her hair and sprayed it lightly. She considered changing clothes, but that was a long and awkward procedure alone.

Paula held the office door open and let Margaret enter with the coffee service. Bob stood. He was in a dark suit, tailored close to his robust body. The fabric looked English and very expensive.

"Bob, what a nice surprise," Paula said. "You never drop in." She offered her cheek to him. He barely touched it.

"Dropping by seemed necessary," he said dryly.

Paula ignored the statement. "Here, Margaret." Paula bustled around, playing the hostess. She cleared off the coffee table and love seat of scattered scripts.

535

She seated herself in the matching upholstered chair and dismissed Margaret.

"Sugar, Bob?"

"Black," he murmured.

"Black." As black as your soul, she thought. He seated himself gingerly on the love seat that was too small and too low for his bulk and height, as Paula knew it would be. It never hurt to set things up physically so it was clear who was in charge.

"We have to have a serious talk," Bob said. "And a rational one."

"Are you implying that I'm irrational?" Paula asked.

He ignored it. "There's a lot at stake here, Paula. We can't lightly just kill off the show's most popular character."

"I warned you before the wedding, Bob. I told you we'd have story problems."

"None of this has been discussed," he retorted.

"Look, in six weeks no one is going to care about John and Lily. Their life is perfect now. And who is going to care? There's no drama in that."

"So we throw in some problems for them."

"How can we? The image we've built up for John and Lily will not allow either of them to enter into an affair. Or even a flirtation."

"I agree. But they both have people in their past. We can throw in an ex or something."

"No," Paula said flatly.

"Let's discuss the possibilities," Bob reasoned.

"No. We do that and the viewer is going to decide Lee and Anne are having trouble."

"Not necessarily."

"Ah, yes. Viewers don't always comprehend the difference between real life and the show. And you can't blame them. Lee and Anne are in the magazines, and on talk shows. The viewers listen to Lee and Anne saying the same things to each other that John and Lily say. The viewers are watching the problems of a real couple. Lee and Anne are playing themselves."

536

"Maybe so," Bob conceded. "But killing off Anne isn't a solution."

"It's the *only* solution. *Love of Life* did it. It was the best way they could think of skyrocketing the ratings. John's grief is going to seem very real to the viewers. They'll be seeing Lee grieve for Anne, his real wife."

"No."

"Bob." She deliberately kept her tone calm and spoke slowly, as if talking to a child. "It is unavoidable that the love life of Lee and Anne intertwine with John and Lily."

"It could be exploited," Bob murmured. "But . . ."

"To the hilt," Paula interrupted. "I'm not in a hurry to get rid of Anne." It was not the truth, but she had to give in a little. "It can take months for her to die. And Lee will be lost for months in grief. Can't you see him crying over Anne's casket? Can't you see him getting involved with all the wrong sorts of women? Oh, yes, Bob. We can exploit this."

Bob shook his head. "I just don't feel right about it."

"The viewers won't dare miss a day of *Dreams*. Anne might die while they aren't watching. The ratings are going to drop, Bob, if we don't do something drastic like this."

"Anne is going to hate us," Bob complained.

"She'll come around, in time. Anne can be managed by you. You're the best, Bob. And we don't have to tell her when she'll die. Or even that she will."

"But the tumor thing," Bob protested.

"It'll work. Lily fell and almost died of head injuries. Only it wasn't just a head injury. She actually blacked out before she fell. So, of course, it was a tumor. And it won't take the doctors a long time to find out." She paused and cleared her throat. "It will work."

She was convincing and knew it. Bob still looked glum, but she could see the wheels turning. The ratings were what counted, first, last and always. He was wavering.

Paula sat back, holding her cup in her right hand. "It will work, Bob," she repeated.

"I don't know," he hedged.

"Okay." She would give a little more. "We don't have to make the decision now. I've done the medical research. We can swing it either way. And we'll decide at the point of surgery if Lily dies or lives."

"And what do I tell Anne in the meantime?"

"Not too much right away. Let's give her time to adjust to the idea. She will eventually see for herself that this is necessary."

"She'll only leave one way," Bob muttered. "Kicking and screaming. I know Anne. I'll have to think about this."

Paula was careful not to smile. She had won. Bob would go for this tomorrow. Like Anne, he just needed time to adjust to the idea.

Chapter Fifty-Three

Paula sat alone in her office. Lauren and Jenny were gone, as was the new girl they had hired. Paula was not impressed with Andrea Majors, but she supposed the young girl fresh out of secretarial school would do.

It was Wednesday, and Gil still had not called. They were to meet Friday night, as usual. They had been established last week, but she felt a need for contact with him now.

The telephone rang. Paula studied the phone, considering letting it ring. It was after hours. But she pressed line one and picked up the receiver.

"Paula Cavanaugh."

"Bob here, Paula." His tone was brisk.

"Oh, hello." She sat up straighter.

"I've talked to Shepard."

"And?" Paula asked cautiously as a ball of dread formed in the pit of her stomach.

"I also spoke to Anne Voll. I laid it all on the line with her and Caleb Shepard."

Paula's fingers tightened around the receiver. "You didn't tell Anne!"

"I couldn't be dishonest with her. If I stab one of my people in the back, then I'll lose the trust of all of them."

"You made a mistake, Bob."

"No. *You* made the mistake, Paula—in not consulting with Caleb or me." Paula closed her eyes against his grim voice. "We'll go ahead with the tumor and a *successful* operation."

"We'll be in trouble," Paula warned. "You know *Love of Life*—"

"*Shtup* that. I don't give a damn about how they handled anything. This is *Dreams to Come* and we handle it our way."

"You mean your way," Paula shot back. "You and Caleb Shepard."

"Feel that way if you must, Paula," Bob said. "But this show is a team effort."

Paula's brain boiled and red flared in front of her eyes. "I won't have it, Bob. You can't disregard me this way."

"I can, and I am."

"Bob, you bastard, I'll . . ."

"Watch yourself, Paula," Bob warned. "Don't push me too far."

Paula clamped her mouth shut. Fire raged through her mind.

She hung up on him. Her broken fingers were throbbing. She shook her head wildly and stamped her feet. Damn Bob Silverstein! Damn Caleb Shepard and, most of all, damn Anne Voll, that stupid, frivolous bitch!

Paula leaned against the desk, supporting herself with her good hand, hot tears blinding her. Damn them all. She picked up an object from the desk. It was small and cold. Her grip tightened around it. Over the love seat was a floating mirror, framed in clear glass and chrome.

She stared at herself. She was old and her hair was dyed, so old and ugly, older than Gil. She drew back her arm and slammed the object into the mirror. It hit with a hard wracking sound, shattering the mirror and scattering shards of glass over the sofa and floor.

Trembling, Paula looked down. It was the glass paperweight she had thrown, the one Gil had given her with the orchid inside. It was broken in half.

Distraught, she moved around the desk and picked up the pieces with her right hand. The embedded orchid was in pieces. Futilely, she tried to force the pieces back together.

The pieces refused to fit. She wiped angrily at her tears, smearing mascara across her face. Sniffling, she picked up the pieces and put them in a desk drawer.

She pulled tissues from a box in the drawer and moved to the love seat, ignoring the crackling of the glass under her feet. There was one long shard of mirror left hanging in the frame. She moistened the tissue and dabbed at the black streaks under her eyes.

She had to get herself together and get out of the office before madness took over. She moved to the phone and dialed Gil's number. She waited, then listened to a recording telling her it was no longer a working number. Damn, she had dialed wrong! She tried again and got the same recording. The stupid phone company! She dropped the receiver.

Paula stalked back to the living quarters. Her heart was quivering, she could feel the adrenalin flowing, creating a rushing sensation just under the skin.

She walked to the kitchen. "Margaret," she said, "I'm going out. I won't be home for dinner. There's a broken mirror in my office. Would you clean it up, please?"

"Yes, ma'am, but . . ." Margaret gestured toward the salad she was preparing.

Paula walked out without another word. She got her purse and her mink coat and called down for her car. If she did not get out of there, if she did not get to Gil, she was going to start screaming.

She drove to the Marina, barely aware of the traffic ebbing and flowing around her. She parked in the street in front of Gil's apartment. She wanted his arms around her, she wanted his understanding and comfort. She hurried up to his second-floor apartment and rang the bell.

She waited impatiently, then pressed the button again. Where was he? "Gil?" she called and knocked. "Gil?"

He wasn't home. Paula's head felt light and she swayed against the door. "Gil!"

She did not hear the man until he was almost upon her. A bucket and mop clattered in his hands, startling her.

"You looking for Mr. Richardson?" the balding man asked. He hitched up the zipper of his coveralls at the throat.

"Yes," Paula said eagerly. "Yes, I am."

"He moved out."

"No, you're mistaken. I'm meeting him here Friday night," she protested.

"This ain't Friday."

"I know that!"

"He moved out Sunday."

Paula could not comprehend this. "Why? Where?"

"Don't know."

"He must have left a forwarding address."

"Not with me he didn't."

"You must be mistaken," Paula insisted.

"I'm not mistaken, lady. I'm the manager and I reckon I know who moves in and out. I come up here to clean the place. He's gone."

She did not believe him until the door was opened and she looked into the empty rooms. She walked slowly back to her car. It made no sense that Gil would move without letting her know, or that he would move at all.

She sat behind the steering wheel of her car for a long time, not knowing where to go or what to do, so tired her body ached. Cradling her arm, she leaned forward and put her forehead against the hard steering wheel. She would go home and go to bed. Gil would surely call tonight.

Joe was home when Paula returned. "Oh, you're back," he said from the bar where he was mixing a drink. "Margaret said you had gone out."

"I came back," she muttered wearily.

"Can I mix you a drink?" he offered.

"Yes, a strong one." She shook her mink off her shoulders and let it slide to the couch. "Have Margaret bring it to my room. And tell her I'll have a tray in bed."

Joe moved toward her. "Paula, are you ill? You don't look very well."

"I'm exhausted."

"Can I get you anything?"

His solicitous attitude annoyed her. "No, Joe. Just—just leave me along."

Paula bathed as best she could, keeping her left hand resting on a towel on the edge of the oversized square tub. She wrapped herself in a white satin gown and robe and swallowed down the drink Margaret had left on the bedside table.

The raw ache in her stomach started acting up again. She rolled her head back and forth over the pillow, trying to ignore the pain. She was not like Naomi, she did not have cancer. She ground her teeth together to keep from crying out.

"Ma'am?" Margaret called.

"Come in." Paula arranged the pillows behind herself and spread the cover neatly over her body. Margaret placed the tray across Paula's legs. "Mr. Seals left the paper," she said.

"How kind," Paula murmured sarcastically. "That's all, Margaret."

There was salad, chicken soup and tea on the tray. Paula picked up the soup and sipped the hot liquid, straight from the bowl. Slowly her stomach began to relax. She set the tray aside, leaving the salad untouched, and drank the tea. Where was Gil?

Paula nudged the newspaper. Reading it was something to do. She scanned the first page and opened the

Times to the third page. She skimmed over the headlines and pictures. A composite drawing leaped out at her: "CON MAN BILKS WOMAN"

The black-and-white drawing faintly resembled Gil. It seemed to grow bigger and bigger before her eyes. She read the text:

Gilbert Richardson, alias Rich Gilbert, alias Richard Daws, alias Darrel Gatlin, has struck again. A known con man who has never changed his successful method of operation has taken three wealthy Los Angeles widows for at least $200,000. There were also reports of missing jewelry, which two of the women assumed they lost while in Richardson's presence.

Con man! Alias. Paula's mind fumbled with the concept. It was not true. It could not be.

Posing as an investment broker who puts together backers for assorted projects, Richardson spends months in a city lining up his victims. Three years ago in Detroit he wooed and dated eight women in a period of six months, leaving the city with well over $300,000. His primary ploy, reported by Los Angeles victims, is his reluctant to accept last minute money to complete a "deal" which is about to fall through because of one investor withdrawing.

Paula ran her hands and fingers over the newsprint as though it were written in Braille.

Los Angeles Police are urging any women who have had dealings with Richardson to contact them.

Never! The shame. She could never go forward and admit she had been taken. She would be the laughing stock of *Dreams*. It would get into the magazines. Anne and Bob and Caleb would pretend sympathy and laugh behind her back. She would lose her self-respect.

Fifty thousand dollars and an opal ring. Even if she reported it, she would never get the money back. Obviously, Gil was a smooth operator; he would never get caught, and she would never tell.

Paula's eyes burned. She was a foolish old woman, no better than the rouged hag at the Bistro. "I loved you," she cried. "I could have given you everything, Gil. Everything."

Her mouth filled with bile. She swallowed it back. Humiliated, shamed, she pushed the newspaper to the floor and pulled the covers up over her head, wishing for oblivion that would not come.

Chapter Fifty-Four

Sally walked slowly through the house she had rented that morning. The lease was signed and she had paid the first, and last month's rent and a deposit that knocked almost three thousand out of her checking account. But what was twelve hundred a month when you were going to be making three thousand a week?

And the house was furnished, so she would not have to buy much. And it was all hers, hers and Jake's. Best of all was the land surrounding the property. It was not in the canyons, but was the next best thing. The acre was situated at the northwest end of the San Fernando Valley at the edge of the hills. There was a stable down the road where they could rent horses.

Sally slipped outside and padded barefoot across a redwood deck that overlooked a pool. California, I love you, she thought. It was December, but the sun was streaming down. It was seventy degrees and pure heaven.

Absently, she wondered why Jake was taking so long. He had promised to be back in an hour with his belongings. Since he didn't own anything beyond a guitar and clothes, it should not be taking him this long.

She was going to buy Jake a car. Living this far out meant two cars were an absolute necessity. Jake was so right for her now. It was a whole new beginning for them both and it was going to be perfect. She did not need old men like Alex LaBarre, not when she had Jake.

"I'm in love," she whispered aloud. "God, am I in love." She spun around and around over the tall, dry grass, head back, hair flying out behind her. She spun until she collapsed in a dizzy, breathless heap.

Sally wished Lauren would understand. It seemed like Lauren, of all people, should know that you had to do what was right for your man. You could not change a guy, you either loved him or you walked out. Lauren should have learned that with Kerry.

Sally did not feel as close to Lauren any more, and she missed that. All Lauren did was work. Paula was really taking advantage of her, but Lauren did not seem to care. If anything, she was thriving in her private way.

Sally picked up a brown leaf, all lacy and thin. She laid it over her eye and gazed at a filtered world. Lauren had been none too happy for her when she got the TV pilot. Joe was furious. But to hell with them both! She and Jake had decided it was the right move to make.

Akron was not so bad after all. He was big time and if he was abrupt about things it was because he was busy. He had made sure she had a beautiful wardrobe and he got a director who knew what he was doing. Sure, the story was corny, but the comic-strip stuff was hot and the money was fantastic.

The pilot had sold and they had two shows in the can now. Akron was definitely not a man to waste time. And the money, the glorious money, it made everything possible. She had even managed to keep up the personal appearances for California Girl, though those had tapered off some and Dick was concentrating on TV commercials now. The decision on whether or not to go nationwide would be made in January. Sally was certain they would get a great big GO!

Sally sat up. She would have to face Lauren tonight.

Sally knew it was wrong to move without notice, but if she had told Lauren, she would have spoiled all the fun. Lauren would have tried to talk her out of it.

Sally stood, brushed off her jeans and headed back to the house. There was so much to take care of. As soon as Jake got back they would be getting the utilities turned on and the telephones in. Sally wanted lots of phones, one in every room. She needed to change answering services, too.

Then they could go shopping for towels and sheets and dishes and stuff. And she could buy anything she wanted and not worry about the cost. "I'll take that. And that. And that!" She pantomimed and laughed out loud. Life was glorious.

Sally heard a car approaching and she sped around the house. It was Jake. She walked down a small incline to the brick-lined driveway to meet him.

He grinned at her through his beard as he got out of the red "Z."

She went slowly into his arms, her eyes sparkling as she gazed fondly at Jake. "I do love you," she said.

"I know you do." He ruffled her hair. "Hey, got any cash on you? I need to buy some things."

"Sure." Sally put her arm around Jake's waist. They were going to be so happy together. They would work and love and live in their new house.

She was going to see to it that Akron got Jake some studio work. And surely with the right connections she could get him some recording gigs, too. And someone to listen to the songs he had written. Then he could get his own recordings out and they would both be famous and rich in spite of what Joe said.

Joe was going to get himself fired if he didn't start cooperating. Jake had already offered to manage her money and take care of all the taxes and stuff she did not understand. It would actually save them money, because Joe was charging extra percentages for managing her money.

Cobb Strong's house was even better than Lauren had expected. It was sixty years old and built of dark stone, trimmed in chocolate brown. It set in the middle of a spacious green lawn, and a few flowers were still blooming in the immaculately cared for beds. There were even a few vegetables left in the garden Cobb tended himself.

She had come straight from work to his house for dinner. He had walked her around the grounds, proudly showing off everything from his prize roses to his compost heap.

"I keep gardening as organic as possible," he said, stopping and glancing at Lauren. "Am I boring you?"

"Oh, no!"

"You're so quiet."

"No, I think this is a wonderful place, very peaceful. It's a little like being back home. My mother is an avid gardener."

"I'm glad you like it here."

"I do."

They smiled at each other. She was struck again by how easy it was to be with Cobb.

"Good," he said. "Lupe should have our drinks ready by now. On the patio. But if you're cold we can go inside."

"I have my sweater," she said, aware of his constant concern for her well-being. It was very nice.

He had been calling her nearly every day since the wedding. But tonight was the first time she had felt free to join him.

Lupe, Cobb's housekeeper, met them on the flagstone patio with a pitcher of drinks and a collection of tiny appetizers on a tray. Lupe defied the usual image of a Mexican maid. She was tall and bony, a sixtyish widow whose voice was soft and lilting. She had been with Cobb for most of his daughter's life.

"Where is Martha?" Lauren asked. "I'm anxious to meet her."

"Oh, Martha is changing. She has changed clothes

three times now. She wants to impress you, I think," Lupe said.

"I'm flattered."

Lupe left on slippered feet. Lauren took her drink and tried one of the fried fish balls. "Hmm, delicious."

"I know," Cobb said, popping two into his mouth. "Lupe is a hell of a cook."

"I'm not," Lauren said. "I just get by."

"You obviously have other talents," he said, giving her a mock leer.

Lauren laughed. "Maybe." She changed the subject back to the housekeeper. "You're very lucky to have a woman like Lupe."

"She's the only mother Martha has known. She loves us and we love her. But it's not the same as—well, as having a wife."

Lauren sipped her drink, feeling very self-conscious suddenly. It would be very easy to love Cobb, for she was incredibly comfortable with him. She knew that if she let it continue, Cobb would become a habit with her.

"You're quiet tonight," he remarked.

"Oh, I was thinking about the show," she fibbed, flushing.

"Isn't Paula making things a little tough on you?"

"Somewhat, I suppose. But it is quite an education. I thought I had everything figured out about soaps, until I started taking Paula's dictation. "I'm learning more every day."

"Still, seven days a week to the show. No one else is that dedicated."

"Paula is. And we've hired another girl now. So I work only for Paula with the outlines and scripts. When those are done I go home and work on my own script."

"I'm jealous, you know. It hasn't left you much time for me."

Lauren felt her cheeks growing warm. "I'm sorry," she whispered, and was immediately annoyed with herself. She should not be apologizing for inconvenience caused by circumstances.

"Well, we'll make up for it." There was a noise behind them and Cobb stood. "Here's my beautiful daughter," he said. "Martha, this is Miss Parrow."

Martha hung back shyly, her head down, but her eyes—a paler version of Cobb's—darted up for glimpses of Lauren.

"Hello, Martha." Lauren held out her hand, which Martha eagerly accepted.

"You're very pretty," Lauren told her, though she was not. The flat-faced features were typical of children with Down's syndrome. "You have your father's eyes and hair."

"Thank you," Martha lisped slightly.

Cobb had warned Lauren that Martha's intelligence level was approximately that of an eight-year-old. Once Martha felt at ease with Lauren she chattered away about her friends at "school."

Lupe served a beautiful dinner, then Martha showed off her paintings, which were very sophisticated considering her intelligence level. Martha played the piano for them, astonishing Lauren again. At the piano, the girl wasn't so big and awkward looking and she seemed to become part of the music.

"She's a marvel," Lauren said to Cobb.

"She can't read music, but she can play anything she hears. There is one small problem though. Once she starts playing for someone it's very hard to get her to stop."

Cobb coaxed and cajoled and finally had to raise his voice to get Martha to stop. Then he gently but firmly sent her to bed. Martha insisted on kissing them both good night.

After she was gone, Cobb turned to Lauren. "I hope the kiss didn't bother you, hope you weren't uncomfortable. She's just so damned loving."

"I wasn't uncomfortable."

"She's not perfect," Cobb murmured. "But she is one

of God's children. And I believe she was sent to me for a purpose."

"You're beautiful together. I can feel the love just flowing through this house."

Cobb raised his eyes to hers, and there was a question in them she was not ready to answer. He was older and settled, she still needed time to sort out her own life before she committed herself to another man. She turned away, then asked Cobb. "What are you and Martha doing for Christmas?"

"We'll spend it here, as always. There will be parties at her school with her friends. What about you?"

"I don't know. My parents wanted me at Thanksgiving and I've been invited for Christmas." She could not go back yet. She was not ready to face them all again.

What are you like, Cobb Strong? Lauren wondered. Are you like Dick Morris. More like Dick than Kerry, of course. Dick and Cobb were the sort who had a strong sense of responsibility. They would always come home, no matter what happened on the side.

Chapter Fifty-Five

The next evening Lauren was in the kitchen when she heard a key in the door. "Sally?" she called. "I'm in here." Lauren licked mayonnaise off the knife she had used to cut her sandwich.

Sally sauntered slowly into the room. "Hi." She was clad in faded jeans and a thin blue shirt. Dirty toes stuck out from underneath the frayed hem of her jeans. Sally looked much as she had the first time Lauren had met her, except that Sally was even thinner now.

"Are you hungry?" Lauren asked. "I'll make you a sandwich."

Sally shook her head. "No." Her eyes did not focus on Lauren when she spoke.

Lauren studied the girl's face, saw the gaunt look there. Sally had not been home in two weeks. "You're losing weight, Sally," she said.

Sally shrugged. "I'm okay."

"Are you?"

"Yes."

"Please have something to eat with me," Lauren coaxed.

"No, I'm not hungry." Her features took on a petulant look.

"Sally, you . . ." Lauren began, knowing she

sounded like a nagging mother but unable to stop herself. "You've been with Jake, haven't you?"

"Sure. What have you got against Jake?"

"I think that's obvious. He's into drugs, he's a bum." Just being around Jake made Lauren feel slimy.

"Jake is going to be a big success. He's good," Sally said.

"Sure he will, if he has a mind left."

Sally edged around the kitchen. "I have to tell you something, Lauren."

"Oh?"

"I—Jake and I have rented a house. So I'm moving out."

"Moving out?" Lauren echoed. "No, not with Jake. Sally, don't jump into this."

"I've already signed a lease on a house."

"Oh, Sally!" The reality of it began to come down on Lauren. "What about this apartment? It's costly and big."

"I'll pay my share of the rent for another month, until you can get another roommate or move."

Lauren sank down at the table. "Sally, don't do this," she begged.

"Hey, it's my life, my guy," Sally flung at her. Lauren lowered her eyes. Sally was right, of course. It was her life. "I'm taking some clothes with me tonight. Tomorrow there's a truck coming for my furniture."

"I won't be here," Lauren said.

"I'll come back."

"All right." An awkward silence fell between them.

"Well . . ." Sally shook back her silky hair. "It's been fun, Lauren. We're still friends, aren't we?"

Lauren smiled weakly. "Of course." But it would never be the same.

Sally followed the moving van from the West Los Angeles apartment to the house at the far end of the Valley. She really did feel guilty about moving out on Lauren so suddenly. But she had left a check for the next month's rent on the kitchen table. She thought that was generous of her, seeing as how she would not be there.

Sally felt light-headed and tired. She was going to have to start sleeping nights instead of hanging around the club listening to Jake play and sing. She dug into her purse with one hand and found an aspirin bottle. She flipped off the top and shook out a red and popped it into her mouth. Too many reds would scramble your brain, so she only took them when it was absolutely necessary, like before a personal appearance or if she fagged out while shooting the TV show.

Sally maneuvered her red "Z" into the driveway behind the moving truck. There was a faded and rusted van parked further up in the brown lawn. She glanced at it, curious. She pulled in next to the van.

"This stuff goes in the master bedroom," Sally told the two moving men.

One of the men looked uncomfortably about. "Lady, what about that dog?" he asked. "Does he bite?"

"Dog?" Sally turned around. There was a shaggy collie lying on the porch.

"Hey, fella," Sally called. The dog flopped his tail on the porch. She walked over to him. He did not get up or growl. "I guess he's harmless," she called back to the man. The dog sniffed at her feet and legs. "Nice dog. What are you doing here, huh? Do you have a name?"

A shadow fell across the doorway. Sally glanced up to see Jake behind the screen. "That's Dog," he said.

"Dog?"

"That's his name, Dog."

"That's awful," Sally said and opened the screen. "Where did he come from? With the van?"

"He belongs to Marco and Bebe."

"Bebe?" Sally laughed. "Who's that."

"Look, honey," Jake said, putting his arm around her. "Marco and Bebe are having a rough time of it. They're both out of work and they got kicked out of their pad. They've spent the last three nights in the van.

557

And it's getting colder now. So I told them they could crash here for a few days. I told them you wouldn't mind."

"I guess not," she murmured, but she was disappointed. She had been looking forward to being alone with Jake, thinking about Christmas in their own house.

"They're really going to appreciate this, honey," Jake assured her. "And I know you'll like them."

Jake propped open the door for the two waiting movers, then Sally followed him and Dog inside. A couple of duffle bags were tossed in front of the stone fireplace.

Sally directed the men back to the bedroom she and Jake had cleaned out. The extra bed had been stored in the garage. She showed the two men where to set up the bed and went to find Jake.

He was in the kitchen. A girl and a guy sat at the breakfast bar. "Bebe and Marco," he said. "This is Sally."

Sally nodded, feeling vaguely apprehensive.

"Wow!" Bebe exclaimed. "You really are the California Girl!"

"Did you think I was making it up?" Jake asked.

"Sort of, I guess." She had a small, pinched face and a frizz of dirty blonde hair. "I thought Jake was putting me on." She looked at Sally with adoring eyes. "You're beautiful."

"Thank you."

Bebe was small, about Sally's size. The guy was also small, with a reddish beard and unkempt hair. He just sat, staring off into nothingness.

"Honey." Jake dropped his arm around Sally's shoulder. "Why don't you run down to the grocery store? There's not much food here."

"Oh. Okay," Sally agreed reluctantly.

Bebe jumped to her feet. "I'll do it for you. I mean, I got to do something around here so I'll feel useful. We appreciate your letting us stay here, and we don't have any money, but I'll do anything you say." She rubbed her fingers together. The nails were chewed to the quick. "You just tell me what to do and I'll do it. Marco, too."

Marco made no response to the mention of his name, nor did he speak. Sally took out a twenty-dollar bill and gave it to Bebe.

"Thanks," Bebe said. "Uh, do you think I could have enough for a little gas for the van, too. I'm not sure I can get back here."

Sally fished out another ten and gave it to Bebe. Why not, she thought. They were Jake's friends and it was important to him that they be treated right.

Bebe left, then Sally got the hammer and nails she had bought and went to the bedroom. The bed was up and the movers were bringing in cartons. After the remaining furniture was in place, Sally paid them. She opened up boxes and found the chrome-framed prints of herself and the ads. She arranged and rearranged and finally got them hung over the bed.

She put away some of her clothes and checked to make sure her treasure box had arrived safely. She tucked it into a bottom drawer.

Satisfied with the room for now, Sally returned to the kitchen. Jake and Marco were passing a joint back and forth. Bebe came in with two grocery sacks. "I got lots of TV dinners and some candy bars," she said and began dumping things on the table. "I got at least one of every kind. Everybody choose."

Sally wrinkled her nose. She hated TV dinners. "I'm not hungry," she muttered. "You guys go ahead." God, that Marco is creepy, she thought. Did he ever talk?

Lauren and Cobb stood back to admire the oversized Christmas tree. A tattered angel grazed the ceiling. Below, the tree shimmered in layers of icicles and the vast array of ornaments. Martha was in bed now and Lupe had gone to her room after serving hot chocolate laced with a coffee liqueur.

559

"It's pretty," Lauren whispered, feeling nostalgia from years past. She also felt a little teary.

"Nice tree," Cobb agreed. "Maybe not as nice as last year's."

Lauren laughed. "You sound like my father. He said that every year."

Cobb smiled across at her. "Come on. The chocolate is getting cold." They sank down on the couch together. Lauren kicked off her shoes and sipped the sweet chocolate.

Cobb put his arm around Lauren and she snuggled down against his bulk. "Oh, I almost forgot to tell you," she said. "I found an apartment today."

"I'm sorry to hear that."

"Cobb!" Lauren popped up.

He pulled her back. "Well, I was sort of hoping you'd show up on my doorstep, a homeless orphan seeking shelter."

The teasing made her uncomfortable; he said too many things like that. She kept her voice light. "Nope, I found a one-bedroom. It's nice, in an older place with large, airy rooms. It's on the top floor and there are trees outside my windows, huge ones. They run across one end of the living room. I'm going to use that for my office."

"Sounds nice."

"It is. I'm getting new furniture, too. I can afford it now. Lots of bright floral prints. I want color around me. And I'll fill the windows with plants."

"I have rooms and windows and plants. You could—"

"Don't, Cobb." She tried to move away but he pulled her back.

"Give me a chance, lady," he said. "I'm trying to work up to asking you to marry me."

Anguish swept over her. "Don't," she begged.

"Why?"

"You're scaring me, Cobb. We don't even know each other."

His blue eyes were imploring. "I think we do."

"Don't rush me. I've been through so much this year. I'm not ready to handle this." She felt suffocated and wanted to move away from him, but she knew he would not understand.

"You mean you aren't ready to handle me?" There was pain in his eyes now.

"You, and marriage," she said. He was dear and good and kind. She liked being with him and treasured his friendship and his easygoing ways. If it was love it was different from any kind she had felt before. She touched his face gently. "I care about you."

"I *love* you," he replied.

She dropped her eyes. She couldn't say it back to him, not yet. "Cobb, we've been seeing each other for a very short time. We haven't been dating a month yet."

Cobb laughed. "You're right. But I feel like I've known you always. Maybe I've been in love with you since that first night we met at that crazy saloon with Kerry and Sally."

Lauren's throat constricted and she squeezed Cobb's hand. "Give me time," she said. Be gentle with me, be kind, she thought. She wondered why it could not have been Cobb who attracted her instead of Kerry. But she knew why. Cobb was older, a quiet, gentle man, while Kerry was like a young male animal, sensuous, powerful, promising everything. A tremor slid over her body.

"Cold?" Cobb asked.

"A little."

"I'll put a log on the fire."

"No, don't. I need to go home. I have lists to make for Christmas and my new place."

"And working and moving," he said for her.

"And working and working, and shopping and shopping," she groaned and stood.

"Hey, that reminds me. Do you know what's going on between Anne and Bob and Paula?"

"Almost nothing. Paula has been very secretive lately, and . . ." Lauren shrugged.

"And what?"

"Tired. Her hand isn't healing fast enough to suit her." There was more, but not to tell Cobb. It was not that she didn't trust him, but he was part of the cast.

"Anne is going around like the proverbial cat who ate the canary."

Lauren indicated that she knew nothing about it and went to the hall closet for her jacket. Cobb walked her out to her car. It was a crisp, clear evening; more stars than usual could be seen in the sky. Red and green lights twinkled on the house next door and a collection of spotlights were focused on a fat, grinning Santa.

They faced each other and Cobb slid his hands inside her coat and drew Lauren close. She accepted his kiss and the pressure of his body against hers. She knew he wanted to take her to bed, but he was not pushing. She was grateful for that.

Cobb was different from other men; sex was not of paramount importance with him. He did not have to prove himself by taking her to bed. She liked that. Cobb was the kind of man she had dreamed about once. Yet when she was with him she found she held back; too often she divided herself in half, so that one part of her participated and one part observed.

Her kisses were warm and enjoyable. She felt safe in his arms. She snuggled against him for a moment. "I have to go," she whispered against the broad solid swell of his chest.

"I know." Reluctantly he released her. "Don't forget that you have promised Christmas day to us. Lupe will go to visit relatives and we'll cook dinner ourselves."

"I wouldn't forget. Good night, Cobb."

"Good night."

He helped her into the car and closed the door. As she drove away she looked in the rearview mirror. He was still standing in the driveway when she turned left.

In her mind, she moved away from Cobb to Paula Cavanaugh. Paula was ill, there was no other explanation for the way she was acting. First they were pushing ahead so everyone could have a few days off at Christmas. Now they were behind and there was no chance of more than one day off.

Paula seldom came in now before ten. Often a decision she made in the morning was rescinded in the afternoon. The way Paula insisted on keeping Lauren in her office was getting downright spooky. The woman was clinging, bossy, and was growing more dependent on Lauren daily.

Lauren found herself put in the place of making necessary decisions about story line and plot simply because Paula was not making them. Sometimes Paula would drift off in the middle of dictation. Lauren would have to pull her back verbally and remind her of where they were going.

It was difficult and trying. Yesterday Lauren had almost walked out when Paula threw a tantrum. She did leave the room, shaking from head to toe. She went into the bathroom because the new girl had taken over her former office. She locked the door and gulped in air until she was breathing normally again.

She and Jenny had both tried to talk to Paula about seeing a doctor. They were sneered at and cursed for their efforts.

Lauren had not quit. The job, the money and the position were too important to her to fling away in anger. She went back to Paula's office and opened the door without knocking.

Paula was standing by the window, overlooking Wilshire, clutching something in her hand. She held it up to the sunlight. It glistened and Lauren recognized it as the paperweight that had disappeared from Paula's desk. It was broken and Paula was crying softly.

Lauren closed the door quietly without being seen. She felt sorry for Paula. She wanted to go to her, but Paula would never allow pity or sympathy. Lauren considered approaching Joe, then decided against it. He had to be aware of his wife's peculiar condition lately. If she went to Joe and Paula found out, the woman would be absolutely furious.

During times like yesterday, life with Cobb Strong was tempting. She would never have to love and lose roommates like Sally. She would never have to live alone, and there would be no bosses like Paula. Life would be simple and quiet and easy. If she had any sense she would grab Cobb and never let go.

Chapter Fifty-Six

It was Christmas eve in Los Angeles. The night temperature was sixty-eight degrees and a breeze blew in off the ocean, clearing the skies. Mechanical Santas bobbed in store windows, machine-driven elves danced in place on rooftops edged in colored lights and fake snow covered a lawn here and there.

In the faded yellow club on Ventura Boulevard a few people with no place else to go gathered. There was little conversation in the club and for the most part people kept to themselves, scattered along the bar and at tables.

Jake played and sang in the woozy, unfinished way people do when they're stoned. No one, including Jake, noticed when he lasped off into nothingness or changed songs in the middle of a chord.

Sally huddled alone in a dark corner as far away from the spotlighted stage as she could get. William Akron had abruptly stopped production on the TV show with lots of meaningless talk about lack of money and the network having second thoughts. It was definite the show would not premiere in January.

"Maybe in the fall, kids," Akron told them with a psuedo-friendly wave of his hand. Somehow the comic-strip shows were suddenly out of style. Two of the ones airing had been canceled. The fickle American public had turned thumbs down.

Sally was scared and she was sick from combining wine and grass and Quaaludes for too many hours. She was dizzy and queasy, and she wanted to go home, but home had turned into a crash pad. Bebe and the silent Marco were still unpaying houseguests. A couple of guys from Utah had moved in last week, bringing unnamed girls in and out at will.

They ate Sally's food, wore her clothes and smoked Jake's seemingly endless supply of grass. When Jake was not working he divided his time between sleeping and giving speeches on the mysticism of orgasms and the necessity of not folding under to the pressures of a capitalistic society. Bebe and Marco and the others treated Jake as though he were a guru, and they his willing followers.

But the truth was they were living off Sally and her earnings. And tonight she had told Jake she was broke. "Broke!" His lips tightened between beard and mustache. "That's impossible."

Hot tears filled her eyes that were already burning from lack of sleep. "I wrote a check yesterday, and that was it, Jake."

"Where did it go?"

"Well, the telephone company for one thing. Have you seen the phone bills? Those—those creeps are calling all over the country."

"So speak to them about it," Jake countered. "Have the phones taken out. Something."

"You do it!" she threw back. "Take the phones out and those people with them!"

"Shit!" Jake muttered in disgust. Then he grinned and pulled her into his arms. "It'll work out, honey. You're still the California Girl. And you'll get more work. And I've got steady pay, too."

His meager salary would not even keep them in food, much less grass. "Make them leave," she begged. "Make them all go away, Jake."

"At Christmas? Can you do that to them?"

When he put it that way, she knew she was licked. She came to the club with Jake instead. The waitress, a skinny rabbit-nosed girl called Sandy, put a glass of wine in front of Sally.

"I don't want that," Sally slurred. "I want to sleep."

"It's from the guy at the bar," Sandy said. "The fat one."

"Him!" Sally made a gagging sound. He had been watching her all evening. He was a creep, a slimy fat creep. He had pig eyes lost under heavy brows. He was swarthy looking with oversized, floppy lips that never stopped yammering. He had already bought two rounds of drinks for everyone, but he wasn't a jolly Santa. There was something mean and cruel about him.

The waitress left the wine and sauntered away. Sally pushed it to one side and hunched down further in her chair. Through half-closed eyes she watched the fat guy leave his barstool and approach the stage. He pressed some bills into Jake's hand and whispered to him.

Sally yawned, hoping the slob was leaving. She wondered if anyone would care if she went into the back and stretched out on some liquor cases. It would be another hour before the club closed and they could go home.

Sally slid even lower in her chair and put her knees against the table. Her head was throbbing and her mouth was dry. She wished for water.

Jake laid his guitar aside and hopped down from the stage, leaving the fat man to fade back out of the lights. "Sally." Jake grasped her shoulder and leaned over her. "Look here." He spread out two one-hundred-dollar bills.

Sally jerked upright. "For your singing?" she gasped. "A tip?"

"Well, no." He began to massage her shoulder. "It's for a little time with you."

"Me?" Sally could not, dared not comprehend the meaning of his words. "Me?"

"Sure. For one night of your time."

A chill trembling began somewhere in the depths of her body and soul. "Jake, no!" She stared at him in disbelief.

"It's easy, and we need the bread," he crooned.

"No. No, I'm not . . . I never!" she protested, images of Patty and her mother filling her mind.

"You do it plenty, and you give it away."

"That's different! My friends—men I care about. Jake, no," she whimpered.

"The difference is money, Sally. Come on. Smile and be sweet. It won't be so bad." His hand urged her to her feet. This could not be happening, Jake would never ask her to do something like that.

Her numbed legs threatened to give way under her. She swayed against Jake, who was suddenly a stranger. She was not that kind of girl, she was not like her sister Patty. She was not a whore!

Horror washed over her in hot thick waves as the fat man stepped back into the light. He licked his oversized lips and stared at her through pig eyes. Grinning, he approached.

Jake's hands grasped Sally's upper arm. "Just be sweet," he coaxed. "It will be over with before you know it."

She yanked free of Jake, crashed into a table, then dodged around it. She stumbled over protruding feet and stumbled outside. The cool night air hit her in the face. Gasping, she ran up the street. Behind her Jake was yelling, but she did not stop or look back.

She careened down the alley toward her car. Somewhere there were keys. In her pocket. She got them out and got into the "Z" and started it. She shoved the shift into reverse, hit the gas pedal hard and crashed into a collection of garbage cans.

Ignoring the clatter of metal against metal, she jerked the car into first gear and sped away, throwing gravel against the buildings. She drove, mindlessly at first, conscious only of the need to put distance between her

568

and the fat man, between herself and Jake's obscene suggestions.

It was incomprehensible that Jake would suggest she prostitute herself when he knew how she felt about Patty. It was the lowest thing a woman could do, it defiled sex and love and friendship. Jake knew she was not like that, yet he had asked her to do it.

Forced to stop for a traffic light, she became aware of the spastic trembling of her body. Muscles jerked and twitched. There was a service station on her right with a telephone booth outside. She yanked the car into the deserted lot. She could call Lauren. She would put her up for the night. But Sally had neither purse nor money.

And she could not drive there with the gas gauge sitting on empty. She had no idea where Lauren had moved to, even if she did have gas.

She could not go home. Her beautiful house was jammed with people, dirty and cluttered. She had been a fool to let them move in. Tomorrow she would kick them out. She would talk to Jake and he would apologize. When it was just the two of them it would be okay again.

She finally drove home after three cramped and sleepless hours in the car. There was no place else to go. The Fiat she had bought for Jake was in the drive, along with the van, a couple of old cars and a pickup truck she had never seen before. She was too weary to feel more than vague annoyance at the thought of someone else moving in.

She would sleep now, she would release her aching body from its agony. Tomorrow they all would have to leave, even if it was Christmas.

Sally stepped over a sleeping body in the living room and made her way to the bedroom. A single lamp glowed, casting a faint light through the open door. She stepped inside and stopped short. Her blood chilled, then waves of horror engulfed her at the sight of Jake and Marco sleeping spoon fashion. Jake had Marco's nude body drawn up against his and his arm was around the man, his hand in Marco's crotch. Bebe was sleeping far on the opposite side of the bed, her frizzy hair buried in Sally's pillow. On the wall above was Sally—pouting, smiling, serious, winsome. Sally in all her moods looked down from the color photographs.

It was as if a steel splinter shot through her head. They took, they used; not just Bebe and Marco, but Jake too. If it was not for her money none of them would be there. "Users! Users!" The word reverberated through her shattered mind as she shook with sick realization.

Jake was a snake, a louse. This surely was not the first time he had been with Marco. Tonight he must have chosen to deliberately flaunt it in her face, to pay her back for running out on him.

She would sell her body and talents before a camera to support him, but not to another man. The rage faded and a strange calmness settled over Sally. She was too sick and too tired to sustain the hot burning anger.

She moved across the room, ignoring the bodies on the bed. She opened a drawer and took out her precious treasure box. She opened the lid, lovingly touched the pewter box Tony had given her and checked the contents. They were all intact, including a twenty-dollar bill she had hidden away. She pulled an armload of clothes from the closet and carried them out to her car.

In the kitchen she found a box and some grocery sacks. She returned to the bedroom and threw in what she could find. She discarded the leather suit Alex had bought for her. There was a nasty tear down the back of the jacket.

She was leaving with something this time, not like before when she left Jake. She had a car and some clothes. She had a future, she hoped, with California Girl. She had a few dollars in her purse, and her pride. She was going. She did not know where, but she was going. She would find Tony or Alex or Lauren. Someone would help her.

Joe Seals awoke at ten Christmas morning. Paula's door was firmly closed and he had no way of knowing if she could come out today or not. He had offered to take her away for Christmas, to the mountains or the beach or anywhere she wanted to go. For his efforts he had received a suspicious look and a refusal even to discuss the possibility.

Despondent, he went to the kitchen and made coffee. He opened the refrigerator. Margaret had left a small smoked turkey there, along with a bowl of dressing, cranberries and plum pudding. The hearty traditional food was a mockery to Joe, as was the tree Margaret had put up on her own. The only gift under the tree was a jade necklace Joe had bought for Paula. It would probably go unopened.

Saddened by the bleakness of the holiday, Joe carried his coffee to the living room. There was not even a newspaper to bring in, not on Christmas day. He flipped on the radio set in an elaborate stereo cabinet. There were church services and Christmas carols on every channel. He turned it off and moved to the bar to fix a Bloody Mary.

The house phone rang, breaking the silence. Joe picked up the nearest extension.

"Joe, it's Sally."

"Merry Christmas, baby."

"Joe, I need help. I've left Jake and I don't have any money or anywhere to go." Her words tumbled out on top of each other. "I've got to break the lease on the house and get those people out and I don't know where Lauren lives and . . ."

"Slow down, Sally," Joe ordered. "First things first. Now, where are you?"

"At a service station on Sunset."

"Go to my office then. I'll meet you there. We'll figure out something."

"Lauren will . . ."

"She's in a one-bedroom place now," Joe said, his

tone level. "And I think it might be better if we get you into a hotel."

"Does she hate me?" Sally asked.

"No, honey. Not that. But—well, I've heard this song before, and Lauren has, too."

"Oh, Joe!" she cried, her voice breaking. "I'm in such a mess. I've ruined everything."

"Go to my office," he ordered.

Thirty minutes later, Joe parked his Mercedes behind the red Datsun. The street was almost empty and there was only the barest movement of traffic. Sally got out of her car and came toward Joe. His heart tightened at the sight of her. She looked like warmed-over death. He opened his arms and Sally rushed into them.

"What am I going to do with you, Sally?" he asked protectively.

"Hold me, Joe. Help me get my head together."

"I will, I will," he said, stroking her matted hair. A warmth spread across Joe Seals. In spite of his cavalier attitude toward her, he did love her. She was such a little gremlin, kooky and sincere, warm and flighty. She was a beguiling little creature in desperate need of his help.

She pulled back. "I'm going to stand on my own feet, Joe. I'll be strong and I'll be good. And I'll listen to you. I won't ever go against you again."

"Yes. Yes." He pulled her back against him. He wanted her safe, wanted to protect her, wanted to make her happy, wanted to feed her and see her eyes shine with laughter again.

Joe's arm tightened around her and he crushed her body against him, burying his face in her hair.

The Christmas sun shone down on Sunset Boulevard. A boy of about fourteen wandered out from between two buildings and rubbed the sleep from his eyes. He sauntered toward the embracing couple in the parking lot to ask for a handout.

Chapter Fifty-Seven

Since Christmas, Lauren had either seen Cobb daily or talked to him on the phone. Tonight she was seated next to him as they drove to Bob Silverstein's home in the hills.

"It should be quite a bash tonight," Cobb said of the twentieth-anniversary party of *Dreams*. "We usually have a little food and drink on the set. But Bob is giving it his all this year. Of course, he'll write it off."

"Maybe he's celebrating the stability of the show," Lauren remarked. The ratings had dropped off after the surge from the wedding, stabilized, then dipped and were now rising as they squeezed every ounce of emotion possible out of the Anne/Lily brain tumor.

"Maybe," Cobb said with a curious look at Lauren. "Just how much do you have to do with the success of this show?"

"Me? What are you talking about?" Her pulse beat picked up in an apprehensive quiver.

"There are lots of rumors stirring about, particularly about Paula's behavior. Word has it that you're carrying the show."

Lauren laughed nervously. "Don't be foolish," she murmured and worked the ring on her right hand round and round. Cobb had given her the emerald for Christmas. Over her protests, he insisted she wear it, if not as an engagement ring, then as an about-to-be-engaged ring.

She stared down at her hand. She was carrying Paula, if not the show. Paula was in a fragile state and Lauren and Jenny protected her from outside pressures as much as they could.

Lauren handled all the studio problems now, without taking them to Paula. If Sue called about even the smallest error or change, Paula would rant and rave for hours. So Lauren simply did not tell her about them.

She took Paula's abuse and stifled her own rage over and over, biting back the kind of scathing comments that would surely get her fired. There were more days than she cared to contemplate when she left Paula's office shaking. She would be fortunate if she made it to her car before she started crying. She told no one that she cried because she was nervous, because Paula put her down, because she cared too much about her job, that she shoved her own self-respect back into a far corner because the position of staff writer meant everything to her. Because when she saw her name roll past on the credit crawls at the end of the show it erased the hell involved in getting there. It was a thrill that would never diminish for her.

"Lauren?" Cobb spoke and patted the seat next to him.

"What, dear?" She scooted over closer to him.

"Don't you think it's time to move that ring from your right hand to your left?"

Not now, she thought, feeling desperate. The pressure of work was all she could handle now.

"Do you really care about me?" Cobb asked.

"Care?" She bumped her cheek against his shoulder. "I adore you," she whispered.

"But do you love me?"

"I think so. If it's not love, then it is the deepest caring I've ever known."

"Don't you want to be with me every day?"

"We're together constantly," she hedged.

"Would it be any help if I told you I wouldn't want you to give up your career? Of course, you'd have to leave Paula's office, but you'd still be doing a script a week at home."

"I don't know when I can leave," she said carefully.

"Does she need you so much?"

"She seems to, yes."

"More than I do?" he asked, looking away from the street toward her.

"Yes, for now," Lauren answered truthfully.

"Would it help if I agreed to having children?"

"We've discussed this before, Cobb. You told me you wouldn't want children, because Martha will be your child for always. And you said you were too old to start over with babies."

"I know what I said," he replied. "Can't I take it back?"

"I suppose."

"You sound reluctant. I thought you wanted children."

Lauren picked at the long dark skirt. "I used to think I'd be a whole woman only if I gave birth. I know now that isn't true." Kerry and Dick and her desire for a career had taught her at least that much about herself.

She was not sure if having or not having babies was the problem anyway. It was her career. She was not sure she wanted to be at home all day. Difficult as Paula was, it was still a challenge. It was exciting and she was honing her craft with each passing day. It was a lucrative profession and the pay would get better and better. One day she would want to set out on her own and try other types of TV writing, maybe a book, possibly a screenplay.

Cobb wanted her to be primarily a housewife. She would be expected to put him, his career and his daughter ahead of her own desires. Her lips drew into a tight thin line. She did not want to be one of those women whose husbands *let* them work.

"Lauren?" Cobb said, breaking silence. "Are you still carrying a torch for Kerry?"

"Kerry?" she repeated the name almost listlessly. "No, I'm over Kerry." But sometimes, and she hated herself for doing it, she compared Kerry and Cobb. It may have been painful with Kerry, but it was exciting. With Cobb there would never be highs or lows. She told herself mature love should be that way, but certain doubts kept creeping in. Sometimes she was able to tell herself she was lucky to have known and loved a man like Kerry Scott. He had shattered her sexual defenses, awakened her and turned her into a vibrant, sensuous being. A lot of women never had the kind of satisfaction Kerry had given her.

It had not been a solid and lasting love, as Cobb's would be, but it had been the ultimate trip. Of course, sex was part of the current problem, too. She and Cobb still had not slept together. There was no driving desire for it in her, no throbbing need to explore sex with Cobb. She was even a little afraid of it with him, fearful of his not satisfying her. She could only envision herself submitting to Cobb Strong.

It was not that he would not want to please her. Cobb went out of his way to please her in nearly everything. But she was deeply afraid he would not satisfy her sexually, that something in her would not respond to him as it had to Kerry and to a lesser degree to Dick Morris.

Cobb turned the car up the hills. At a wide stretch in the road just before a curve he pulled over on the shoulder. He turned to Lauren. "Marry me," he whispered without touching her. "Don't keep me waiting. My life is half over now, probably more."

"Cobb," she choked.

He leaned over and kissed her. "I love you, Lauren. I want to be more than your friend."

She hid her face against the smooth silken fabric of his tuxedo jacket. "You are the best friend I have ever had," she murmured.

"It isn't enough, though. Not for either of us." He took her hands and she was forced to raise her head to face him. "Let me put this ring on your left hand. Let me announce our engagement and turn this party into a real celebration."

Lauren nodded very slowly and carefully. "But we can't set a date. Not until Paula . . ."

"Paula what?"

"Oh, settles down and gets the splints off her hand."

Cobb grinned. "I'll hold you to that. The day the splints come off we set the date. Oh, Lauren!" He drew her into his arms and she gave herself up to his long, searching kiss.

I'll never hurt him, she vowed, confident in the knowledge that he would inflict no pain upon her either.

The Silverstein home was a 1920 Moorish-style house, that almost but not quite qualified as a mansion. It lacked the required projection room considered standard equipment in Hollywood industry homes.

There was a prescribed swimming pool, covered now with a deck to provide a place for dancing. The rooms were filled with trendy furniture that included life-size ceramic dogs and sickly green Oriental statues.

Bob's fluttering wife, Sheila, resplendent in a bright green silk pajama outfit, directed Cobb and Lauren to the patio that lazily circled between house and pool and cabana.

It was a catered affair, and the area was dotted with waiters and waitresses in matching brown velvet jackets and red bow ties. An elaborate spread of food included bouquets of edible vegetables. A bread tree, looking like a child's attempt to build a giraffe from assorted bakery breads, dominated one table.

Cobb scooped two glasses of champagne from a passing tray. "To us," he said and they lightly touched glasses. The ring on Lauren's left hand made her feel self-conscious.

"To us," she answered as he adored her with his eyes.

She drew away, hating herself for the doubts prickling at her conscience and looked around at the milling crowd. "Is there anyone who isn't here?" she asked. There had to be a hundred people present already and it was still early.

Bob Silverstein and Caleb Shepard were holding court in a white gazebo nearly obscured by clinging passion vines. All members of the cast were on hand, as were their spouses and even some of their children.

Lauren sighted Paula and Joe on the far side of the pool dance floor near the combo. Paula looked thin and brittle in a black gown that hung too loosely from her shoulders. She had been negotiating her new contract through Epstein with Bob. It was not going well, and the effect showed in the deep lines etched on Paula's face. Dark shadows underneath her eyes gave them a bruised look.

Paula was asking too much of Silver Productions this time, Lauren thought. She swore she would settle for no less than complete story control this year. Lauren wished Paula would not put herself through a battle she could only lose. The strain was tremendous and signs of it became more evident every day.

"Hey, hey!" a voice called, making Lauren and Cobb turn around. It was Sally Rook, looking like a designer's dream in coral chiffon.

"Sally!" Lauren cried. "You look terrific." She was far different from the girl she had seen three weeks earlier. The beaten, unhappy look was gone and Sally was glowing.

Hugs and kisses were exchanged, then Sally took a possessive hold on Lauren's arm. "Let me steal your girl for a minute," she told Cobb. He politely moved away to speak to Rose Jardine and her husband.

"I can't believe you, Sally," Lauren enthused. "You snap back faster than anyone I've ever known."

"You won't believe how well things have gone,

Lauren. You know that Joe rented an apartment for me?" Lauren nodded and Sally rushed on. "And he had the police kick Jake and his friends out. Yuck!" Sally made an expressive face of distaste. "I salvaged what they didn't steal. It cost plenty to get the house cleaned up, but Joe got me out of the lease."

"Were you—are you still hurting over Jake?"

"No, not really. The hardest thing was facing what a fool I made of myself. Once I did, the pain went away." There was a grace about Sally, a maturity Lauren had not seen before.

"You've had one hell of a bad year with men," Lauren told her.

"Haven't we both?" Sally laughed. "But that year is past and this year is going to be perfect. You've found a guy, haven't you?"

"Cobb? Yes." But for reasons she did not understand herself, she failed to mention to Sally anything about their engagement.

"This time I'm going to get it all straight. Joe has my permission to hit me if I foul up," Sally said and laughed throatily.

Lauren was deeply pleased for Sally. She was obviously off the pills. She could tell that just by looking. Her ability to recover was fantastic.

"Did you know my TV show went down the tube?" Sally asked. "Joe says I'm lucky. He doesn't think they'll ever show them. And did you hear about California Girl? It's going nationwide!"

"That's wonderful, Sally. I'm happy for you."

"Dick calls me all the time. He said this week to be sure and give you his best."

"Tell—tell him I think of him, too, with good thoughts."

"I will," Sally promised.

The tempo of the music increased and Sally began to wiggle her shoulders and hips. "I gotta dance!" she announced. "Who can I grab?"

Lauren looked around. "How about him?" she asked,

579

pointing to a young man who was probably someone's son.

"Not bad," Sally said as she left Lauren. "See ya!"

Sally flitted away in a swirl of coral. Lauren searched the crowd for Cobb and spotted him standing alone by a potted palm tree. The expression on his face was somber. He stood between two groups of people, all of whom had their backs to him, intent on their own conversations. Cobb looked lonely, and she felt responsible in some perverse way that made her uncomfortable.

Chapter Fifty-Eight

Joe touched Paula's arm. "Are you cold?" he asked.

"No," she replied, but she had her left arm drawn up right against her body, as though it were still in a sling.

Joe cleared his throat and made an effort at conversation. "I don't know why Bob insisted on having an outside party in January. He's damn lucky it didn't rain again today."

Paula did not answer. Joe was not sure she had heard him. He shifted uneasily. Her fingers were wrapped so tightly around her glass the knuckles were growing white. "Why don't we get a plate of food and take it inside?" he suggested.

"I'm not hungry."

"Margaret says you haven't eaten in two days."

She did not even look at him, but shrugged silently, as if brushing away an insect. "I'm fine."

"Paula." He touched her at the waist.

"Get your hands off me! Quit crowding me," Paula said, a shudder slipping over her body.

"Excuse me for living," Joe retorted, wondering why he bothered to make an effort to be kind.

"I have to talk to Bob," Paula announced.

"Paula," Joe said. "Don't start anything tonight. Let Epstein take care of the negotiations."

"That bastard!" She spat it out. "All he knows how to do is give up. I think Bob is paying him a kickback."

"Paula!" Joe was aghast.

The nostrils of her thin, rigid nose flared. "They're out to get me. Look at Silverstein and Shepard!" she hissed. "They're talking about me."

Joe glanced toward the gazebo. Bob and Caleb were surrounded by people and they were laughing, probably over one of those dirty jokes Caleb delighted in telling. "They're just telling jokes, Paula," he said.

Paula's face was pinched and pale. "They're laughing at me!"

"Why don't we just go home?" Joe asked. "It's not much of a party anyway." Joe was aware, if Paula was not, that no one had approached them with more than a nod or hello since they arrived. He had seen it happen before with people on their way down. It had happened to him. The word was out, the stench of failure was in the air and no one in Hollywood wanted any association with failure.

"Excuse me," Paula said. "I must go talk to Bob." The muscles across Joe's shoulders stiffened into taut lines. He jammed his hands into the pockets of his black trousers. Nothing or no one could stop Paula now. She did not want him, had no need of him and would never accept help or take a compromise solution. It was hopeless.

Joe stood watching his wife weave her way through the throng. She moved fast, plowing through as if she did not even see any of them, or as if they were small nuisances to be shoved aside.

Paula took hold of the railing leading up to the gazebo. Bob, wearing a camel-colored tux with brown velvet trim, greeted Paula with a jovial smile, but his eyes were hard and dark. Joe could not hear what was being said. He felt as if he was suspended in some dark place watching a silent movie.

Bob's hand reached down toward Paula's. The figure in black stopped. She raised her splinted hand to her

582

face, swayed against the railing and abruptly pitched forward. A woman screamed and Bob leaped toward Paula, catching her before she hit the steps.

Joe, his heart racing, pushed his way through people and noise. Kneeling, he took Paula's limp form from the supporting hands and cradled her against his body. "Paula! Paula!" he said. Her face was pale, immobile. "Paula!"

Bob's hand gripped Joe's shoulder. "Let's get her inside."

Joe nodded and swept Paula up, astonished at the lightness of her body.

"Everyone back!" Bob directed, and the authority in his voice opened a pathway along the edge of the dance floor. Joe carried Paula and from somewhere Sally appeared and hurried along beside him.

Inside, Bob and his wife, Lauren, Cobb and Sally all hovered over Joe and Paula. Joe laid the inert form on a brown suede couch. "Paula." He slapped her face gently. The black mascaraed eyelashes flickered briefly as nerves in her eyelids jumped. He slapped her again. "I can't get her awake," Joe said, his throat tight with fear.

"I'll call am ambulance," Sheila volunteered.

"No," Bob said. "A car will be quicker."

"I'll go with you," Lauren offered.

"Me, too." Sally's hand rested sympathetically on Joe's shoulder. "Get me your keys, I'll bring the car around."

Sally hurried through the double door. Joe was aware of the others standing around him in awkward silence. Sheila tried to press ice cubes wrapped in a linen napkin on Paula's forehead. Paula twisted her head away.

"Paula," Joe said loud and firm. Her eyes fluttered open. She stared vacantly at nothing. "Paula!" She closed her eyes, sliding back into her private blackness.

"There's something really wrong with her," Bob said. He looked up at the sound of a car. "That's Sally. Come on, Joe. I'll help you."

"I can manage," Joe said. "Get the back door open for me."

Joe laid his wife gently in the back seat of the Mercedes. He covered her with a car robe and turned to Sally. "You drive," he ordered. "There's a hospital not far from here, at the bottom of the hill."

Lauren stepped forward. "I'll go, too." She reached for the door handle and a hand came out and grabbed her wrist.

"Stay here," Bob Silverstein said, his tone commanding.

"I have to go," Lauren protested.

"No." Bob's grip tightened painfully. He herded Lauren toward the house. Caleb came outside, looked to Bob, nodded and put his arm reassuringly around Sheila's shoulders.

Confused, Lauren tried to pull away from Bob. But it was too late, the car was moving. "Cobb?" Lauren turned to her fiancé of one hour.

Bob Silverstein stepped between them. "Cobb, you follow and report back to us as soon as you know anything."

Cobb nodded. Lauren had the impression of Bob as some army general whose troops obeyed without question. Cobb strode off into the night toward his car without a backward look.

Dazed, Lauren watched Cobb fade from sight, then she turned her eyes on Bob. "You have to stay, Lauren," he said. "If Paula can't carry the ball, then it's thrown to you."

"Me?" She frowned, not understanding.

Bob's arm came around her waist. "Let's go inside where we can talk."

She nodded, there was nothing else to do. Bob guided her through the house and into a handsome office lined with bookcases. He closed the door behind them, shutting out the sounds of the party and its music.

He pointed out a chair to her and moved to a tea

cart. He poured two brandies into snifters. "Looks like you may need this."

Lauren moistened her dry lips and took the glass, her eyes anxious as she glanced around Bob to the door.

"You'd be of no help at the hospital," he reminded her, his tone gentle.

"I suppose not. But what difference does it make to you?"

"The show!" he said. "*Dreams*. We don't know what's wrong with Paula or how long she'll be out of commission."

Lauren sipped the brandy. It burned her throat as she swallowed. Her mind was clearing and beginning to function. It was show biz, she thought ironically. The show had to go on.

"Plans have to be made," Bob continued. "Someone has to take over."

"Well, I'll help all I can, of course. But who can do outlines and—"

"You."

"Me?" Lauren came to her feet. The brandy sloshed in the glass.

"Sit down." Bob's voice had dropped to a smooth, soft tone. "Paula is in trouble and you know it better than I do."

Lauren shrugged, her loyalties torn between the show and Paula.

"I talk to Paula," Bob went on. "I read the scripts and the outlines. They're different. Better. That's your doing, isn't it?"

"I—I assist," Lauren said.

"You've been more than assisting her. She's ill, physically and I think mentally. I've been very apprehensive about signing her for another year."

Lauren's first thought was that if Paula went, so did her job on the writing staff. A new head writer would bring in her own people. A protest rose to Lauren's lips. "She—she has been ill, but—"

"She's sick and she's old," Bob said, moving across

the Oriental rug and standing before Lauren. "Look, I want to make you an offer, and I want you to give it serious consideration."

She stilled. "Yes, sir."

"We don't know how long Paula will be out. Meanwhile, the show continues, with or without her. While she's out it will be up to you to keep everything going."

"Alone?" Lauren gasped. She didn't have the experience or the knowledge.

"Caleb Shepard can stay in town. He can give you guidance on the outlines and he can take over part of the script writing."

Courage stilled in Lauren's chest. "I—I guess I could do it, with Mr. Shepard's help. But not alone. I'm too young, too new."

"Ah." Bob smiled down at her like a father. "Your youth is what attracts me. You're bright, you learn fast. You're talented, and best of all, you're young. If you can carry the show while Paula is gone, then I'm going to offer you the position of head writer."

The enormity of the situation slammed into Lauren's brain. "This is too much to take in." She ducked her head. "And . . ." He might not like this, but she had to ask. "How can you push Paula out while she's ill?"

"Because she's been on her way down for almost a year now. She's been well paid, and if she's managed her money properly, she is now quite well off."

"I suppose she is, but to do it behind her back, when she's down . . ." Lauren shook her head. It went against everything she had been taught. You helped the one who was down; you didn't kick him.

"It's known as survival, my dear," Bob said, beginning to pace back and forth over the rich Persian rug centered over a hardwood floor. "Television is a cold, hard game and you do what is necessary. I own *Dreams,* or rather my production company owns it. And any company man worth his salt cuts his losses. Otherwise, he doesn't survive."

Lauren nodded. It made sense. *Dreams* wasn't one

job. There were forty-plus actors, five directors, assistants, electricians and camera men, wardrobe workers, technicians, grips. Yes, it was a company; it was big business.

"The show needs you," Bob continued.

Lauren raised her eyes to his. "This isn't something off the top of your head, is it? You've considered it, even while you've been negotiating over Paula's new contract."

"It's been there in the back of my mind. Tonight simply made the decision urgent."

"I don't know," Lauren hedged, still struggling with her own feeling of disloyalty.

Bob came over and laid his hand on her shoulder. "We'll help you. We'll give you an office at the studio, with a staff. Naturally, you can't start out at Paula's six-thousand budget but I think a three-hundred-thousand budget would be a good beginning."

Three hundred thousand. It was more money than Lauren could comprehend.

"You would pay your writing staff out of that, but I'll cover your administrative staff and office."

A new emotion stirred, an ache without a name. Lauren's chest swelled with longing.

"You want it, don't you?" Bob asked.

"Yes," she breathed. "Yes!" She wanted it. It was not as though she had set out deliberately to do Paula in. The woman's problems and illness were of her own doing. Lauren hardened herself to the misgiving stirring in the back of her mind.

"I can do it," she said, the truth of the pronouncement astonishing her. She was fully capable of tackling the job and giving it her all. Such a sense of confidence was a new and heady feeling, an invigorating one. Lauren stood. "I'll give it my best effort," she promised.

"Good." Bob smiled and held out his hand. She laid hers in his. The shake was firm. "We'll move you into the studio office Monday morning. If you can handle it, the job is yours."

"I can do it," she said again. Exhilaration hit and she went giddy. She had to suppress a nervous laugh.

"Then let's get down to work," Bob said. They spent the next hour talking and making notes on what must happen on the show during the following month.

Lauren was gathering the notes when a knock sounded at the door. "Come in," Bob called.

Cobb Strong, looking a little worn, stepped inside. "She's hemorrhaging internally," he said without preamble. "An ulcer. The doctor was furious, said she'd been bleeding for at least four days."

"Oh." Lauren went to Cobb. "That's awful."

"Yeah." Cobb glanced at Bob. "It'll be a long recovery, she'll be in the hospital for at least three weeks. And she won't be fully functional for some time."

Bob clapped Cobb on the shoulder and winked at Lauren. "This young lady and I have everything in hand. Now, if you two will excuse me? I'll get back to my guests. Lauren can tell you all about it."

"It?" Cobb asked as the door closed behind Bob Silverstein.

Lauren sighed heavily. Her eyes shining as brilliantly as the emerald on her hand, she gazed fondly at Cobb. "It's up to me now. I have to take over."

Cobb's expression did not change. "I guess if it has to be, but damn it, I resent it. We never had a chance to announce our engagement tonight. This will delay our wedding."

The wedding! She had completely forgotten it. She had not thought of Cobb from the time she'd stepped into the room with Bob, not until Cobb returned. "Cobb, there's more," she said.

"Oh?"

"Bob offered me Paula's job."

Cobb's head snapped back. "As head writer?" He was incredulous.

"Yes," she said, her answer bringing spots of color to her cheeks. She wanted Cobb's approval, wanted him to

588

be happy for her. Instead he looked as though she had just told him the world was ending.

"That's impossible," Cob declared flatly.

Lauren stepped back. "You don't think I can do it?"

"Hey, it's not that. But being head writer—that's an all-consuming job. It makes you a slave. I mean, staying home and writing a script a week is one thing. That gives you an interest, sort of a hobby, but—"

"Hobby?" Lauren said, her voice hollow. "Hobby? How can you think of my writing as a hobby?"

"No, honey, I didn't mean that exactly," Cobb retracted rapidly. "I mean, this is more than part-time work."

"Writing is, is . . ." Lauren searched frantically for an explanation. "Writing is my life. It is as important to me as your acting is to you. I'm very serious about my career."

Cobb tried to take her in his arms. She turned away, her eyes moist with unshed tears. "I want this, Cobb. I want it."

"What kind of life will you have? You know the sort of hours Paula puts in."

"I know, I know." She threw up her hands. She worked for Paula, she put in the hours, too.

"I'm against it!" Cobb stated flatly.

Lauren's beseeching eyes met his, asking for understanding.

Chapter Fifty-Nine

Lauren called Joe Sunday morning to inquire about Paula's condition. "The doctor has been unable to stop the bleeding," Joe told her. "She's in surgery now."

"I see," Lauren said slowly, with mixed reactions that made her feel guilty. "Are you going to the hospital?"

"I don't know," Joe replied. "She doesn't seem to want me around."

Feeling like a traitor, Lauren asked if she should go over. "No, don't bother," Joe told her. "They won't let you in today. Maybe Monday or Tuesday evening."

"I'll send flowers," Lauren promised, her mouth so dry she could barely talk. She had rehearsed it over and over and there was no way the words would sound right. "Bob says I have to work out of the studio. He hopes that between Caleb and myself we can keep the show going. I don't know what to tell you about Jenny and Andrea."

"I'll think of something," Joe said, his tone disinterested.

Lauren was glad to hang up. She would send flowers, of course. It was always the thing to do, whether people needed them or not. Bob was speaking with Germain and Mel today, visiting both of them personally to reassure them and solicit their assistance.

Caleb Shepard had returned to his mountain home to pack some clothes and was checking into the Beverly Hills Hotel tonight for as long as Lauren needed him.

By five Monday Lauren was certain she would need Caleb forever. She had slipped into Paula's office early in the morning, unseen, using her own key. She did not know if taking outlines, scripts and notes she needed was stealing or not, but she felt like an ordinary thief. She was sure no thief was ever this nervous. Her hands were slick with perspiration for hours.

At the studio Sue Bergman ushered Lauren into an office bare of everything except the most functional furniture. Venetian blinds, layered in dust and spotted with fly specks, let in a sickly bit of sun. The desk was rickety and the strange typewriter was sluggish to her touch.

Caleb, gallant and calm, talked her through the day. He discussed story and character personalities and helped her get the first outline off the ground.

Cobb dropped in and became hurt because she would not go out to dinner with him. All she wanted to do was go home and try to sort out a reasonable work schedule. She wanted to change the routines to fit her habits and speed.

The most logical thing seemed to be to work at turning out three outlines at the beginning of each week. One each for Caleb, Mel and Germain. If she could do them in two days it would leave her the rest of the week and the weekends to turn out two scripts. Cobb was not going to like her working weekends, so she would have to find a way to make him understand it would last only until she was faster and more sure of herself.

Bob Silverstein was as encouraging and supportive as Caleb. She was grateful for the rare opportunity he had given her. And if she made it, if she proved herself capable, she would be head writer by the time Paula had recovered.

And it might as well be her as someone else. Bob had told her the job would not go back to Paula under any circumstances. If they had to they would go outside and hire an another experienced writer.

She covered her typewriter shortly after six and sat back. She wanted to go home, as she had told Cobb. But the worst of the day still faced her. She had promised herself she would drop by the hospital.

She went straight from work, steeling herself into a controlled exterior calmness that was denied by the fluttering in her stomach. A nurse directed her to Paula's room. "Only five minutes," the nurse cautioned. "She's in a very weak condition."

Lauren took a deep breath and opened the door to the private room. At first glance she thought she had the wrong room. The figure on the bed was too small. Lauren tiptoed nearer the bed, barely breathing.

The familiar blood-red nail polish was gone from the clawlike nails. Free of makeup and in repose, Paula's face was that of a stranger. Her flesh was a cold, pale, colorless mask. The dark shadows under her eyes spread down on her cheekbones. The mouth was nothing more than a gaping hole. Wrinkles crisscrossed, rose and fell, resembling nothing so much as a topography map.

Lauren was struck by the helplessness of the creature on the bed, unable to defend herself against anyone or anything. The bitter taste of guilt lay on Lauren's tongue. She was one of those people, one of the backstabbers, one of the conspirators out to get Paula Cavanaugh.

She could not do it, could not talk to Paula. She eased back from the bed. Paula's eyes fluttered open and focused immediately on Lauren's face.

Lauren's hands formed into clenched fists. "Hello, Paula."

"Lauren. Hello." The voice was stronger than she had expected, the eyes clearer.

"How are you?"

"Shitty. What did you think, that I'd be up dancing a jig?"

"Of course not," Lauren soothed gently. Always agree with Paula, never cross Paula. Accept the blame whether you are at fault or not. You were always wrong and she was always right.

"Why are you here?" Paula asked.

"To reassure you," Lauren said. "So you'll know we're keeping everything going."

"You damn well better keep it going." Lauren's eyes concentrated on the tube going into Paula's nose. It was a revolting sight. "Anyone who messes up my show will find themselves fired."

"Yes, Paula," Lauren murmured through stiff lips. "I suppose that bastard Shepard will be taking over while I'm here."

She could not meet Paula's eyes. "He—he seems to have control of the situation."

"That old goat. He'll have the story so fouled up it will take me months to get it back together." Paula rolled her encumbered body back and forth as far as the tubes would allow. "I want daily reports. I want copies of everything."

"I don't think you're strong enough, and we'd have to clear it with your doctor," Lauren said, surprised at how smoothly the words came out. "I think you should concentrate on resting and getting well."

"Just who in the hell do you think you are that you tell me what to do? I took you in when you were nothing. I made you, I taught you."

Lauren's fist opened and closed and she could feel her face burning. She had made it under her own efforts, with her own sweat, she had dug and written and gotten very little help from Paula.

"I have to go, Paula," Lauren said, speaking very carefully and very slowly in order to keep from lashing out at the fallen Witch.

"Daily reports!" Paula screamed as Lauren walked to the door. "Daily reports. If you don't do as I say, I'll . . ."

Lauren closed the door on Paula's tirade. Anger flowed where guilt and sympathy once dwelled. Lauren's determination was strengthened, driven to new heights by that anger, shored up by the memories of Paula's vicious outbursts, by the snowballing effects of Paula's put-downs and sneers. Lauren had taken everything Paula could dish out for a year. She would never be in that position again. This was her chance and she was grabbing it.

Chapter Sixty

The crush of wilting flowers had been removed. The assorted makeup, creams and expensive gowns and robes were packed and waiting. Paula was going home. Her doctor was highly displeased, but three weeks was Paula's absolute limit. She could not stay in the high bed another second.

She was anxious to be back at work. Primarily, she wanted Lauren out of the studio and back in her penthouse office where she belonged. The girl was getting completely out of hand. In spite of repeated calls to Lauren, Sue, Bob, Epstein, Joe and Jenny, the demand for daily reports had never been met.

Paula turned hard, glittering eyes on the notepad at her side where she had listed her accumulated grievances against them all. They were up to something, all of them. She had to get out of the hospital to take care of them, because no one could conquer Paula Cavanaugh.

The door opened and Paula looked up. Margaret peeked in. "Are you ready, Mrs. Seals?"

"Yes," Paula replied curtly. "Where's Joe?"

"In the car, ma'am."

"That fool! You'll never be able to carry all this yourself."

"I'll get a nurse, ma'am. Excuse me." Margaret backed out of the room.

Paula was pushed toward Joe's Mercedes in a wheelchair by a nurse. Margaret and an orderly trailed behind with her luggage.

"Joe!" she barked, infuriated by his stupidity. "For God's sake, why don't you have the trunk and doors open? I want to get home."

"Yes, Paula." He obeyed, but with annoying slowness.

Joe's driving was abominable. "I think you're going out of your way to find bumps and dips," Paula complained. "Every one you hit hurts me."

"Sorry," Joe muttered without looking at her. He was being strange, and something about him was not normal.

"Do you have to drive so slowly?" Paula asked angrily, shifting cautiously. Her body was not accustomed to much movement.

"It's the law," Joe replied.

"Worm!" she mouthed. "Jenny is in the office, isn't she?"

"Yes, Paula."

"And?"

"She's there," Joe said with a shrug. "I haven't talked to her today."

Paula's eyes narrowed to slits. The bastard was up to something. Her gaze moved down to her left hand and she tentatively flexed her fingers. The splints were gone at last, but the incision running from between her breasts to her navel was an irritating replacement. An ulcer, a stinking, stupid ucler! Still, it was a relief to find out that was all it was. She was ashamed of herself for having foolish thoughts about cancer.

She had let fear rule her, which was never a wise thing to do. It wouldn't happen again. Gil had taught her another lesson; with him she had denied her own philosophy of never putting your hopes into another human being. He had taken her, but she had let him. It would not happen again.

Paula glanced up. "Joe! That light is red!"

"I see it!" he hissed, tight-lipped. He hit the brakes, jolting Paula.

"Be careful! God, when are you going to learn how to drive?"

Joe threw up his hands. "Do you want to drive this car?"

"Don't be absurd." She turned to the back seat. "Margaret, do you have my diet sheet?"

"Yes, ma'am."

"Are you sure you don't want me to hire a private nurse, Paula?" Joe asked. "You're still weak."

"I have Jenny and Margaret. I don't want some medical person taking over my home and my business."

Settled in her bed by Jenny and Margaret, Paula immediately began issuing orders while Joe watched. Margaret scurried off to do Paula's bidding and Jenny stood nervously at attention. "What's wrong with you?" Paula demanded. Jenny was always so placid.

"Nothing."

Paula's lips tightened. Jenny was lying. "Get Lauren on the phone. I want her back here Monday morning."

"I'll get her," Jenny said and moved toward the bedside telephone.

Joe moved from the doorway into the room. "Later, Jenny," he said. "I want to talk to my wife."

Paula shot him a hard look. "Not now, Joe. I'm busy."

"Jenny, excuse us, please." The forcefulness of Joe's voice made Paula look up.

"Yes, sir," Jenny murmured.

"Jenny!" Paula yelled, but she was already out the door. "Jenny!" she screamed, the effort sending a shooting pain through her incision. "Damn!" She clutched herself. "What in the hell do you want, Joe?"

Joe tugged at his jacket. For the first time Paula realized why Joe looked so odd. He was wearing a pin-striped suit she had never seen before, and with a conventional tie. "So what is it?" she asked again.

"I'm leaving you, Paula. In fact, I've already left."

"You're leaving me?" Paula asked with a wry smile. "*You* are leaving me?"

"Yes."

She did not believe it. "Why?"

"I've moved in with Sally Rook. We have a small apartment."

"Sally!" Paula snorted. "What a sick couple you two will make!"

"Perhaps in your eyes," Joe said. "But I think it will work out fine."

"How?"

"We need each other, which is something you don't know about, Paula. You don't need anyone."

Paula was torn between shock and laughter. "Well, why are you standing here? Go!"

"I thought you might like to say good-bye."

"So good-bye. Get out, good riddance. You're a drag on me. You're a loser, a nuisance, you're a . . ."

He was walking away from the foot of the bed. At the open door he paused. "Good-bye, Paula. I'm sorry for what might have been."

"Don't be stupid."

"Good-bye."

She sank back on the pillows stacked at her back. Her breasts heaved with indignation. How long did he think that brat would stay with him? Not long, that was for sure. Needed him. He thought Sally Rook needed him? She would use him and take off with the first young stud who wiggled his behind at her.

Need. Need. Need. It was a luxury only weak people allowed themselves. "Jenny?" she cried. Where was that woman? Paula fumed through an interminable wait, punctuated by the ringing of the doorbell.

Jenny returned, an apprehensive look on her face. "Mr. Silverstein is here," she said.

"Good." Paula was not surprised. Bob was probably

ready to go down on his knees to her, not that he would admit it. But having her out for three weeks had surely taught him a few things.

Paula ran a hand over her hair and smoothed the bedclothes. Jenny kept standing at the door with the most curious look on her face, almost one of pity.

"Are you all right, Jenny?" Paula asked.

Jenny dropped her eyes to the floor. "Yes, Paula."

"Then show Bob in, please."

"Yes, Paula."

Paula lifted her chin, a small smile of triumph played over her lips. Bob would come in crawling, anxious to get her back on the show, ready to meet all her demands on the new contract. It was going to be sweet.

...life. I'm one night of your time.

A chill trembling began somewhere in the depths of her body and soul. "Jake, no!" She stared at him in disbelief.

and she had been so involved ... Cobb's obscene suggestions.

It was incomprehensible that Cobb would suggest she prostitute herself when he knew how she felt about Pete. It was the lowest thing a man would do, it de-

Chapter Sixty-One

Lauren glanced up from her desk as her secretary came in. Assigned to Lauren by the studio, the woman was pushing Lauren's patience. Over sixty and vague, Erma Landtroop had hair dyed a garish red, wore girlish dresses and tottered around on shoes with three-inch heels.

She was a sweet lady and well meaning, but she had to go. Lauren had figured out quickly enough that the woman had been shoved off onto her because no one else wanted her and no one had the guts to fire her because she was so close to retirement.

"Yes, Erma, what is it?" Lauren asked impatiently.

"There's a man to see you. From the show. Cobb Strong."

Lauren slowly laid aside the carpet and drapery samples she was considering for her office. "Send him in, please."

Lauren stood, smoothing the soft wool skirt of her three-piece suit. She tugged the vest down and took a deep breath. She was proud of the suit, awed a little by the Saks label, but determined to look and dress to suit her new income level and position.

Erma toddled off and Cobb walked in moments later, his expression hopeful. Lauren went around the desk to meet him, a sad, painful feeling swelling up in her breast as she accepted his kiss.

She stepped back and raised her eyes to his questioning gaze. "I did it," she whispered, "I signed the contract with Silver Productions this morning."

Gloom settled over his rugged features. "I had the feeling you would," he said. His fingers stroked her arm through the silky fabric of her blouse.

"I'm sorry, Cobb," she murmured. *Sorry.* The word struck a chord and reverberated through her mind. Here she was, apologizing again for doing what she knew was right for herself. She stiffened her spine. Those words would never pass her lips again.

"You know you can't have it both ways, Lauren. Me and the show."

"I know." She slipped the emerald ring from her finger, expecting sadness but finding instead relief. "Here." She held the ring out to him.

His eyes held firmly to her face, as though he was memorizing her features. "I don't want the ring back, Lauren. Wear it, please."

"Cobb." She reached out to him and touched his square-cut chin with her fingertips. "I do care about you."

"And I care about you," he answered, and there was nothing else to say. Caring was not loving. The truth lay open before them. There was no need to discuss the impossibility of a life together.

"Well." He cleared his throat and tried to smile. "I'll see you around."

"Lots," she said, her throat filling with tears.

"Bye, Lauren."

"Good-bye, Cobb." She turned away to hide the tears in her eyes. The door closed behind him with a soft click. She would always care for Cobb, always treasure his friendship, but it wasn't enough to base a marriage on. Lauren knew she had shed another piece of her butterfly cocoon. She closed her eyes and leaned against the desk. Her lashes lay sooty on high cheekbones emphasized with powdered blush. The makeup man on *Dreams* had taken her in hand last week at Lauren's request and told her what cosmetics to buy and how to apply them for the best results. The effect was stunning, giving her color and balance and making the green eyes larger and brighter than before. Sleek sophistication fit Lauren Parrow well.

Lauren took a deep breath to steady herself and opened her eyes. There was a multitude of problems facing her today. Rose Jardine wanted two weeks off to do a character role in a movie, the new Katherine was being temperamental and demanding more depth in her character and Sally's old role of Janie was finally being recast.

She exhaled slowly as her thoughts turned to Sally. She seemed happy enough with Joe, enthusiastic about their relationship. But then Sally was always ecstatically happy at the beginning of any new relationship. Even though Sally did seem slightly more mature, and she had to credit Joe with a stabilizing influence, Lauren considered their involvement with each other sick. Sally's twenty years to Joe's fifty-six was absurd. Maybe she had found a father figure as Paula had once suggested she needed, but Lauren knew it would not last. Sally was too sexual to stay with a man like Joe.

Lauren knew she had outgrown Sally, who had yet to come to terms with herself as a woman. Sally was still a girl, living out her fantasies, still playing games with life and herself.

Sally, for all her talk and independent ways, did use people. She had to have someone around to lean on and use, people like her Tony and Alex, Lauren, and now Joe. Sally was simply not the free spirit she envisioned herself as being. She was still a searching child.

Lauren smoothed her skirt under her as she sat down at the desk. She pushed the fabric Sue had sent over to one side, and picked up the budget sheet she had started working on at home last night.

Three hundred thousand dollars was a small fortune,

but on the other hand it presented some problems. Even after well over a hundred thousand a year was subtracted for Mel and Germain, there was a lot of money left. Of course, there were all the deductions for federal and state taxes, Social Security and hospitalization that came directly out of Lauren's share. Bob Silverstein had suggested that she take out disability coverage, too, a vital necessity for the single self-employed person.

Taxes were going to eat her alive until she found a way to shelter part of the income. She knew the first thing she must do was buy a house or a town home and she thought she would prefer the latter because of the low maintenance required on her part.

It was obvious she was going to have to get a business manager to make some of these decisions for her. The only one she knew was Ed Epstein and she wondered how he would feel about taking her on after what had happened with Paula.

Lauren had not seen Paula again since the day in the hospital. There had been one hysterical phone call from Paula after Bob fired her. The woman was screaming and making wild accusations, holding Lauren responsible for her downfall, saying Lauren had deliberately set out to destroy her.

The call had jarred Lauren badly, throwing her momentarily into the throes of guilt. Then she became angry with herself. She had no reason to feel guilty. Yes, she felt sorry for Paula, but she had not deliberately set out to destroy her and take her job. She had nothing to do with the destruction of Paula's life. Paula had done that to herself and Lauren had protected her as long as she could.

Paula had her chance and her time. Now it was Lauren's turn. It was as Bob said, the show needed a young influence to keep it in step with today's life. If Lauren had not accepted the job someone else would have taken it. She knew the show, she had endured a year of Paula's tirades and vicious outbursts. And in spite of Paula, she had learned her craft. She could handle this job and do it well. *Dreams* belonged to her now and she would nurture it. She would give her all to keep the show a success.

She had nothing to be ashamed of and no need to apologize for her actions. She had come to terms with herself and she liked this woman she had found. And one day she would find a man, too. Someone willing to share her life on an equal footing. No more ego-driven men like Benji and Kerry, who viewed women as a reflection of their own ego, to be cast away and pulled back at will. Nor like Cobb Strong, who, as sweet and good as he was, still wanted his woman sitting at home playing wife, subjugating herself to his career and wishes. The right man, whoever and wherever he might be, was her personal dream yet to come. Meanwhile, a full, rich and busy life was laid out before her.

Lauren shook herself mentally. There was work to be done. She buzzed her secretary. "Erma, would you find out when it would be convenient for Mr. Silverstein to see me?"

There were many things she had to take up with Bob, including Erma. Either the woman had to go or else another secretary be added to pick up the slack caused by Erma's inefficiency.

Lauren's mind plunged back into the daily problems of getting a soap opera written. They would continue, day in and day out, all-consuming, worrisome and satisfying, as long as she could keep the ratings up.

Paula Cavanaugh was alone in her office. The phones were not ringing, the typewriters were silent. She shook out a menthol cigarette and tapped it on the desk. Vivid red nails gleamed in the sunlight filtering in through the windows. She poured a glass of sherry and moved to look out over Wilshire Boulevard, her street of banks and churches, her symbol of power and success. She inhaled deeply, strengthened by the sense of power she always attained from this vantage point.

On her desk behind her was a presentation for a new

605

soap opera Paula had tentatively titled *Shadows of Love.* She was going to offer it to the other networks where she still had some connections, though she supposed she should get herself an agent to tout her around town.

Not that the bastard would do any real good, but agents were one of the necessary evils in the business. She would be back on top again, bigger and better than ever. She had been down before and survived, and she would survive this time.

She had a hundred ideas, for TV movies, for night-time shows; all she had to do was get them on paper and get them circulating. She would be cautious this time, careful. She would not sign any contract until it met her specifications.

In this business a woman could not be too careful; there was always someone waiting to knock you down and take your place. Ungrateful backstabbers like Lauren Parrow. She had badly underestimated Lauren, thinking her to be rather naive and as loyal as Jenny.

Lauren Parrow would find out what it was like to work in a place where power makes all people nervous, where everyone feels insecure and inadequate, living in constant fear of falling ratings. She would find out you had to protect yourself first, last and always, because no one could be trusted.

One hand stroked unconsciously over the black silk dress and the incision underneath. Paula exhaled a stream of gray-blue smoke. "You'll find out, Lauren," she said aloud to the empty room. "You'll find out."

Lee Trent sat alone by the pool of the new home Anne had somehow conned him into buying. He admitted to himself that it was easier to give in than to fight her. There was a steady plop, plop, plop of tennis balls being hit, coming from behind the tall hedge that separated the pool and court.

Lee raised his face to the weak winter sun. He was drunk in a dull quiet way, and he knew it. He wanted another drink, one that would lift him, but it was too much trouble to go inside after one. He was also fat; he had put on another ten pounds since the November wedding.

"Hi, Daddy," Reenie called from the patio. He watched her walk toward him, her breasts bouncing under a tight white tennis dress. "Want to go a couple of sets with us?"

"No, thanks," Lee murmured.

Reenie stopped beside his chair. "What's the matter with my daddy?"

Disgust crossed his face. "Don't use baby talk with me."

Her eyes widened in innocence. "Man, are you in a foul mood!"

"What if I am?"

"So be that way. Ta-ta." She waved baby fingers at him, just like her mother. She got more like Anne every day. Reenie never sneaked into his bed now, and Anne always had some excuse for avoiding sex.

Glowering, he watched Reenie walk away. The tennis dress was too short to be parading in. She should not be showing off her enticing little rear end like that, especially in front of the new tennis pro who came three times a week to give Anne and Reenie lessons.

Lee could not stand him. His name was Kevin, "Kev" to Anne and Reenie. "Kev says, and Kev told me . . ." All the damned time it was "Kev" this and "Kev" that. "Kev" was young, tall, broad-shouldered, bronzed by the California sun that also bleached his hair to a golden brown. He never wore underwear underneath his thin white tennis shorts. It was obvious he had something to show off.

Lee slipped on his sunglasses and closed his eyes. There was just one thing that puzzled him. Reenie and Anne had gone to one hell of a lot of trouble to get him. He could not figure out what they wanted with him.